SUMMER KISS

He stilled her with a hand on her shoulder. Her skin was as warm and smooth as he'd imagined, her shoulders pliant, strong and soft as only a woman's could be. Slowly he turned her to face him. His hand went to her hair next, taking a thick section in his palm. His fingertips skimmed her neck, coming to rest beneath her chin. Her lashes fluttered once. Then her eyes opened wide. There was surprise in their depths, but she wasn't backing away.

He glided his thumb over her bottom lip. Perhaps it was the catch in her breathing that had him raising her chin a little more, and turning her face slightly. Or perhaps this had been inevitable since the first time he'd kissed her, when he'd thought she was Laurel.

"What are you thinking?" Liza whispered.

"I'm thinking to hell with counting backward," he said as he lowered his head and covered her mouth with his. . . .

Books by Sandra Steffen

THE COTTAGE

DAY BY DAY

317 BEULAH STREET

COME SUMMER

Published by Zebra Books

COME SUMMER

Sandra Steffen

ZEBRA BOOKS
KENSINGTON PUBLISHING CORP.
http://www.kensingtonbooks.com

ZEBRA BOOKS are published by

Kensington Publishing Corp.
850 Third Avenue
New York, NY 10022

All Kensington titles, imprints and distributed lines are
available at special quantity discounts for bulk purchases for
sales promotion, premiums, fund-raising, educational or in-
stitutional use.

Special book excerpts or customized printings can also be
created to fit specific needs. For details, write or phone the
office of the Kensington Special Sales Manager: Kensington
Publishing Corp., 850 Third Avenue, New York, NY 10022.
Attn. Special Sales Department. Phone: 1-800-221-2647.

Zebra and the Z logo Reg. U.S. Pat. & TM Off.

First Printing: April 2004
10 9 8 7 6 5 4 3 2 1

Printed in the United States of America

For the newlyweds,
Doug and Karianne

CHAPTER 1

Other than Millie Prescott's three cats watching from the windowsill next door, nothing stirred on the cul-de-sac at the end of Desert Moon Drive. It was too early in the morning to be stirring. It was too early in the morning to be *up*. The sun was already blinding; the sky was clear—but then it seemed the sky was always clear in Nevada. It was the reason people moved here.

Liza Cassidy was leaving, this time for good.

"I'm not so sure this was a good idea, Liza." Denise Bailey, of Bailey Brokerage & Associates, gestured feebly with her right hand. "Technically, it isn't your house anymore."

Denise had been Liza's friend since childhood, and more recently, her real estate agent. Liza wasn't ignoring her out of rudeness. It was just that her thoughts had turned inward, her attention on the tiny yard surrounding the house where she and Laurel had grown up.

Plus, Denise was wrong. Liza needed to be here today. She needed to leave from here, because this was where it had all started. Laurel had known it, and had put it into words in one of her letters.

Sometimes, Liza, she'd written, *what we think is the end is really just the end of the beginning.*

The house on Desert Moon Drive was the beginning of the beginning for the Cassidys. Built in the fifties, it was a modest, single-story house. Like the others on this block, the exterior was stucco. Most of the neighbors' little yards were stone and gravel. Liza's mother had insisted on grass. Never mind the fact that Nola Cassidy forgot to mow it half the time, and the other half of it burned up in the scorching heat of the Nevada summer. Kids needed grass, she'd said. And this yard had grass. It also had a fountain, which Liza's mother had called a bubbler, like the one Nola had had growing up in Madison, Wisconsin. The plastic pink flamingo next to it was as tacky as always. Liza was of the opinion that her mother had stuck it near the front steps to serve as a warning of the bright colors visitors would inevitably encounter inside.

They'd had a lot of visitors. Nola had had a lot of friends, and every one of them was as nontraditional and unconventional as the interior of her house. And as her daughters.

Shading her eyes against the glare of the June sun, Liza glanced all around. The Cadillac parked in the driveway looked as out of place here in this neighborhood as the four-karat rock on Denise's ring finger. How many times had she become exasperated with Liza throughout this process? How many times had she said, "But it's a good offer, Liza. You can't allow the buyers' personalities to enter into your decision."

As far as Liza was concerned, that was the only thing that should enter into her decision. This house needed a new family. Only someone who understood the personality of the house itself should live here. She'd refused to sell to the highest bidder, a woman who'd looked at it with dollar signs in her eyes, as if all she saw was how a few upgrades would add to the market value when she turned around and sold it for a tidy profit.

This house was a home, not a tidy business deal. The

Bullards, a young couple who worked on the strip to support their rambunctious brood, were moving in later today. Their three urchins would surely mar every last inch of the newly buffed hardwood floors. Those little boys with their adorable dimples and cowlicks were going to be so happy here, just as Nola and her precocious daughters had been happy here.

They *had* been happy here.

No matter how right the Bullards were going to be for this house, everything would change with their arrival. Of course, everything had already changed. Liza stared at the house, her feet rooted to the sidewalk, her gaze glued to the place over the front door where her mother's sign had hung.

NOLA REDS.

"You have a burning need to go through it one more time, don't you?" Denise asked.

Denise was very astute. She'd graduated from high school with Liza fifteen years ago. Denise had married well. She and her stuffy husband and their two well-behaved children lived in a big house with high ceilings and not much personality, if you asked Liza, in one of the new gated communities that were springing up around Las Vegas. Not that Liza would ever say it out loud. To each his own. Besides, Denise had earned her commission on this house, and then some.

Liza took a deep breath. "I'll only be a few minutes."

She let herself in through the front door. Pocketing the key, she was suddenly uncertain which direction to go first. She'd left some of the furniture for the new owners. The belongings that didn't fit in the back of Laurel's old car had either been stored or sold. The house smelled of floor polish and pine cleanser, foreign scents in a house that had once carried the aroma of her mother's perfume, acrylic paints and whatever casserole happened to be bubbling in the oven. All of Nola Cassidy's casseroles had tasted the same, due largely to the fact that condensed cream of mushroom soup was the main ingredient in each of them. Liza and Laurel had taken over the cooking as soon as they were old enough to work the stove. Still, to this day, Liza's favorite comfort food was tuna noodle casserole made from her mother's simple recipe.

That was the first thing she would cook when she reached the Atlantic Coast and found a place to stay. For now, she strolled through the living room with its purple walls and stenciled ceiling, and on into a short hall. Her mother's room had been at the far end, Liza's on the right, Laurel's on the left.

She paused in the middle. The girls had never had a canopy bed, nor had they wanted one, and nothing in either room, or in the entire house, had ever been pale pink or pale yellow or pale anything. Nola Cassidy had been a self-taught, wonderfully gifted artist, and it was like she'd often said—artists simply didn't do pastel. At least not the red-haired, flamboyant artist who had, at barely eighteen years of age, fled the lush greenery of one of the prettiest towns in the Midwest to fulfill her passion to become a dancer. She'd ended up a showgirl in Vegas.

Oh, and pregnant.

The father—even thirty-three years later, Liza still thought of the man who'd sired her as *the* father, not *her* father—had been a dashing Frenchman. To hear Nola tell it, he'd spoken barely a lick of English, but evidently was fluent in the language of love. His name had been Pierre, and he'd moved on long before Nola had started her daily morning tête-à-tête with the toilet.

The pregnancy had forced Nola's dancing career into a temporary hiatus, but it had been the stretch marks and ruined stomach muscles, the result of carrying identical twin daughters with a combined birth weight of almost twelve pounds, that had made her leave the profession permanently. Nola Cassidy may have been a little ditsy at times—she *had* stepped off a curb and had gotten run over by a bus, something many women thought might happen to them one day, but few actually experienced—but my, how she'd loved. One thing she'd never been was bitter. So, when her dancing career ended, she'd started helping with makeup and costumes.

Before long, she was designing and creating costumes that were works of art. She'd been carrying one of her creations with her the day she'd died. The bus driver thought he'd hit a woman and some sort of live exotic bird. Liza had laughed about that. It had been a welcome respite to the tears.

It hadn't been uncommon for Nola to bring the head-dresses home. In the early days, she'd put them on the console table outside Laurel and Liza's bedrooms to work on them—until the time Laurel let loose a bloodcurdling scream in the middle of the night about monsters in the hall, that is. After that, Nola kept her creations in her own room. The truth was, Laurel hadn't been any more afraid of that costume than Liza was. She'd simply been mischievous. Oh, Laurel had been a stinker. They'd both been. They were Nola's girls, after all.

No, Laurel hadn't been afraid of that headdress. Until she'd gotten the diagnosis, she hadn't been afraid of much of anything. She'd rarely cried, either, not even when the head-aches that had been plaguing her had gotten bad enough to send her to the doctor. She'd cried when the diagnosis had come in. All three of them had, for Nola and Liza had been with Laurel when the neurologist delivered the news. The empathy in his deep voice hadn't made his words any easier to grasp. A slow-growing tumor was putting pressure deep inside Laurel's brain. Without surgery, she would die. With surgery, she would most likely die. There had been other options, trials, studies, treatments that offered a slight exten-sion of life, along with horrible, grotesque side effects that would have robbed her of her independence in the months she had left.

There had been no question in Laurel's mind which op-tion she would choose. She would live until she died. Period. That had been almost six years ago. Laurel had been gone nearly five.

Finding herself standing in the middle of her old room, Liza knew she would have done the same thing. Through the win-dow she saw Denise head for her Cadillac and air-conditioning. She wasn't rushing Liza. That Denise was all right.

Liza turned in a complete circle. The walls in her old room were painted the colors of the ocean—dark blues and vivid greens and the murkier shades of deeper water. There were schools of fish and even an old shipwreck, and on her ceiling a mermaid seemed to float in translucent water. Leaving her bedroom behind, she strolled into Laurel's.

Every wall in this room was covered with murals in the lush greens that made up the tropical rain forest. There were fronds and vines and birds and monkeys. The ceiling was a canopy of trees. Liza stood in the middle of it all, peering at the distance between the two rooms. How many times had hairbrushes and hangers and the occasional shoe gone sailing between rooms during those heated, volatile moments of anger and angst? The house had been noisy. How could it have been anything else with three hormonal red-haired artists living and breathing and growing strong under its slate roof?

It had been Nola who had insisted the girls have their own rooms, Nola who had insisted that her identical twin daughters have their own identities. There were no look-alike outfits for them; they'd grown up happy and close. They'd started out at UNLV together, but had ended up transferring to colleges in different states. Born first, and according to Nola, squalling, Laurel had begun to make a name for herself in the fast-paced world of newspaper journalism in Chicago. Liza had been quieter and for a long time, weaker. "Not weaker," Nola would often say. "Sickly." As if that was better.

Liza had outgrown that, though, and had settled in wine country along the California coast where she sold her pottery and artwork from her tiny studio that doubled as her apartment.

No matter where she and Laurel lived, this house had always been home. No more.

The Cassidys were down to one. And Liza was moving on.

Life without Laurel had been inconceivable. At times it

still was. They'd all cried a lot those first months after the diagnosis. They'd gotten a second opinion. And then they'd cried some more. A lot more. One day, Laurel's tears stopped. She'd looked at Liza and said, "I'm dying. But I'm not dead yet." She'd said it again, louder. By the fourth time, Liza had joined in. Nola had rushed in to see what the commotion was about. Soon, all three of them were laughing and singing as they danced around the room. It was amazing the way the saddest times had a way of transforming themselves into the most vibrant and vivid and poignantly beautiful memories.

That day was a turning point for Laurel. She'd taken stock of her life, and had set off to be the curator of her own contentment. Those were her exact words. Laurel had always had a way with words, which was why she'd insisted upon going out East to write the novel that was inside her. Out East. She couldn't have come to California with Liza. Oh, no. Laurel had to seek her inspiration on the rocky Atlantic coast, with its unsullied landscapes and the constantly heaving ocean. It was like Liza had said: The Pacific Ocean heaved, too, all the time, in fact. But Laurel had made up her mind, and when that happened, there was no changing it. She was going east alone, and had used every feminine wile she possessed to extract a promise from Liza and Nola not to visit unless she invited them. She needed to do this her way, and no amount of argument or pleading or bribing could budge her.

She'd come home, once at Thanksgiving and again for Christmas. She'd looked good, so good in fact that there had been something almost ethereal about her. Although she slept a lot, she swore the headaches were no worse. After that, they spoke on the phone. And Laurel wrote letters, one nearly every week. As far as Liza knew, that novel never did get written, but those letters were works of art unto themselves, the words lyrical. Week after week Nola and Liza read about the spray of the ocean, the howl of the wind, the ever-changing salt marshes, and the people Laurel met. Liza felt as if she knew Addie and Rose Lawson, two elderly sisters everyone in the small town of Alcott, New Hampshire, called "the aunts"; and Skip Hoxie, a former sea captain; and Matilda Kemper, an old woman who'd buried three husbands. Laurel hadn't befriended many young people. Perhaps because she was dying, she'd felt a greater connection with other old souls. She wrote about one young person, though. His name was Jack McCall. From nearly three thousand miles away, Liza and Nola saw Laurel falling in love with Alcott, and with Jack. Late at night, Liza reread those letters, putting them to memory.

One week, no letter arrived. Fear and dread-filled days passed—one, and then another, and another. Laurel didn't answer her phone. Nola and Liza waited. And then, after nearly three excruciating weeks, the final letters found their way to Nola's and Liza's mailboxes. Liza had known it was the final letter before she'd opened hers. It had been postmarked in Boston, not the tiny town of Alcott, but it was more than that. Maybe there was something to the research about identical twins and a kind of telepathy that existed between them. Regardless of how she'd known, her fingers had shaken as she'd opened the envelope, unfolded the crisp stationery and stared at her sister's loopy scrawl.

My dearest Liza.

She'd crossed off the My dearest, so it read simply:

Liza. No sense getting maudlin, right? Aw, hell, if I don't have a right to be a little maudlin, who does?

She'd started again.

My dearest Liza,
Well. This is it. The end of my beginning. What do I say to the sister who has understood me (most of the time), encouraged me, cheered me, angered me, and loved me?

Bless you.

And thank you for being in the other half of that egg. And for letting me rant and dream. And thank you for loaning me that little black dress before you'd even worn it, the one I never returned. Thank you for lying to Mom for me. And you're welcome for all the times I returned the favor. Thank you for granting my wish these past months. Lord knows I probably wouldn't have been able to keep such a promise if the situation was reversed.

It's been a truly amazing final year. Do you know what I've learned, Lize? No one, and I mean no one, stops exploring until they're dead. Maybe not even then. I'll have to get back to you on that. Sorry. It's not funny, I know. But I'm not sad. Not like I thought I would be. Back to what I discovered.

I came here to explore my life. And at the end of my quest, I find myself back where I started. Somehow, I think it must be the same for everybody. Everything I thought I knew is false, and it's as if I've reached this place inside me for the first time only to discover that I've been here before. I just didn't know it. Now, I know. And what I know, what I recognize, what I am, is the very thing I've always been searching for, what we're all searching for. What I am, Liza, what we all are, is love.

I know, I know. I could have left you anything, money, jewelry, a winning lottery ticket, and I leave you my puzzling philosophy about life.

I'm sorry for shutting you out. I don't know why, but I had to take this journey alone. Or maybe I'm selfish, and wanted to hoard this blessing I call life to myself as long as possible. I'll leave you to your own conclusions after you sort everything out. God knows you wouldn't take my word for it anyway.

I need you to do me one last favor. I need you to meet Jack. Go to the lighthouse on the Isles of Shoals next Wednesday at noon. You should be awake by then. He'll be waiting. You'll recognize him—tall, dark and brooding. He'll be angry. That's his MO. Give him a kiss for me. (Gracious, no one can kiss like Jack McCall.) There are blanks he'll fill in for you. Once you've met him, you'll understand why I love him so. Even I don't know why I couldn't explain everything to him. Do that for me, okay?

Oh, and my car? It's yours. And Gran's ruby ring. I can't give you back that little black dress, because I lost it. But you already know the story, just like you know the story of how I lost my first tooth and my virginity. You know all my stories, except for the ones I've left out these past eight months. Jack will fill you in on those.

You're going to love Alcott. And I love you.

Take care of Nola. Tell Jack I tried. And don't forget, give him that kiss from me.

She'd signed it with a flourish of loops and curves that spelled, simply, *Laurel.*

That letter, along with all the others, were in a tin in the back of Laurel's old car. Liza was taking them to Alcott with her. She had a long drive ahead of her, and probably should get started pretty soon.

Dazedly, she strolled out to the hall. She peeked inside her mother's old room, but didn't go any farther. Instead, she opened the door to the attic and climbed the steep steps. It was stuffy and sweltering at the top. She strolled around an old trunk she was leaving for the Bullards, her thoughts turning inward again.

She'd gone to the island on that Wednesday at noon just as Laurel had instructed. She'd waited at the lighthouse all afternoon. The love of Laurel's life hadn't bothered to show up. That evening, Liza had found his number in a phone book, and dialed it up from her hotel room. A woman with a soft, sultry voice had answered. "Hello?" she'd said, and then, "It's okay, Jack-honey. I've got it."

Liza had frozen.

The woman prodded her with another soft, sultry "hello" before Liza lowered the phone. Well, well, well. Laurel's ashes hadn't even settled, and Jack-honey had already moved on.

That had been the end of it for more than four and a half years, and would have been for longer if her mother hadn't been thinking about something else instead of looking out for approaching buses. After the shock of losing Nola had dulled slightly, Liza had come back here to sort things out and decide what to do with the house on Desert Moon Drive.

She hadn't been sleeping well. The therapist she saw in Santa Rosa said it was perfectly understandable. Neither of them knew what to make of the dreams she'd been having for six months, more particularly the fact that a red-haired little boy had been the star in each one. The psychologist had suggested that perhaps subconsciously Liza wanted a baby because she was yearning for a strong physical and emotional bond now that Laurel and Nola had died. The explanation had made sense, until Liza had discovered Laurel's autopsy report along with every important document, every letter of recognition and artistry award, every receipt, and every birthday card Nola had ever received. It had taken Liza two weeks to go through everything in the attic. It had taken only a matter of minutes to read the autopsy report the neurosurgeon evidently had sent after Laurel died. Liza had no idea how it had ended up here in the attic, unopened. Nola had probably had her reasons. Perhaps it had been sadness, or forgetfulness. The reasons weren't important, not anymore.

The autopsy report was.

Once again, Liza's hands had shaken as she'd opened it. According to the official report, Laurel had opted to have the surgery. That was surprising, shocking, because she'd been adamant about *not* having it. Twenty-eight-year-old Laurel Cassidy had died during surgery. All her organs were donated per her wishes, and her body was cremated. Other than the brain tumor, she'd been extremely healthy. In fact, the only other scar had been the result of her recent cesarean section.

Those last three words had staggered Liza.

Laurel had given birth?

When?

How?

And she hadn't bothered to tell Liza? Why the hell not?

Liza had fumed. She'd ranted. She'd implored the heavens. And every night, for two more months, she'd dreamed of a little boy with dark auburn hair, the exact color hers and Laurel's had been when they were small.

Two months before, the dreams stopped as abruptly as they'd started. Liza had to find out why they'd started, why they'd stopped, and what it all meant.

She would have had her answers a long time ago if Jack McCall had bothered to show up that day. Thinking about that, she descended the attic stairs and swept out of the house.

Denise met her on the sidewalk. Taking the key from Liza's outstretched hand, Denise said, "Now are you ready?"

Liza looked back toward the house. Was she ready?

She had a sudden memory of the day Laurel had left. The hot Nevada sun had pummeled the burnt-up grass in the yard much the way it was this morning. Liza had known what Laurel was doing when she'd looked all around at the sidewalk where the two of them had played jump rope, and tattled on the Walsh boys for burning ants with their grandmother's magnifying glass. That last morning, Laurel had taken it all in, putting it all to memory—the house, the yard, the sign over the door. She'd looked at Liza and their mother last, and with a hug, a wink, and an all encompassing grin— Laurel had always hated good-byes—she got in her car and drove away. She hadn't looked back.

On a similar morning nearly six years later, Liza, too, looked all around one last time. There was the front walk, the inviting little house, the brown grass, the bubbler and pink flamingo.

Liza's gaze returned to the front stoop. Without stopping to analyze her actions, she rushed up the sidewalk and plucked the gaudy pink flamingo from its perch. After stowing it in the back of Laurel's old car, she rubbed the dust from her hands and climbed behind the wheel. Now, she was ready.

Waving to Denise, the last Cassidy drove away. She didn't look back, either. She looked forward. She was going to Alcott, New Hampshire, with its heaving oceans and unsullied landscapes.

Give Jack a kiss for me, Laurel had written.

Liza didn't know who she was more angry with, her darling, daring, deviant sister, or Jack-honey McCall. "Give him a kiss?" she muttered to the dash. No way in hell. A punch in the nose, now that was a distinct possibility.

It would take at least four days to drive to the East Coast. That should give her plenty of time to decide just how much she hated Jack McCall.

CHAPTER 2

As it turned out, Liza didn't think about Jack McCall very much. She thought about Laurel, and Laurel's child.

Her sunglasses had come off five hours into the trip. The windshield wipers came on shortly thereafter. She didn't see the sun again until she crossed into Pennsylvania. By the time she reached eastern Massachusetts, it was cloudy again. But the colors! Not even California wine country had so many shades of green.

Green wasn't the only color Liza noticed.

Since leaving Nevada, she'd counted twenty-two redheads, sixteen of which were genuine—she could spot the bottle variety from thirty paces away. Of those sixteen, three had been children. She hadn't realized she'd been keeping track until the fourth day into her journey.

The trek across the country took longer than she'd expected, compliments of an engine light that had come on just before something started hissing under the hood. The Ohio state trooper, genuine redhead number nine, who'd pulled up behind her steaming car had been extremely helpful, but it was still seven o'clock on Friday evening before she had her first glimpse of the Atlantic Ocean.

She inched her way along Route 1 with the hoards of

other tourists and weekend residents intent upon reaching
their destinations before the sun went down. The teenage
girls in the car ahead of her waved to the locals sitting on
their porches. Some waved back; others sat, arms folded,
seemingly content just to watch the summer traffic pass
them by.

Liza followed the road toward Portsmouth. Alcott was
twelve miles south of there, slightly off the beaten path, and,
in Laurel's words, breathtakingly simple.

An old church with a gleaming white steeple sat at the
village's outskirts, exactly as Laurel had described. Moments
after passing it, Liza came to a sign welcoming visitors to
Alcott. She didn't know where Jack McCall lived, but in a
town of less than three thousand people, it shouldn't be too
difficult to find him.

Half a minute later, she had to rethink that assessment.
People were everywhere. Craft booths and food trailers were
set up in the centers of the main streets. Sawhorses blocked
through traffic, and people dressed up like Pilgrims directed
cars to tree-lined streets where the sidewalks were filled with
children on bicycles and roller blades, dogs on leashes and
smiling, bantering adults trying to keep everything straight.

According to the banner overhead, she'd happened upon
the Twenty-Second Annual Alcott Art Festival. Eager to take
it all in, she rolled down her window and immediately heard
people laughing, dogs barking and music playing. The scent
of slow-cooking corn dogs, fried dough and roasting seafood
wafted inside, and suddenly Liza wanted some of everything.
A marching band serenaded her as she passed. On the next
corner, a man dressed in a Scottish kilt played a bagpipe and
winked as she drove by. Liza surprised herself when she
laughed out loud.

No wonder Laurel had loved it here.

She spied a parking space up ahead about the same time
that the sun found a hole in the clouds. Squinting, she fumbled on the seat next to her for her sunglasses, then settled
for lowering the visor.

She happened to glance out her window, straight at a little boy with a splotch of dark red hair. Liza went perfectly still.

Every scent, every sound, every image faded, and there was only him, standing in a ray of yellow sunshine on the sidewalk a dozen feet away. He was young enough not to mind having his hand held by the woman he was with. His T-shirt hung loose from thin shoulders. His face wore a serious expression and his head was covered by a spattering of fuzz that might become curly after his hair grew back.

After it grew back.

A shock ran through Liza as the reality of that soaked in. The boy must be ill to lose his hair like that.

The car behind her laid on the horn. She jumped, coming to her senses enough to take her foot off the brake. Heart racing, she drove to the corner, then sat at the curb clutching the steering wheel with both hands.

For days her subconscious mind had been counting people who had red hair. She could stop counting, for she'd had her first glimpse of Laurel's son.

Forcing herself to breathe, she told herself she was jumping to conclusions. She couldn't be certain it was Laurel's child. So this boy had auburn hair—okay, auburn peach fuzz—and happened to be about the right age, and was in Alcott. That didn't mean he was Liza's nephew. The autopsy report had said that Laurel had delivered a child by cesarean section. It didn't say the child had been a boy, or that he had red hair.

The child Liza had seen tonight had been frighteningly pale. He'd noticed her, too. And for that brief instant when their gazes had locked, she'd seen recognition in his eyes. She'd recognized him, too, for he was the little boy from her dreams, a child who looked remarkably like she and Laurel had when they were small.

Laurel's son.

She pressed the heels of her hands over her eyes, slowly dragging her fingers down her face. Clutching the steering wheel again, she checked for traffic, then coasted to the end of the next block. She'd planned to get a room in a bed-and-breakfast inn right here in Alcott. Still shaking, she drove aimlessly out of town. Eventually she came to a nondescript hotel halfway between Alcott and Rye. She'd stayed here nearly five years ago after Jack McCall hadn't bothered to meet her at the lighthouse. The names she would call him upon her first meeting were getting less complimentary all the time.

Liza needed to think.

Laurel had loved Jack, truly loved him. And if Laurel had had a child . . .

There were no ifs about it. Laurel had had a child. Tonight, Liza had seen him with her own two eyes. And if Laurel had loved Jack McCall, he was her child's father. Liza would have to be careful what she said to him. She would think about that later. Right now, one thought remained in her mind.

Laurel had a son.

He wasn't an obscure notion, a figment of her imagination or a hazy character in a dream. He was real, and he was in Alcott.

He was also probably very ill.

She pulled into a parking space in front of the hotel. The lot wasn't full. There was good reason for that. People who came to the seacoast wanted views of the ocean and glimpses of the salt marshes and unsullied landscapes. According to the brochures she'd picked up at the New Hampshire state line, visitors to the towns on or near the seacoast had their choice of a wide assortment of quaint bed-and-breakfast inns within walking distance of old grist mills and weathered salt-box houses surrounded by picket fences. This hotel had a total of twenty-four rooms. Half of them faced the highway, the other half faced the parking lot. Either way, the view was dismal. Built along a wide spot in the road, the two-story building sat next to a gas station and a mom-and-pop diner that had seen better days.

Laurel had a son.

She and Nola should never have kept their promise not to visit Laurel during her last months. Liza should have been with her when she'd given birth, when she'd faced brutal brain surgery, when she'd died. If only Laurel had told her . . .

Was that why she'd wanted Jack to meet Liza at the lighthouse that day? To tell her about their child? He should have come, damn it. Why didn't he?

Liza didn't want to deal with questions, with yesterday, with doubts and regrets, nor with tomorrow, with worries and logic. At this moment in time, she wasn't all that thrilled about dealing with today.

She needed a place to hole up for the night. Rolling up her window, she reached for her purse and headed for the room marked OFFICE.

The clerk glanced at her as she entered. Sporting a sparse goatee that made his chin look weak and pointed, the young clerk told whoever he was talking to on his cell phone to hold on for a second. He riffled through a basket and procured the correct forms. By the time he ran Liza's credit card, he'd picked up his phone conversation again and resorted to pointing to the place for her to sign. When everything was in order, he handed her a room key along with a flyer that contained a coupon good for a complimentary breakfast at the restaurant next door.

Hooking the strap of her bag over one shoulder, Liza left the office and trekked across the asphalt parking lot toward her room on the first floor. It was windy here, and even though it was June, the air felt cool on her skin. Her mother would have called it sweater weather. Homesickness came out of nowhere, dowsing Liza, leaving her shivering and her chest aching.

She was thirty-three years old, and she wanted her mother. Or her sister. Preferably both. But they were gone. And Liza was on her own.

Laurel had a son, and he was very sick. Kids didn't lose their hair from the flu. Liza didn't know if she was up to this, but it seemed she didn't have a choice.

The breeze smelled of gasoline and greasy foo— pealing combination on the best of days. Heartsi... longer hungry, Liza stole to her room where she kicked ...er shoes and tossed off her hat. After locking the door and drawing the shades, she freshened up in the tiny bathroom, then stripped down to her panties. Just before crawling into bed, she wadded up the breakfast coupon and flung it, hard, across the room. She didn't plan to be up in time for breakfast.

She lay down on her back, the covers pulled up to her neck, the wind outside howling about something. Her eyelids fluttered a few times, then closed.

The child from her dreams was real.

Liza had seen him, and he was hauntingly beautiful. Tomorrow she would find him again—Laurel's son.

The atmosphere in Alcott was festive the following day, and the streets and sidewalks were even more crowded. Liza felt better today. The sunshine helped, but it was more than that. She was rested and clearheaded. And she had a plan.

She found a parking space a few doors down from the sheriff's office. She would walk up to Jack McCall and introduce herself. After a brief explanation, she would inquire after his son. His and Laurel's.

Liza knew from Laurel's letters that Jack was the town sheriff. She rehearsed what she would say as she hurried toward the weathered clapboard building that housed the sheriff station. She would keep it short and sweet, concise and to the point. She would begin by extending her hand and saying, "I'm Liza Cassidy. I understand you used to know my twin sister, Laurel."

Or should she mention Laurel's son first? No. Better save that until after the introductions and explanations, until after . . .

Her thoughts trailed away when the door didn't budge. It was locked. The sign in the window read, CLOSED FOR THE PARADE. BACK AT ONE. IN CASE OF AN EMERGENCY, CALL 911.

Liza stared at the sign. Those introductions were going to have to wait. Again. Could nothing ever be simple?

She spent the next hour strolling from one craft booth and art display to the next. The wind was playful today, fluttering through the hem of her long, loose dress, feathering through her hair. Most of the time, she had to keep a hand on top of her wide-brimmed hat to keep it from blowing away, her purse hooked over one shoulder as she examined pottery and watercolors and oil paintings.

Keeping her eyes open for a man in a sheriff uniform and a child with auburn hair, she drifted along with the crowd. She ate a corn dog and drank a tall glass of lemonade, then tried the sheriff station a second time. Finding the door locked and the sign still in the window, she wandered to an old white bench near the corner, slightly off the beaten path, where she could wait for Jack McCall to return.

As long as she kept her head turned, she had an unob-structed view of the street and all the people in it. Taking off her sunglasses and adjusting her hat, she leaned her head against the building, soaking up the sunshine. It was lovely, and so relaxing, she could have dozed easily. In fact, she was so relaxed that at first she thought she was imagining the ten-tative brush of a small hand on her arm. She turned her head and found herself looking into the serious face of the child she'd seen last night.

Laurel's son.

His eyes were blue, was her first thought, not green like the Cassidys'. He held her gaze bravely for a moment, but Liza wasn't fooled. His fingers quivered against her arm, as if it had taken all his courage to get this close to her.

"Hello," she said softly.

He stared at her in silence. She wondered where he'd come from. Since there were no other adults nearby, she de-cided he must have wandered out of one of the stores or away from the group of people in Pilgrim attire who were practicing some sort of reenactment farther down the street.

"Are you lost?" she asked.

He shook his head solemnly.

"I saw you last night," she said, hoping to lure his smile out of hiding.

He nodded.

And she said, "I was hoping I'd see you again today."

He seemed tall for his age, but he didn't smile, and he still didn't say anything. He stood there looking up at her, and when he'd worked up more courage, he touched the sleeve of her dress, and then her arm just below it.

Liza's throat closed up.

She wished she knew more about children. He was wearing a brown baseball cap. With his head covered, he didn't look much different than any other little boy.

Again, he touched her arm.

"Are you checking to see if I'm cold?" she asked.

He looked up at her in surprise. "Hell, no. I mean heck, no. I'm checkin' to see if you're real."

Something went warm inside Liza, and she laughed. "I'm real. As real as you."

He tilted his head slightly, as if pondering that. A moment later that smile she'd been waiting for surfaced. It was tentative, precious. She wanted more.

"Tommy!" a man called.

The child's eyes went round.

"Tommy?" That voice came again, louder and slightly frantic. "Where are you?"

Without a word, the child darted away, behind the building, toward that deep, resonant voice. Strangely bereft, Liza followed from a distance. She peered around the corner and discovered an alley where more people in Pilgrim and Native American costumes were practicing a skit.

Although she couldn't see the man, she heard that deep voice again. "Where were you?"

"Over by the bench on the sidewalk."

"You scared me."

Silence.

"I thought you were lost. Don't ever run off without me again. Got it?"

More silence.

"Tommy?"

"I'm not a baby."

"You're four."

"I'm almost five. I can read. Everybody says I'm older than my years."

"Nobody's older than their years. I'm waiting for you to promise not to run off again."

There was another stretch of silence, and finally a deep sigh. "I promise."

So, Liza thought, his name was Tommy. Thomas. She wondered if that had been Laurel's choice or Jack's. The boy had a lot of spunk. He'd gotten more from Laurel than the color of his hair. That lingering sadness evaporated like tears on an onrushing breeze, and in its place was pride and an indefinable feeling of rightness.

Laurel had a son. Of course he was no ordinary child!

A man toting a musket stepped aside, and Liza was able to see a dark-haired man in a sheriff's uniform hoist the boy onto his back. Tall and dark, the man was strong, his movements sure and practiced, as if he'd done this many times.

She knew she was looking at Jack McCall.

She recalled one of the last things Laurel had written about him. *People here in Alcott think Jack's angry. Often, even Jack thinks he's angry. But he isn't, Liza. His thoughts run deep, that's all. He's the most decent man I've ever known. Sometimes, my heart aches, knowing I waited until my life is almost over to meet him.*

Liza sighed the way Tommy had earlier. She probably should have marched right up to Jack and introduced herself. If he'd been alone, she would have. But he wasn't alone. He was with Tommy and a woman wearing Native American attire, the same woman who'd been holding Tommy's hand last night. Almost as tall as Jack, she had straight brown hair nearly down to her waist. She said something to Tommy, adjusted his shirt, then tugged playfully at his cap. Shoulders nearly touching, she and Jack walked away with the ease of two people who'd known each other for a long time.

Liza wondered if they were married. It would explain why Jack hadn't shown up at the lighthouse that day. It would explain why another woman had answered his phone.

It wouldn't explain why Laurel hadn't told Liza she was pregnant. And it still didn't explain what was wrong with Laurel's son.

Liza hurried back the way she'd come, past the bench to a corner craft booth on the village's main street, where balloons bobbed and a man with a ponytail was doing caricatures in coal. She waited, blending in with the small crowd watching the artist. She didn't have to wait long for Jack to stroll by, the woman at his side, Tommy riding piggyback style. Oblivious to her presence, they passed within a few feet of her. She followed as far as the center of the sidewalk, then stopped abruptly, forcing people to veer around her to keep from running into her. She stood there, the wind toying with her dress and hair, her eyes on the tall man and woman and the pale child growing smaller in the distance.

They were almost a block away when Tommy turned around. As soon as he spied her, he lifted a skinny arm and waved.

Liza waved back, tears burning her eyes and throat. And since her other hand had already gone to her mouth, she kissed her fingertips and extended them to him.

She couldn't tell if he was smiling. Somehow, she doubted it. But he touched his cheek as if he'd caught the kiss, then he turned around and rested his head tiredly on his father's shoulder.

Liza didn't move until they were out of sight.

* * *

Jack McCall swiped a piece of lint from the hood of his freshly waxed '67 Ford. It hadn't needed waxing. He'd needed something to do.

He wished Eve would get back with Tommy. The house was too quiet without him.

Jack could have ambled next door to see what his father and brothers were doing. He'd seen Brian pull in an hour ago, Carter not long after. Jack wasn't in the mood to be worried about, prayed for or razzed. And that was what they would do, starting with his father, Saxon, the worrier; Brian, the preacher; and Carter, the family badass.

One at a time, they were fine. Hell, they were a godsend. In his frame of mind, Jack was better off alone, that was all. He patted his pocket. He sure could have used a smoke, though.

A lot of people said he was moody, a lot more, downright ornery. He didn't care how the gossip ran. He had a town to protect, a son to raise. And he would raise Tommy.

He sure wished Eve would get back with that boy.

Leaning against the hood of his old truck, he crossed his ankles, disrupting the family dog's snout from his boot. Tanner looked up at him and simply moved over a few inches, putting his snout back where he figured it belonged.

This was the last house on the outskirts of town. Jack couldn't see the ocean from here, but he could smell it.

It was just another day like every other day. He told himself the restlessness in the pit of his stomach would pass. A man had to take stock of his life every now and then, that was all, and Jack's life wasn't bad. He had a comfortable house; a job he enjoyed; a father and two brothers who were good with Tommy; an old, classic car; and a loyal dog. And he had his son.

Once, he'd wanted more. He'd wanted Laurel.

He'd more or less come to terms with the fact that she just plain hadn't loved him and Tommy enough to stay. Sometimes the anger still crept up on him, but usually he could keep thoughts of her at bay. And then, last night at bedtime, Tommy had told him he'd seen his mother. Here. In Alcott. He'd been very matter-of-fact about it, as if he'd seen a whale or dolphins, two of his favorite sightings, out beyond the harbor.

Although Tommy was getting stronger, his condition was fragile, and Jack didn't want to upset him, so he'd let it go. And yet it was that simple mention of Laurel that had started this restlessness in the pit of Jack's stomach. He'd tossed and turned most of the night. When he wasn't tossing and turning, he'd dreamed. That was worse.

It was impossible. Laurel had left, and they hadn't heard from her once in nearly five years. It couldn't have been her that Tommy had seen. Most likely, it wasn't anyone. Tommy had probably made her up, like an imaginary friend.

Jack didn't know what the hell he was going to do about that. He didn't even know if he *should* do anything about it, but unless he found some way to burn off his frustration, tonight would be a repeat performance of last night's restless tossing and turning and burning and useless yearning. Maybe he should walk on over and pick a fight with Carter, after all. If he worked at it hard enough, he could get Brian to join in.

Jack didn't want to fight. He wanted sex. Pure, raw, earthy. Just him and a dark room. And Laurel.

Damn, he needed a cigarette.

He shoved himself away from the hood of his truck so fast Tanner's snout thudded hollowly on the cement floor. "Sorry, boy."

The old yellow Lab found his feet and followed Jack out of the garage and into the side yard, past an old basketball hoop, a rope swing and the fort Carter and Brian had built for Tommy last fall after the diagnosis. It hadn't been played with much.

Yet.

Tommy was better. He was getting stronger every day. That was all that mattered. He was getting his appetite back. In fact, he'd been polishing off a thick hamburger and fries tonight at supper when he'd told Jack he'd seen his mother again.

"It was her, all right," Tommy had said with his mouth full. "Last night I thought maybe she was an angel. But she wasn't. She was real. I know, because I touched her."

Jack and his father had shared a long look across the table. Saxon McCall came over every night and cooked supper for Jack and Tommy. A retired builder with a bushy white beard, Saxon had shaken his head, his way of suggesting that Jack ignore Tommy's little bombshell.

Jack took the unspoken advice. He'd learned a lot from Saxon McCall, who'd raised his three sons by himself after their mother had died. Moodiness ran in the family, at least in the men. So did being alone. The McCalls shared a passing family resemblance and a penchant for restoring old cars. Saxon had an Edsel; Brian, the pastor over at the Pilgrim Church of God, was working on a vintage red Corvette, something the busybody old biddies in his congregation were up in arms about. Bad-boy Carter, the youngest of the McCall boys, as people still called them, had driven his restored Harley into town two months ago, just before Tommy had gone into remission. Carter was just conceited enough to believe he had something to do with it.

Jack was just terrified enough to leave Carter to his illusions. Jack's youngest brother insisted he wasn't leaving until the doctors were confident the remission was going to stick.

Before Tommy had gotten sick, Jack hadn't been superstitious. Now, he appreciated any help he could get. His father and brothers had gotten him through a hell of a year, the worst year of his life. Maybe some day he'd figure out a way to repay them. He didn't like being in anyone's debt, but he'd barter with the devil if it meant Tommy stayed healthy.

The boy was better now. He was starting to cuss again, a good sign if you asked Jack. After all, only the good died young.

Right now, Tommy was with Eve, visiting Addie and

Rose Lawson. Eighty-six and eighty-eight years old, the aunts loved Tommy. Everyone did.

But nobody loved him as much as Jack.

He gave Tanner fresh water, scratched behind his ears for a minute, then ambled into the house. Although it was only seven-thirty, it was shadowy inside. Eve and Tommy would be back any minute. Then the house would be noisy again, the way a house where a little boy was growing up was supposed to be.

Dropping into the most comfortable chair in the living room, Jack propped his feet on a footstool and aimed the remote. There was nothing like a good race to take a man's mind off emptiness. He turned up the volume until the cars sounded like they were boring through the living room. In the back of his mind, he wondered what he would say to Laurel if she ever really returned.

"Go to hell" came to mind.

He was wasting his time even thinking about it. She wouldn't come back. Why would she? Why now?

And if she did?

He wouldn't give her the time of day. She didn't deserve it. She didn't deserve a passing thought.

He crossed his ankles and bent one knee in an effort to give his body a little more room in jeans that were suddenly too tight. He swore under his breath, because his body never had listened to his brain where Laurel was concerned.

Liza parked in front of the last house on Mill Street. After double-checking the number, she gathered her purse and her courage and strode up the narrow sidewalk. A yellow dog was sound asleep in a waning patch of evening sunshine, and didn't so much as move as she stepped around him.

She'd found three McCalls listed in the phone book. Jack's residence hadn't been difficult to locate. The house was a weathered Cape Cod with freshly mowed grass, some scraggly, overgrown lilac bushes from an earlier generation, and not much else. It didn't give her much insight into the man who lived here.

At the stoop, she took a deep breath, smoothed a hand over her long, green dress, then knocked softly on the door. It swung open a few inches on quiet hinges. She looked all around her, and then at the portion of the house that was visible through the opening. She could make out a hall table that held some old newspapers and fliers and the small brown baseball cap Tommy had been wearing when she'd seen him earlier today.

"Hello?" she called.

She listened intently. No one was out and about in the neighborhood. They were all probably at the art festival or at a related activity at the baseball diamond or the horseshoe tournament or the karaoke contest downtown. Someone was home at this house, though. A television blared from a nearby room. No wonder her knock went unanswered. Who could hear it with all that racket?

She tried again, harder and louder this time. Again, no one appeared. The door opened another foot.

"Hello?" she called a second time.

Nothing.

She didn't know what to do next. She couldn't very well leave the door hanging open. Did she dare go inside? She stood in indecision for a moment. She wanted to talk to Jack. She needed to find out what was wrong with Laurel's son. And she couldn't do that if she left now.

Following her instincts, she called out again, then stepped over the threshold and closed the door. As soon as her eyes had adjusted to the shadowy interior, she continued to the doorway of a living room, where the racing noises were coming from.

Toy trucks and stuffed animals were strewn about, but there was no sign of Tommy himself. She saw his father, though. Jack McCall was stretched out in a leather easy chair, apparently sound asleep.

"Hello," she said, singsongy. "Mr. McCall?"

Her voice was swallowed up by a crash on TV. Jack didn't so much as stir.

Now what? Liza thought. Should she leave? Or try to wake him? The booming noises on the television hadn't accomplished that. How would she?

Her eyes took in the simple furnishings. It was a comfortable-looking room, a little lacking in color, perhaps, but not without character. The sofa was leather, like the chair, the lamps were mismatched and the end tables were water stained and a little cluttered. An upright piano sat beneath a high window, the top covered with framed photographs. It was a man's house, a man's room. Even the photos were mostly of boys and men. In fact, there were only two pictures of women in the entire collection. One was an old black-and-white wedding picture. The other was a photograph of Laurel.

It drew Liza like a warm fire on a chilly day. She found herself staring at a photograph depicting one of the memories Laurel hadn't shared with her. The picture had been taken on a windy day. Laurel was standing on some rocks, the ocean behind her, her chin-length hair blown back away from her face, her loose-fitting shirt pressed tight to her pregnant belly. She was laughing, and the light in her eyes took Liza's breath away.

She looked happy—beautifully, ethereally, breathtakingly happy.

Liza was reminded of something Laurel had written. *Do you know how many women dread their thirtieth birthdays, Liza? I most likely won't live to see mine. And the ironic thing is, I'm happy. How could I be happy when my life is going to be over far too soon? I'm not happy about that, but I'm happy about the life I've lived, the life I'm living right now. When it comes right down to it, life isn't measured by the number of breaths we take, but by the moments we experience that take our breath away. And my life takes my breath away every day.*

"Jack?" Liza said, a little softer than before. She side-stepped a toy and tried again. "Mr. McCall?"

She bent over. Somehow her hand found its way to his arm. She touched him tentatively, the way Tommy had touched her. Jack's skin was warm and tan and covered with a spattering of short, coarse hair. He was no longer in uniform, and had the face of a renegade—tough and lean. He had a broad forehead, a square chin and a straight nose. His mouth was wide and frowning, even in sleep. His eyelashes were dark where they rested, the skin beneath them darker yet. He looked like he needed to sleep.

Sighing, she pressed the power button on the remote lying on the arm of his chair. Instantly the room was completely quiet. In that same instant, he opened his eyes. And looked right at her.

There had been no fluttering of his eyelashes, seemingly no effort to focus. Even in the shadowy room, she could tell that his eyes were blue. Like Tommy's.

She tried to speak, but no words formed. She could only stare at him, tongue-tied, heart knocking, mind blank.

He stared, too. And on a shuddering breath, he said, "It *is* you."

He reached a hand to her cheek.

"Tommy was right. You are real."

"What?" She wet her lips. She tried to speak, swallowed, and tried again. "I . . . I'm . . . sorry. For barging in here like this. I didn't know what else to do."

His gaze roamed her face, homing in on her mouth. "I know what to do."

He raised up slightly. And it occurred to her that he was going to kiss her.

Dismay reared up inside her. She had to straighten. She had to speak. She had to back up. She had to do something before it was too—

His mouth covered hers.

He kissed her, and it was rough, a possessive meeting of mouths and heat and hunger. He kissed her, and it was urgent, a mating of air and need and instinct. He kissed her, and it was demanding and rousing and devouring. He kissed her, and it was too late to back away, to speak, to straighten.

It was too late to resist.

CHAPTER 3

Jack didn't know what the hell he was doing.

Okay. He knew. He was doing what he'd dreamed of doing last night. And a thousand other nights. He was kissing Laurel, just as he'd known he would when he opened his eyes and saw her leaning over him, her face close to his. He had no business kissing Laurel, when he should have been asking her where the hell she'd been for so damn long.

It didn't matter. Nearly five years of misery abated in one crushing kiss.

His throat tightened and his chest constricted. He was either having a heart attack, or seeing Laurel again had blown a hole through his chest. That didn't matter, either. Need was all that mattered, and it came out of nowhere—the need to touch, and taste, and remember. He thought he'd remembered everything—every detail, every nuance—but his memories hadn't done her justice. But then, memories never did.

More. He needed more. More of her sighs, her little moans. More of her lips. More air. More time. More of her. More of this. And more is what he took, of everything.

Her lips parted on a gasp. He took advantage of her surprise, tilting her head for better access. He slid his tongue into her mouth, touching hers, stroking, retreating, stroking again.

He couldn't keep his mouth off hers, or his hands. Her lips were soft and wet and full, her skin smooth, her body warm and pliant and strong. Somehow she ended up across his lap. Maybe her knees had given out. Maybe he'd dragged her there. It was just one more thing that didn't matter.

Liza heard a gasp. It must have come from her. The room was spinning, and she in it. She was shocked at her eager response to a man she didn't know. It had happened to Nola with her Frenchman. It had happened to Laurel. And now it was happening to Liza.

His hand covered her breast. Moaning, she arched into it, and cried out when his lips kissed a path down her neck.

She'd been prepared to punch him in the nose despite Laurel's specific instructions to give him a kiss for her. Instead, she'd done exactly as Laurel had said. And then some. Oh, Laurel had been right. No other man could kiss like Jack McCall.

God. Laurel.

Liza had to stop this, this crazy spinning out of control, this passion. She placed a hand on his chest in an effort to push herself away.

"Jack."

His muscles flexed beneath her hand. He groaned. She whimpered. She wasn't like this. She'd never been like this with a man she didn't know.

"We have to stop."

"I know." His words came out on a rasp, a deep, husky, masculine sound that turned into a moan as his hand covered her breast again and his mouth came down again. This time she turned her head, breaking the kiss before it spun out of control. He made a sound of frustration, but at least she could think, and breathe. A little.

She drew away slightly.

He opened his eyes. "I can't believe you're here."

She didn't speak. She couldn't.

"God, Laurel, what took you so long to come back?"

One thing began to make sense. He thought she was Laurel. But that didn't make sense at all. How could he think she was Laurel, when Laurel had been dead for nearly five years?

Liza tried again to get up. How had she ended up sprawled across his lap? She moved, first one way and then another, attempting to straighten, to ease off, to inch over, but it wasn't easy, for every place she put her hands for leverage got her in deeper trouble. His thighs were hard, his chest broad and muscular, and everything in between dangerous and swollen and straining one seam or another. He kissed her again—her face, her cheek, her chin and jaw.

"Jack. We have to stop."

"I'm trying, damn it." His mouth covered hers again, the kiss pure, raw, earthy.

He called that trying?

She wrenched herself away. After more scrambling, she finally made it off his lap, although none too gracefully. Next, she found her feet. When they were finally firmly underneath her, she stared at him, and he at her. "Jack, I . . ."

He wiped his mouth on the back of his hand and looked at her as if he'd just caught a whiff of something unpleasant. "You what?"

The question was snide, his sudden anger stinging but no less potent than his passion had been but a moment ago. Evidently, the man had switches, and he'd just flipped one.

He stood. Even with the large leather ottoman between them, he seemed too close, like a cougar on the prowl, his next meal in his sights.

Liza took a step back. "This isn't what you think. I knocked on your door. It wasn't closed tight, and it opened by itself, so I came in. And you were asleep. I tried to wake you. But then you woke up on your own. And you, that is, we . . ."

His eyes narrowed, his gaze dropping from her mouth to her shoulders to her breasts. His stare was bold, but the look in his eyes the next time they met hers sent a sourness to the pit of her stomach, for it held anger and contempt.

"I can explain."

"That would be a first, wouldn't it? By all means, Laurel. Explain."

She shuddered inwardly, then looked him in the eye. "That's just it. I'm not—"

The door burst open. "I'm home!"

Liza spun around.

Footsteps shook the entire house, rattling anything not battened down. "Who's here, Dad? Whose car is that?"

Jack opened his mouth to reply the same instant Tommy burst into the room. The boy stopped so quickly, the soles of his shoes squeaked on the hardwood floor. Although very thin, he was energetic, full of vigor.

"See?" he said, looking askance at his father. "I told you!" He looked up at Liza next, and then back to Jack. "She is so back."

Liza swallowed. "Tommy—"

"Son," Jack said at the same time.

A gasp drew all three of their gazes to the doorway where a tall woman with long, straight brown hair stood, stark and still, her face pale except for a splotch of red on each cheek. "Laurel!"

Liza felt as if she'd just been caught with her hand in the cookie jar. Or worse. She knew how this looked. Her clothes were askew, her lips swollen, her hair mussed. She dared to glance at Jack. Just as quickly, she looked away, for the evidence was even more telling on him.

If everyone would just let her explain.

"What are you doing here?" the other woman asked.

It had been nearly five years, but it took Liza only a moment to place that voice. This was the woman who had answered the phone that day when Jack-honey had failed to meet her at the lighthouse on the Isles of Shoals. There was intensity in the woman's gray eyes. There was also recognition. She thought Liza was Laurel, too.

Laurel was dead. This man had fathered her son. Why didn't he know Tommy's mother had died?

For a fleeting instant, Liza hoped. Just as quickly, the hope was extinguished, for she'd read the letter from Laurel's surgeon, had read the autopsy report, had read the reports regarding the organs she'd donated. It was Liza who had spread Laurel's ashes to the wind over the Pacific Ocean just off the California coast.

Laurel was truly gone, and had been for a long time. Liza knew that for a fact. She felt it in her soul. She didn't know why these people didn't know.

She needed to think. She needed to sit down. How long had it been since she'd gotten what she'd needed?

Tommy sidled closer. Placing his hand tentatively in Liza's, he said, "I knew you'd come back some day."

Her heart turned over, and tears wet her eyes. She caught the look the tall woman cast at Jack. He was angry, and the other woman was sick at heart.

Finally, Liza found her voice. "Are you two married?"

The woman's gray eyes widened.

"Eve and I?" Jack made it sound like a rhetorical question, as if it was too absurd to require any more explanation.

So her name was Eve. Liza didn't recall Laurel mentioning anyone by that name. But then, her darling sister had left a lot out, hadn't she?

Eve looked hurt. Jack seemed oblivious. And it occurred to Liza that not everyone would be happy if Laurel had indeed returned.

It still didn't make sense. Liza's thoughts swam. She wished someone would say something.

Jack finally filled the ensuing silence. "Eve, I'll walk you out."

Eve didn't appear to want to leave, but she nodded and said, "All right. That would be nice, Jack."

Jack spoke to Tommy as he passed. "I'll tuck you into bed in a few minutes."

He didn't speak aloud to Liza, but his expression spoke

volumes. She had some explaining to do. And she'd better not be thinking about making a run for it until he was good and satisfied with her answers.

The instant they were alone in the room, Tommy released her hand and climbed onto the big, comfortable-looking couch. The leather creaked slightly, his legs sticking straight out from beneath his baggy shorts, his hands folded neatly in his lap. She marveled at his patience.

Liza was aware of the low, hushed tones of the voices out in the foyer. Uncertain when she'd have another chance to get this close to the boy, she perched at the edge of the middle cushion, and smiled at him. He studied her with curious blue eyes. "Eve and Dad are best friends. They aren't married. He's never been married to anybody. Not even you."

He thought she was his mother, too. Laurel, she said to herself, what kind of mess did you leave behind? Deciding to wing this for now, Liza said, "My mother didn't marry my father, either."

Tommy looked at her for a long time, as if pondering that, then slowly nodded. "Why didn't she?"

"I don't believe he ever asked her to."

"Did my dad ever ask you?"

Oh, boy. This was dangerous territory. She wanted to touch him, to take off his adorable blue baseball cap and rub her hand across the wispy hair growing on his head, to pull him onto her lap and press a kiss to his scalp. She'd never considered herself maternal. She certainly wasn't one of those women who oohed and ahhed over young children and wanted to hold every baby they saw. This instinctive reaction to Laurel's son came as a complete surprise.

He was precious, and she couldn't lie to him. Had Jack asked Laurel to marry him? That, she didn't know. But she knew with certainty that he hadn't asked *her.* "No," she said. "Your father never asked me to marry him."

That was about all Liza was certain of anymore.

She stood slowly. Smoothing a wrinkle from her dress, she walked to the far side of the room, trying to think of something to say. She wished she'd paid more attention to children over the years. What did adults talk about with young children? Were four-going-on-five-year-old boys too young to be interested in sports and cars? Was there such a thing as an age when boys were too young for that?

She stopped in front of the piano again, studying the photographs. One photo in particular caught her attention. In it, Tommy was in a hospital bed, hugging a stuffed whale. His head was bald, and he wasn't smiling, but he looked as if he had been moments before the photo was taken.

"Do you like whales, Tommy?"

His silence drew her around.

"Tommy?"

His eyes were closed, his head tipped back slightly, his mouth open a fraction of an inch. She tiptoed closer and very gently removed his baseball cap. His eyes moved beneath his lids, but didn't open. She reached out and smoothed the wispy hair on his forehead.

A thud of footsteps and the rustle of clothing drew her gaze to the doorway. Jack stood in it, looking at her, an unreadable expression in his narrowed eyes.

"He's ill," she said softly.

"He was."

She straightened. "How ill?"

"Just about as ill as a child can be."

She closed her eyes for a moment, dreading what was coming next. "Cancer?"

"He had leukemia." Although quiet, Jack's voice was hard.

"Had?" She latched onto the past tense.

Jack ran a hand through his hair, making it clear that he thought he was the one who should be asking the questions. But he answered. "He's in remission." He glanced at his son. In four long strides, he reached Tommy. "This isn't a conversation we should be having over a sleeping child."

He scooped the boy into his arms. Tommy snuggled closer. He obviously trusted this man.

Jack McCall would have earned that trust.

He seemed to think she'd earned his derision, too, for he looked at her, and with a curl of his lips, said, "I'll get him tucked into bed. Will you be here when I come back? Or will it be five more years before you show up again?"

Liza didn't appreciate the insinuation or the bitter edge in his voice. Since she'd done nothing to deserve any of this, she straightened her back and gave an affronted little snort. "I guess you'll just have to find out for yourself, won't you?"

She'd surprised him. And angered him. She held her ground and his gaze as he neared. Careful not to touch her, he took Tommy's hat from her on his way by, a symbolic gesture if she'd ever seen one. She waited to turn around until after the sound of his footsteps faded.

Alone in the room, she wasn't at all certain who'd won that round. But she knew she'd received no satisfaction from getting the last word.

Jack bit his cheek so hard he tasted blood. He didn't know who the hell she thought she was, making him feel guilty for being sarcastic. She deserved it. Four years and eleven and a half months, she'd been gone. There had been no phone calls, no postcards, not one single word in all that time. What did she except? The welcoming committee? He wasn't falling for her feeble excuses, her secrets again. As long as he stayed mad, he could pretend to ignore the heat lying in wait where she'd sprawled across his lap.

He carried Tommy through the short hall and into the first bedroom. The boy stirred when Jack removed his tennis shoes and the rest of his clothes, and woke up enough to use the bathroom and brush his teeth. Wearing a plain, clean white T-shirt and superhero underwear, he padded into his bedroom and climbed into bed. Jack whisked the covers up to his neck and kissed his son's smooth forehead.

Tommy stood for the nightly kiss. Just in case his father decided to linger, he turned his head, and Jack knew his son had something else on his mind. He'd turned a small ear toward the hall, listening so intently it was almost comical. If Jack could have laughed, he would have.

At the sound of footsteps out in the living room, Tommy visibly relaxed. Jack heard those footsteps, too. They had the opposite effect on him.

"Dad?" Tommy had never called him Daddy, going directly from Da, his first word, to Dad when he was a year old.

He would probably call him worse things someday. Jack looked forward to that, for it meant Tommy would grow up strong and healthy and obstinate and belligerent and moody like the rest of the McCalls. It meant he would grow up.

"Eve asked me to tell you good night," Jack said. "Did the two of you have fun tonight?"

Tommy shrugged.

"Was Miss Rose feeling better?"

Again, the boy shrugged. And Jack knew Tommy didn't want to talk about Eve or Miss Rose.

"Don't make her mad, Dad." Tommy stared up at him.

Jack cleared his throat, feeling defensive.

Without waiting for his father to reply, Tommy said, "And don't make her leave."

Laurel had left of her own free will. Left, hell, she'd waltzed away without a backward glance or a second thought. Tommy didn't care about that. He only cared that she was back. This boy didn't ask for much. Even when he'd been the sickest, he'd withstood the pain with a dignity that far surpassed his years. Now he didn't want his father to make Laurel angry. He especially didn't want his father to make her leave.

Jack sighed. "I'll try, Tommy."

"You gotta try real hard."

His son knew him well. "All right."

"Promise?" Tommy was looking at Jack with a spellbinding intensity, his eyelids slipping lower.

In the face of his son's innocence and weakness, Jack felt

small and weighted down with responsibility. "I promise, son."

He'd spoken in the nick of time. Tommy grinned for half a second. And then, he was asleep.

Before he'd gotten sick, Tommy had fought the sandman tooth and nail. Nowadays, each time he went to sleep reminded Jack of a steel door slamming down on cement. Jack was learning not to panic when it happened. Tommy would awaken in the morning, rested and energetic. Every day that the cancer stayed away was a good day. Maybe, in a hundred years, Jack would take it for granted.

For now, he had to force himself not to hover. He rearranged the blanket and turned out the lamp. It was time to face the music out in the living room. Casting a glance at his sleeping son, he strode from the room, pulling the door closed behind him.

Liza turned the moment she heard Jack's footsteps in the hall. They stared at one another, each of them hesitating. She wished she knew what to say.

He spoke first. "You look good."

Liza doubted there were many men in the world who could make a compliment sound like a sin. If he thought she was going to thank him for it, he could think again.

"What are you doing here?" he said.

The tone of his voice sent a chill over her. Hugging her arms close to her body, she said, "There is a lot I don't understand, a lot I don't know. Until a few months ago, I didn't know anything about this. My sister died five years ago, and then my mother got run over by a bus last winter, and I'd been having dreams about a red-haired little boy."

He planted his feet, legs apart, arms folded, as if bored.

Oh, that attitude!

Liza knew she'd been rambling. She tried again. "I didn't know what the dreams meant. How could I? But then I read the autopsy report. By then the dreams had stopped."

He continued to look at her, obviously unmoved. "Let's keep this about Tommy, shall we?"

A slap wouldn't have opened her eyes any wider. Okay, as far as explanations went, hers hadn't been terribly clear. He didn't have to be nasty, though.

"What about Tommy?" she asked.

Jack came a few steps closer, but only a few. "I don't want him hurt in any way."

"Neither do I." Before he could say something derisive, she said, "You said he's in remission. What exactly does that mean?"

Deftly, he turned on a lamp. "It means there's no sign of cancer cells. It means his white and red blood cells and platelet counts are normal. It means the treatments were successful and the pills he continues to choke down every day are working." His words were as clipped as his movements.

"That's good." His face was stern, causing her to say, "It *is* good, right?"

"Of course it's good." He took a deep breath, and swore under it. "I don't know what you're doing here, or why you came back. I sure as hell don't know what you expect me to say. But I just promised Tommy that I wouldn't do or say anything that would make you leave Alcott again. And *I* keep *my* promises."

Meaning she didn't. Oh, he had a lot of nerve. But of course, he thought she was Laurel, and evidently Laurel hadn't been honest with him about her illness. "I thought you wanted to keep this about Tommy."

Anger glittered in his eyes. Score one for her.

"I don't want you upsetting him. I want him as happy as a clam every day from now on. No stress. No disappointments. No losses, no worries, no scares. Understand?"

She didn't understand much of anything, but she understood that he thought she was Laurel, and she understood that the worry in his face and in his voice was real. It almost made it possible to excuse the anger and the implication that she would do anything to hurt that child. "Are you saying his condition is precarious?" she asked.

"I'm not taking any chances. Who knows what havoc emotional upheavals can cause?"

"How long?" she asked.

He hesitated, measuring her. It was obvious that he didn't know what she was asking.

"How long was Tommy sick?"

"It started eight months ago."

Eight months, she thought. That was when her dreams of a red-haired child had begun. "And his remission? When did that begin?" She knew the answer before he spoke.

Two months.

"Two months," he said. "The chemo knocked the cancer cells out of him, and nearly took him with it."

Two months ago, the dreams had stopped. The coincidence gave her a sense of confidence she didn't even try to explain.

"Are you staying at the captain's cottage again?"

Liza hadn't realized that she'd started to pace until she heard the question. She looked over her shoulder at Jack, regarding him quizzically. Laurel's letters had always contained a return address, but she'd never referred to it as a captain's cottage.

"Or aren't you staying?" he asked.

She didn't appreciate the attack on her character. Again. "I have a room at the Alcott Hotel out on Route One."

"I see. Tommy's going to want to see you. It's probably best if you keep your distance. We wouldn't want a repeat of . . ." His voice trailed away and his gaze trailed to the easy chair where he'd kissed her.

"We wouldn't want that," she said, snide in her own right.

This was getting them nowhere.

She took a step toward him. Holding out one hand gently, palm-side up, she said, "I'm not who you think I am, Jack."

That humorless curl of his lip was back. "Surprise, surprise. You never were."

Her shoulders went back and her chin came up. Loyalty to Laurel kept her from lashing out. "Be careful. You don't strike me as a man who would enjoy eating crow."

She turned on her heel so fast her dress swirled around her legs. She left the living room without a backward glance, her annoyance increasing with every step she took.

How could Laurel have loved him?

Liza fumed all the way to the foyer. The man was a jerk. A condescending, egotistic, nasty, tainted, cross, annoying, unpleasant, insufferable, arrogant, irksome jerk!

He sure could kiss, though.

She was shaking as she threw open the door. She'd been here only twenty-four hours, and she'd already been kissed senseless and had her character attacked. At this rate, it was going to take her a long time to get to the bottom of the truth.

Jack stood, feet apart, eyes narrowed, waiting for the door to slam. It wouldn't be the first time Laurel had left mad as a wet hornet, slamming the door so hard it rattled its hinges.

Tonight it closed quietly, with barely a click. Somehow, that seemed even more ominous.

Some of his anger evaporated, leaving conflicting emotions. The greatest was guilt. Damn it all to hell. Why should *he* feel guilty? She was the one who'd left *him* all those years ago. She'd professed to love him more than she'd ever loved anyone. She'd sure changed her tune after Tommy was born. He'd never forget the day she'd stood in this very room, eyes hauntingly deep, but dry, her voice shaking as she'd confessed that she had some important business to attend to. In Boston. She'd said she wasn't certain she was meant to raise a child. As if it just plain wasn't in the cards. And if he didn't hear from her within a month, she told him to just forget her. Just—as if it would be simple, or even possible.

She'd left. And he'd been tied up in knots, waiting to hear from her. Day after day, he'd waited, until the weeks turned into that month she'd named, and the months had turned into years. And then, just like that, she'd waltzed back into town. And her only explanation was that she'd been having some dreams?

Dreams, hell. Meeting her had been a nightmare.

He knew that wasn't true. He'd loved her. Together, they'd created Tommy. Losing her had been the nightmare. And now she was back, and he was tied up in knots all over again.

He fumbled in his pocket for a cigarette, then stalked outside for some much-needed air. He hadn't bummed a cigarette in almost five years. He'd gotten through Tommy's treatments without one. He should be able to get through Laurel's return. Now, if only he could think of some way to get through tonight.

He heard voices in the yard next door. He had good hearing. As a single father, he'd learned to tell the difference between his newborn son's cries of hunger and fear and just plain boredom. He'd learned to pay attention when a little boy was too quiet or not quiet enough. As a lawman in town, he could tell when a tourist was lying, when one of the regulars at Dusty's Pub had had enough to drink, or when something was amiss around Alcott.

Everything seemed normal in the neighborhood tonight. Dusk had given way to darkness. Night insects were starting their chorus, and those voices next door were getting closer. There were lights on in his father's house, but no yard lights between here and there. Beneath the sliver of the moon, Jack could make out the outline of his father and brothers as they entered through the gate in the picket fence, Saxon in the middle, Brian on one side, Carter on the other.

Jack trudged down the steps. At the bottom, he took a couple of deep breaths, his eyes on the red glow of Carter's cigarette. He didn't look away until Carter had crushed it beneath his boot.

"Hey, Jack," Carter said. "I'm getting ready to take my Harley for a spin. Wanna ride along?"

"No, thanks."

"You sure? A little wind in your hair can go a long way in taking the edge off everywhere else."

"Maybe some other time."

Brian looked at Jack. "You okay?"

Jack shrugged.

The pastor of the Pilgrim Church, Brian was only a year younger than Jack. Having a single, thirty-four-year-old preacher wasn't going over real well with some of the Elders of the church. Being a McCall wasn't helping, either.

"That looked like Laurel's car," Brian said.

"It was."

"No shit?" The youngest of the McCall boys, Carter was thirty-one. One of these days, somebody was going to have to tell him.

Saxon said, "Then it's true. Tommy wasn't making her up."

Jack shook his head.

"Is Tommy sleeping?" Saxon McCall was a big, burly man with a booming voice and a soft heart. He was easy to see because of his white beard and hair.

"Yeah," Jack said. "He's out for the night."

"How did she look?" Brian's white cotton shirt stood out, too.

Jack answered without moving. "About the same, I guess."

And Brian said, "Did she tell you why she left?"

"No."

"How about why she came back?" Carter asked. "Did she tell you that?"

"She didn't get around to explanations."

Carter wore his usual black jeans and dark T-shirt, and Jack had to rely on the tone of his youngest brother's voice and the occasional glimpse of white teeth as he said, "I wasn't around when she was in Alcott the last time, so I never had the pleasure. From the looks of you, I'd say you've had some pleasure already, and she just got here."

"Go to hell, Carter."

"I'm planning to."

Pastor Brian cringed. "Guys, come on."

"Oh, lose the halo," Jack and Carter said at the same time.

"Boys," Saxon said, as if they were all adolescents. He looked closely at Jack. "She really didn't tell you why she came back?"

Jack shook his head.

And the youngest McCall brother asked, "How long is she going to stay?"

"I don't know that, either."

Carter started back toward his motorcycle parked in the driveway next door. "Instead of jumping her bones next time you see her, maybe you should ask her."

Talk about roaring silences.

Saxon eyed his boys. Fifteen years ago that statement would have landed Carter on his back. Jack wouldn't have been careful about it, either, taking Brian down with them. Before Jack had time to think about doing the same thing tonight, Saxon scooped a basketball from the ground and flung it, hard, toward his firstborn. Jack caught the ball out of self-defense, then froze for a moment.

"Work it off," Saxon said.

"We're too old for this." Jack bounced the basketball once, twice, three times.

"Speak for yourself," Carter said.

"You saying you want to play a round?" Jack asked.

Brian and Carter eyed each other. "You game?" Brian asked.

"I'm always game," Carter replied. "I guess my motorcycle ride could wait."

Together they ambled toward the cracked cement beneath the net. Jack followed with the ball.

The game began. They were a little rusty. None of them was dressed for basketball, but then the game they played didn't have a lot in common with the usual version. There wasn't much light. There was a lot of cussing and a series of grunts. And then they got serious. It was two against one.

Whoever had the ball was the opponent, and they all took turns handling the ball.

Saxon knew his sons. Jack needed something to do to burn off his frustration. He could either do it by working up a sweat playing basketball, or he could prowl the floors of his house all night, old wounds and regrets and unanswered questions eating a hole through his insides.

A good game of two against one usually worked wonders.

The boys played rough, breathed heavy, and broke every rule. Looking up, Saxon wondered if their mother was watching from heaven.

The stars were starting to come out, and so were the mosquitoes. Slapping at one of the bothersome, bloodthirsty nuisances, he reached into his pocket and drew out his pipe. He lit it, took a few good puffs, then rocked back on his heels to watch the show.

A lot of it *was* show—the grunts, the three-point shots, the passes and double-dribbling were mostly theatrics. Saxon pulled a face, because Jack's elbow in Carter's chest had been real. So was the thud the basketball made when it bounced off Brian's head.

Saxon took a puff on his pipe and blew a smoke ring. The McCalls were a tough lot. Their physical bruises would heal. The emotional kind were trickier.

Laurel was back. He'd liked that girl. He hadn't liked what she'd done to Jack, though. Now she was back and Tommy was in remission. Jack had good reason to be riled up. Not that he needed a reason. Being riled up was another McCall trait.

Carter had been riled for a while now, since shortly after he'd ridden his Harley back into town. He was itching to be anywhere else. Brian, "Brother Brian," Carter called him, wasn't any too happy, either, although he wasn't admitting it.

None of his boys were happy these days. Sooner or later, they'd wake up and figure out what they needed.

Saxon already knew. Knowing came with age. There had to be something good about getting old.

He puffed some more on his pipe, the smoke choking the mosquitoes. The skirmish underneath the hoop was winding down, three separate sets of frustrations eased somewhat, at least for now.

Tomorrow was another day.

CHAPTER 4

The shopkeepers in downtown Alcott were rolling out their awnings when Liza hurried past just before noon the following morning. Most looked twice at her. A few gaped.

Liza had been awakened early by church bells. She'd dragged a pillow over her head and tried to go back to sleep, but by then her mind was awake, and it was no use. Groggily, she'd showered. After drying her hair and putting on another of her long, flowing summer dresses, she'd driven to Jack's house. Nobody was home. Now she was on her way to the sheriff station to try to find him. She had to talk to him.

The last time she'd tried to talk to him hadn't gone so well. Today it would be different, because today she was prepared. Still, the thought of facing him again was disconcerting, and she wanted to get it over with. Once she'd explained everything, or at least everything she knew, Jack would have to decide how to explain it to Tommy. It seemed to Liza that the longer the charade continued, the more upset Laurel's son would be. And Jack had said it was possible that any upheaval could be dangerous to Tommy's health.

She had to tell Jack the truth. It wouldn't be easy, because no matter how angry he was, there had been something much stronger than anger in his kisses when he'd thought she was Laurel.

He didn't know Laurel had died. And she dreaded being the one who had to tell him.

If Laurel had been here, Liza would have told her exactly what she thought of her secrets. But then, if Jack had bothered to show up at the lighthouse that day, much of this could have been avoided.

What was done was done. Soon this would be over, too.

Church must have let out; the sidewalks were filling up with men, women and children in their Sunday best. The sheriff's office was directly in front of her. Thankfully there was no sign in the window today. Liza took a deep breath and opened the door.

A heavyset woman with a round face looked up the moment Liza entered the small office. "I heard you were back in Alcott, Laurel."

News traveled fast in small towns.

Liza said, "Is Jack here?"

The woman eyed Liza curiously and shook her head. "No, he's not. You grew your hair long."

Actually, she'd always worn it long, but this wasn't the time or the place to try to explain. "Do you know where Jack is?" she asked.

The woman studied Liza for another long moment. Finally, she said, "He's out on a call."

Liza's disappointment must have shown on her face. The other woman's expression didn't soften, exactly, but she did say, "Is this an emergency?"

It was important, but it wasn't an emergency. It only felt like one. "I suppose not," she said quietly.

"In that case . . ."

Liza could well imagine what had been left unsaid. It seemed everybody in Alcott thought Laurel had walked out on her newborn baby and his father, and nobody had heard from her in all this time. They didn't seem to think she should expect any favors from them.

Except she wasn't Laurel.

And Laurel hadn't walked out on them. She'd died.

Liza massaged her temples.

"Are you still having those headaches?"

Liza clasped her hands in front of her and shook her head. "Just tense, I guess." Sighing, she turned to go.

"Laurel?"

Liza paused at the door.

"I'll tell Jack you're looking for him."

Liza glanced over her shoulder, and this time it was easier to smile. "I would appreciate that. Thanks."

She closed the door behind her and headed back the way she'd come, past food trailers and craft booths and stores that resembled quaint little cottages and weathered old fishing shanties. She'd gotten as far as the corner when she saw a tall woman helping two elderly ladies cross the street.

All three of the women paused, for Liza had inadvertently blocked their path. "Hello, Eve," Liza said.

Eve nodded, her expression carefully schooled. "You remember Miss Rose and Miss Addie."

Liza didn't, but she remembered reading about them in Laurel's letters. In their late eighties now, they were obviously sisters. Both had white hair and wore old-fashioned dresses with lace collars, white sweaters and small Sunday hats. One was slightly taller, and clung tightly to Eve's arm. She didn't let her frailty keep her from looking down her nose at Liza. The other one carried a huge assortment of cut flowers. Rounder of face and body, she appeared less severe. "You must excuse us, Laurel," she said. "Samantha Bell needs these flowers. They're from our garden, you know, and all the proceeds from today's sales will go to the Pilgrim Women's Society to aid the church."

Just then, the sterner sister faltered. Her knees wobbled, and her entire body appeared to be turning to liquid, like melting wax. Somehow, the other sister and Eve managed to keep the poor woman on her feet. In the process, the flowers were transferred into Liza's arms.

A younger woman whom Eve called Samantha rushed over to help. Leaning heavily on Eve and Samantha, the frail woman and the rest of the little entourage slowly made their way to a bench in the shade in front of the flower shop. Liza stopped near the table, out of their way.

"Could you hurry with those flowers, miss?" a woman wearing a nautical summer sweater said.

Liza glanced at her.

Another woman with coifed platinum hair and a Boston accent very much like her friend's said, "We're expected at a luncheon in Newburyport in less than an hour and those flowers would be a perfect hostess gift."

Realizing they were speaking to *her*, Liza cast a quick look at the four women huddled in the shade behind her, then at the flowers in her arms. After another few seconds spent in indecision, she placed the flowers on the table and drew out some greenery, bluebells, sweet williams, daisies and poker primroses. Quickly she put together a pretty bouquet. Sliding the stems through the rubber topper on a water-filled plastic vial, she set the bouquet in a rack and started on another arrangement using delphiniums, lilies of the valley and more bluebells. She did four small arrangements in all before she realized how quiet the people watching had become.

Finally, one woman said, "You do that beautifully. How much, dear?"

Rather than stammer, Liza said, "I think we should ask the woman in charge."

Leaving Eve with the two elderly women, Samantha Bell squeezed up to the table beside Liza. She was the kind of woman that always got a second look, and not because she was pretty. Her eyes were close-set, her mouth a little too wide for her face, her dishwater blond hair tucked behind ears that stuck out slightly.

Smiling at her customers, Samantha said, "The first two

bouquets are always for the dear ladies who grow the flowers. Laurel, would you mind taking this one to Miss Addie, and this one to Miss Rose? And then come back and show me how you did that."

Liza didn't mean to stare. It was just that, other than Tommy's, Samantha's was the first genuine smile she'd received in days. Liza liked her instantly.

"Are you going to stand there all day?" Samantha's nudge brought Liza to her senses.

A bouquet in each hand, she traipsed to the bench where she'd been instructed to present the flowers to Addie and Rose. She hesitated before them, trying to remember if Laurel had written anything in her letters that might help her determine who was who. She couldn't recall anything specific. Taking a chance, she extended a bouquet to each lady.

After a slight pause, Addie and Rose accepted the flowers, then promptly switched with each other. The kinder of the two looked up at Liza with faded, watery eyes. "It's been a long time, Laurel."

The other sister made a harumph sort of sound and then said, "I suppose you're staying at the captain's cottage."

Everyone seemed to know that Laurel had lived there during her stay in Alcott. Now that Liza thought about it, it was interesting that she hadn't lived with Jack.

Feeling several pairs of eyes on her, Liza said, "I haven't made any solid plans. If you'll excuse me." She darted around the table, intent upon making a hasty retreat.

"Laurel?"

Liza had never had so much trouble with her own identity. Her exit thwarted, she stopped, turning slowly. Eve stood next to Samantha, who had paused in the middle of arranging another bouquet. Both looked at Liza. Samantha said, "If you decide to stay, and you need a job, come to the flower shop and see me."

Liza's throat felt thick, but she said, "I'll think about it."

Again, Samantha smiled. And Liza thought people really needed to change the way they measured beauty.

"Where are you going?" Samantha asked.

Until that instant, Liza had had no idea. "To the captain's cottage."

The next time Samantha spoke, it was very, very quietly. "Captain's Row is that way." She gestured with her thumb.

Liza refrained from rolling her eyes, but just barely, then promptly changed direction.

Samantha began putting together more bouquets, but Eve watched Liza walk away. "That was strange," she said. "Did you notice—"

"I noticed," Samantha said, handing another bouquet to a waiting customer.

"She didn't seem to know Addie and Rose."

"And just now she didn't know her way to the cottage. There's something different about Laurel," Samantha said.

Eve stared at the speck in the distance that was Laurel's pale blue dress. What had happened to the bright colors she'd worn? Her hair was long now, too, but it was more than that. There was an air of quiet about her that hadn't been there before. She seemed softer, more reserved. Five years ago, she'd laughed easily and often. She'd been lively, and at times downright bold, and yet she'd remained secretive, keeping to herself much of the time. Although she'd been friendly to most everyone, the only people she'd gotten close to were people who were old or dying. And Jack. That had been a nightmare for Eve. Somehow, Laurel had known. Instead of gloating, she'd been kind. She'd been an enigma. She still was, for now, she rarely spoke and barely smiled. Her expression was guarded, her demeanor uncertain.

It was almost as if she wasn't Laurel at all.

Jack took his foot from the accelerator, allowing the patrol car to coast down the hill, allowing himself another opportunity to absorb the fact that Laurel was truly back in town.

He'd been following her for a while. She was walking

south toward Captain's Row, a street where once-majestic mansions formed a curved rim on the southern edge of town. Technically it was called High Street, for it was the only street in town with a view of the ocean. Regardless, everyone in Alcott referred to it as Captain's Row, because of the former sea captain who'd built his huge house there before the turn of the last century.

Jack had been calmer after the basketball scuffle with his brothers last night. His thoughts had been clearer, but no less intense. Seeing Laurel again had been a shock, and yet, surprisingly, he'd slept. Since waking up, he'd gone over everything she'd said. It hadn't been easy, because she'd rambled, which was strange. Laurel had always spoken her mind clearly and concisely. He'd never met a more stubborn woman, that was for sure. Five years was a long time. Perhaps his memories had become part fiction. He remembered her hair, though, and he knew for a fact that he hadn't seen another woman with hair exactly that color since she'd left. No other woman had the ability to cause his hormones this much commotion just by walking down the street, either. Damn, but the commotion felt good.

He really needed his head examined. He could do that later. Right now, he had to get to the bottom of what she was doing back in Alcott.

She wasn't walking fast. Her gait was smooth, her hips swaying just enough to be interesting. Before she'd gotten pregnant, she'd worn short skirts and high heels. In a hurry most of the time, there had been an eye-catching swing to her hips. Her point of gravity had shifted as Tommy had grown inside her. She'd still been in a hurry, though.

She wasn't hurrying today. In fact, she seemed to be moving slower all the time.

She turned suddenly and glared at him, her hands settling on her hips. He wondered how long she'd known he was there. Obviously, she didn't appreciate being followed. He took perverse satisfaction in that.

Pulling up next to her, he leaned over the seat and opened the passenger door. "Get in."

"Is there a law against walking in this town?"

Perhaps her gait had changed, but she still didn't let him intimidate her. "I heard you were looking for me," he said.

Liza stared at Jack. He certainly wasn't apologizing for tailing her. Even in his tan uniform, he looked more like a renegade than a man of the law. He'd lived a life that hadn't always been kind to him. It had left him slightly jagged around the edges, the complete opposite of the kind of men she dated, when she bothered to date at all. She'd had a few serious relationships over the years, but they'd been with starving, struggling, striving artists, long of hair, pale of skin and full of angst.

"Are you getting in or aren't you?"

Jack McCall was full of himself. She gritted her teeth, held her tongue, and got in.

Many of the houses in Alcott were surrounded by picket fences. The houses on this street were surrounded by waist-high stone walls that were crumbling in places. The huge houses had probably been imposing in their day, but now looked old and tired. She continued to watch out the window, wondering if she would be able to tell which house had been Laurel's residence during her stay here.

At the end of the street, Jack turned onto a narrow lane that disappeared around a dense arborvitae hedge that was permanently bent from the predominate winds. They emerged on the other side, and there it was, the last house on the street. Originally, the house had most likely been built as a summer house or guest quarters for the big mansion next door. Smaller than the other houses on the street, it sat alone, private and tranquil and weathered. Overgrown rhododendron bushes flanked the front steps.

Liza couldn't take her eyes off the shiny, plastic pink flamingo next to the stoop. Heart beating in her throat, she waited for the car to come to a complete stop, then got out.

Sometimes it still surprised her just how much she missed her sister.

Its shingles weathered to a dull gray, the cottage had a slightly untidy look to it. It sat on a knoll that overlooked the ocean, perhaps a half mile in the distance. The Atlantic was a deep, dark blue, the sky a hundred shades lighter. Sea birds rode the invisible air currents, heading toward the water. Far below, a large sailboat skimmed across the horizon. She watched it disappear, the wind billowing through her clothes, tangling her hair.

Her mother used to say, "God whispers in the desert and yells near the sea."

Nola had needed the whispers. Laurel and Liza had come alive near the sea.

Sometimes, Liza, it seems as if you're standing here beside me, Laurel had written. *If you were, I know what you would say. "Sure, the Atlantic Ocean is beautiful, but it's on the wrong side of the country, because everyone knows that the sun is supposed to SET over the ocean, not RISE."*

Liza was smiling when she turned.

Her smile changed, for Jack stood a few paces away, feet apart, eyes squinting, face in a perpetual scowl. For a moment, she'd forgotten he was there.

While she'd been staring at the ocean, remembering, he'd been staring at her. She had to force herself not to fidget.

"I have a friend back in California who's a sculptor," she said. "She would love to do you in bronze."

"So that's where you've been? California?"

Liza nodded, uncertain how to begin.

Jack McCall was a man of few words. He wasn't an easy man to talk to. He glanced at his watch, letting her know he had other things to do. He wasn't an easy man, period.

"Do you want to see the inside?"

Again, he waited for her to nod before opening the door. Being careful not to touch him, she went in ahead of him.

The cottage looked even smaller on the inside. It was just cluttered enough to be charming. There was a fieldstone fireplace on one wall, ashes from a long-ago fire filling the base. The throw on the back of the chintz sofa had been a Christmas present from Laurel's old college roommate. One of Liza's paintings hung on the wall. One of their mother's design sketches of a headdress was on another. Cobwebs filled the corners of the room, and layers of dust covered every surface. Even the magazines strewn about were old. It was as if time had stood still here.

"Nobody lives here anymore?" Liza asked.

"Skip Hoxie gave it to you."

Liza jumped. She hadn't realized Jack had come up so close behind her. Laurel had talked about Skip Hoxie when she'd come home that last Christmas. At ninety, he'd been as bald as a cue ball and bawdy as sin. He'd worked on a whaling boat in his youth. In later years, he'd ferried a boat to Nantucket and Martha's Vineyard, but had come back to Alcott to retire. He'd taken an instant shining to Laurel, telling her all his old stories. She'd written many of those stories down, and yet she hadn't mentioned that he'd left this cottage to her.

"I'm surprised it hasn't been repossessed or sold at a tax sale."

Jack's silence drew Liza's gaze.

There were three doorways off the living room. One led to a tiny kitchen, another to an old black-and-white-tiled bathroom. Jack was peering into the third, which led to a small bedroom. Liza found herself standing in that doorway near him.

She didn't like putting him through what he was undoubtedly remembering. "Someone's paid the property taxes, haven't they?" she whispered.

He shrugged. As if uncomfortable with the conversation, he went to the window and looked out.

"It was you, wasn't it, Jack?"

He didn't reply one way or the other. He didn't have to.

Walking closer, Liza was pretty sure she knew why he'd done it. He'd hoped Laurel would return.

She didn't stop to think before she reached out, laying a hand on his arm. He might have been tall, dark and brooding when Laurel had known him, but the years since had hollowed him out. Life had a way of doing that.

She sighed. "Jack, I know this isn't easy for you. Believe me, this isn't easy for me, either."

Jack felt the gentle hand on his arm. All it took was one touch, and he wanted more. He wanted everything. It had been this way from the start. He'd made the first move their first time. After that, he and Laurel had been neck and neck in that department. Their appetite for each other had been voracious and insatiable. His body was heating, remembering.

He stared at her hand. Her fingers were long, her nails unpainted. She was wearing the ruby ring she'd gotten from her grandmother. She'd never let him put his ring on her finger, that was for damn sure.

God, he'd missed her. He hated himself for that. He wanted to hate her. Hate her for what? She hadn't broken any promises, because she'd never made a single promise to him. She'd made no demands on him, either, and she wouldn't allow him to make any demands on her. She'd set something free in him that first summer. He hadn't felt that way since.

Until now.

He covered her hand with his, slowly bringing it to his mouth. He kissed her knuckle, his gaze on her face. Perhaps of its own volition, her fist opened. One by one, he uncurled her fingers the rest of the way. Slowly he moved her hand to his chest, pressing her palm slightly above his heart.

Her breath caught. Beneath his thumb, her pulse jumped. He knew the feeling, for his blood was making a whooshing sound as it left his brain. Their eyes locked, and it was just like the previous night all over again. Taking a step toward her, he lowered his head to kiss her.

She wrenched herself away and took a backward step. His hand tightened around hers, and one step was as far as she got.

Her eyes were wide and green and held something uncertain and infinite and indefinable, something he'd never seen before. It was almost as if he was looking at a stranger.

Or she was.

"Last night . . ." she said, her voice thick, her throat convulsing on a swallow.

"What about last night?" He couldn't help it if his voice was gruff.

"When I told you I'm not who you think I am. I wasn't lying, Jack."

He remembered when she'd told him that. His reply hadn't been kind.

He moved his head an inch one way, and then the other. His eyes remained fixed on hers, her hand in his. Understanding dawned like a fist to the jaw. His mouth dropped open, his hands falling to his sides.

The long hair. The loose-fitting dresses. Her walk. The way she'd rambled through an explanation that had made no sense. The way she'd looked at him last night, as if seeing him for the first time. And the way she'd looked at Tommy.

She wasn't Laurel.

He must have said it out loud, because she shook her head. "No, I'm not Laurel."

And he said, "Then who the hell are you?"

CHAPTER 5

A cloud drifted in front of the sun, casting the world beneath it in shadow. The somberness seemed fitting somehow.

The moment of truth had arrived.

Liza tried to calm her nerves. Since there was no way to soften reality, she kept her gaze and her voice steady as she said, "I'm Liza Cassidy. Laurel was my identical twin sister."

He stared at her, still as stone, everything about him intent upon her. A lifetime passed before he spoke. "Was?"

She bit her lip, then slowly nodded. The thing she hated the most about death—she hated a lot of things about death—but the thing she hated the most was having to use the past tense. Laurel was. Laurel had been. Laurel used to.

She reached into her pocket, taking out a photograph of the three Cassidy women that had been taken a year before Laurel's diagnosis. She looked at it for a moment before handing it to Jack.

He took it. With a steady hand, he brought it closer to his face, studying the picture carefully.

"Laurel died, Jack."

She watched his expression change with his changing emotions. First came shock, then denial, and finally, inevitably, acceptance, as if deep inside, he'd known. He cleared his throat, but even then, it seemed to cost him a great deal to find his voice.

"When?"

"Nearly five years ago now. It happened right after she left Alcott. All this time, I thought you knew."

His eyebrows shot up. "You knew about me?"

"Well, yes. She wrote about you. In her letters home each week." Liza looked past him, out the window where more clouds were gathering offshore. "I take it she didn't talk about us?"

"Us?"

"Our mother and me. Didn't she tell you anything about her past?"

"Laurel mentioned a mother and sister out West somewhere. I figured you were estranged. She said she'd been a reporter. She must have been good at it, because a lot of people opened up around her."

"She was good at so many things. She ran in marathons and could dance and swim and she was so funny. She was a great conversationalist, too. But you probably knew that."

He wound up staring at the bed. "Laurel and I never got around to doing a lot of talking."

Suddenly Liza didn't want to be having this conversation in Laurel's former bedroom. She spun around and went out into the living room. After a time, she heard the floor creak on the other side of the room.

"How did Laurel die?" The question sounded heavy, as if it had been dredged from a place deep inside him.

"She had a brain tumor."

"Cancer?"

"No. But just as deadly." Liza kept her back to Jack, her gaze on a ship far out to sea. "I guess I shouldn't be surprised she didn't tell you about it in the beginning. She didn't tell many people. Laurel grew to accept her fate, but she hated the very idea of seeing pity in people's eyes. You probably have a thousand questions. I know I do. Most of them would have been answered a long time ago if you'd bothered to show up at the lighthouse on the Isles of Shoals as she'd requested."

"What are you talking about?"

She turned around slowly, baffled. Jack stood across the room, his skin tan above the collar of his beige sheriff uniform, his eyes stark and steady and very, very blue.

"I'm talking about the letter from Laurel."

"What letter?"

Liza's mind reeled with confusion. "The letter she wrote just before she underwent her brain surgery."

He continued to stare blankly at her.

Liza floundered, uncertain where to begin. "Actually, there were three letters. One to me, one to our mother, and one to you. She left them with her surgeon, along with explicit instructions to mail them if she didn't survive."

Jack's back was ramrod straight, his mouth set, his jaw clenched. "I never received a goddamn letter from Laurel."

It required effort on Liza's part to keep from ducking her head. She dropped to the sofa so quickly, dust rose around her. Jack's voice had been bitter, but the look in his eyes was as naked as the truth. "You never received your letter." The reality of that was still sinking in, causing her to think out loud. "Dr. Green told me he put them in the mail personally."

The letters to Liza and her mother had arrived intact all the way across the country, and yet the letter to Jack hadn't made it less than a hundred miles? How could that be?

Nola and Liza had flown to Boston to meet with the neurosurgeon shortly after receiving their final letter from Laurel. There had been compassion in the doctor's eyes as he'd explained about the depth and location of the tumor, the size, and how very sorry he was. He remembered his patient with fondness and a touch of exasperation. That was Laurel, all right. Most people loved her. A few disliked her. No one was indifferent to her.

Dr. Green had honored Laurel's wishes and followed her final instructions. Liza didn't understand why one of the letters hadn't been delivered. All this time she'd been angry at

Jack because he hadn't bothered to meet her at the lighthouse that day. And all this time, he hadn't known.

She jumped to her feet. "Just once I would like fate to co-operate."

Jack was still trying to make sense of this new information. "This letter Laurel wrote to you," he said. "What did it say?"

Liza cleared her throat. "In a roundabout way, she said good-bye. I brought it to Alcott with me. You can read it if you'd like. Laurel left me her car, Gran's ruby ring, a few dozen letters, and twenty-eight years' worth of memories."

"And a nephew."

There was a long pause while she formulated her response. "I didn't know about that until I read Laurel's autopsy report a few months ago."

He looked stunned. "Why didn't she tell you she had a child?"

She sighed. "Why didn't she tell you she was dying?"

They stood on opposite sides of the small room, gazes locked. Jack spoke first. "She should have told us."

Liza sighed again. It was becoming a habit. "I agree. I think that was why she wanted us to meet at the lighthouse. She wanted us to tell each other the things she hadn't been able to tell us herself. She was dying when she met you. You never suspected that she was ill?"

He paced as far as the sofa, then back to the other side of the room. The soles of his shoes left tracks in the dusty floor. "I met Laurel on the ferry ride out to the Isles of Shoals. We spent the day together, and I invited her to Alcott. I wasn't at all certain she would come. Looking back, I was never certain of anything when it came to Laurel. I knew she had headaches. She told me they were nothing to worry about. Did she tell you she tried her damnedest to keep from falling in love with me?"

"She said it was bigger than both of you."

Actually, Laurel had written that she couldn't stop thinking about a man she'd met while spending the day at the Isles of Shoals. *It's fate, Liza. We were conceived because our mother fell for a Frenchman who'd gotten lucky at blackjack. And now I can't seem to keep my hands off a dark and brooding man named Jack. Nola's Frenchman got lucky in more ways than one. But I feel lucky, too, lucky to have met Jack McCall.*

Nola and Laurel had believed everything was fate. Liza thought it would have been easier to believe in fate if she weren't the one left behind to pick up the pieces.

Jack was quiet. And Liza knew that before her stood a man who was facing the harsh reality of loneliness, and had been for a long time.

"Yeah, it was bigger than both of us, all right." His expression was grim as he said, "That didn't keep her from shutting me out. She kept to herself, holing up alone out here for days, weeks at a time. She wouldn't move in with me, and she wouldn't marry me."

"Not even after she knew she was pregnant?"

Jack made no reply, as if that was private.

Liza chose her next question carefully. "I take it neither of you planned that? I don't mean to pry, Jack. I'm only trying to understand."

His answer had a lot in common with a snort.

"Laurel was stubborn," she said. "But when she loved, she loved with everything she had. We'd known about the tumor for a year before she died. Initially, there was talk of treatment. Although it might have prolonged her life slightly, it would have left her weak and bedridden, her body wracked with horrible, grotesque seizures that would have required mind-numbing medication. She opted for a higher quality of life, and vowed to live in dignity until she died, savoring every second until the end came naturally."

"I thought you said she had surgery," he said.

"We didn't know about that until later. The last Mom and I knew, she'd refused to have that, too. Surgery promised to be brutal. Although that type of surgery had been performed before, it was still experimental in nature. It would have taken a miracle for her to survive it *and* come out of it whole."

Jack knew more than he'd ever wanted to know about experimental procedures and risks and prognoses. "Then why did she do it?" he asked.

They answered at the same time. "Tommy."

Jack stared at Laurel. No, not Laurel. This woman was Laurel's twin sister. There was a long, brittle silence before he said, "You said your name is Liza?"

With a smile that held more sadness than anything, she said, "I think it might be a little late for a formal introduction."

He didn't know what to say, because last night had been the time for formal introductions, and last night, instead of giving her a chance to tell him who she was, he'd dragged her across his lap and kissed her. He didn't know how she could make light of that, but he appreciated it. He should apologize. He wasn't any better at asking for forgiveness than he was at asking for permission.

Laurel was dead. He'd wondered, suspected, feared, dreaded. Often, when he'd awakened in the night, it had seemed like the only plausible explanation. He should have known she wasn't being honest with him that last morning when she'd told him she had some soul-searching to do. She'd said she wasn't sure she was meant to raise a child. God, he should have read more into that. He didn't know she was dying, but he should have known she'd loved Tommy. He should have believed in that, at least. Hadn't he watched her hold their son, feed him, cherish him?

But he'd gotten angry when she'd left. And anger made a man stupid.

"Are you all right?" she asked.

He hated questions like that.

"How are you feeling now?" Liza asked.

She sounded like a shrink. He began to pace again.

Laurel had once told him that every emotion he ever experienced was either a prelude or sequel to anger. Now that he thought about it, she'd sounded like a shrink, too.

He stopped abruptly and took a long, hard look at this woman who said her name was Liza. She held perfectly still, letting him look as long as he needed. Next, he studied the photograph again. Although the sisters bore an incredible likeness, he saw subtle differences, nuances, really. They dressed differently. Wore their hair differently. Smiled differently.

The woman in this room today wasn't Laurel. She was telling the truth about that.

"Jack?"

He started. "What? You want to know how I feel? Laurel left me, and in the process, she left me wondering. She put me through hell. And now I find out she's been dead all this time. How do you think I feel?"

She waited a moment, and then asked, "What will you tell Tommy?"

He thought it was wise of her to change the subject. Raking his fingers through his hair, he said, "I have to tell him the truth." He hoped it didn't stinking kill him.

Jack knew it was up to him to make sure it didn't.

Saxon McCall's back door led directly into his kitchen, which was where Jack found his father. Whatever had been for lunch was congealing in a pot on the stove. He could hear Tommy playing over the television noises coming from the next room.

"You're back early," Saxon said without looking up from the crossword puzzle he was working at the kitchen table. "What's a seven-letter word for *without words?*"

Jack's silence finally drew Saxon's gaze, but it was probably his expression that held it.

"You on duty, or off?"

"On," Jack said. It was slow in and around Alcott today.

The festival was winding down. Norma knew where he was, and would two-way him if a call came in, just like she always did.

"What's wrong?" Saxon asked.

Now there was a question. "That woman," he said to his father, "the one I thought was Laurel? Turns out she isn't."

Two deep lines formed between Saxon's eyebrows while he waited for Jack to continue.

"Her name is Liza Cassidy. Liza, not Laurel. Laurel was her twin sister."

The kitchen clock ticked loudly. Jack counted seven ticks before Saxon said, "Was?"

Grief ripped through Jack as he said, "Laurel died, Dad."

"Are you sure?"

"Ninety-nine point nine percent sure. Laurel had headaches, remember? And she slept a lot. People said it was normal for a pregnant woman to be tired. There was a lot more to it, and a hell of a lot she didn't tell me. She had a brain tumor. I don't think her sister's lying about that." He showed his father the photograph Liza had shown him. While Saxon studied it, Jack said, "How's Tommy been this morning?"

Saxon scratched his bearded chin. "He dumped out his toy chest, didn't play with a single thing, then argued with me about picking everything up. After I won, he ate a good lunch. Now, he's watching *Free Willy*. I don't know what we're gonna do if that old tape ever wears out." He paused, lowering his voice. "He's been asking about his mother."

"What did you tell him?"

"I told him what I know. What I knew. I said she was funny and kind and she loved him, and that whatever it was that she had to do had to be very important, or she wouldn't have gone." Very slowly, Saxon pushed the photograph toward his son. "I always figured she had something big to do. I never figured it was this. You might as well get it over with."

His father was right, of course.

Jack had spent the past fifteen minutes trying to figure

out what to say to Tommy. He entered the living room without a clear plan.

Tommy's favorite movie was playing on the VCR, but he wasn't watching it. His scalp showed through the fine hair covering his head; he was thinner than he'd been a year ago, but not as thin as he'd been six months ago. Jack swore he was growing again. All arms and legs these days, he was sailing a toy boat across a turbulent, imaginary ocean.

He glanced at his father. As if sensing that something grave was about to happen, he scrambled to his feet. "Have you been fightin'?"

Only with the devil, Jack thought. Jack lowered to his haunches close to his son. "I've been thinking."

"Grandpa says that'll get ya in trouble. Know what else he said?"

"What?"

"He said I'm insolent." The boy peered around his father in order to see the TV. "This is the good part where Willy gets free."

Jack reached for the remote and turned the movie off. "You've seen this a hundred times. Right now, there's something I have to tell you."

Tommy stared up at him without blinking. Right from the start, this child had had a direct gaze. It was almost as if he could see deep inside a person. At times like this it was disconcerting. Right now, Jack needed all the composure he could get.

"You know how we thought the lady who was here last night was your mom?"

"Yeah." Tommy sidled a little closer.

"It turns out she isn't your mother."

"Is so."

Jack shook his head.

"Uh-huh. You saw her. We both did."

"She's your mother's sister, Tommy."

Tommy narrowed his eyes. It was what he always did when he was gearing up to argue.

Jack didn't give him the chance. "They were identical twins." He showed Tommy the photograph Liza had shown him. Pointing to the woman with shorter hair, Jack said, "This is your mother, Laurel. And the other one is her twin sister."

He could practically see the wheels turning behind Tommy's blue eyes. "How do you know?"

Right then, Thomas John McCall was very much his father's son. "I know. I just found out this morning. It's true, son."

Jack knew Tommy wanted to argue. He wanted his mother to be alive. What kid didn't? But Tommy also knew his father never lied. Still, he thrust his chin out stubbornly and asked, "What's *her* name, then?"

It reminded Jack that Tommy was his mother's son, too.

"Her name is Liza Cassidy. She's your aunt. You can call her Aunt Liza."

Tommy was accustomed to having uncles, not aunts, and it showed in his expression. "She's really not my mother?"

"She really isn't your mother."

The boy was quiet while he thought about that. He looked up at Jack, his blue eyes full of hope and longing. "Does she know where my mother is?"

Other than a muscle working in Jack's jaw, outwardly nothing moved. Inside was a different story. When would he learn to expect wisdom and intelligence from this precious little kid? Finally, Jack said, "She died. Not long after she left Alcott."

Jack held his breath, gauging Tommy's reaction. The boy stared at the photograph for a few more seconds, then quietly handed it back to his father. There were no explosions, no temper tantrums, no tears. There was only a sad kind of acceptance as he said, "Think she and Cody know each other, then?"

Jack's throat closed up so tight he didn't see how it would ever reopen. Tommy had met Cody Archer in the hospital the previous winter. They had become fast friends. They'd had a lot in common, right down to the same form of cancer: ALL, acute lymphoblastic leukemia. They could both pronounce it. Cody, who was a little older, had taught Tommy how to spell it. They were both bright, both urchins, and were known as the holy terrors of St. Marks Hospital. On their good days, their antics and laughter carried up and down the corridor. Jack would never forget the afternoon he'd stepped off the elevator at the third floor and into an eerie silence. He'd found Saxon sitting with Tommy, his expression grim. Tommy was crying, and Saxon was patting his back. A few days earlier, Cody had taken a turn for the worse. He'd contracted pneumonia, and had died shortly after noon that day. His room was empty, and all his family had gone. It was one of the few times throughout all of Tommy's treatment that he'd been inconsolable. Jack had held his son, aching, too, tears squeezing from his closed eyes, tears for a six-year-old boy who had suffered, tears for his family, and tears of shame because he was relieved that it hadn't been Tommy.

Tommy hadn't mentioned his buddy in a while. His uncle Brian had told him that Cody had gone to heaven. Jack didn't know what *he* believed anymore, but he knew that little kids were not supposed to see death up close. They sure as hell weren't supposed to accept it without flinching, the way Tommy was accepting the news that his mother had died.

He stared into his father's eyes for a long time. Jack prepared for a hundred difficult questions.

And Tommy said, "Do we have any ice cream at our house?"

The last thing Jack had expected to do was laugh, but it blasted out of him, rusty and choppy, like an engine in dire need of an overhaul. On the heels of his laughter, emotion flooded his chest with so much force, it was all he could do to keep from grabbing Tommy up and holding onto him too tight. He settled for lifting the boy off his feet and rubbing his whisker stubble against Tommy's smooth cheek. Tommy's quick hug made Jack wonder who was comforting whom. Jack's throat closed up all over again.

Somehow, he managed to say, "We can buy some. Any flavor you want."

As soon as Jack set Tommy back on his feet, the boy scooped his toy boat off the floor. "Let's go."

"Want a piggyback ride?" Jack asked.

"Nah. I'm not tired today. Can I ride to the store in the cruiser?"

"Yes."

"Can I sound the siren?"

"No."

"That's what I thought. I wanna take Shamu with me."

Jack ruffled the short tufts of auburn-red hair sticking up on Tommy's head. Shamu was the stuffed whale he'd gotten from Cody's mother shortly after her son had died. Tommy hadn't played with it in a while. Jack sighed. His son was getting better. That was what mattered most.

"Dad?"

"Hmm?"

"What does insolent mean?"

Saxon's voice carried from the kitchen. "It means you're a McCall."

Jack should have known his father had been listening. Reaching for Tommy's hand, he said, "Being insolent isn't something to be proud of, because it means you're overbearing and insulting. The next time Grandpa tells you to pick up your toys, you might as well do it the first time."

"Cuz he's more insolent than me?"

"Because when you're over here, he's in charge," Jack said, making a valiant effort not to grin.

Of course, Tommy saw right though him.

Jack was six-two, and weighed 185 pounds. Every last ounce of him was putty in this little boy's hands.

* * *

Liza heard the door bang shut next door. Holding very still, she was able to sit undetected while she watched three generations of McCalls heading this way across the side yard.

The oldest carried a folded newspaper, and had a beard and a full head of white hair that was a little too shaggy to look civilized. Jack's hair was dark and short and neatly styled, and yet there was something in him that looked uncivilized, too. Tommy, with his knobby knees and boyish lope, looked more beguiling than uncivilized. They spoke amongst themselves. Although she couldn't hear the actual conversation, they sounded normal and happy. She wondered if Jack had told Tommy about Laurel.

They were at the gate in the picket fence between the two yards when they noticed her sitting on the stoop at Jack's back door, their overweight yellow dog lying near her feet. They slowed in unison, then resumed walking, Saxon on the left, Jack on the right, Tommy in the middle, all three of them quiet suddenly.

She waited until they were almost upon her to stand up.

"Liza Cassidy," Jack said, "this is my father, Saxon McCall."

She held out her hand. "It's nice to meet you, Mr. McCall."

"Call me Saxon," he said, shaking her hand. "Welcome to Alcott."

Tommy stared openly.

She looked to Jack for some sign. He nodded once.

So, she thought, Tommy knew that Laurel had died. Pointing to a stack of photo albums, she said, "I thought Tommy might want to see pictures of his mother when she was his age."

Tommy was still staring up at her. "Dad says you're not my mom."

She looked at him, and said quietly, "That's right, Tommy, I'm not."

He continued to stare at her for so long, she wondered

what he saw. Finally, he held his toy out to her. "See my new sailboat? The aunts gave it to me. And it isn't my birthday for three more weeks."

With her heart in her throat she took the toy, turning it this way and that. "It's a sloop, and a pretty good replica, too."

Pleasure lit the boy's eyes from the inside, making Liza glad she'd known that. "I'm gonna have one when I grow up."

"When your mother lived in Chicago," she said, "she had a sailboat on Lake Michigan."

His interest peaked, Tommy asked, "What kind?"

"A little catboat with a bright orange sail." She'd sold it before she'd come out East, along with the majority of her other worldly possessions. "Orange was her favorite color."

He took the sailboat back. "Catboats are for sissies."

Liza burst out laughing. In a million years, she hadn't expected to, not today. She sat on the top step again. Smoothing her dress over her knees, she said, "Your mother was a girl, but she was certainly not a sissy. Once, when we were ten, she stood up to the neighborhood bully who said our corner lemonade stand was his. His name was Billy, but Laurel and I called him Bubba. He was two years older and a lot bigger, but not very bright, you know?"

She had Tommy's undivided attention, and was completely focused on him in return. Therefore, she didn't know that he wasn't the only McCall watching her. Saxon had lowered stiffly onto an Adirondack chair on one side of an outdoor table, and Jack settled into another chair close by.

"What did the bully do?" Tommy asked.

"He didn't like being challenged by a girl, so he named the terms. Besides the rights to our lemonade stand, which Laurel and I had spent all morning setting up, he said the winner of a race around the block got all the lemonade he wanted plus all the money from sales, and the loser had to eat dog poop."

Tommy stared at her in waiting silence.

Liza feigned an interest in her chipped fingernail. "Your mother and I made nine dollars and fifty cents each that day."

She knew the exact moment Tommy understood the meaning behind her blasé statement. It hadn't taken him long to figure it out. He was Laurel's child, all right.

"Did Bubba eat dog poop?"

She pulled a face. "Bullies are never as good as their word."

Tommy's disappointment was comical. Liza laughed again.

"What's so funny?" Tommy asked.

"You are." She happened to glance at Jack and Saxon, and caught them looking at her. Suddenly self-conscious, she was glad she hadn't told the rest of the story, for Laurel had won that race because she'd tripped the bully when he'd started to gain on her. The only reason he hadn't beaten her up was because Nola had intervened. They'd gotten a lecture about fair play, but both Laurel and Liza had known that their mother was secretly proud and relieved that her girls were learning to take care of themselves.

"Liza? Aunt Liza?" Tommy jostled her from her musings.

"Yes?"

"Why'd you stop talking?"

"I was thinking."

"Oh no, more thinking."

She smiled. "You remind me so much of your mother."

"Was she insolent, too?"

Liza stared at him, amazed at his language and comprehension skills. He'd said that word yesterday, too. He was old beyond his years, just like Laurel and Liza had always been. A new and unexpected warmth spread through her. "Sometimes, I suppose she was very insolent."

"You've got pictures of her in those books?"

Liza glanced at Jack for permission before reaching for the first album. He nodded, and it occurred to her that Tommy was having an easier time with this than his father was.

"Just a minute." Tommy scampered up the steps and disappeared inside his house. He returned, a stuffed black-and-white whale under his arm where his boat had been. Without saying a word, he sat down next to her. Saxon spread out his newspaper, and started in on his crossword puzzle. Liza opened the first album.

The air was a pleasant seventy-eight degrees, the sky partly cloudy. If she concentrated, Liza could feel something soothing on the ocean breeze, like the brush of a gentle hand. Somewhere, a radio played, and a lawn mower rumbled a block away, but other than birds and a bumblebee or two, all was quiet at this end of Mill Street. Just as quietly, reverently almost, Liza began to put her childhood memories into words.

Jack sat a short distance away. He noticed the breeze, too, but he felt anything but soothed. Holding very still, he took a deep breath and tried to relax. It was no use.

When Tommy had first perched next to Liza, he'd been shy and stiff, keeping a careful distance between them. Bit by bit, he'd inched closer. Now, he was touching her, sometimes leaning against her as he peered at the photos. She didn't seem to know a great deal about children, and yet she appeared to be enjoying Tommy's closeness.

Settling back in his chair, fingers steepled beneath his chin, Jack looked closely at her. She had a narrow nose, a wide mouth and green eyes. Her hair was windblown and it waved past her shoulders, the ends nearly touching the top of Tommy's head. She looked so much like Laurel, it was easy to imagine what might have been.

Although he couldn't make out the images clearly, he could see some of the photographs as she pointed to them. In the first album, Liza spun her tales around all three Cassidys. An artist, Nola Cassidy sounded like a nutcase to Jack, but she must have done something right, because it looked as if her daughters had had a happy childhood. And the woman hadn't raised dummies or weaklings, that was for sure.

In the more recent photographs, there was only Liza and her mother. Tommy studied those for a long time, and Jack thought it had been wise of Liza to bring the albums over, for they gave Tommy visual tools to help him comprehend the situation.

At one point, Tommy looked up from the albums, straight at Jack. "Weren't you going to buy ice cream?"

Jack started. "We were going to go out for some, remember?"

Tommy looked from his father to Liza, his indecision obvious.

"Why don't you go get some, Jack, and bring it back here?" Saxon suggested.

Because Jack didn't want to leave, either, that's why. He clamped his mouth shut. He admitted it to himself. That didn't mean he liked it.

Norma's voice came over the two-way radio. "Jack?"

He grabbed the radio from the clip on his belt. "Yes, Norma?"

"Pete Dixon is here about a permit to park in a restricted area. I told him we're only open today because of the festival, but you know Pete."

"I'll be right there." To Tommy, he said, "I'll swing by the grocery store after I get off duty." After glancing at Saxon, who nodded, his way of letting Jack know he would stay with Tommy, Jack found his feet. "What flavor?"

"Superman! What kind do you want, Aunt Liza?" That easily, Tommy accepted that she was his aunt.

Her voice was huskier when she said, "Superman-flavored ice cream is okay with me, too."

"You like Superman ice cream?" Tommy said.

"Why do you ask?"

"What flavor?" Jack asked.

She relented. "Cherry, strawberry or blackberry frozen yogurt. Perhaps something of that nature?"

"Real ice cream for me. With nuts," Saxon said, his pencil poised over a blank box on the newspaper.

"I'll see what I can do."

Jack had started toward his car when he heard Saxon say, "Hey, Liza? You wouldn't happen to know a seven-letter word for *without words,* would you?"

"Don't tell him," Tommy said. "Grandpa learns big words from working his crossword puzzles, then he uses 'em on the rest of us."

Jack stopped in the shade. Looking back toward his house, he saw a woman and child poring through photo albums on the stoop off the kitchen, an older man hunched over his newspaper, an old yellow dog sound asleep at his feet. It might have been just an ordinary family on an ordinary day in an ordinary small coastal town.

"Try tacitly," Liza said.

Saxon gloated when it fit, and Tommy said, "I told you not to tell him."

Liza laughed out loud.

It was as if a fist had wrapped around Jack's windpipe. And he faced the fact that there was nothing ordinary about any of this.

Liza was enjoying herself, her laughter too rich and joyful to be fake. You could tell a lot about people by their laughter. No two people laughed exactly the same way. Jack knew because he collected laughs the way some people collected coins or autographs or ancient art. Laurel's laugh had been deep and sexy, playful and sultry. Saxon's always came from the vicinity of his knees. Brian hadn't laughed much since he'd become the pastor at the Pilgrim Church. Carter laughed loud and often, but he didn't mean it. Liza's laughter was lilting and resonant, blending with Tommy's high twitter.

She chose that moment to look his way, her gaze meeting his from thirty feet away. She said something to Tommy, and a second later, his son waved comically, wholeheartedly. Liza smiled at the boy's antics, and Jack felt as if he'd gotten too close to an electrical power line.

It was a relief when she turned her attention back to the

photo albums. Gritting his teeth, he turned on his heel, walked to his cruiser and got in.

Work. He was going back to work. And then he was going to buy ice cream. He could have used a cigarette and a stiff drink. A good fight would suffice. An hour between a woman's sheets would be even better. He listed all the reasons he wouldn't do any of those things. He was a father and a sheriff. It was the middle of the day. And this was Alcott. He didn't smoke or fight anymore. He rarely drank. And he'd learned to live without sex.

Or at least he'd stinking thought he had.

CHAPTER 6

"There we were. My buddy Steven and me and three gorgeous women in an inflatable raft at a bend in the Colorado River."

Liza looked up from her sketch pad to find Carter McCall shading his eyes as if peering into distant rapids. Tommy was napping in the shade, and Saxon, Brian and Jack all appeared to be listening to Carter's latest tale.

"Ahead of us was white water as far as the eye could see. Back on shore were three jealous boyfriends." Carter gave Liza a reckless grin. "It took some hard paddling and fancy maneuvering, but we finally made it to safety. That was some ride!"

"These three jealous boyfriends," Brian said, "were they the women's, or your buddy Steven's?"

Luckily, Tommy was sound asleep, and didn't see the one-finger salute Carter gave the pastor of the Pilgrim Church. Even Jack grinned at that one.

Carter launched into another story, and Liza returned to her sketch pad, her right foot moving in small half circles. It had been a pleasant afternoon. Carter was funny enough to do stand-up. She had the pain in her side to prove it. Although he tried not to be, Brian was nearly as funny, but much drier. Saxon was so serious, it was comical. She didn't know if Jack had a sense of humor or not. He'd returned twenty minutes ago, a grocery sack under one arm. He'd covered Tommy with a corner of the lightweight blanket, then disappeared inside where he stashed four containers of ice cream in the freezer and changed into faded jeans and comfortable shoes before joining the group lounging in his side yard. He hadn't said much more than "hello" to anybody. His family seemed to accept it as commonplace.

Liza had grown up surrounded by women: her mother, her sister, her grandmother and friends. Even the family parakeet had been female. Men had always seemed so mysterious, with their deep voices and five-o'clock shadows and interesting quirks. They could spend hours in dank, cobweb-infested basements and garages and enjoyed smelly things like cigars and didn't mind getting grease under their fingernails. They could lift heavy furniture and open stubborn jars. She wouldn't allow herself to think about how a man could make a woman feel in bed.

Her hand paused over her sketch pad, hazy images moving through her mind like the first brushstrokes of watercolors on canvas. The shimmering images lasted but a moment, just long enough to slow her thoughts and her heartbeat. Chiding herself, she returned to the sketch.

Looking very much like the knave he portrayed in his stories, Carter sat back in the lawn chair, slouching slightly, legs apart, knees poking through holes in his jeans. He was a little younger than Liza. She couldn't tell how much. He had the McCall features, except for his hair, which was chin length and stuck behind his ears. Brian appeared very clean-cut, with his short hair, navy chinos and white cotton shirt, the sleeves rolled up on his forearms; but the brothers weren't so different. Carter jiggled one foot. Brian sat ahead, toying with a rubber band he'd found in his shirt pocket. Saxon, wearing old Wranglers, strummed his fingers on the picnic table. Only Jack sat perfectly still, serious and intense.

Liza wondered if he made love with the same kind of single-minded intensity.

There she went again, imagining his mouth moving across her lips, to her neck, slowly kissing his way lower, his hands gliding over her skin, his fingertips warm, sure, deft. Her vision cleared, and she found herself looking right at him. He stared back at her, his breathing deep, his gaze steady, his expression inscrutable. He was the first to look away.

Did he dislike her? Was that it? How could he? He didn't know her, and he didn't strike her as an unfair man.

She set her foot in motion again and forced her gaze elsewhere. Brian was listening to Carter, who'd launched into another tale of debauchery and adventure. Saxon had started another crossword puzzle. Tommy and Tanner were both still sound asleep on the superhero blanket they shared.

The McCalls were an interesting lot. None of them pounded their chests or readjusted anything in public, and yet there was enough testosterone in this yard to fire off a cannon. They were all tall, and all had dark blue eyes and chiseled features. There were differences, too. Brian's hair was lighter, Jack's mouth was wider and Carter's eyes were deeper set. Tommy and Saxon had both dozed off earlier, not long after Carter and Brian had sauntered over. Brian had remarked on Liza's likeness to Laurel, and both of them had offered their condolences for her loss. Liza appreciated it. She appreciated their easy camaraderie even more.

She'd learned a lot about the group dynamics of these men. Saxon was wise, and Brian was itching to laugh at Carter's off-color jokes. Carter wanted everyone to think he was the family rebel. She hadn't quite figured out what he was hiding. She'd learned more about Tommy's illness, too. According to Saxon, the child was on daily, low-dose chemotherapy, and would be for at least another year. Other than the cancer's return, infection was the biggest threat to his health. Brian assured her that Tommy's type of leukemia,

ALL, was the most common form among children, and had the highest success rate for remission and cure.

She stared at the sleeping child, thinking about what he'd been through. Jack rose to his feet like a spring wound too tight, as if he couldn't sit still another second. Taking that as her cue, she began gathering up her pencils and photo albums.

Tommy opened his eyes and sat up, all in one motion. "Hey, Tanner." He jostled the old dog. "It's time to get up." A crease in one cheek from the blanket where he'd slept, Tommy looked all around and said, "We're up!", as if they wouldn't have noticed on their own. "What are you doing?" he asked Liza, pushing his feet into his shoes.

"I should be going." Slowly, she straightened.

"What about your ice cream?" the boy asked.

"Maybe another time."

He darted to Liza, shoelaces trailing on the ground. "Then you're coming back?"

Suddenly, the side yard was utterly silent. Saxon looked up from his crossword puzzle. Carter and Brian were looking past Liza, at Jack. It was Brian who finally broke the awkward moment. "Of course she's coming back, buddy."

"She's your aunt," Carter said. "That means she's family."

The pointed look Brian and Carter cast toward Jack went over Tommy's head. It didn't escape Liza, though. She tore off the final sketch. Gliding down to his level, she handed it to her nephew.

It was of him, sleeping on the blanket in the shade with Tanner. Tommy studied it. Without warning, he threw his arms around her, crinkling the drawing between them. She'd held a baby once, but she hadn't hugged a child Tommy's size since she was that small herself. Perhaps she had some maternal instinct after all. Or perhaps her surprise simply gave way to joy, because her arms found their way around his narrow back. Eyes closed, she inhaled the scent of popsicles and soap and grass and fresh summer air. When she opened her eyes, Jack was looking at her, his expression locked up tight. She wished she knew what he was thinking, but a woman with any sense at all knew better than to ask.

The hug was over as quickly as it began, and Tommy darted off to show everyone else the sketch. When he got to his father, Jack made him hold still long enough to tie his shoes.

Liza left the other sketches on the rustic wood table. Smiling all around, she said, "Thank you all for a wonderful afternoon."

All but one of them said good-bye.

Darkness hadn't quite fallen when Jack turned on the outside faucet, cranked up the pressure, and aimed the nozzle at the melted ice cream that had pooled on the bottom step. Tommy was asleep. Jack was trying to wind down, too.

The crafters had packed up their merchandise hours ago. The annual art festival was officially over. Already, Alcott was nearly back to normal. Nothing had really changed in the past twenty-four hours. Tommy was in remission. Laurel was gone. Trees were green and the sky was blue. Thunder rumbled in the distance. Make that sky gray. Dark gray.

Nothing had really changed in Jack's life or in his world, and yet one question continued to plague him. Why hadn't Laurel told him she was dying?

Why?

There was no plausible answer. Liza had said that when Laurel loved, she'd loved with everything she had. That brought Jack to the real reason he was climbing the walls tonight.

He was often angry. But he wasn't unkind or inhospitable. Today, he'd been both.

Saxon, Brian and Carter had all left soon after Liza had. None of them had said a word about his behavior. It was just as well. He had nothing to say in his defense.

He'd stared for a long time at the sketches Liza had done. She'd captured the real Saxon dozing in his chair, arms folded across his chest. The sketch of Tommy and Tanner napping on the same blanket was good enough to frame. The ones of Brian and Carter were interesting likenesses, too.

She hadn't drawn him.

Even Tommy had noticed. Frustration tore at Jack. It was going to be a long night.

"You mad at your sidewalk, Jack?"

Recognizing that voice, he eased the pressure he was exerting on the nozzle, and turned around. Eve Nelson strolled toward him. Giving him one of those grins that always made him feel like there might just be some order in the world after all, she stopped well out of the way of the streaming water.

He started to relax, really relax, for the first time all day. "Tommy dumped his ice-cream cone earlier. Thought I'd spray off the cement before the ants move in for good."

She came a little closer. "Is Tommy asleep?"

He gave her a curt nod.

"And you're restless."

He didn't bother trying to deny it.

"If you'd like me to sit with Tommy for ten minutes while you go run twenty miles, go ahead."

"Very funny." But he was glad she'd stopped by. Spending time with Eve was like pulling on an old sweatshirt on a cool day. She was comfortable, agreeable, practical. She was everyone's friend, the kind of woman everybody could depend on. It was one more thing that never changed in Alcott.

"Do you have time to talk?" she asked.

Something in the tone of her voice made him look closely at her. The sides of her hair were pulled up and secured with shiny clips. She wore brown sandals, loose-fitting chinos and a white cotton T-shirt. She looked the way she always looked. Jack could feel himself relaxing a little more.

"Is something wrong with one of the aunts?"

She shook her head. "Rose has been a little under the weather, but that isn't what I wanted to talk to you about."

"Your sister?"

Again, she shook her head. Shooing away a mosquito buzzing around her head, she redistributed her weight to one foot and said, "It's about Laurel."

Jack felt his spine straightening, one vertebra at a time. "Eve, she isn't—"

"I know what you're going to say. Please, just hear me out. There's something different about Laurel, Jack." She combed her fingers through her long, straight hair the way she often did when she was thinking about something important. "At first, I couldn't put my finger on what it was, but this morning, she didn't know Addie and Rose. And then she didn't know the way to the captain's cottage." Eve faced him, earnest and intense. "Call me crazy."

"You're one of the most sane women I know."

She smiled at him the way she'd been doing since they were ten years old. "Wait until you've heard what I have to say and then tell me if you still feel the same. I mean, I know that scientists supposedly haven't cloned humans yet, but I don't think that woman is Laurel."

"She isn't."

Eve stared wordlessly at Jack. Her feet were rooted to the sidewalk, making it impossible for her to sidestep the water running in little rivulets toward her. She was pretty sure her mouth was hanging open. She couldn't help it. She'd expected him to argue, or at the very least show surprise. "What did you say?"

"She isn't Laurel. Her name is Liza."

"Liza?"

"Liza Cassidy."

"Cassidy?" She clamped her mouth shut. Surely, she sounded like an imbecile.

"She's Laurel's twin sister. Laurel died," he said. "Not long after she left Alcott."

Jack's voice had dropped in volume, causing Eve to lower her voice, too. "That's what we thought, isn't it? I'm sorry. I know how you felt about Laurel."

He bent over the spigot and turned the water off. His shirt

was out and unbuttoned, his jeans faded to nearly white. He had a washboard stomach, a broad chest and wide shoulders. When he straightened again, she had to look up slightly to talk to him. Once, she'd told her sister he was the only man in Alcott tall enough for her. But that wasn't true. There were other men taller than her five-feet eleven inches. She would have wanted Jack if he'd been a foot shorter. She'd known it when they were both in the third grade.

They'd grown up together. They'd walked to school together and played together. He'd tutored her in geometry, and she'd helped him through broken dates and broken promises. When other boys were teasing her about being all arms and legs, he'd accepted her exactly as she was. To this day, he considered her his best friend. He'd been on the verge of falling in love with her for so long. And then Laurel had arrived in town. It was as if lightning had struck, thunder had rumbled, and cymbals had clanged, all in the same instant. By the time the crescendo was over, Eve had lost him to a woman she couldn't even hate. She knew, because she'd tried. Then Laurel had left. And Eve had helped him through that, too.

She sighed. Yesterday, when she'd thought Laurel was back, it had seemed as if lightning had struck all over again. She'd spent the night tossing and turning, and had spent today worrying. But Laurel wasn't back. Of course she wasn't back. Lightning never struck the same place twice.

Talking while he rolled up the garden hose, Jack said, "Today, I told Tommy his mother is dead."

Eve remained quiet as she thought about that. Telling Tommy about Laurel's death couldn't have been easy for Jack, but then nothing about this situation had ever been easy. "How is he?"

"I was worried about him, but he handled it okay. He's one strong little kid."

She could feel herself melting on the inside. "He takes after you."

Jack glanced at her again, and she went weak in the knees, flushed with heat at something as ordinary as the affection in his expression. "Good old Eve."

She felt an instant's squeezing hurt, and averted her gaze so he wouldn't see. When she was able to speak, she said, "Tommy has a doctor's appointment tomorrow, doesn't he?"

"Yeah."

She waited, giving him time to invite her to go along. He didn't, of course. She'd offered once, early in Tommy's treatment, but he'd declined, saying he didn't want to take advantage of her goodness. How on earth could a woman throttle a man for that?

"I dread putting him through it."

"You just said he's a strong little kid. The report came back fine last month and it will again this month. Tommy's stamina is already returning. Every time he has good results, you'll breathe a little easier. As long as his ANC stays over a thousand, his immune system will be adequate and he'll be able to start school in the fall. And then next year he'll be in my first-grade class and all this will be a distant memory. I'm helping Brian at the church office tomorrow morning, and I'm taking Miss Rose to the doctor in the afternoon. Call me when you and Tommy get back from his appointment, okay?"

"What would Alcott do without you?"

She flushed as if he'd just said she was beautiful.

And he said, "You're right about Tommy. He is getting stronger. Dad said he hauled out every toy he owned and showed Liza."

"Liza?"

"That's her name. Laurel's identical twin sister."

Yes, she'd caught that. "She's been here today?"

For a moment his gaze sharpened. "She showed Tommy old pictures of Laurel."

Eve must have been good at schooling her expression, because his eyebrows lowered into place. Of course she was good at it. Good old Eve had had years of practice.

Taking a deep breath, she adjusted her smile. "She's staying, then? In Alcott, I mean?"

He hoisted the garden hose over his shoulder. "I haven't asked her about her plans."

Eve didn't understand the reason for his grim expression. "Is something wrong, Jack?"

"No. Yes. I don't know." And then, quieter, he said, "I owe her an apology."

Thunder rumbled again. Again, Eve waited, this time for him to invite her in. For a moment, she wondered what she would do if he ever returned her feelings for him.

When. When he returned her feelings. Not if.

"Whom do you owe an apology, Jack?"

"Liza." The distant thunder made his answer sound ominous to Eve.

"For what?" she asked.

He shrugged, and she knew he wouldn't elaborate.

Choosing her words carefully, Eve said, "Then maybe you should apologize tomorrow. If it'll make you feel better, that is. I'd wait until after you get back from Tommy's doctor appointment and you're breathing easy again."

His grim expression brought out her smile. Apologizing was difficult for most people. Once, when they were both seventeen, she'd stuck her hands on her hips and told him he'd sooner have a tooth yanked out without Novocain than ask for forgiveness. He hadn't denied it. Knowing him, he still wouldn't.

Thunder rumbled again and darkness was falling fast. They spoke of mundane things for a few more minutes. After extracting a promise from him to call her when he and Tommy returned from their appointment in Manchester the following day, she hurried the two blocks to her house.

Eve wasn't normally prone to gloominess, but after unlocking her back door, she was glad she'd left a light on. Lamplight or not, she was still coming home to an empty house. It was a nice house. Small, but nice. It was plenty big enough for just her. Her and her shadow.

One of Thoreau's writings drifted through her mind. *There's no companion as companionable as solitude.* Thoreau most likely hadn't been a thirty-five-year-old virgin who'd been hopelessly in love with the same man all his life.

She gave herself a mental kick and insisted she stop feeling sorry for herself. Besides, this wasn't hopeless. Striding to the window, she watched it rain. She was feeling a little lonely, that was all. She thought about calling her sister, but it was after nine, and Brooke was probably trying to convince Sophie it was time for bed. Samantha would be busy with Ben and Mariah. It seemed that all her friends were either working on having a baby, already had children, or at the very least were working on their first divorce. And here Eve was, still single. She was a late bloomer. There was nothing wrong with that.

Eve and her sister had been born after their parents had given up hope of having children. Francine and Edgar Nelson had been pleased to have a family. Eve and Brooke had been loved, but to Eve, her parents had always seemed old. They'd been kind and proper, the house tidy and quiet. When they'd died suddenly, six months apart, ten years ago, they'd left everything to their daughters. It had been up to Brooke and Eve to divvy things up. They'd attacked the problem very pragmatically, splitting everything, even Steven. Since Eve hadn't had a burning desire to live in the house where they'd grown up—her burning desires had always lain with Jack, and Brooke had a husband and daughter, it had seemed more practical for her to live in the old Victorian house on Bridge Street. Eve had purchased this small bungalow on West Briar Street with her share of her inheritance. Eventually, she planned to move into Jack's house anyway.

She stood at her bedroom window for a long time, watching the rain and thinking about the course her life had taken. She'd had it all charted out at a young age. Graduate from high school at the top of her class. Obtain her teaching degree, also at the top of her class. Obtain a position teaching elementary school. Marry Jack. The first three had fallen into place right on schedule. The fourth matter was taking much longer than she'd planned. Eve was patient—most of the time. Meanwhile, it wasn't as if her life had no meaning. She led a quiet life, but a good one. To outsiders, it probably seemed as predictable as her parents' had been.

Rain pelted the roof. Like the gust of wind that bent the branches on the tree in her tiny front yard, something flared inside her. She felt a momentary panic, as if she was already old.

Good old Eve.

She doubted Jack had ever referred to Laurel in that manner. And now Laurel's twin sister had come to Alcott.

Lightning struck with so much force it split the entire sky in half. Eve jumped. The lights went out without so much as a flicker. Heart racing, she went in search of candles, telling herself it didn't mean anything.

It was just a storm.

Jack's tires splashed through the puddles in the patched asphalt parking lot of the Alcott Motel. His headlights competed with the glare of fluorescent lights around the perimeter of the building. Circling the entire structure, he counted seven cars. Not one of them was Laurel's old Chevy.

Where could Liza be at two o'clock in the morning?

He strummed his fingers on the steering wheel and stared at the wet pavement. The storm had finally hit with a vengeance at shortly after eleven, taking out half the town's power. That was probably why Carter had come tooling in next door earlier than usual. Jack hadn't wasted any time roping him into staying with Tommy for a little while, while Jack went out.

Liza was new in town. Where could she be? His foot came off the brake at the same time it occurred to him where he would find her.

He turned his Scout toward Captain's Row.

He drove with his window down and his radio off. The storm had blown out to sea, taking most of the clouds with it. Stars were out, and the moon was a crescent in the sky. There was something honest about the middle of the night, a kind of reverence that didn't exist any other time of the day. It had to do with the dark sky and the silence. No matter what else had changed over the past million years, night hadn't. It blanketed all of humanity's supposed progress, leaving only those elements that had always been real: earth, sea, wind and sky. It was the one time of the day when his mind cleared and he could breathe. Problems seemed smaller and life almost made sense.

He turned his lights off at the end of the street. He wasn't certain what he expected, but felt sure he would know when he saw it. Leaving his Scout near the first arborvitae bush, he walked the rest of the way.

Laurel's old car was parked in front of the cottage. He'd been right about that. The power was out on this side of town. He didn't see any candlelight in the windows. Liza didn't have a key, so unless she'd jimmied a lock, she wouldn't be inside, anyway. Without making a sound, he ducked around the side of the cottage where the rhododendrons and azaleas grew wild.

He was still in the shadows when he saw her.

She stood near the edge of the property, arms spread wide, back arched, her face tipped toward the sky. She was dancing, humming to herself, her movements so fluid he couldn't take his eyes off her.

A long time ago, the small backyard had been an English garden designed to please the guests of the people living in the big house. All that remained were some scraggly rose-bushes and the hundred-year-old flagstones where Liza twirled, her filmy dress weaving and fluttering around her legs. There was such joy in her movements. It was as if the soft breeze was her music and the night was her partner.

He wondered what she was thinking about, imagining, dreaming of. A man? The moon? This moment in time?

She'd been wearing a blue dress earlier. This one looked silver, the fabric gauzy and translucent. One sleeve had slipped off her shoulder, baring her throat, her collarbone, and a few inches of creamy skin beneath it.

A gentle breeze continued to move over her, sifting through her long hair and fluttering through the hem of her dress. That same breeze lifted his hair off his forehead and billowed through his shirt. It was as if the flowing rhythm and crooning melody of her movements had found their way inside him. He reacted in the most fundamental way.

He backed away jerkily, one step and then two. Turning on his heel, he left as quietly as he'd arrived.

Liza stopped humming. She wasn't sure why she stopped moving. There hadn't been any sound to disturb her. It was more a sense that she wasn't alone. Goose bumps tap-danced up and down her arms—from the breeze, not from unease. Holding perfectly still, her breathing slightly ragged, she opened her eyes in time to see Jack McCall slip away through the shadows and disappear into the night.

It was a long time before she moved.

Liza drove slowly, the radio tuned to her favorite late-night talk show. Steering around a fallen limb, she turned onto Mill Street, then parked her car at the curb in front of Jack's house. She'd been heading for the Alcott Motel, when suddenly, she'd turned around and driven this way. Before she could talk herself out of it, she got out of her car, crept up the steps, lifted her fist and rapped on his door.

The lock scraped a moment before the door was pulled open. Jack stood in the foyer, his feet bare, his shirt flung over his shoulder. Candlelight flickered behind him, too faint to shed much light on him.

"Why did you leave?" she asked.

"You saw me?"

"Wasn't I supposed to?"

She was a little surprised when he shook his head, not by his answer, but that he'd answered at all. "Are the fine citizens of Alcott aware that their sheriff is a Peeping Tom?"

He gaped. "I'm not. I didn't go there to spy. I went because I wanted to apologize."

She pushed her sleeve up where it belonged on her shoulder. "Nobody wants to apologize. It's the hardest thing on the planet to do."

Jack did a double take. She could have been angry with him for intruding on her private dance in the moonlight. Instead, she made him feel understood. And that felt dangerous. It just so happened he was in the mood for danger, and had been all day. "Would you like to come in?"

She shook her head. "And waste that sky?" She backed up, turned and glided down the steps of his front stoop.

He didn't have to think twice before he followed her. Barefoot, he paused on the sidewalk and started to speak. The quick shake of her head made him stop.

She looked all around, and finally up at the sky. "Do you hear it?"

"Hear what?" he asked, his voice as quiet as hers had been.

"Silence."

He listened. He heard the silence; sensed the tranquillity; saw sheer, unspoiled beauty. He wasn't looking at the sky.

She opened her eyes and caught him looking at her. It was as if she'd known he would be. He put on his shirt. Leaving it unbuttoned, he walked close enough to see her more clearly, but not close enough to touch her. What he saw in her eyes made him wish he'd moved a little closer after all.

CHAPTER 7

Liza stepped lightly over the moon shadows stretching beneath the widespread branches of the oak tree in Jack's front yard. "You must have gone to the captain's cottage for a reason tonight," she said. "Why did you leave?"

He'd been expecting a question along those lines, although not in a voice so sultry and deep. She placed her hand at the base of her throat. When her sleeve started to slip off her shoulder again, she moved her hand there, edging the fabric back into place. It took a little doing to regain his train of thought.

"You looked . . ." He searched for the right word. "Untroubled."

"So?"

"I didn't want to . . ." What was wrong with him? Now, he couldn't even talk?

"What?" she whispered. "You didn't want to frighten me? Don't worry; I had my mace, my stun gun, my forty-four and my machete, not to mention my secret weapon."

He hadn't expected to smile tonight. "Maybe I'm the one who should be afraid.

"I went to the cottage to apologize. After I saw you dancing, I didn't want to intrude."

"That's nice," she said, turning her head to look at him.

He made a sound that was half snort. *"Nice* isn't a word people normally use to describe me."

"I didn't say you were nice. I said you did something nice. There's a huge difference."

"Then my reputation is intact."

She didn't try to hide her grin. And it occurred to Jack that she somehow sensed that this bantering wasn't common practice for him.

"My mother used to call this skylarking," she said. "It means romping with words."

He tried the word in his mind. He'd never heard of it, but it seemed appropriate, made even more fitting by the lateness of the hour and the darkness of the night.

"I'd forgotten that," she said. "Once people are gone, you forget so many things, no matter how hard you try not to. My mother was an amazing woman. Spirited and funny, warm and sometimes forgetful, she had a word for everything. She and Saxon would have gotten along fabulously."

Saxon was a McCall, and didn't get along *fabulously* with anybody, but Jack left Liza to her illusions. "I don't remember much about my mother," he said, surprising himself.

"How old were you when she died?"

"I was seven." She wasn't looking at him. Perhaps that was why he continued. "Saxon raised Brian, Carter and me. Most of my memories of our mother are of the stories Dad has told us. Her name was Emmaline. The pictures in my mind are exact replicas of the photographs of her smiling, holding one or another of us. The only thing I really remember is her laugh."

She turned slowly, facing him.

Until now, he hadn't realized when he'd stared collecting laughs. He shook his head slowly. "I don't usually talk this much."

"It's the dark," she said. "And the quiet, and the moon and that sky. Even men who never talk open up under these conditions."

"A lot of men talk to you in the middle of the night, do they?"

She didn't seem to mind that he had no business asking a question like that. "Not to me," she said. "They used to talk to my mother."

"I see."

Liza took a deep breath of air scented of pine needles and azaleas and rain-soaked earth. "It isn't what you're thinking. It wasn't what the men who knocked on our door in the middle of the night were thinking, either. There was a sign over the little addition on the side of our house when I was growing up in Vegas. *Nola Reds.* It was the name of her costume design studio, but those men didn't know that. At least once a month, some truck driver looking for the way back to the expressway, or some salesman or middle-aged Joe Shmoe who'd gone for a drive because he was tired of the noise and neon on the strip saw that sign and the light in Nola's studio, and thought, *what the heck, as long as I'm lost.* Ultimately, he'd knock on our door expecting a . . . well, you know. Laurel and I used to hide behind a ficus tree in the hall outside our bedrooms to get a glimpse of them. Without fail, their faces fell when they took one look at the red-haired woman opening the door, a foghorn in one hand, a can of pepper spray in the other. Nola never let them in. There were two comfortable chairs and a small table on a little patio in front of her studio. She used to tell them that if they behaved themselves, they were welcome to sit and have a cup of coffee and cookies or coffee cake. Often, they ended up bringing out pictures of the family. Before they left, Nola usually knew the names of their children and pets. And the men had remembered his wives' favorite flower or perfume."

Sometime during the telling, Liza had meandered to the street, and Jack had followed. They leaned against her car, his ankles crossed, her arms folded beneath her ribs.

"Don't get me wrong," she said. "I'm not saying that talking to Nola turned them into paragons of virtue. I mean, obviously, they weren't above paying for sex. But my mother liked to think that they went back to their hotel rooms and called their wives, and maybe thought twice before deciding to risk such a proposition again."

"Did she ever have to use the spray?"

"Where do you think *I* learned?"

Jack couldn't be certain she was kidding. "Were you ever afraid?"

"Of those men? Of the night? Of the dark?" She shook her head. "Most people aren't really afraid of the dark. They're afraid of the unknown. What are you afraid of?"

He ran a hand through his hair. The grass was cool and wet beneath his feet, the air pleasant on his face and arms. Liza was looking at the sky again, so he did, too. A thin cloud drifted in front of the crescent-shaped moon. Liza watched it, quiet, as if his reply was optional. Perhaps that was why he said, "I was never afraid of anything. Not storms or heights or the dark or flying or ghosts. Tommy's doctor appointments scare the spit out of me."

Hugging her arms close to her body, she said, "It's like being trapped on the roof of a burning skyscraper with a basket of wriggling puppies, and the only way off is over a narrow plank stretching between buildings that sways and bows with every step, and you just know that one wrong move will bring everything crashing down."

He stared at her.

She gave a little shrug and bit her lower lip. "It's a recurring dream I have when I'm facing great responsibility. Go ahead and dread putting Tommy through painful tests and uncomfortable procedures, but there's no need to be worried about the results."

Liza could tell he didn't believe her. It was there in his stance and squared shoulders.

"You know those dreams I mentioned when we first met?" she said. "The ones I was having before I even knew Tommy existed? Their origin coincided with the onset of Tommy's illness. And I stopped having them when he went into remission." She pushed herself away from her car and faced him. "I don't understand it, either, but they mean something."

"You think they were a sign." The man obviously didn't have a lot of faith in such things.

"Last night I slept soundly," she said. "Believe what you want, but Tommy's cancer isn't back."

She didn't know what was going on in the dark vagaries that made up Jack's mind, but she was pretty sure the lines next to his mouth had softened somewhat. This street was quiet. Dogs didn't bark at the moon. Cats didn't yowl from fences. It was as if everyone and everything slept except them. The night felt like a secret the two of them shared. It was doing strange things to Liza's mind and body. Worrisome things. Delicious things.

The way he slid his hand into his pants pocket gave her a perfectly good reason to look where she was looking. And it wasn't her fault the moonlight made his faded jeans practically glow. She was glad the lightning had taken out the streetlight, glad for the relative darkness, because it meant he couldn't see the flush creeping across her face.

He drew his hand from his pocket and reached toward her, a skeleton key held loosely between two fingers and his thumb. Slowly he reached for her hand. As she opened her fingers, he placed the key, warmed by his body heat, into her palm. She curled her fingers around it and opened her car door.

"Liza?"

It was amazing how wonderful it felt to be called by her own name. "Yes?"

"What were you thinking about?"

Her mind floundered. Perhaps he'd seen her blush after all. Perhaps he'd sensed what she was thinking, feeling. "When?" she asked, stalling.

"When you were dancing in the moonlight."

She tossed her hair over her shoulder and hiked one foot onto the floor of her car. "I doubt you would believe me if I told you. Besides, I wasn't dancing." Sliding into her car, she settled herself behind the steering wheel.

"What would you call it?"

"I'd call it embracing the night."

He stepped back and closed the door.

Through the open window, she said, "Tuna casserole."

"I beg your pardon?"

"You asked me what I was thinking about in the dark behind the captain's cottage." She gave him something her friends back in California called her take-it-or-leave-it look. "I was thinking about tuna casserole. It was what my mother always made for Laurel and me for new beginnings—a new school year, a new job, a new adventure. I was thinking how fresh the air smells, how friendly the moon is and how hungry I am for tuna noodle casserole. Will you be able to sleep now?"

"I think so."

"I'm glad." She started the car and drove away without saying good-bye.

Jack watched until her taillights disappeared. He didn't know where she was going. He didn't know if she would use the key. He didn't even know if she knew what it would unlock. Only time would tell. It was a strange thing to be thinking about as he entered his house, because time hadn't been his friend this past year.

Carter was conked out on the couch. Leaving him there, Jack blew out the candle. Using the beam of a small flashlight, he checked on Tommy. Next, he made his way to the bathroom. Finally, in the dark of his own room, he undressed and stretched out on his king-size bed.

The mattress was blessedly soft, the sheet smooth, his pillow down-filled. *Skylarking.*

The sky was dark beyond his windows, and he could feel himself relaxing, his eyes closing, his mind easing. *Embracing the night.*

His eyes closed. His breathing slowed, becoming deep and even. *Nola Reds.* Even his thoughts came slowly.

Tuna noodle . . . The last thought went unfinished. Jack was asleep.

Tommy sat quiet and still on the blue vinyl chair in the reception area in the pediatric oncologist's wing in the hospital in Manchester. Waiting. Jack sat next to him, doing the same.

Until the diagnosis, Tommy had never had any use for a security blanket, had never had an attachment to a special toy or a bottle or pacifier. This morning, his eyes big in his narrow face, he clutched the stuffed whale beneath one arm, keeping his other hand tucked firmly in his father's.

Jack used to try to distract him with books or games. Tommy hadn't fallen for the ploys, preferring to sit perfectly still, quietly watching the other patients—some with hair, some without—all waiting for their names to be called. Jack had no idea what Tommy thought about as the seconds ticked slowly by. It was as if he retreated to a place deep inside himself. Jack had learned not to intrude, but he did it without letting go of his son's small hand.

"Megan Donahue?"

A pudgy twelve-year-old girl carrying a stainless steel bowl rose shakily to her feet. Leaning heavily on her mother, the girl followed the nurse from the room.

Minutes ticked slowly by. Finally, another nurse appeared.

"Thomas McCall?"

Father and son stood in unison. Hand in hand, they followed the nurse through the labyrinth of familiar hallways to the examination rooms. Full of smiles and chatter, the nurse took Tommy's weight, temperature and vitals. Then it was time for the part they dreaded.

The needles and vials were brought out. Tommy's lip quivered.

There wasn't anything Jack wouldn't have given to let it be him instead.

Tommy handled the pain of having his blood drawn with a few tears but no tantrums. Afterward he accepted Jack's hug and restored his dignity with a tissue from the box on the stainless steel counter, then waited quietly on his father's lap for Dr. Andrews to come in.

They always talked during this portion of the wait. Tommy had slept through the storm the previous night, but viewed the ensuing power outage as an adventure this morning. He'd tried every light switch, and pretended they'd traveled back in time to an era before electricity had been discovered. Tommy rattled on about how he was going to change history and be the one who discovered it. "After I have my birthday," he said, "cuz nobody'd believe a four-year-old could do something that smart."

A knock sounded on the door.

Tommy clamped his mouth shut, his imaginative adventure forgotten the moment Dr. Andrews entered the small, cheerfully decorated examination room. The actual results wouldn't be available this quickly. The report regarding white and red blood cells and platelet counts would be mailed. But Dr. Andrews had taken a look at the slides under the microscope. And both Tommy and Jack watched the oncologist's expression closely.

The fair-haired doctor tugged at the bill of Tommy's baseball cap and smiled at Jack. "Everything seems fine. So far so good."

Tommy slid from his father's lap . . . and Jack released the breath he'd been holding for what felt like a decade.

Kevin Andrews was Jack's age. He'd graduated from Yale, and he looked it. Of average height, he was slender and wore imported shoes and wire-rimmed glasses. Having amassed his vast net worth the old fashioned way—per a rumored eight-figure inheritance—he'd become a physician not because of the earning potential but because he loved medicine.

On the day that the results had come in verifying that Tommy was indeed in remission, Jack had grasped the man's hand. Voice shaking, he'd said, "You ever need a kidney, you come see me."

Dr. Andrews had accepted the powerful handshake without flinching. "That makes eighty-two kidneys that are mine for the asking."

Jack hadn't known what to say. Kevin Andrews had treated eighty-two children with leukemia. Eighty-two desperate families. Eighty-two boys and girls of various ages, nationalities and backgrounds, every one precious in his or her own right. Jack didn't know how many of those little kids were still alive today. And he hadn't asked. Tommy was in remission. His counts looked good. Jack hadn't known who to thank, but humbling thankfulness had filled him.

They went over Tommy's diet, his maintenance therapy of daily low-dose chemotherapy, and what to do if the test results showed that Tommy's absolute neutrophil count, called ANC for short, was below a thousand, that magic number that indicated that his immune system was able to fight off infection. As long as his platelet counts remained high enough, he wouldn't bleed to death if he cut his finger or skinned his knee. With an ANC above a thousand, a cold probably wouldn't kill him.

Jack knew the statistics. Ninety-five percent of children who received state-of-the-art treatment immediately after diagnosis of acute lymphoblastic leukemia, called ALL, entered complete remission. He also knew that complete remission and a complete cure were two very different things. Tommy wouldn't be considered cured for a long time. Until he was, there was always the fear of relapse.

But not today.

Today, Dr. Andrews said everything looked fine.

They said good-bye to the doctors and staff in the pediatric oncology wing of the hospital in Manchester. Tommy ran ahead to the elevator. The minute they set foot in the parking lot, Jack swung his boy up over his head in the sunshine. Tommy squealed with delight.

Without realizing it, another laugh had just been added to Jack's memory.

"Think the 'tricity's back on at home?" Tommy asked from his father's back, where he liked to ride after these appointments.

"Probably," Jack said. "You hungry?"

"Yeah."

Jack was, too. In fact, he had a sudden and unusual craving for tuna casserole.

It took all Liza's might to drag the large trunk into the center of the room. Swiping the dust from her hands, she stood, catching her breath and the cross breeze. It was two o'clock in the afternoon. Perspiration dampened her face and clung to her neck and midriff. Her jeans and long-sleeved shirt weren't helping.

She'd driven directly from Jack's house to the captain's cottage last night. She'd passed a utility truck on her way, its yellow light flashing, a man in a lit hard hat up the pole at the corner. By the time she'd discovered that the skeleton key did indeed fit the lock perfectly, as she'd suspected, and had opened the door, the electricity had been restored in this part of town.

She'd meandered through the rooms of Laurel's old cottage, switching on lamps, picking up this, looking through that. Although small, the cottage had lots of amenities. The ancient refrigerator had been emptied and unplugged, anything edible in the cupboards evidently thrown out. Otherwise, the little house appeared to have gone untouched for a long, long time.

The thought of returning to her dark hotel room hadn't been appealing, so at three A.M., she'd stripped the sheets from the bed, loaded them into the old washing machine, then dragged the first trunk closer to the lamp. While the washer completed its cycle, she'd discovered photographs of

Tommy as an infant, plus newspaper clippings, receipts and junk, another reminder that some of Nola's traits had carried over to Laurel.

Liza distinctly remembered taking the bedding from the dryer a short time later. The last thing she recalled was stretching out to smooth a wrinkle from the mattress cover. She'd opened her eyes seven hours later, a kink in her neck and a crease in her cheek.

She'd been sitting on the edge of the bed, stretching, when she saw the horrible little mouse scuttle from behind the antique bureau. She was outside before she'd thought to scream. Even now, hours later, she was still shivering at the very idea that she'd spent the night in the same room as a mouse.

She'd gone back to her hotel room for a shower and change of clothes. Taking her time, she'd put gas in her car, had breakfast at the restaurant next to the motel, and stopped at the little grocery store on the highway. The whole time, she told herself mice were harmless. What did people say? "They're more afraid of us than we are of them. They're like squirrels, only smaller, not so different than gerbils and hamsters, some of children's favorite pets."

Gathering her courage, she'd returned to the cottage. Groceries in tow, she'd gone to the kitchen where she'd put together two separate lunches. Next, she'd propped the doors and windows open. Watchful of anything furry that moved, Liza resumed the daunting task of sorting through Laurel's old things.

She didn't know what she was searching for, but she was certain that Laurel would have left behind more than knick-knacks and photos and newspaper clippings. From the second trunk, she removed shells wrapped in yellowed tissue paper and magazines about pregnancy and books dealing with childbirth. Even after all this time, it was hard to believe Laurel hadn't shared any of that with Liza.

It took both hands to lift the tome entitled *Alternative Medicine As the Cure: The Risks and the Benefits*. No matter what Laurel had said about acceptance, she hadn't wanted to die. Liza carried the book to the table where she opened it slowly, reverently, as she imagined Laurel had.

Liza was closing the book when two shadows, one tall and one small, fell across the threshold. "Why'd you throw this bread on the ground out here, Aunt Liza?" Tommy stood in the doorway next to his father.

Motioning them in, she said, "I'm feeding a mouse. Hopefully, outside."

Tommy entered ahead of Jack. "Why do you have those rubber bands around your ankles?"

She shrugged. She'd heard of mice running up people's pant legs. "A woman can't be too careful."

"You've seen a mouse?" Jack asked.

She nodded.

"I thought burning buildings was your phobia."

She felt the strangest inclination to grin.

"Something sure smells good, Aunt Liza."

She laughed, bypassing grinning altogether. Tommy and Jack had just come from a doctor appointment. Tommy looked happy and energetic in his shorts and sandals and baseball cap. Although more dressed up, Jack appeared calm, too. They must have gotten good news.

She lowered the lid on the trunk and said, "You're just in time. The famous Cassidy tuna casserole smells ready."

The casserole was good. Tommy ate two helpings, but he was too busy asking questions to bother with compliments. It awarded Jack the opportunity to watch and listen. Laurel hadn't cooked much, preferring to have most of her meals at Cooper's Cafe in the village square. The rest of the time, she'd eaten sandwiches made from whole wheat bread, or warmed up canned soup. Those days she'd probably been too sick to go anywhere. She'd never come out and told him that. She'd never told him her mother had fixed casseroles that all tasted alike, either. She'd shared very little about her mother and sister, or her past, or even the present. Looking back, Jack realized that she'd been keeping her distance. It was as if she'd tried not to become too attached. Or perhaps she'd done it to keep him from becoming too attached to her.

She'd been dying. She should have told him. He should have guessed.

"Jack?"

Liza's voice drew him from past regrets. Her nod in Tommy's direction alerted him to the fact that his son was falling asleep at the table, his chin propped in one hand. Jack scooped the boy up and carried him into the bedroom. By the time he'd removed Tommy's sandals and covered him with the clean sheet, the child was fast asleep.

Liza watched from the foot of the bed. Wondering if Laurel had laid Tommy on the bed when he was a newborn baby, she said, "How old was Tommy when Laurel left?"

"Two weeks."

She'd had so little time with her child. Liza thought of one of Laurel's letters. *Time isn't measured by the number of breaths we take, but by the moments that take our breath—*

Something streaked into the room, inches from her right foot. Liza shrieked. Scrambling madly to the top of the antique dresser next to the bed, she said, "It's the mouse! Did you see it? Where did it go?"

Jack got down on all fours and peered under an old desk. "There's a knothole in the floor next to the wall. It probably went in there." He looked up at her and darned if he didn't say, "It probably just wanted to say thank you."

"For what?" she yelped.

"For the peanut butter sandwich."

"You mean . . . ?"

He nodded. "He was carrying dinner."

She peered over her shoulder, out the open door where the pieces of sandwich she'd put out to lure the mouse outside were slowly drying in the sun.

"You know what they say," he said, rising to his feet. "Once you feed them, they're pets."

She dropped her face into her hands. Men simply did not understand the seriousness of these situations.

"Tommy will sleep for an hour, at least," Jack said. "That should give us plenty of time to go through more of Laurel's things. Was she always such a pack rat?"

She rolled her eyes at his drollery. Apparently all the McCalls were comedians. "Do you think you should move Tommy out to the sofa?" she asked.

"He'll be fine."

She looked at the little boy, who hadn't stirred or flinched despite her shriek of terror. Indeed, he did look as though he was sleeping peacefully.

She slid off the bureau. Head held high, she left the room.

Jack followed more slowly. Wavy tendrils of Liza's hair had escaped the intricate braid. One side of her cotton shirt had come untucked, but she still wore rubber bands around the ankles of her jeans. Her fear of a helpless little mouse made her seem very human.

And it made him feel very alive.

"Okay," he said. "Let me get this straight. Your mother entertained would-be johns in the middle of the night but wouldn't let you and Laurel date until you were sixteen."

"She didn't *entertain* those men. She talked to them. And no, she wouldn't. What about you?" Liza placed another stack of magazines next to the knickknacks already filling the low table. "Did your father have many rules for you and your brothers?"

"He had three. No booze. No sex. No fighting. We broke them, of course, sometimes all in the same night."

"There's no need to brag." She peered deeper into the old trunk, her voice echoing slightly as she lifted a metal box. "You do realize that what goes around comes around. Children always have to outdo their parents. Look."

She placed the locked metal box on top of the stack of magazines, then returned to the trunk to search for the key.

They'd been sorting through the items in the captain's cottage for an hour. She wouldn't say Jack was opening up, exactly, but he appeared to be having an enjoyable time, despite the circumstances. It almost felt as if they were becoming friends.

"I've gone through everything in this trunk," she said. "There doesn't seem to be a key to the strongbox."

Jack took over. Shouldering her out of the way, he positioned himself in front of the metal box and took a small file from his wallet.

"You spy on people and pick locks," she said. "What, exactly, do the bad guys around here do?"

"Drugs, drinking, speeding, theft, wife beating."

Her shoulder was touching his upper arm. And something was happening to the air she was breathing. "It's the same old same old everywhere."

He shrugged, continuing to work the file into the lock.

"Do you feel old or young?" she asked.

"You ask strange questions."

"That isn't an answer. Come on. Old or young?"

Judging from how long it took him to reply, he was having trouble deciding. "Old, I guess."

She sighed. "Me too. Picasso said it takes a long time to be young. Laurel was born first, but I was born older. Our mother often said I was the sensible one. According to her, my first words were *careful* and *no-no* and *hot,* and were uttered as warnings to Laurel."

Liza wondered what her mother would think about what she was doing today. It didn't feel sensible to be telling Jack her innermost feelings. It didn't feel sensible to be standing so close to him, either. My, but it felt good. In fact, it had been a long time since anything had felt this good.

She wasn't sure what was happening between them. They had little in common other than love for her deceased sister, a kind of peace with the night, and Tommy. Perhaps they were simply two lonely souls whose paths had crossed. It was even possible that their paths had crossed for a reason.

She'd thought she was the end of the line for the Cassidys. Oh, she had good friends here and there. But Tommy was family. Where was Jack in all of this? *What* was Jack in all of this? Another friend? Perhaps. Perhaps more. The thought should have been more terrifying than a little mouse. And yet it wasn't.

Just then the lock clicked, drawing their gazes to the metal box. Jack lifted the lid. Heads bent close, they peered inside where a bound notebook with a leather cover had rested undisturbed for nearly five years.

"Laurel's journal," she whispered.

On top of the notebook was an envelope, and on the front, in a swirl of loops and curves, were the words *My darling Jack.*

Jack didn't move.

Liza reached for the journal, but stood in indecision. She wanted to read Laurel's thoughts and stories. Suddenly, it didn't feel like her place to do so. Slowly, she put the journal on the table near Jack's right hand, then went to the kitchen to award him some privacy.

Back home, dirty dishes weren't a priority. Today, she rummaged in a low cupboard, blew the dust off a bottle of dish soap and turned on the tap.

She took her time cleaning up the kitchen. Although she couldn't help listening intently for the slightest sound coming from the next room, she kept her back to the doorway. She was drying the last plate when the floor creaked behind her. Only then did she turn. Jack stood, feet apart, eyes hooded, expression inscrutable once again.

"What did she say?" she asked.

"She left a quit claim deed, signing the cottage over to Tommy, and she named me the executor until his twenty-first birthday." He folded the document, then tucked it into his shirt pocket.

Laurel had entrusted their son into Jack's capable hands. Liza wasn't the only Cassidy who'd been sensible. Laurel had loved Jack. And Jack was obviously shaken from the affirmation that she'd not only loved him, too, but she'd trusted him with their son's life, as well as with this property.

There was a sign there somewhere for Liza. It was like advice to wear a sweater or watch her step or proceed with caution. "Have you read any of her journal?"

"Just one entry."

"And?"

He left the room abruptly. When he returned, he had the bound pages with him. "You take it," he said.

She looked at the journal, and then at him.

"And when you're finished," he said, "bring it back to me."

Her heart filled up, and so did her eyes. Placing the journal with her purse, she returned to the living room to continue sorting. Tommy woke up a short time later. Liza gathered up her purse and keys and Laurel's journal, and prepared to leave.

"What are you doing, Aunt Liza?"

Jack noticed that Liza peered into the bedroom where the mouse had last been spotted. "I think I'll spread a blanket in a shady spot and do some reading."

"At our house?"

She shook her head. "Not this time."

And Jack knew she needed to do this reading alone. He pressed a hand over his shirt pocket, the paper crinkling inside. He'd heard an attorney was hanging her shingle in Alcott. Tomorrow, he would pay her a visit.

They all left the cottage together. Liza turned right at the end of High Street. Jack turned left.

"Where are we going?" Tommy asked.

"To the hardware store to buy mousetraps."

CHAPTER 8

"I'm telling you, Randy Burke is having an affair with Kate Stavinski."

"Not Randy!" Janet Powers exclaimed.

Eve pretended to be working on the minutes from the meeting while Melissa Meyers cast pointed glances up and down the long table. "Her kids are at camp and his repair truck has been seen parked in front of her garage three afternoons this week alone," Melissa said. "And nobody has that many appliances go bad in one week."

"Gertie!" It wasn't the first time the old fisherman seated near the window of Cooper's Cafe had tried to be heard over the voices of the women who had gathered for the monthly Pilgrim Women's Society meeting. "What's a person gotta do to get a refill around here?"

Eve watched the gray-haired waitress trudge to the counter for the coffee carafe. Clearly Gertie didn't appreciate the interruption, even if she was supposed to be working.

They usually held their meetings in the parson's study next door to the church. Since the roof had leaked during the storm the night before last, and the carpet in the parson's study was still spongy, Eve had suggested they move the gathering to Cooper's this morning. The official portion of the meeting had broken a record, lasting a mere eight and a half minutes. Motions had been made, seconded and quickly voted upon. Normally, the members weren't so agreeable, but today, they had more gossip than usual to share.

"I don't know what this town is coming to," Melissa exclaimed. "People having affairs in broad daylight. Lawyers in fishnet stockings and high heels."

"A man or a woman?" Janet asked.

"For heaven's sake, Janet! A woman, of course."

As if it would have taken the grapevine this long to spread the word if a cross-dresser had moved to Alcott. Eve cleared her mind and tried to visualize fields of daisies swaying on a gentle breeze.

"You've seen the new attorney?"

"My Fred has."

Melissa's Fred had a wandering eye. Apparently she was the only person in Alcott who didn't see how perfectly it went with the rest of him.

"Does the word *floozy* mean anything to you?" Melissa asked.

Samantha Bell leaned over and whispered in Eve's ear. "Does the word *shrew* mean anything to you? That tape recorder's off, right?"

Eve nodded at her closest friend. During the school year, Eve didn't attend these meetings, but during the summer she filled in as secretary-treasurer. The group did a lot of good for the community, taking meals to shut-ins, organizing fund-raisers, visiting the sick. It was just all this gossip. Sometimes it got to her.

"I heard that the Cassidy sister stayed at the captain's cottage the other night," Joyce Sturgis said. "And yesterday Sheriff McCall came into the store and bought mousetraps. It seems she spotted a mouse there." Joyce made a point of looking all around. "Now how do you suppose Jack knew that?"

Yes, sometimes the gossip got to Eve.

Her fields of daisies were withering in her mind, and it

was getting more and more difficult to maintain a smile. If only she could come up with a reason to leave gracefully without making a scene.

Eve Nelson helped. She accommodated. And she did it all with seemingly little effort and a ready smile. In all her thirty-five years, she'd never so much as caused a ripple on the surface of the Alcott gossip pool. Laurel Cassidy's arrival in town nearly six years before, her affair with Jack, her pregnancy, and then the way she left apparently without a backward glance had kept the gossip going for a long time. Already Liza Cassidy's arrival had brought a lot of speculation.

Eve wished people would stop talking about it, because every time she heard Jack's and Liza's names linked, her scalp tingled. For a moment, she pictured her head exploding.

That would definitely cause a scene.

Short of exploding, she wouldn't know how to begin to cause a scene. Not that she wanted to. She didn't. And yet . . .

The group had grown quiet. By the time Eve noticed, the reason for everyone's discomfiture had stepped into her line of vision.

"Good morning, ladies," Brian McCall said.

"Reverend." Miss Addie smiled sweetly, oblivious to the sudden tension in her fellow society members.

Eve hid her smile. No wonder a hush had fallen over the fine and upstanding members of the Pilgrim Women's Society. Brian's last sermon had dealt with the ills of gossip, and he'd just caught them with their tongues wagging.

He glanced at Eve last. "Got a minute?"

"Of course." She left some money on the table and followed Brian toward the door.

Behind them, Janet Powers whispered, "Reverend Peters never traipsed around town in tight jeans and worn work boots."

"I heard tithing is down. That's why he's working as a handyman on the side."

"What will he do next?" Melissa grumbled, her whisper sharp enough to penetrate steel. "Become a calendar model in a G-string and tool belt?"

"I move that Melissa brings her calendar to the next meeting!"

"Samantha! Shh. He'll hear you!"

That, they quieted. Eve sighed.

Keeping her eyes straight ahead, she preceded Brian out the door. Out on the sidewalk, she squinted against the sudden brightness of the sun. "Did you need something, Brian?"

He shook his head. "I was walking by and saw you sitting there. I know you can only take so much of them."

She stared at him, wondering how he'd known that. "You're a godsend."

"That makes one of you that feels that way."

"They mean well."

"No, they don't." His voice was resigned.

Hilda Meyers, her two grandchildren in tow, crossed the street in front of the cafe. "Hi Miz Nelson," the children called.

"Hello, Eve dear," Hilda said. "Reverend." Her greeting to Brian was much less cordial.

Eve waved and smiled.

Brian's eyebrows rose slightly after they'd passed, but he made no comment. After an awkward moment, Eve said, "Give them time. Half the members of the congregation wiped your nose when you were small. They're having trouble viewing you as a man of God. It would help if there was a bald spot in the middle of that four shades of brown hair of yours."

"Five shades of brown." But he smiled.

She thought, why couldn't she have been attracted to him? He was nearly as tall as Jack, and nearly as good-looking. She sighed again.

"Is something wrong, Eve?"

She hesitated for a moment. Brian had been a grade behind her and Jack in school. Until a year ago, he'd been upbeat and good-natured, at least for a McCall. Eve knew about the financial difficulties he was having, because she helped out in the church office a few mornings a week. It was only until things picked up and he could afford to hire someone permanent. She thought about the trouble he was having appeasing the people at church.

"I'm fine," she said. "But I think it might help people accept you as pastor if you would start looking for a good, solid woman and settle down."

"By good and solid, do you mean a pious three-hundred pounder?"

Long used to that McCall attitude, she said, "I was thinking more along the lines of a woman who could help out in the church office and sit on committees, and stand quietly, proudly at your side. A lot of pastors' wives do volunteer work. There must be someone in this town you find interesting. How about Kate Stavinski's sister, Amy? I'll bet she'd enjoy teaching Sunday school. And the entire family is musically inclined. She could play the organ at weddings and Sunday services."

Brian saw Eve's mouth moving, but it wasn't easy to hear everything she was saying because his ears were ringing. He could have blamed it on the car sputtering past, in dire need of a new muffler. Except he didn't lie, at least not to himself.

Face it. The only organ you want the woman you marry to play is the one below your belt, and not just on Sunday.

He clamped his mouth shut to keep from saying it out loud. He'd been having crass thoughts for months. Preachers were supposed to hear voices from heaven. His came straight from the gutter. He'd identified the problem. He hadn't had sex since he'd started working with Reverend Peters when the old pastor announced his imminent retirement last year. A year was too long for a man to go without sex.

His eyes focused; the ringing had ceased.

Eve was still talking. "Besides, they have plenty of other things to gossip about," she said. "Thanks to Kate Stavinski's broken appliances, Liza Cassidy's existence, and the new attorney setting up practice in town, your name has barely been mentioned all morning. I'm not saying I expect you to be happy that they're gossiping, but surely you're entitled to feel relieved."

She smiled. And Brian couldn't help smiling, too. Tall, thin, and kind to the bone, Eve Nelson was a gem. Some things never changed.

"Did you want me to type up the notes for Sunday's sermon?" she asked.

"That would be a great help. They're on my desk."

"I'll have them ready for you by the end of the day."

"Good old Eve." Without another word, he sauntered away.

Very slowly, Eve turned her head and watched him go. It was obvious from his loose-jointed swagger that he didn't feel her eyes boring into his back. He climbed behind the wheel of his '66 Corvette—another thing of which the members of his congregation didn't approve—and drove away without seeing the look on her face. Good old Eve saw red long after the candy-apple-red convertible disappeared around the corner.

The first thing Jack noticed about the new law office was that the door stuck. The second was the mess. And what was that smell?

The lower portion of the building had been vacant for years, the space used as a catchall for the various upstairs summer tenants who had come and gone over the years. Jack stepped around a pile of rubble and called out, "Excuse me. Is anybody here?"

Nobody appeared. Music was playing. Evidently, somebody was here . . . somewhere. Following the sounds deeper into the building, he noticed it wasn't just any music. Whoever was back here liked rap, and evidently the louder the better.

He hadn't gone far when he saw a young woman bending

over a large carton, her hips moving to the beat of the music. Rap music had a lot of beat.

"Excuse me!" Jack called again.

The wiggling stopped. The woman twisted around to face him. Her dark hair was almost black. It was chin length, but it stuck out, as if she'd frozen it and broken it off. From behind, he'd dubbed her to be in her early twenties. Now that he saw her face, he put her closer to thirty.

Her dark eyebrows arched as she glanced at his badge. "Don't tell me they already sent out the posse."

That cynicism made him think she might be closer to thirty-five. He couldn't place her accent, but it sure wasn't East Coast. "I'm Jack McCall," he said loudly.

She teetered over to the cluttered desk and switched off the CD player. Jack didn't know many women who listened to rap music and wore ruby red lipstick and platform sandals to unpack boxes.

"I'm here on personal—" He stopped and adjusted his voice to the sudden quiet. "This is a personal matter. Could you tell me where I might find Natalie Harper?"

She rotated a kink from between her shoulders. "Have you checked the French Riviera?"

He wasn't certain how she expected him to respond, and when uncertain, Jack remained silent. She muttered something under her breath that sounded suspiciously like a complaint that nobody in this town had a sense of humor.

"What can I do for you, Sheriff?" Natalie swiped her dusty hand on her thigh. And waited.

"*You're* Natalie Harper?" He stood near the doorway, all shoulders and sulk, but his response was right on cue and pretty much what she'd expected.

"You're quick, aren't you?"

He didn't seem put off by her sarcasm.

"Look," she said. "I have a lot to do. There's unpacking and renovations and cleaning and airing. I'm pretty sure something crawled under this building and died."

He didn't comment. And he didn't leave. Obviously, Natalie thought, the man couldn't take a hint.

"You said your name is Jack McCall?"

He nodded and ventured farther into the room.

Upon closer inspection, Natalie saw a bleakness about him, a kind of fatigue a person didn't acquire overnight. Tired or not, he'd noticed her legs. He didn't seem all that impressed. She thought they were going to get along just fine.

"As you can see, I'm not officially open for business. Would you care to make an appointment for next week or the week after?"

His grip tightened around a folded document. Natalie knew people who claimed they could see auras. Unfortunately, she had to rely on instinct. She hadn't always been a good judge of character. There was nothing like the school of hard knocks to hone a woman's life skills. She'd sized up Sheriff McCall a minute and a half ago. He was a decent man with more than his share of worries. Whatever was on his mind wasn't going to wait until next week or the week after.

"I'll tell you what," she said. "If you don't mind conducting business under these conditions, I have a few minutes right now."

"You're really an attorney?"

She traipsed to the desk again and brought back her framed credentials. He read them, and then he studied her, sizing her up in return. She must have passed, she thought, because he unfolded two sheets of paper and handed them over with a steady hand.

She scanned them both, then looked at him. "A quit claim deed and a last will and testament. What would you like to know?"

"I just discovered them yesterday. They were dated nearly five years ago. Are they legal?"

She read the first document over, word for word. When she was finished, she said, "In order for a quit claim deed to be legal, it needs an original signature. This one is signed in blue ink. It must be notarized by a licensed notary public, and witnessed. This has a raised seal and two more signatures in black ink." She handed the deed back. "It appears to be completely legal."

His face showed relief.

"Apparently, the previous title holder made certain the *i*'s were dotted and the *t*'s were crossed. Deeds can be recorded out of order any time. It must, however, be recorded with the Register of Deeds Office at the county seat in order to show up on a title search."

"And the will?"

She studied that next. "It also appears to be legal. Is Thomas John McCall your son?"

He nodded.

"Is Laurel Cassidy deceased?"

"Yes."

Natalie paid close attention to the sheriff's expression as she returned his papers. A lot of people would have been halfway through their life stories by now, as if her representation somehow included Psychology 101. Sheriff McCall said very little. That was even more telling.

"Do you have a copy of her death certificate?"

"I know someone who does."

She nodded. "As long as these signatures are authentic, both documents are perfectly legal and would hold up in any court of law."

The breath he released was extremely telling. "How much do I owe you?"

"No charge."

His eyes widened, and she thought he would be a very attractive man if he ever smiled. Not that she cared. Natalie Harper was immune to men, attractive or otherwise.

She followed him from the room. "What do you think of the place?"

"Truthfully?"

So, she thought, he did have a sense of humor after all. She cast him a small smile. "Not so truthfully that it hurts."

"You're going to need a little help if you want to be open for business by next week or the week after."

"A little help? I could use a frigging miracle." She'd visited the property two years ago. She hadn't been ready to purchase then. Recently, she'd contacted the former owner again. The woman had sent her dated photographs and had assured her nothing had changed. The previous owner obviously was a lying sack of shit. Natalie wasn't often wrong about people anymore, but this one had slipped past her radar. She had everything documented. The former owner wasn't off the hook, but Natalie still had a mess to deal with, which seemed to be her lot in life.

"The building has a good, solid structure," Jack said, looking around. "It just needs a good handym—person."

Natalie Harper wasn't a feminist or an activist. She was an independent woman who believed in equal rights. She also believed in calling a spade a spade. She needed someone who could lift heavy loads and reach high places and wield a hammer and power tools and a paintbrush. "You wouldn't happen to know a good handyman, would you?" she asked.

He stopped short of the door and almost smiled, as if he'd just gotten the punch line to a very old joke. "It so happens I do. He's fixing the roof over at the rectory this morning."

She peered up at the water stain on the ceiling. "You know someone who mends roofs?"

"I'll be seeing him later. Want me to tell him to stop by?"

"No. I'll handle it. I'll need his name and number."

"His name is Brian."

"And his last name?"

"McCall."

"McCall?" It was like pulling teeth. "Any relation?"

"He's my brother."

"What about references?" She smiled when her question hit its mark. "No offense, Sheriff, but the Boston Strangler probably had brothers, too."

"Brian's honest and hardworking. I'd trust him with my

life, and my son's life. A lot of people don't think he knows a soul from a hole in the ground, but our father taught him everything he knows about carpentry work."

"Your father's a carpenter?" she asked.

"He was before he retired. He's strictly old school. Always claimed there were only two things he couldn't fix."

Natalie watched him, eyebrows raised slightly.

And he said, "The crack of dawn and a broken heart."

She shook her head. "And is your brother strictly old school, too?"

"You strike me as a woman who would want to make up her own mind." He scribbled a phone number and address on a piece of paper, then left while Natalie was trying to make sense of the information. What did a hole in the ground have to do with fixing the crack of dawn?

And people said Texans talked funny.

It was early evening when Liza parked her car at the curb in front of Jack's house. Insects buzzed, and a couple of houses down, children's voices were raised in play. She'd spent the remainder of yesterday reading Laurel's journal. One page in particular played over and over through her mind.

My precious Thomas,

I count your fingers and toes each morning. Ten of each. So perfect. You grasp my finger gently but tightly. Already, you have good instincts. You curl your foot when I count your toes, ticklish! I swing you up and then I cradle you close, my precious, happy baby. All the while, you watch me with those clear, steady eyes of yours. Looking back at you, I wonder if you know. Your mother is dying.

I fill my senses with you, the softness of your wispy hair beneath my fingertips, the smoothness of your cheek, the delicate, sweet-smelling skin underneath

*your chin where the doctor assures me your neck will
be. I press my lips to your round tummy. I breathe in
the scent of you, and I memorize the sound of you, the
utter perfection of you.*

*I touch your palm. Again, you curl your fingers
around mine, gentle but firm. You're holding on. And I
so yearn to let you. But I must leave you today. I'm
going to try to come back, my sweet, sweet child.
Come what may. If I can't return, know that I've had
two weeks to love you. It seems like so little time. But
love isn't measured by time. The purest love isn't measured at all.*

*As I watch you, I smile, and it occurs to me that you
were born knowing exactly what you need. So cry
when you're hungry, rest when you're tired, and laugh
when you're tickled. And know that your mother loves
you for all time.*

There was something lyrical and haunting in Laurel's
writings. Reading them made Liza ache inside. Needing to
talk to somebody, she'd called two of her friends back in
California. With their help, she'd made arrangements to sub-
let her tiny art studio that doubled as her apartment. Her
mail was being forwarded to the post office here. One by
one, she was tying up the loose ends of her former life. With
the money she'd received from her mother's life insurance
policy and the sale of the house on Desert Moon Drive, Liza
had enough to live on for a few years or more, providing she
wasn't too extravagant, so it wasn't worry that was causing
her to feel so unsettled. Rather, she felt strangely lost. It was
as if what little roots she had left were dangling in the
breeze.

She paused for a moment to collect herself. In an hour,
darkness would begin to creep across the sky. And then silence would descend. Already the western horizon was
streaked with faint touches of lavender, peach, coral and
gray. Back in California, she'd watched the sun set over the

ocean nearly every night. It *rose* over the ocean here—at least, that's what she'd been told. It seemed as if she'd been on the East Coast for a long time. In reality, she'd been here a mere five days.

Light and shadow were different here. It had been too long since she'd taken out her art supplies and captured those elements on canvas. Tomorrow she would begin. She wasn't sure what she would paint.

Jack's dog looked up as she neared. Getting up stiffly, he hobbled over, wagging his tail in greeting. Liza bent down and scratched his knobby head.

Jack was waiting at the door when she straightened. He opened the door wider. Carrying Laurel's journal beneath one arm, she went inside.

"Did you read it all?" he asked.

"Yes." She left the journal on the kitchen table. Next to it she placed the final letter Laurel had written to her.

"Did you see the attorney?" she asked.

He nodded. "As strange as it sounds now, Laurel left everything in order."

It was true, Jack thought. Everything was becoming clear and was beginning to make sense, except what had happened to the final letter she'd sent to him. Maybe it would arrive mysteriously thirty years from now, one of those strange stories that made the national headlines.

Just then Tommy came bounding into the room. "Hey, Aunt Liza. Guess what?"

"What?"

"You don't hafta be afraid of that little old mouse anymore."

"Why is that?" she asked.

"Me'n Dad set traps."

"You mean mousetraps?"

Jack was nearly as surprised as Tommy by the suddenness of the question and seriousness in her voice. As if he thought it was possible that they didn't have mousetraps where she came from, Tommy explained. "The mouse tries to eat the cheese and, *snap!*" The words were accompanied by a graphic pantomime.

"When?" She spoke in a suffocated whisper, turning to Jack.

"Yesterday," he said.

Her face pale, she rushed outside.

"Where's Aunt Liza going?" Tommy asked.

Jack reached for Tommy's hand. "My guess is she's going to the captain's cottage."

"But why?"

"What do you say we go with her and find out."

Liza got in her car, and Jack and Tommy squeezed in with all the things she'd brought out East with her. She grasped the steering wheel tightly, as if holding on for dear life. Her shrink back in California had told her this might happen—that one of these days some little incident would creep up on her and all the sorrow would ambush her and she would overreact. She was probably scaring Tommy. She looked at him in the rearview mirror. He seemed more curious than upset. Jack probably thought she was certifiable. Maybe she was.

No one spoke during the drive to Captain's Row. She pulled into the driveway in front of the cottage, not far from the pink flamingo.

Jack was the first one out of the car. "I'll go in and have a look."

Tommy unfastened his seat belt then raced after his dad. Liza followed much more slowly. The two males marched into the bedroom. Liza stayed near the painting she'd done for Laurel a long time ago.

She jumped when the trap snapped.

"Nothing in this one," Tommy said as he followed his father out of the bedroom and into the kitchen.

Again, Liza listened. This time, there was no snap. There was only a stretch of silence. And then Tommy said, "Uh-oh."

Liza shivered.

In the kitchen, Jack hunkered down and was peering inside the cabinet beneath the old sink. Bent at the waist next to his father, Tommy stared at the evidence.

A moment later, Jack heard the outer door close.

"What was that? Is Aunt Liza cryin'?"

"I wouldn't be surprised."

Tommy stared deep into his father's eyes. "I thought she didn't like mice."

"She doesn't." Jack stood. Walking to the window, he looked out and saw Liza heading toward the back of the property. She stopped where she'd danced in the moonlight a few nights before, and stood looking out over the ocean.

This wasn't really about the mouse. Reading Laurel's letters must have brought back Liza's losses, her dashed hopes and sorrows.

"Tell her, Dad." Tommy had joined his father at the window.

"Tell her what?"

"Tell her we wouldn't kill a mouse for just anybody."

Jack almost cracked a smile. "I have another idea."

"What're we gonna do?" Tommy returned to his perch in front of the cabinet beneath the kitchen sink.

"We need a small box."

"What for?"

"For the mouse."

"Why?"

Jack explained what he planned to do, and Tommy was quick to comply.

They made an unusual procession, Tommy solemnly carrying the small box out in front of him, Jack following with the shovel he'd retrieved from a hook outside the cottage's back door. Tommy placed the box on the ground. Jack dug a hole, no small feat in the hard earth. When it was deep enough, he set the tiny cardboard box in it, then tossed in the first shovelful of dirt.

Tommy instinctively tucked his hand into Liza's. Both looked on quietly. When it was over, Liza whispered, "Thank you." Her gaze went to Jack. Sniffling one last time, she released Tommy's hand, then walked regally toward her car.

Jack and Tommy stared after her. Birds were singing, and the breeze billowed through her slacks and hair.

Making a sound universal to men, Tommy said, "I don't understand girls."

"I don't think we're supposed to, son."

But Jack was sure of one thing. It would be a hell of a boring life without them.

CHAPTER 9

"G'night, Aunt Liza."

Aunt Liza. She took a moment to savor the distinction, slowly returning Tommy's smile. She was sure she wasn't imagining that the tufts of his hair were sticking up more than usual. Neither he nor Jack had brought up the mouse incident during the hour they'd been back at their house. Perhaps holding all his questions and comments inside was the reason for Tommy's wild hair. More likely, he needed a haircut. Still terribly thin in places, his hair was growing. He was getting better. She hadn't had a dream about him in months. The child wasn't invincible—no one was—yet the regrowth of Tommy's hair was concrete evidence of his resilience. It was wonderfully reassuring. Liza knew who she wanted to paint.

After leaning down to kiss Tommy's cheek, she eased away from the twin bed with its superhero sheets. Leaving Jack to the ritual of tucking his son in, she meandered out to the living room. Again, she was drawn to the photographs on the old upright piano.

She picked up each in turn, studying them all carefully. There were similarities in bone structure and facial expressions among several of Jack's family members, as there were

among her own relatives. And she knew she was ready to unpack some of her family photographs.

Although Liza's relatives were gone, and the house on
Desert Moon Drive was another family's home now—the
Cassidys' roots more delicate, perhaps, than those of the
McCalls—her family lived on inside her. And in Tommy.

Family. It was a simple word for something that was far
from simple. Family began as a basic unit of two or more
people. It became so much more: a place to grow up in, to
grow out of and away from. Somehow, along the way, family
became something to come home to. It was a foundation to
hold onto, to cherish, even when the memories faded into
faint hues of loved ones who were no longer here. Family
was where everyone began, and if a person was lucky, it
never truly ended, living on not only in memories, but in new
generations.

The Cassidys lived on in Liza. And in Tommy. He drove
home the fact so innocently and profoundly every time he
called her *Aunt* Liza.

A floorboard creaked in the hall. Liza looked over her
shoulder as Jack entered the living room. She didn't think it
was her imagination that he appeared more rested, more un-
hurried and more smoldering.

"I've been thinking," she said.

"I've been thinking," he said at the same time.

She motioned for him to continue at precisely the same
moment he motioned to her. They both smiled, her more
than him, but that was her way, and his.

He stood at the far end of the piano. "You first," he said.

Very gently, she touched her finger to middle C, once,
twice, three times. "I read somewhere that Walt Disney was
afraid of mice. Don't you find that ironic? I wonder if
Mickey Mouse came to him in a nightmare." She glided her
fingers up the scale. "Never underestimate the power of
dreams."

Jack didn't see what he could add to that, so he said what
he'd started to say when he'd entered the room. "We haven't

talked about your plans, about whether you're considering staying, or if this is just a visit. Either way, I want you to know you're welcome here."

With one finger, she played "Twinkle, Twinkle Little Star." He had no idea what she was thinking, but she seemed to be smiling, so he continued. "You're welcome to stay in the captain's cottage." He paused. "Now that it's safe."

"You call that safe?" She tossed her hair and lifted her chin the way Laurel used to. The shock of it hit Jack full force, the déjà vu experience feeling like a sledgehammer on his head.

He wondered if she was aware of the smile that stole across her face just then. He wondered if she had any idea what that smile of hers was doing to him. "We could always call an exterminator," he said.

Then he added, "Are you certain you have enough little boxes?"

He'd eased away from the piano, but had glimpsed enough of her face to see her smile widen. She knew what she was doing, all right, and was enjoying it very much. She was teasing him. And he was enjoying it, too. Would wonders never cease.

"I appreciate the offer, Jack. And I might take you up on it, at least temporarily."

Darkness was falling on the other side of the windows. He should have been thinking about turning on a lamp. But Liza didn't mind darkness and shadows. Her resemblance to Laurel was uncanny, but their personalities were very different. Laurel had been bold and at times demanding. Liza was subtle. Laurel had worn bright colors. Liza made her own kind of statement in more subdued shades.

Tonight she wore a pantsuit. The top was made from the same gauzy fabric as the slacks. Both pieces were the color of walnut shells. The outfit brought out the auburn highlights in her hair and made her skin look warm and rich and so, so smooth. The top was sleeveless, the pants loose enough to allow for movement, but tight enough to stir his imagination.

They fell slightly below her waist, hugging her hips, delineating the length of her thighs. The two pieces met without overlapping. If a man watched closely, and was lucky, he got an occasional, momentary glimpse of pale, bare skin.

Jack had been watching closely all evening.

She was strolling away from him, toward the kitchen. On her way to the door, she glanced at Laurel's journal, but said nothing. She was leaving, as she often did, with little preamble and no fuss. Jack followed her out the door.

She paused on the stoop overlooking the side yard. "All teasing aside, I appreciate what you and Tommy did tonight."

He distributed his weight evenly an arm's length behind her. He settled his hands on his hips and said, "It reminded me of when I was a kid."

"You gave mice funerals when you were a child?"

He heard the humor in her voice. "Brian used to bury every bird that flew into our picture window, every stray cat that unwittingly tried to cross a busy street. Even roadkill got a proper burial at our house. Saxon always complained about mowing around so many crosses."

"Then Brian was destined to become a preacher."

He hadn't thought about it, but maybe it was true. He didn't really want to talk about Brian. Jack didn't want to talk at all—surprise, surprise. He didn't feel much like fighting for a change, either. And a beer wasn't all that appealing. That left one activity.

The stoop wasn't wide. Liza stood a step ahead of him and half a step over. Although he couldn't see her expression, he glimpsed a partial silhouette of her face when she turned her head just so. She wasn't wearing heels tonight. It made him feel very tall, and strong, and invincible. Or maybe that was the result of desire.

The first firefly of the summer flashed in the darkening sky. Liza saw it, too. "We didn't see fireflies in Vegas. Nola always said the neon was too much competition."

Another one flashed. And Jack said, "Saxon used to tell us they were little photographers flying around snapping our picture. Carter never went outside at night without combing his hair."

"So many stories and memories. You're lucky to have so much family."

Until Laurel left, and Tommy got sick, he'd taken luck for granted. Now, he took nothing for granted, certainly not the fire inside him right now.

Liza's shoulders were slender and straight, the skin slightly tan but not freckled. He wondered if it was as soft as it looked. His voice was slightly deeper when he said, "You can borrow them whenever you want."

"You mean it?"

"Saxon can always use help with his crossword puzzles. And you're welcome to spend more time with Tommy. Just clear it with one of us first, so we know where he is."

"How about tomorrow?"

Why did he get the feeling he'd been set up? He didn't remember the last time he'd felt like grinning so many days in a row. He didn't remember the last time he'd been in this particular predicament so many days in a row, either. What was it Brian had told boys in the youth group to do?

Count backward.

Nine hundred ninety-nine, nine hundred ninety-eight . . .

"I was thinking I'd like to take him to the beach," she said. "He loves the ocean. And I'd like to paint him."

Nine hundred ninety-seven . . . "He tires easily."

"I'll see that he doesn't overdo it."

Nine hundred ninety-six . . . "What time tomorrow?"

"Noon?" She started away from him.

He stilled her with a hand on her shoulder. Her skin was as warm and smooth as he'd imagined, her shoulders pliant, strong and soft as only a woman's could be. Slowly he turned her to face him. His hand went to her hair next, taking a thick section in his palm. His fingertips skimmed her neck, coming to rest beneath her chin. Her lashes fluttered once. Then her eyes opened wide. There was surprise in their depths, but she wasn't backing away.

Nine hundred ninety . . .

He glided his thumb over her bottom lip. Perhaps it was the catch in her breathing that had him raising her chin a little more, and turning her face slightly. Or perhaps this had been inevitable since the first time he'd kissed her, when he'd thought she was Laurel.

Nine hundred ninety-five . . .

Or was it ninety-four?

"What are you thinking?" she whispered.

"I'm thinking to hell with counting backward." He lowered his head and covered her mouth with his.

Her lips parted and his tongue found the tip of hers. It was a kiss of discovery, and while it made no promises, it lowered their eyelids and slowed their breathing, a joining of mouths and sighs, full of intimacy and possibilities. Even when it broke gently, and their eyes opened, neither drew away.

"Counting backward?" she whispered.

He nodded. "It doesn't work, anyway." Her eyes were green, her lips wet from that kiss.

She couldn't have known what he was talking about. She swayed slightly. It was all the invitation Jack needed. He kissed her again, a little less gently, a little more deeply, a connection of two lonely people who'd somehow found their way to this place, to this moment. He wanted to grind his hips against hers, to take her to bed, or take her right here on the ground. But they were in plain view of the street, and of Jack's father's house, and of anybody who might be looking. So he held himself back.

And he kissed her again.

The spring was back in Eve's step. It was a pleasant evening and she was feeling optimistic. She'd had dinner at Samantha's, as she often did. It had reminded her that she had wonderful friends in Alcott. Jack was one of them. That hadn't changed.

She was on her way to visit Miss Addie and Miss Rose. Okay, Jack's house wasn't exactly on the way, but it was close enough to warrant dropping by. As long as she was in the neighborhood, and all. She smiled to herself. She hadn't talked to him in a few days, and was looking forward to catching up with him, as she'd been doing since they were kids. She'd run into Kate Stavinski in the grocery store earlier. Kate had mentioned how crazy her week had been, what with all the damage her appliances had suffered from the electrical storm.

There, Eve had told herself. Contrary to what the grapevine claimed, Randy Burke really had been fixing appliances at Kate's house all week. Kate Stavinski was no more having an affair than Jack was.

A muffler backfired a block away. Eve jumped, then looked all around, as if it was possible that someone had fired a gun in Alcott. She smiled as she imagined telling Jack what she'd been thinking. He would shake his head and tell her she'd been reading too many of the suspense novels she checked out from the library every summer. That was how well she knew him.

Lights were on in several of the houses she passed. Eve had less than half a block to go. Already, she could see a portion of the side of Jack's house. In fact, it looked like he was outside. She peered closer to make certain it was Jack and not one of his brothers. It was Jack, all right, and he was on the side stoop, directly beneath the light. The yellow glow of the outdoor bulb made his hair appear black. Why was he leaning over that way?

Eve's steps faltered. He wasn't alone.

She came to an abrupt stop.

He was with a woman who had long, red hair. Neither of them were moving. And there wasn't enough room between them to pitch a cat through.

Eve darted off the sidewalk. Her ankle turned on the uneven ground, shooting pain up her leg. Righting herself, she hobbled to the cover of a maple tree. Leaning heavily on the rough bark, she looked a second time. And then she closed her eyes.

"Here, dear, drink this." The delicate teacup rattled in its saucer as Addie Lawson placed it on the antique table next to Eve.

Eve felt like a fool.

She didn't want to drink sweetened tea. She wanted to climb through a knothole and pull it in after her. But Rose and Addie hovered over her, and they were so worried about her. Dutifully, she took a sip and shuddered at the sickening sweetness.

She had no memory of how she'd come to be standing on the aunts' wide, Victorian porch on Briar Street, her finger pressed to the doorbell. She must have hobbled over here. Not even the pain in her ankle could erase the pain of seeing Jack kissing another woman.

Miss Addie's perpetual smile had fled the instant she'd opened the door and seen Eve. Bodily removing Eve's finger from the bell, she'd called, "Sister, come quick. Our sweet Eve is crying."

Sweet Eve. Good old Eve. She really was a fool.

Addie and Rose had led her to an old chintz chair with a ruffled skirt and silk needlepoint pillow. Rose had handed her an old-fashioned handkerchief, and Eve had started blubbering and rambling about what she'd seen. "It's as if history is repeating itself. And there wasn't even any lightning." She was rambling, but she couldn't help herself. "I haven't heard from him in days. He promised he'd call after Tommy's last appointment, but he didn't. And now he's kissing her."

"After everything you've done for him!" Rose said.

Addie nodded sympathetically.

It brought Eve to her senses. She stared at the two little old ladies who seemed to get smaller every year. "What have I done for him?"

Two years older than Addie, Rose complained more and smiled less. "Sister," she said, "bring the decanter of cooking sherry. We'll add some to Eve's tea."

"Yes, I do believe that's a wonderful idea, Rose."

Suddenly it all seemed so clear to Eve. The two old ladies bustled around, speaking to each other, about her, as if she wasn't there. Eve stared at the rug beneath her feet. It wasn't the vibrant, Oriental variety, but an old wool carpet that had withstood years of foot traffic with seemingly few signs of wear. It was utilitarian, comfortable, nondescript. She was like the rug—serving a purpose, blending with her surroundings, pleasant enough, accommodating, but always going unnoticed, a good base or backdrop for something prettier, brighter and more colorful.

It wasn't only Jack who didn't see her.

As if to prove it, Addie entered the room in her stately lavender dress that had probably been in style thirty or forty years ago, her gray hair springy from a recent perm, a decanter of amber-colored liquid in her arthritic hands. She and Rose were discussing how much to give Eve, as if Eve were a child, or worse—as if she weren't even there.

Did no one see her, truly see her? How could a woman who was nearly six feet tall be invisible?

She sat back in the old chair and looked around the old room. Rose and Adeline Lawson had lived in this house on Briar Street their entire lives. They often spoke about their parents, and former neighbors and old friends who had died. Once or twice a year Addie reminisced about her old beau, a young officer who had been killed in the Battle of the Bulge. Rose never mentioned a man. Eve wondered if she'd ever been in love. Perhaps not; perhaps that was why she was so curt, so dry and brittle. Tears stung Eve's eyes. Was that the way she would end up, drinking tea from genuine china cups, scowling, wearing old dresses with organza collars, carrying lace handkerchiefs in her pocket, attending community meetings and growing flowers for other people's bouquets?

There was a clink and the sound of liquid sloshing. And then Rose was pressing the cup and saucer into Eve's hand, and Eve was taking a sip of sherry-laced tea. It was nauseating. But she took another dutiful sip, then looked into Rose's faded, deep-set eyes. "What did you mean, after everything I've done for Jack?"

Rose lowered stiffly into the adjacent chair and straightened the doily on the table. "Why, you've practically raised Tommy."

"No, I haven't. Jack won't let me. I've been a friend to him, to both of them."

"Yes, you have," Addie said, patting Eve's hand. "You've been a wonderful friend to them. You're a wonderful person."

"He doesn't see me."

"Perhaps if you dyed your hair red."

"That seems drastic," Rose snapped.

"No more drastic than the last time, Sister. What was it Papa used to say? Drastic situations call for drastic measures."

"Papa never said that."

"He most certainly did."

Eve tuned out the ensuing argument. In her mind she saw Jack kissing Liza Cassidy. Liza's hand had gone to the side of Jack's face, her fingers slowly gliding through his hair. It was beautiful, or it would have been. If it had been Eve instead.

She'd never even touched his hair. And she'd certainly never been kissed by him.

"It's time to be daring. Before it's too late again."

"There's nothing wrong with Eve or her hair."

Both women turned to Eve. Addie said, "That's true. But I think it's time she put the move on her man."

Her man? Eve thought.

"What move?" Rose asked.

"You know." There were two splotches of color on Addie's cheeks. "It's what they call it in *Cosmo.*"

"You read *Cosmo?*" Eve asked.

"Adeline!" Rose said at the same time.

"I might have happened to glance at it by mistake the other day at the beauty parlor. And it's a good thing I did. Eve needs to buy something called an Enya CD. I think he's related to that Presley boy who was so popular years ago. And she simply must buy some candles, and a bottle of wine."

"But I don't drink."

Both old women looked at Eve's empty teacup, then quietly resumed their conversation.

"And a push-up brassiere."

"Adeline, really! What would Mother say if she heard you?"

Eve might as well have been watching a tennis match.

"I wouldn't normally recommend something of this nature," Addie said. "But Eve isn't getting any younger."

It was happening again. They talked as if she weren't even in the room. And her scalp was tingling again the way it did when she imagined her head exploding. Something flared inside her. She'd had enough.

Enough!

She pushed to her feet, staggering slightly as pain shot up her right leg. More careful, she took a slow step.

"Where are you going?" Addie asked.

"Home," she said, hobbling toward the door.

"But your ankle!" Rose exclaimed. "Sit back down, Eve dear, and we'll call someone to drive you."

Eve dear looked down into the lined faces of these two kindly old women. In an effort to put them at ease, she smiled slightly. "It's only a few blocks to my house. I'll be fine."

Hobbling to the door, she bid the aunts good night. They stood in the open door, wringing their hands and watching her navigate the porch steps. Head held high, Eve made her way toward her house. Other than a dog barking in the distance, Alcott was quiet for the night.

Eve hadn't gone far when it occurred to her that Rose and Addie knew about her feelings for Jack. Something else nagged at the back of Eve's mind. It was something Addie had said about drastic measures. There was a thought in the back of Eve's mind. She tried to concentrate on it and bring it into focus. She blinked several times in an attempt to chase away the dizziness. She was a pathetic thirty-five-year-old spinster who got tipsy on two ounces of cooking sherry and hadn't been successful keeping her innermost feelings from two old ladies who would do anything for her.

Anything except see her for who she really was.

With pain eking up her shin, she concentrated on putting one foot in front of the other. She hobbled into her little house that felt so much like her little life. Sinking onto a dining room chair, she told herself to stop feeling sorry for herself. Her house was adequate. It housed her antique dining room set, the only furniture she'd splurged on in her entire life.

Her entire quiet, adequate, pathetic life.

A tear rolled down her face, landing on the smooth table-top. Refusing to shed another, she hiked her foot onto another chair. Elevating her ankle helped. Already, it throbbed less. She studied her ankle. She didn't have small feet by any means, but she'd always had thin ankles. She'd always thought she had nice legs. A lot of good it did her. Her right ankle wasn't thin tonight. It was swollen and it was sore. It was probably sprained, or at the very least, strained. Her sister Brooke had sprained her ankle once and had hobbled around on crutches for a week with her ankle in an ace bandage.

Eve didn't have an ace bandage. And the drugstore was closed. All the stores in Alcott were closed. In fact, the only store open this time of the night was the convenience store out on Highway 1. Rising shakily to her feet, she reached for her keys and hobbled to her car. Driving to a convenience store to buy a bandage wasn't exactly thrilling, but it beat feeling sorry for herself all alone in her adequate, pathetic house.

Natalie Harper didn't pay much attention to the tall woman sitting in a plastic chair near the door of the convenience store. Natalie was on a mission. Once a year she put on a leather skirt and spike heels, bought a pack of cigarettes and a bottle of Captain Morgan, then went back to her place and proceeded to get trashed. She'd considered *not* doing it this year. She considered *not* doing it every year. But it was pretty damn difficult to break tradition.

By the time she'd selected and then paid for her items, the tall woman was hobbling out the door ahead of her. She glanced at Natalie, smiling kindly and a little sadly.

Her face looked slightly familiar. Natalie tried to place her.

As if thinking the same thing about Natalie, the woman said, "You're the new attorney in Alcott, aren't you?"

Natalie was in no mood to strike up a conversation with a stranger in a deserted parking lot. Not tonight. "I'm Natalie Harper, yes."

"Eve Nelson." As if sensing Natalie's irritable mood, Eve started toward the only other car in the parking lot.

"Did you hurt your ankle?" Natalie asked. Mentally, she kicked herself for opening her mouth.

The woman turned carefully. "I twisted it earlier." She glanced down at Natalie's spiked heels. "How on earth do you manage to walk on those? I'd fall off them and break something for sure."

Natalie shrugged. "It's an acquired talent. I don't wear them often anymore. Not this high. But birthdays only roll around once a year." She clamped her mouth shut with so much force her teeth gnashed.

"Happy birthday."

"It's not my birthday. I stopped having them years ago."

It was obvious that the tall, plain woman didn't know what the hell Natalie was talking about. Who could blame her? Natalie opened the pack of cigarettes and shook out one before offering one to Eve.

"No, thanks. I don't smoke."

Natalie didn't either anymore. Except once a year. It was part of the tradition.

"Jack used to smoke, but I never have. Not once. Can you believe that? I'm pathetic, I know. It's no wonder I'm invisible."

Natalie lit up and took a long draw on her cigarette. "If you're invisible, doll, why can I see you?"

Eve did a double take. No one called her doll. She was curious about something, but didn't see how she would dare to ask. Her scalp started to tingle again, reminding her that she had to do something. She'd made a fool of herself in front of the aunts. Why not in front of a total stranger? "Would you do me a favor?"

Natalie didn't commit one way or the other.

And Eve hurried to say, "Don't worry. I don't want free legal advice or anything. I just wondered . . . what do you see when you look at me?"

Natalie looked Eve up and down so thoroughly, it was all Eve could do to keep from fidgeting. Finally, Natalie said, "I see a woman who could use a stiff drink."

Eve's mouth dropped open. "I don't drink."

The pointed glance Natalie cast at the brown paper sack under Eve's arm didn't go unnoticed. "Actually," Eve said, "I don't drink, well, not usually, at least not until tonight. I bought this wine, but that's a long story. I actually got dizzy on a jigger of cooking sherry a while ago. That's how good I am at holding my liquor. I'm pretty sure I sprained my ankle, and I saw the man I've loved all my life kissing another woman, and then two little old ladies were citing advice from *Cosmo,* and—"

"Sugar, I think you've earned a drink. And so have I."

Eve gaped. Her grandmother used to call her "sugar."

Natalie Harper was the most ungrandmotherly, unmatronly woman Eve had ever seen. Stunning, and taller than Eve in those spiked heels, she wore a tight leather miniskirt and so much makeup it was difficult to determine her exact age. She teetered away toward her car. Not many women could pull off a walk like that on five-inch heels, and she wasn't afraid to leave the top buttons undone on her blouse.

"You know, you could give lessons."

Natalie turned. "Excuse me?"

"I mean, I could use a few lessons. More like a crash course. Attracting a man 101. And you're right. I have earned a drink. And do you know what else? I don't feel like drinking alone." She thought about her sister at home with her husband and daughter, and her friends who were at home with their husbands and kids, and her quiet, empty, adequate house waiting for her. Before she lost her nerve, she blurted, "Would you like to come back to my house and have a glass of wine?"

Natalie didn't reply immediately. And Eve wondered if perhaps she needed to make her birthday toast alone.

Finally, Natalie said, "I already have a date."

"Oh, well . . ."

"With Captain Morgan here." She held up the brown paper bag in her hand. "I doubt the captain would mind sharing me. Just tell me you're not one of those Sunny Suzys who says crap like 'Snowflakes are snowmen that fall unassembled to the ground.' "

"The term *Sunny Suzy* nauseates me."

Natalie smiled for the first time. "I think you and I are going to get along just fine."

"You live here? No wonder you're depressed."

"I'm not depressed. I'm pathetic. There's a huge difference."

"Whatever you say, sugar. Cheers."

"Cheers." Ice cubes clinked as Eve lifted her tumbler and

took another sip. Natalie had said rum was an acquired taste. The flavor was strong, but Eve thought it tasted a lot better than cooking sherry–laced tea.

They were sitting in her living room, Eve on the sofa, her ankle wrapped in her new ace bandage, her foot propped on a pillow, and Natalie in an overstuffed chair, smoking another cigarette. Eve had tried one, but had wound up snuffing it out after two horrible puffs. She decided to perfect one vice at a time. She could hardly believe she was doing this.

The bottle of rum was leaving a mark on the coffee table, and Natalie's shoes were tipped onto their sides near the back door. A cupboard door hung open and chairs were out. Except on those occasions when Tommy or her niece visited, it was the messiest her house had been in ten years. She really *was* pathetic.

Natalie seemed more interested in smoking than in drinking, and Eve was still working on her first glass of rum. Maybe it was a pathetic attempt to get drunk, but she figured she had to start somewhere. She'd told Natalie more than she'd ever told anyone, about how she and Jack had always been friends, and how she watched Tommy whenever she could and how Jack always unclogged her sink and changed the oil in her car when it needed it. She told her about Jack's family, about Tommy's leukemia and Jack and Laurel, and now Jack and Laurel's identical twin sister. She told her about the aunts' advice, too.

"I hate to say it, Natalie." Were her words slurred? "But I think they might be right. I think I'll lose him again unless I do something drastic."

"Are you sure he's worth the trouble?" Natalie asked.

Eve nodded. They both grew quiet. Eve wondered if Natalie was thinking about her dreaded birthday. "I'm doing most of the talking."

"I don't mind." She spoke through a cloud of smoke.

"Do you really hate your birthday so much?"

"My birthday is in October."

Something about the information didn't make sense to

Eve. She took another sip from the glass in her hand. Although she didn't enjoy the taste, she rather liked the way the captain warmed a path to her stomach.

"I really appreciate all your help tonight," Eve said. "All the listening you've done. I'd like to return the favor."

"It's not necessary."

"Isn't there anything you want? Anything you'd like to know about Alcott?"

Natalie exhaled a breath of smoke. She cocked her head slightly, thinking. Finally, she said, "What can you tell me about a local handyman named Brian McCall?"

"Brian? He's Jack's brother."

"Yes, I know."

"Jack is the man I'm trying to, er . . ."

"Seduce?"

Eve probably blushed three shades of red, which was as good a reason as any to take another sip of rum. "Brian is a decent man. He's an excellent carpenter. All the McCalls are." And then she added, "But Natalie? I've never actually tried to seduce Jack."

"Maybe it's high time you did."

"But how?" Her cheeks even *felt* hot now.

"Be yourself. Be sensuous."

"Yeah, right." She paused. "You're serious. Go on."

"Open the top button on your blouse. Dab on some perfume. Leave your underwear in the drawer. Be coy."

She couldn't possibly do any of those things. Why, she wouldn't know where to begin. "You think that would work on Jack?" She hated how small her voice sounded.

Natalie snuffed out her cigarette. "He's a man, isn't he?"

Eve drained her glass of rum, smacked her lips. Placing the empty glass on the table, she made herself more comfortable on her sofa. "I'm glad I ran into you tonight."

"You're not so bad yourself."

Eve's eyes were drifting shut. She was powerless to help it. "I mean it. Melissa Meyers saw you the other day and told everyone at the Pilgrim Women's Society meeting that you look like Erin Brockovich, but without the kids or the cause. I really can't stand Melissa Meyers."

Natalie held perfectly still. Her mind whirled. Suddenly, she felt very chilled.

Eve's eyes were closed now, and her words were slurring together. "I think you're an amazing woman," she said quietly. You're jusht what thish tired town needs. What I wouldn't do . . ."

Natalie looked at Eve.

". . . for a walk like . . . yours, or for half . . . your cour— cour . . . courage."

"I'm not that brave, Eve."

A tense silence enveloped the room. Natalie looked closely at Eve, then called her name.

Eve snored softly.

Natalie shook her head. Eve was under the table after one glass of rum. Sighing heavily, Natalie looked at her own full glass, and rose to her feet.

She covered Eve with a crocheted afghan. Eve didn't so much as stir. Natalie gathered the glasses, recapped the bottle and carried everything into the kitchen. She dumped her drink down the drain, only to pause as she thought about some of the things Eve had told her. Natalie had met Jack McCall, and although he wasn't *her* type, Eve didn't have bad taste in men. And it didn't sound as though he treated her badly. He serviced her car and fixed her plumbing when it needed it, didn't he? Did he really have no clue that she wanted more from him?

Eve Nelson really was a nice person. Sometimes, small towns succeeded in squeezing the life out of nice people. Tonight, Eve had gasped her first breath in years. Natalie had a feeling more would follow. Eve was sweet and kind. It wouldn't be easy for her to break out of the mold the town had put her in. Too bad there wasn't somebody around to give her a hand.

Natalie had an idea, then spent the next several seconds

trying to talk herself out of it. In the end, she couldn't think
of a good reason not to do it.

She opened the cupboards in Eve's nondescript kitchen
and took out peanut butter, coffee grounds and a slice of
bread. She put together quite a concoction. When she was
finished with her handiwork, she scribbled a note.

*Here's drinking to you, kid. Let me know how it turns
out. Natalie.*

She slipped into her shoes and reached for the doorknob,
only to look over her shoulder at the nearly full bottle of
Captain Morgan. Erin Brockovich, indeed. She tottered over
to the sink and snagged the bottle.

Then she let herself out.

CHAPTER 10

Eve was up and ready when she heard Jack's knock on her door. Forbidding herself to hurry for once, she practiced her demure smile in the hall mirror. Then she opened the door. The morning air felt cool on her neck where her shirt lay open. Jack stood on the other side of the threshold, tall and dark and lean in his sheriff khakis, his eyes a tad hooded. It was early, after all.

A real smile took the place of her practiced one. "Good morning." Being coy was going to take some practice. "I appreciate you stopping by to take a look at my drain before work, Jack."

"No problem." He strode past her and into the kitchen, his metal toolbox clanking as he placed it on the counter. Noticing that she'd followed more slowly, he said, "What happened to your ankle?"

"I twisted it last night. It's better this morning." Everything seemed better this morning. In a softer voice, she said, "Did you sleep well?"

"I was up late reading."

"A mystery?"

He thought for a moment. "I guess you could call it a mystery."

He didn't elaborate, so she said, "What do you make of my kitchen sink?"

He glanced at the water sitting in the sink, and then tried the switch. The garbage disposal made a horrendous, laborious sound.

"See what I mean?" she asked after he'd turned it off. "It sounds terrible. It seemed fine yesterday. I don't know what I did." She felt her cheeks grow warm. Jack was rummaging through his toolbox, therefore he didn't see her blush. For once, she was glad he wasn't looking at her.

"You probably didn't do anything," he said.

He couldn't have known how right he was about that.

"These things get plugged sometimes, that's all."

The note from Natalie crinkled as Eve slid her hand into her pocket. "I suppose you're right."

Be coy, Natalie had advised.

Coy. Cute, coquettish, playful. Right. Eve eased slightly closer. Not close enough to get in the way, but close enough to appear to be trying to see what he was doing and perhaps even help. And maybe close enough for him to get a whiff of the perfume she'd dabbed on her wrists and neck before he'd arrived.

He took a deep breath. Eve held hers.

"Do you smell something?" he asked.

She wet her lips and refused to tremble. "Why, I don't know."

"It smells like cigarette smoke."

She wanted to stomp on his foot. "Are you experiencing a nicotine craving again, Jack?"

He shrugged. "Must be."

Considering the early hour, he was acting extremely good-natured. Kissing redheads must agree with him. The thought renewed Eve's resolve.

"Have you used any drain cleaner?" he asked.

And completely undo Natalie's efforts to help?

She knew as well as he did that harsh drain cleaners weren't recommended for use in garbage disposals. Eve simply started to shake her head, but then she remembered she was supposed to be acting coquettish, so she batted her eyelashes, which were heavy with mascara this morning, and decided to throw in a little helplessness, too. "Should I have?"

He glanced at her, and her heart fluttered wildly.

"It's better that you didn't," he said, returning to the matter at hand.

Once again she'd gone unnoticed.

He held a plunger in both hands. "Better stand back. This could splatter."

She stood back. And it did splatter. It didn't unclog her drain, however.

"How long has the disposal been acting sluggish?" he asked.

"It worked perfectly until this morning."

He fiddled with something under the sink. After disconnecting a wire, he reached inside the drain. "What did you try to put through here?"

"Oh, you know. The usual stuff." Actually she had no idea, until he scooped coffee grounds and soggy bread and something that smelled suspiciously like peanut butter and God only knew what else out of the drain and into the old enamel pan she quickly provided.

"If this doesn't work, I'll have to take the trap apart."

She had a sudden image of him lying under her sink, all stretched out, his back arched slightly, a knee bent, his shirt untucked, a portion of his washboard stomach showing. *Please,* she prayed, focusing on the drain, *stay clogged.*

After wiping his hand on several paper towels, he tried the plunger again. Next he fiddled with something under the sink, then flipped the switch. Eve held her breath. The disposal labored noisily.

Jack looked at her. She slanted him what she hoped was a coy smile. His eyebrows drew down. The disposal continued to churn until he flipped the switch. In the ensuing silence, her smile broadened, for her first prayer had just been answered. She owed God and Natalie, big-time.

He glanced at his watch. "I'll have to come back later."

"Later?" Her eyelashes fluttered.

"I'll be late for work if I take this apart now."

"We can't have that." She smiled, and batted her eyelashes again.

"Did something splatter into your eye?"

She blinked, this time from surprise. What? And then, "Oh." She took a step back. "Maybe."

He stacked his tools near the toolbox. "I'll leave these here, if it's all right with you."

"Of course. What time do you think you'll be back?"

"After supper."

She noticed he didn't ask whether she had other plans. It wouldn't have occurred to him. That was how much he took her for granted. That was what she got for being available for the past thirteen years. What a depressing thought! But it was her own fault. Now it was up to her to open his eyes where she was concerned.

With a smooth, natural swagger, he ambled toward the door. "I swear I smell cigarette smoke."

She limped after him. "Last night a friend who smokes stopped by." She purposefully hadn't specified the gender of her *friend,* hoping he would be jealous.

Jack didn't bat an eye.

Sara Kemper's rusty van inched slowly by, her son Seth tossing the morning newspaper. Waving to the boy and his mother, Jack said, "Seth has quite an arm. He'll be a great pitcher by the time he gets to the varsity team next year."

"Providing Roy doesn't break his arm and his spirit between now and then," Eve said.

Jack and Eve shared the kind of look that only years of friendship, of knowing the same people and sharing the same views, could bring. Although there were many things she would change about herself if she could, she wouldn't change that. Suddenly she felt better. All around town people were getting ready for work. Dogs were let out, newspapers brought in. Birds were singing and the air contained that glorious, dew-kissed scent she'd always loved. It was just another June morning in Alcott. She and Jack talked about ordinary things, him on the sidewalk, her on the top step of her little, adequate front porch. Jack mentioned that several streetlights had been busted a few nights ago. He thought it had the markings of teenagers with nothing better to do, and Eve agreed with him. She asked after Tommy, like she always did. She missed that little boy, and it warmed her heart to hear about him.

Jack said, "This morning at breakfast he asked Carter about women."

"Oh, dear."

Jack nodded. "At least Carter gave him the abridged version."

"That's good, I suppose, but . . . Jack? Who do you suppose taught Carter?"

Jack did something he rarely did. He laughed. Their old camaraderie was securely in place, their conversation natural and easy. Several cars went by, drivers waving as they passed. Certainly none of them saw anything unusual. Why would they? Jack was exactly like he always was: quiet and a little gruff, but kind and decent and good to her.

Eve was the one who had started to change.

"I was wondering," she said, running her fingers through her long, straight hair, "if Tommy might like to spend the afternoon with me today."

"It's nice of you to offer," he said.

She nearly melted at the compliment.

"But Liza's taking him for the afternoon."

"She is?" She'd spoken quickly. Too quickly.

He looked at her, his eyes narrowed slightly. Since Eve wanted Jack's perception of her to change from that of merely a friend to something better—a goddess, perhaps—

not something worse—such as an old sea hag—she said, "That's nice of her. What's she like?"

He shrugged.

And she said, "Is she anything like Laurel?"

"Yes and no."

Short of prying, there was nothing more she could do to uncover the extent of his feelings for Liza. Eve's second prayer was that Liza Cassidy would decide not to stay. While she was at it, she said a prayer for Tommy's continued recovery.

Too soon, Jack glanced at his watch and said, "I'd better get to work."

She smiled again. "I'll see you tonight."

He'd already started down the sidewalk, only to glance over his shoulder. "Tonight?"

That quickly, he'd forgotten her.

Trying valiantly not to let her hurt feelings show, she said, "I can call a plumber if you're too busy."

Evidently her mention of plumbing jogged his memory. "I'm not too busy for a friend like you, Eve." His tone held a degree of warmth and concern as he added, "I'll stop over after supper. Take care of that ankle."

"I will."

Very carefully she made her way inside her house, favoring her right ankle and nursing her hurt feelings. Jack was interested in Liza. That much was obvious. It wouldn't be the first time Eve had been overlooked in favor of another woman he'd just met. But this time, she wasn't just going to roll over and pretend she didn't mind. This time, she was going to fight for her man.

She looked in the mirror in her foyer, stopping and staring. Her darkened eyelashes made her gray eyes look big and luminous. Jack hadn't seemed to notice. He hadn't seemed to notice her perfume or that she'd left the top two buttons of her pale blue blouse open at her neck, either. What would it take to make him see her, truly see her? Miss

Addie had said that drastic situations called for drastic measures. Just how much nerve did Eve have?

It occurred to her that she wasn't so much afraid as she was uncertain. What she needed was a plan, and maybe some tips. She didn't dare ask her friends for advice. She had her pride, after all. And she didn't know Natalie well enough to ask her. Eve wondered if there were how-to books in the library, but that would require signing them out beneath Barbara Spitzley's watchful eyes. She thought about the magazine Miss Addie had read at the beauty parlor. Suddenly, she knew where her first stop would be this morning.

Liza Cassidy, prepare to meet your match.

It was almost ten o'clock by the time Eve finally left the beauty shop. Friday mornings weren't good days for getting right in and right out, because Annette Porter had a standing appointment for her "do" every Friday at eight-thirty. And Annette Porter loved to talk.

Eve had a few minutes of peace when Betty put Annette under the dryer. It gave Eve just enough time to look through that coveted magazine, under the guise of searching for a new hairstyle, of course.

By the time Betty was finished, Eve had sacrificed two inches off the bottom of her hair, and she'd wound up promising to contribute a pan of brownies and two loaves of banana bread for the upcoming bake sale, but the visit was worth it, for she'd memorized all ten surefire ways to get her man. A few of them were simply too bold for Eve. She couldn't leave the house without underwear, and she didn't think she could call Jack just before going to sleep at night and whisper sexy things over the phone. Couldn't she get arrested for that? The jury was still out regarding thongs, too. But her wardrobe could use some updating, and she needed to buy some eyeliner and lip gloss and shoes, definitely shoes. And she had to learn to play hard to get—but not too hard. Natalie had been right. She needed to learn to be more coquettish. It seemed that strong, silent men gobbled that up, hook, line and sinker.

Excitement ran through her as she navigated the library steps. Her excitement froze, along with the rest of her, when the door opened, for Liza Cassidy was descending the steps directly in front of Eve.

"Hello." Liza stopped a step up from Eve, and smiled. "It's Eve, isn't it?"

Eve returned a greeting, but there was no enthusiasm in it. She couldn't help it. For all intents and purposes, Liza was the enemy.

Noticing the bandaged ankle, Liza skipped to the top of the library steps and held the door for Eve. "Time to make a switch?" she said.

Eve felt her eyes widen in surprise. Realizing that Liza was referring to the books she was returning, she recovered enough to say, "As a matter of fact, it is."

"What do you like to read?" Liza asked.

Since it would have been completely rude to say nothing, Eve said, "Suspense thrillers, mostly." Her failure to ask a similar question in return seemed terribly obvious and almost mean to Eve.

Liza's smile faltered.

Eve felt nasty, and she'd never been nasty in her life. She told herself that Liza was the one who had been kissing Jack last night. Liza, who was pretty in an exotic sort of way, and new and interesting and . . .

No, Eve couldn't befriend her. She stood, feeling slightly awkward, facing her, mute.

Liza looked closely at her, probably finding all her flaws. "You probably hear this all the time."

Eve braced herself for the usual comments about her height. How's the weather up there? Did you play basketball in high school? How's your sister, Olive Oyl?

People were really funny.

Liza smiled and said, "You have beautiful hair."

Eve was pretty sure her mouth had dropped open. Tears stung the backs of her eyes. "I just had it trimmed."

Liza smiled again, and Eve knew it was genuine. "It shimmers with your every move," she said. "What I wouldn't give for hair as straight as yours."

Eve didn't know what to say. Deep down she knew that Liza Cassidy would be easy to like. That didn't mean she deserved Jack, did it? Remembering how she'd felt when she'd seen Jack and Liza kissing last night, Eve renewed her resolve and said, "Thanks, but I'd better go in or Barbara will accuse me of trying to cool the outdoors."

She limped up the final step and walked through the door Liza held. She didn't look back. And she tried not to feel guilty. She'd thought acting snotty would be more fun than it actually was. She hadn't enjoyed it, and she certainly wasn't proud of it. Winning Jack was going to be even more difficult than she'd imagined.

She had to stay focused. Jack was coming over after supper tonight. She had a lot to do to get ready. In her mind she recited the last sentence from the article she'd practically memorized. *All is fair in love and war.*

And this was both.

Pounding.

Racket. And more pounding.

Who in the hell was making all that racket?

A war was raging inside Natalie's skull, complete with cannons and bombs and Chinese gongs. She winced every time the pounding set off another explosion.

She opened one eye and dragged a pillow over her head. It muffled the sound, but not the pain. She tried to go back to sleep. When it became apparent that the hammering wasn't going to go away, she removed the pillow, eased back the covers, and slid one leg over the side of the bed. When she had both feet under her, she walked rather wobbly over to the window. The empty bottle rolled away when she happened to kick it on her way by. Strangely, the volume of the pounding didn't lessen now that the window was shut.

The sun was high. What time was it, anyway? She squinted at her watch. Jesus, it was after ten o'clock.

Holding her stomach with one hand and her head with the other, she trudged to the bathroom and grimaced at her reflection. Her mascara was smeared and her skin looked pasty. She looked like she'd been on the losing end of a nasty fight. But it was over. As bad as she felt every year on this morning, yesterday was always worse. She wouldn't have to deal with it again for another 364 days.

She splashed her face with cool water, then switched to warm. When her face was scrubbed free of makeup, she brushed her hair and her teeth. She grumbled every time a new round of pounding and banging and crashing rent the air. Whoever was making all that racket was going to get a piece of her mind. She glanced at her nakedness, then backtracked. First she would shower. And it might be more fortuitous to put on some clothes.

She emerged from the small bedroom partially awake and fully dressed in leggings and an oversized fuchsia and orange T-shirt. She brewed a pot of strong coffee and took her first sip, cursing whomever was responsible for that racket. There ought to be a law.

Natalie was at the top of the stairs when she realized why the hammering hadn't decreased in volume when she'd closed the window. It was coming from her own building.

Coffee in one hand, cell phone in the other, she descended the stairs, emerging into the back alley. Following the noise, she stepped through the open door at the back of her own offices. She hadn't gone far when she came upon the man responsible for the noise. He was bent at the waist, his back to her, so that all she could see was a tool belt and faded jeans that covered a pair of long legs and a somewhat bony, but still interesting, derriere.

She turned on her phone and pressed the nine and the one. "Hold it right there." She winced when her voice echoed inside her head.

At least the pounding stopped.

"What do you think you're doing?" she asked.

The man looked at her upside down first. There was confidence in the way he straightened and faced her. He had the nerve to grin.

"Don't make any sudden moves," she said. "I'm one digit away from having you arrested for trespassing."

He eased the hammer into the loop on the tool belt. "You'd be wasting the call. My brother is the sheriff."

Of course he was. The family resemblance was unmistakable—the bone structure, the straight nose and square chin. This McCall lacked the desolation and worry lines the sheriff possessed. He wasn't lacking in anything else.

Oh, hell.

He was still trespassing, and by God, she didn't have to be gracious.

"Didn't my brother tell you I might drop by?"

"No. You're Brian McCall?"

He nodded.

"I'm Natalie Harper."

He waited a moment, and then said, "I know."

"Of course you do."

"You're the new attorney."

This was the part where people normally said she didn't look like an attorney, to which she normally answered that she didn't want to look like an attorney. It was the reason she practiced law in small towns, where she wasn't expected to conform to the way her colleagues expected her to dress and talk and behave.

Brian McCall was in no hurry to say anything at all. A sudden breeze forced her gaze back to the door, which was still open. "I know for a fact that door was locked."

"I'd have the lock changed if I were you."

"And why is that?"

"Because every guy who ever attended Alcott High School knows how to jimmy it."

"Is that so?"

He wasn't the least put off by her sarcasm. He peered around the room. "I lost my virginity here."

"Were you by yourself or did you bring a date?"

He had a lopsided grin. It made him look relaxed and sinuous, like a tomcat stretching languidly in a patch of sun. "Take two aspirin and a tall glass of cool but not cold water. Stay away from coffee. The caffeine will make your headache worse."

"You're an expert on hangovers, too."

Again that grin. "I've had a few. What did you drink, anyway?"

She noticed he spoke softly. She would be darned if she would allow herself to appreciate it. "That's none of your business."

None of this was any of his business, which was what she was about to say when he asked, "Was it a private party?"

She looked at him dazedly for a moment before comprehending the question. "A friend joined me," she said.

"Anybody I know?"

"Eve's from Alcott, so I assume you know her."

"Eve Nelson?"

The credulity in his voice gave Natalie a feeling of superiority. Now that was more like it. "See there? You do know her."

He looked genuinely concerned now. "Eve doesn't drink."

Natalie thought about some of the things Eve had told her last night. She wondered if she'd discovered the plugged drain yet. Natalie hoped Eve hadn't minded a little "help." She wasn't sure what Eve needed, but she knew it wasn't a ruined reputation. "You're probably right. Sipping one glass of rum over ice hardly constitutes drinking."

He grinned at her again, cocky. And she realized she'd inadvertently told him what she'd been drinking, after she'd informed him that it was none of his business, which just went to show that hangovers weren't conducive to clear and quick thinking.

"I'm still having trouble picturing Eve sharing a bottle of rum with anybody."

"Do you think I'm lying?"

"Are you always this agreeable?" he asked.

Natalie wished the man would stop answering her questions with a question. That was *her* trademark.

"Did you tell her nobody puts ice in rum?" he asked.

Natalie shrugged. "How well do you know Eve?"

"Like the back of my hand. I've known her all my life. She's a real gem. She likes everybody."

"Nobody likes everybody. It's humanly impossible. Now why don't you tell me what you're doing here? If you say you're the answer to my prayers, I'll finish dialing nine-one-one, and I don't care if your brother is the sheriff."

"Maybe you should go take those aspirin before we get started."

She'd already taken two aspirin. "Get started doing what, pray tell?"

He eased into a grin he had no business using on her in her condition. "I like the way you think, but we just met, and Jack said you needed a handyman. Where would you like me to begin?"

She cast a pointed glance at the debris he'd already started tearing out. She traipsed to the desk, returning with a notepad and pen. "You can begin by writing down the names and phone numbers of people you've worked for. And then you can tell me why I should hire you."

He jotted several names on the paper. Handing the notepad back to her, he said, "You should hire me because I need the work and you need the help."

Eyebrows raised slightly, she said, "At least you're honest."

"You don't know the half of it."

"Are you experienced?"

His expression changed and his voice deepened as he said, "Not lately, but isn't it like riding a bike?" He clamped his mouth shut so hard she knew he hadn't been talking about making repairs and renovations. He had the grace to appear contrite. And then he adopted a professional manner and launched into a lengthy and in-depth recital of the rotting steps, leaky faucets and dry rot he'd repaired and a dozen other skills he'd evidently acquired over the years. It seemed he could do a little of everything from plumbing to painting to window glazing to roofing. And a little of everything was what this building needed.

"One final question."

"Yes?" he said.

"What do you see when you look at this place?"

This time he didn't blurt the first thing that popped into his head. Taking his time, he went from room to room, looking the entire place over. She turned her phone off and took another sip of her coffee, then followed from a distance. He picked up her shingle, read it, and then peered around as if envisioning the best place to hang it.

Alcott didn't have a historical society. A woman she'd spoken to in nearby Portsmouth said it was a crying shame, and cited that as the reason that so many of Alcott's oldest homes had either been altered beyond recognition or left to crumble. The woman had insisted that the reason Alcott didn't draw new businesses and chain stores had to do with a sad lack of good parking, a necessity when turning a town into a tourist trap. But the residents of Alcott seemed to like their town just the way it was, which suited Eve. Her house had been built by a wealthy merchant in the late seventeen hundreds. Although it had been converted into offices, with a small apartment on each of the two upper floors, the exterior still bore the grand federal style in which it had been built.

She took another sip of her coffee, curious to hear what Brian would have to say about the place. Finally he stopped looking at crown molding and flooring and said, "I see an old building that's been changed and then neglected. Somehow it survived, not entirely intact, but not beaten, either. With some elbow grease, paint and furnishings it could begin a new life as a quiet, tasteful, but far from boring law office. I'd go so far as to say that with a little tender loving care it might even be exactly what this town needs."

Halfway through the recitation, he'd looked at her. She got lost in his dark blue eyes.

Like hell she did.

Swallowing, she said, "How long do you think it will take? God willing and if the creek doesn't rise, I mean."

"Two weeks. Less if I put my mind to it."

"Put your mind to it, Mr. McCall."

"I already have."

She'd expected another cocky grin. Instead, he seemed dead serious. As disconcerting as that was, she believed he would do his best on this project. And he was right. She definitely needed help getting the offices ready to greet clients.

They agreed upon a price, and that ended the interview. The deal was sealed with a brief, firm handshake. Brian McCall got busy. Before long a truck made a horrendous beeping sound as it backed into the alley and unloaded a huge trash receptacle. Natalie went up front to do more unpacking, and Brian began hauling debris outside. While he worked, he whistled. It sounded to Natalie a little like "Amazing Grace." She noticed he didn't do any more hammering. For that she was thankful. By eleven-thirty, her headache was better and he was making a dent in clearing the place out. Shortly thereafter she caught herself humming the same tune he'd been whistling earlier. She turned on the stereo and inserted a CD.

And that was the end of that nonsense.

CHAPTER 11

Tommy unbuckled his seat belt as soon as Liza parked the car in Saxon's driveway. "Dad's here, and he brought the cruiser. And there's Uncle Carter's Harley. I love it when he brings the hog." He pushed the door open and ran on ahead, into his grandfather's house.

Liza followed, her arms full of everything Tommy forgot: his beach towel, the toy pail filled with rocks and shells, his shovel and toy sailboat, the sunscreen and his bright orange sunglasses. She'd never spent an entire afternoon with a child, and it had been idyllic and slightly exhausting. She'd set up an easel for each of them. When Tommy grew tired of painting, they'd waded in the ocean, and collected seashells and fossils along a narrow stretch of white beach between Rye and North Hampton. All the while Tommy had kept an eye out for whales on the horizon. Never mind that an old man walking his dog had insisted that whales were never spotted so close to shore. Tommy believed it was possible, and Liza didn't see any reason to discourage him. What good was an afternoon at the seashore if one couldn't believe in magic and dream of possibilities?

Liza was on the verge of believing in such things herself. She'd awakened early, for once. Perhaps it had been excitement to begin her day. Or maybe she'd finally slept enough. The motel room had looked even more dismal in the morning light. Unwilling to stay there another day, she'd loaded up her car and checked out. If Jack's offer still stood, she was going to stay at the captain's cottage until she found something else, something more permanent.

Tommy's voice reached her before she entered Saxon's cozy old kitchen. "We didn't see any whales, though. Or dolphins, neither. But we saw sailboats and a tanker and three lobster boats. And look. I found this sand dollar." He shook it. "Hear that? Aunt Liza says there's a surprise inside. She says it's a *legend,* so it's gotta be true, right?"

Jack was hunkered down at Tommy's level. Tommy rattled on, excited about his afternoon. Carter slouched in a chair at the table, his feet propped on a chair across from him. Brian was doing something at the kitchen counter, his back to the table. All three of them looked up as Liza entered. Carter and Brian smiled. And Jack almost did. Something went warm inside her. Starting in that sensitive spot between her shoulder blades, it moved downward and outward, and downward again, all the way to her fingers and toes. Jack had done it all with a look, and the hint of a smile that called to mind a dusky evening and a long, tender kiss.

"Dad? What about the whales?"

Jack ruffled the boy's hair. "You need a haircut, buddy."

"Can we go see them? Can we?"

"We'll ask Dr. Andrews at your next appointment. If he gives you the okay to ride a boat twenty miles out to sea, I see no reason not to do it."

"For my birthday?"

Jack stood, lifting Tommy up in the process. "You have it all figured out, don't you?"

"That's what Aunt Liza said." Tommy shook the sand dollar close to his father's ear.

Just then Saxon entered the kitchen. He glanced around the room somewhat grumpily, as if he'd just awakened on the wrong side of an unscheduled nap. Nodding at Liza, he eyed

Carter, whose boots were propped on a painted kitchen chair; and Brian, who was spreading peanut butter and jelly on bread. "Can't you smell that roast in the oven?"

Brian put the top on his sandwich. "I'm not staying that long. I have to practice my sermon for Sunday. I'm trying a new approach."

"I thought you were going to do that this afternoon."

"I worked on Natalie's offices this afternoon."

"Natalie who?" Saxon said.

"Natalie Harper?" Jack said at the same time.

"The new attorney?" Carter said.

Taking a huge bite out of his sandwich, Brian simply nodded.

"Grandpa, guess what?"

Tommy strained to get down, and Jack set him on his feet. The child instantly ran to his grandfather. Noticing that Liza's arms were still full, Saxon motioned for her to transfer all the beach items into his hands.

"Grandpa, I said, guess what?" Tommy held tight to his new prized possession, the sand dollar.

"You saw the president."

"Nope."

"The vice president?"

"Nope."

"An alien?"

"No."

"Captain Hook?"

He giggled.

"Tina Turner?"

"Grandpa!"

Jack pulled out a chair for Liza at the kitchen table. Carter's feet thudded to the floor. Hauling his feet out of the way, Carter told Liza, "It's a contest. Saxon tries to get Tommy to lose his train of thought, and Tommy plays along. They'll be a while."

Liza lowered into the chair, and Jack sat in the one next to Carter. Brian was still eating, leaning against the counter, his jeans dusty, one scuffed work boot crossed over the other. Saxon was still guessing as he put things away, and Tommy was still shaking his head in that superior way inherent in this family.

"Has he been this way all afternoon?" Jack asked quietly.

"Energetic, you mean?" She nodded. There were freckles across the bridge of the boy's nose despite the sunscreen she'd applied repeatedly throughout the afternoon. He'd slept for an hour beneath the shade of the umbrella and had awakened bright-eyed and raring to go again. Then he asked questions—she'd never heard so many questions. Sometimes it was hard to believe he wasn't even five years old.

He traipsed over to Liza. Accustomed to having his choice of laps, he crawled onto Carter's. "I didn't see anybody famous." Holding the sand dollar close to his own ear this time, he shook it, listening to the rattle.

"Then it's not someone you saw." Saxon scratched his bearded chin. "It must be something you did."

Tommy nodded sagely. "You'll never guess."

Liza suspected that Saxon never did.

"I might as well just tell you," Tommy said importantly.

"What are you waiting for?" Saxon asked.

Liza laughed, and Tommy said, "I made eleven dollars."

"Doing what?" Jack asked.

"Shining shoes?" Saxon asked.

"People don't wear shiny shoes at the beach." Not about to go through the entire ordeal again, Tommy placed the sand dollar on the table very carefully. Drawing several crinkled bills from his pocket, he blurted, "I sold my painting."

"What painting?" Saxon asked.

"You did a painting?" Brian said a second later.

Liza laughed again. The McCalls were enough to make anybody dizzy.

Tommy said, "Aunt Liza did one, too. But a fat lady wearing a big hat offered me ten dollars for mine. It was a picture of a whale."

"I thought you said you made eleven dollars," Brian said.

Tommy looked at his aunt. They shared a secret smile before he slid off Carter's lap and said, "Would you make me a peanut butter sandwich, too, Uncle Brian?"

Saxon grumbled, "Can no one smell that roast?"

Jack looked at Liza again. "You upped the fat lady's bid?"

If she'd been sitting closer, she would have swatted his hand. "You have to pay for good artwork."

"And was it good?"

Somehow, she didn't believe he was talking about Tommy's painting anymore. The air heated, the room quieted. He'd done it all with one innocent question delivered in a voice that was anything but innocent. If she'd been sitting closer, he would have heard the quick breath she took. If she'd been sitting closer, she might have lowered her voice to a whisper and said what she was thinking.

"Take a look at this." Saxon dropped the newspaper in front of Carter. It was open to the classifieds.

"I have a job," Carter said.

"You tend bar at Dusty's every night and play pool until all hours."

The room was quiet all at once.

Peacemaker Brian said, "I could use a secretary, but you'd look funny in a skirt."

Although Carter's tight expression eased slightly, he didn't smile. Shoving his hair behind his ears, he glanced at Liza, shrugged at Jack, and finally spoke to Brian. "I don't type."

Liza's gaze was drawn to Carter's hands. Most people noticed faces, but as an artist, she knew that hands were just as telling. They required the most skill to paint. Jack's hands were large, the knuckles slightly bony. There was a blister on Brian's right palm. Carter's hands were callused and thick. They weren't the hands of a man who did nothing but tend bar and play pool.

In an obvious attempt to fill the silence again, Brian said, "So. What are you doing tonight, Jack?"

"I told Eve I'd take the trap apart underneath her kitchen sink."

Carter stood. "I'm taking the hog for a spin."

"What about the roast I'm fixing for supper?"

Carter gave his father a long, layered look. He left without slamming the door, but everyone knew he'd wanted to.

The adults all looked at Saxon. The burly patriarch shook his head. "Know what I like about experience? It lets me recognize a mistake when I make it again." He continued to mumble to himself as he ambled to the oven.

Thinking about what he'd said, Liza said, "Jack, I've been wondering about something."

He looked at her, and she was struck all over again by how easy he was on the eyes. "What have you been wondering about?" he asked.

"I seem to have gotten off on the wrong foot with somebody."

Through the open windows, they heard a voice from central dispatch coming from the patrol car. "I'll be right back." With obvious reluctance, Jack went outside to take the call.

Brian poured himself a glass of milk, and Saxon said, "Who?"

She looked across the kitchen. "Eve Nelson."

Saxon put the roast back in the oven and closed the oven door. And Brian said, "Are you sure?"

"Pretty sure. What's she like?" Liza asked.

Bored with the adult conversation, Tommy went off to play.

"She's a good girl," Saxon said.

"Eve's not a girl. She's a godsend," Brian said. "She's sweet and kind."

"Would you say she's standoffish?"

Just then Saxon's phone rang, too. "I rue the day Alexander Bell invented that contraption." But he ambled into the next room to answer it, grumbling all the way. That left Liza and Brian in the old kitchen with its rooster wallpaper and noisy refrigerator.

"Standoffish? Not Eve," Brian said. "She likes everybody."

Remembering Eve's reluctance to talk to her that morning on the library steps, Liza thought out loud. "Nobody likes everybody."

Brian looked surprised. "You're the second woman to tell me that today."

They talked for a few more minutes, then Brian went outside. Liza's head was spinning. Maybe she'd had too much sun. Or maybe she wasn't accustomed to the way men's minds worked. Deciding she would ask Jack about Eve later, she went outside, too.

"That was Ben Barkley," Saxon said from the dining room. "He's coming over later for a game of canasta." He stopped and looked around his kitchen. His empty kitchen.

Tommy was making motorboat noises in the den. Carter roared out of the driveway on his motorcycle. Saxon felt bad about saying the wrong thing. Again. He could see Jack talking to Liza through the open window of her car, and Brian was easing into his Corvette. At least his oldest two seemed happy today. That mellow whistle of Brian's was something he hadn't heard in a long time. And Saxon hadn't seen Jack like this since Laurel had first come to town.

After Liza drove away, Jack came inside to say good-bye to Tommy, then he got in the cruiser and left, too. He had something to do at the station, and then he was going back over to Eve's to work on her sink.

Saxon had always suspected the girl had feelings for Jack. It wasn't anything she'd said. In fact, he'd never heard anybody mention them in that way, and that was saying a lot in Alcott. Saxon just had a feeling in his bones, not unlike the way he could feel it in his bad knee when it was going to rain. Liza must have noticed something in Eve's manner today, too.

Uh-oh. Jack was going over to Eve's later.

Saxon sat down with his crossword puzzle. One man and two women always spelled one thing.

Trouble.

* * *

There wasn't anything unusual about the plate of warm brownies on Eve's table, or the pitcher of sweetened tea that she knew Jack liked. There wasn't anything unusual about the fact that he'd already helped himself to both, either. And there certainly wasn't anything unusual about the way it made Eve feel to see him enjoy them.

He'd walked over with Tommy and their dog. She'd missed that child, and it was wonderful to see him, too. His presence made Eve glad she'd opted for subtlety.

She'd been busy all afternoon, shopping and scheming. She'd turned the radio to the usual oldies station and had greeted Jack and Tommy at the door with a warm smile. She'd watched Jack closely to see if he noticed anything different about her. Subtle or not, there *were* changes. She'd secured one side of her hair above her ear with a gold clip. The other side hung long and straight. Liza had said it herself. Eve's hair shimmered with her every move. Sometimes tendrils swung into her face, so that she had to smooth them away slowly, sensuously, and maybe even seductively.

After the results it had garnered this morning, she'd given up on batting her eyelashes. She was wearing makeup, though, and shiny lip gloss that tasted like strawberries. According to the magazine she'd purchased in Portsmouth that afternoon, femininity began at the tips of women's feet. She'd painted her toenails and showcased them in the new strappy sandals she'd bought today. Her fingernails were tinted, too. The idea was to let Jack notice subtle differences without realizing anything had changed.

Subtlety was the key.

She still wore the ace bandage, so she had an excuse not to wear her new lime green dress. Lime green! The salesgirl had insisted she looked great in that color. It *did* deepen the color of her eyes. Tonight she wore a new, sleeveless lime green blouse with a vee neckline and a pair of low-rise jeans that felt like they were going to slide off her hips any second.

If Jack had noticed, he hadn't said. That wasn't unusual, either. He was comfortable with long stretches of silence.

She'd once told her sister he was like a window. If she wanted to catch a breeze, she had to be standing in front of him on those rare occasions when he opened up. So far, Tommy had talked more than his father. Liza Cassidy's name had come up. It seemed she and Tommy had spent the afternoon at the beach. And apparently she was moving into the captain's cottage for the time being. Since Eve didn't want to spend her time with Jack and Tommy talking about another woman, she hadn't encouraged the conversation. And once again, Jack had grown silent.

She and Tommy went out to her little front porch. She settled next to him on the top step. He balanced the plate of brownies on his lap and held his new sand dollar carefully in one hand. Tanner sat below, alert for once, as if guarding Tommy.

She read the book she'd bought for him on her shopping excursion. It was beautifully illustrated, and was about a boy and the sea. When she'd finished reading to him, he took it from her and started at the beginning. Leaving him to look through it by himself, she returned to her kitchen. There, she wondered what the experts would suggest she try next.

"Eve, hand me that pipe wrench, would you?" Jack's voice was slightly muffled, coming as it was from beneath her sink.

He was lying on the floor, his back arched slightly, a knee bent, his shirt untucked, a small triangle of washboard stomach showing. Eve was staring. It was a scene straight out of a fantasy. Only he was real. And he was here, in her kitchen, flesh and blood, sinew and muscle, male through and through.

"Eve?"

She came to her senses. "A pipe wrench. Right."

Rather than go around, she stepped over him, straddling him in a sense as she reached for the item he'd requested. Next, she bent over, so she could see his face. "Where would you like it, Jack?"

She wet her lips, and tasted strawberries. Holding her position, she waited for her sensual voice to filter through to his brain.

"Just lean it up next to the cabinet."

His thick brain.

He made a few grunting noises and applied pressure to the wrench. The tool slipped, Jack swore, and water shot from the loosened connection. He jerked out of the spray so quickly Eve didn't have time to move out of the way. His knee came up, knocking her good foot out from under her. She went down like a house of cards.

He bumped his head on the cabinet, but his hand shot out to steady her, so that she landed with a soft thud, one leg straddling his. "Are you all right?" His voice was deep, their faces close. Closer than they'd been in . . . maybe ever.

"Did I hurt your ankle?"

His hand was warm, his fingers strong where they encircled the bare flesh of her upper arm.

"My ankle?" she said. And then, "Oh. It's . . . no." She lowered her eyelashes in a manner she hoped was alluring.

"Can you get up?"

She looked up at him, her eyes delving into his. Her heart was in her throat and something delicious fluttered deep in her stomach.

He stared. "Are you sure you're all right?"

"I believe I'm sure, yes." She wet her lips, wishing he would kiss her.

He looked at her as if baffled by her behavior. And then he looked at the way she was just sitting there, so still. "Can you move?"

"I think so." To prove it, she moved her shoulders slightly, and she hoped, provocatively.

She'd dated in college, and a few times since. The guys she'd gone out with had been all hands, and Eve had spent most of the dates fending them off. Being the aggressor was new to her, and exciting.

Jack eased to one side, leaving her little choice but to drag her leg across, and off, his. Unencumbered now, he climbed to his feet. To her immense satisfaction, he offered her his hand. Placing her fingers in his, she rose fluidly to her good foot, then stood there for a moment, heart beating, her hand still in his. Her gaze trailed to his mouth. For a man, he really had a beautiful mouth.

"Where do you keep your towels?"

She blinked. "My towels?"

He stepped back, pointing at the puddle on her floor. "I want to wipe up that water before I clean the trap out and put the pipe back together."

Her hand fell to her side. "In the top drawer." She'd answered by rote. Uncertain what else to do, she hobbled to a chair and sat down.

Tommy loped in, his new book under one arm, the empty plate under the other. Sighing, he said, "You can't trust a dog to guard your food."

She smiled in spite of herself. "Want another brownie?"

He shook his head, and she thought he was getting tired. He brought the book to her and climbed onto her lap. Breathing deeply, she relished the warmth, the little-boy smell of his hair, the weight and feel of him. And she knew this competition had nothing to do with Tommy. He responded to love no matter who it came from. Grown men were trickier. According to the magazine articles, they reacted to visual stimulation and responded to sensual stimuli.

Jack dried up the water and finished fixing her drain. When he was finished, he tried the disposal. "Good as new."

He dropped the wet towels in the sink and began gathering up his tools. They were leaving, and she hadn't made any progress whatsoever. She hugged Tommy out on the porch, thanked Jack for fixing her sink, then stood and watched father, son and dog start for home.

Jack looked over his shoulder. "Eve?"

"Yes?" Maybe there was hope after all.

"Tommy loves the book." He hoisted the boy onto his back.

"I'm glad." She smiled.

"Maybe you should have your ankle examined."

She shrugged. "I'll take it under advisement. Good night."

The trio continued toward their house on Mill Street. Returning to her kitchen, Eve faced the fact that wearing makeup and subtle though feminine new clothes wasn't working.

She carried the soggy towels to the laundry room. Although it was a little sore, her ankle held her weight just fine. It didn't need examining.

She took the clip from her hair and hiked her jeans higher on her hips. If anything needed examining, it was her head, because she wasn't giving up.

Somebody was knocking on Natalie's back door.

It had been going on, on and off, for five minutes. Whoever it was, wasn't going to go away. She finally traipsed through the newly cleared-out rooms. After peeking out a nearby window, she heaved a sigh and threw open the door.

Brian McCall stood in the dimly lit alley.

She folded her arms. "Oh. It's you."

"Were you expecting someone else?"

His mouth hinted of a smile, but the set of his chin suggested a stubborn streak. It had been a while since she'd come upon a man as stubborn as she was. "I figured you were either a desperate door-to-door salesman, or a Jehovah's Witness."

"Close but no cigar. I saw your lights. May I come in?"

"Didn't you get enough this afternoon?"

He mumbled something she couldn't hear. From the way he clenched his jaw, she assumed that was a good thing.

"It's late, Brian. What are you doing here?"

He eyed her with a calculating expression. "I was going to replace the doorknob and lock tomorrow." He held up a carton containing several mechanical pieces. "But even in a small town, a woman can't be too careful."

"You never know who might break in," she said sardonically.

"I knew you'd see it my way."

She still didn't invite him in. "It can't wait until tomorrow?"

"Would you prefer I wait until tomorrow?"

She stuck her hands on her hips and redistributed her weight to one foot. "I had a woman professor once who spent an entire semester discussing the psyche of, and warning us about men who answer questions with questions."

The comment seemed to amuse him.

With a dramatic flourish, she stepped back and motioned him in. Leaving him to his task, she continued making notations of room dimension and carpet sizes, mentally calculating where she would place her office furniture.

He tinkered with the doorknob, talking as he worked. "I should be able to start painting the walls tomorrow."

"I'll be gone most of the day." She jotted a notation in her notebook.

"What color paint do you want me to use?"

She pointed to a paint chip she'd circled on a color chart, and the notations she'd made on the sketch on her notepad. "I opened an account at the hardware store in the town square."

"Then that's where I'll get the paint. Where are you going tomorrow?"

"To Boston to oversee the loading of my old office furniture."

"You practiced law in Boston?"

She nodded. "I was junior partner in a very prestigious, high-profile, high-powered, high-pressure law firm." The antique pieces had been hers to begin with, and she'd insisted on taking them with her.

"You don't sound like someone from Boston."

"You don't say."

Obviously perfectly happy to share his wisdom, he said,

"Most Bostonians—and people from around here, for that matter—have a unique way of omitting their *r*'s. They say motah for motor and pahtnah for partner. Would you hold this?"

She put down her notepad and went to the door, holding the doorknob from the other side. Even then, the old device was stubborn about coming off.

"Did you attend college in Boston, too?"

"The University of Texas."

"Why did you leave?" he asked.

"Texas or Boston?" Natalie grasped the knob with both hands to keep it from turning.

"Take your pick."

And she said, "I left the firm because I didn't like who I was becoming."

The fact that she'd chosen to answer that question made Brian even more curious about the one she hadn't answered. "That's admirable, Natalie."

She held perfectly still, either surprised or uncomfortable with his praise. He wished he knew which.

"Plus, I was asked to leave."

Brian looked more closely at her. Her hair was almost black, and medium length. It was cut in layers around her face, brushing her cheekbones and brow. She wasn't movie-star beautiful, but her face was memorable. He didn't know any real men who preferred plastic over natural anyway. Her eyes were brown and expressive, her lips lush and full. It was easy to imagine them on his, among other places. He almost said it out loud. Before he embarrassed himself, insulted her and risked getting fired and sued, he said, "Why did they ask you to leave?"

Finally the old handle and lock came off in his hands.

"Who knows." She shrugged. "Maybe they didn't like my religion."

Brian had a feeling what they didn't like was her insolence and her attitude. It so happened he liked both just fine.

He held the new doorknob to the door, measuring its fit. Both he and Natalie were on their knees, their faces close, the door partially between them.

"Are you Presbyterian?" he asked.

She rolled her eyes.

"Catholic?"

"It's really none of your business."

Oh, that attitude. "Baptist?"

This time she looked at him with a critical squint.

"I'm just making conversation. You're the one keeping secrets."

The doorknob slipped from her fingers, dropping noisily to the floor. She fumbled for it, but he was the one who finally located it and picked it up. He finished securing it, and moved on to begin installing the dead bolt. "I guess we can do this the way Tommy does this."

"Who's Tommy?

"My nephew."

"Ah yes, Thomas John. Do what?" she asked.

"Play twenty questions. Lutheran?"

She studied her chipped fingernail.

"Mormon?"

He thought he glimpsed a slight smile.

"Jewish? You might as well answer, because I haven't even gotten started with the Eastern religions."

Shaking her head, she said, "Let's just say I'm a practicing vegetarian, and leave it at that."

"You don't like meat?" slipped out before Brian could stop it.

She looked him in the eye and had the nerve to smile. It was that old I-know-something-you-don't-know look of a woman begging for trouble. "I didn't say I don't like it, Brian."

He swore the air heated ten degrees. "Are you saying you do?"

"I don't partake."

"Ever?"

She smiled, victorious. "That is none of your business, either. Go home, Brian."

He stared into her eyes for interminable moments. Finally, he motioned to the apparatus not yet installed. "What about the dead bolt?"

"This lock will suffice for now. I'll move something heavy in front of the door if necessary."

They both peered around the nearly empty room.

"I'd be happy to stay and protect you."

She cocked her head. "That's very chivalrous of you."

"Know what I think?"

Her eyes widened as she waited.

"I think you're tempted."

She found her feet. "Don't let it go to your head."

That wasn't where it was going.

Brushing the dirt from her knees, she said, "Take a cold shower and call me in the morning."

He stood, too. "You're the boss."

Natalie closed the door as soon as Brian stepped into the narrow alley that ran along the back of the properties adjacent to the town square. From a nearby open window, she listened until his mellow whistle faded into the distance. She resumed her earlier task. It was a long time before she realized she was humming.

She didn't know what was happening to her. She hadn't been inside a church in ten years, and yet the song she kept humming was "Amazing Grace."

CHAPTER 12

Tommy surged to his feet with the force of a small tidal wave. Water sluiced down his thin body and splashed out of the claw-footed bathtub.

Bathing Tommy was a lot like trying to bathe a cat.

Wrapping the towel around him, Jack lifted the boy to the bath mat. Tommy wriggled through the quick rubdown, then dropped to the floor, and went to work poking his damp feet into the legs of his pajamas. By the time Jack had sprayed down the bathtub and replaced the special soap that contained no dyes or perfumes, Tommy was sticking his head into his pajama top. Jack worked a comb through that clean, wild auburn hair.

With more important things on his mind, Tommy raced into his room, picked up the sand dollar and shook it. "Hear that? There's a surprise inside. Aunt Liza told me about the sand dollar's legend."

Jack turned on the Batman lamp, and Tommy climbed onto his bed, where he sat cross-legged. It was Aunt Liza this, and Aunt Liza that. In fact, he talked about Liza almost as much as he talked about whales.

Tommy was fascinated with his sand dollar, too. Every kid growing up on the seacoast had seen them. Most had held one in his or her hand sometime or other. Jack remembered the day he'd found his first one. It was shortly after his mother had died, and Saxon had taken Jack, Brian and Carter to the ocean, probably to escape the cloying stillness that had descended upon the house. Jack had discovered the small object that had resembled a crisp white cookie sticking out of the sand. He shook it, then promptly crushed it to see what had been rattling inside. To this day, he remembered how delicate the broken pieces had felt in his fist as he'd run over to Saxon. Uncurling his fingers, he'd said, "It was pretty, but then I broke it."

Saxon's hair and beard had been black then, his blue eyes sad. He'd grown silent in the weeks since Jack's mother's car accident. To a little boy, that silence had been as terrifying as the empty place at the table and in the kitchen and on his mother's side of the bed.

He'd thrust his hand toward his father. "Put it back together."

"I can't, son. No one can."

The idea that his father couldn't fix something had been new, and Jack hadn't liked it. "I ruined it."

"But look what you discovered inside."

"What did I discover?" Jack had asked.

"Why, magic, of course."

"Magic?" seven-year-old Jack had said.

Saxon picked up one of the tiny items that had rattled inside. "Look here. See these five little figures? Some people say they're doves. Others think they're angels."

Jack had leaned closer. They did look a little like angels.

"You're a lucky boy today."

"Why?" Jack had asked, mesmerized.

"You broke through the crusty outer shell and found the angels inside. If a sand dollar has angels, I guess we probably do, too."

Saxon had grown less quiet in the days, weeks and months that had followed. And Jack's fear had evaporated on the onrushing ocean breeze. He hadn't felt that kind of fear again until Tommy's diagnosis.

It was strange, the things a man remembered.

He recalled the day he'd taken a sand dollar to school. His third-grade science teacher told the students the name and scientific classification, then he'd explained that a sand dollar had once been a living creature called a sea urchin. Long before it washed ashore, it had died, and everything except its fragile skeleton was gone. Mr. Simon had busted the skeleton's shell apart, and Jack had nearly been busting at the seams to hear Mr. Simon tell the class about the angels.

The teacher had held up the five pointed objects inside, and called them *teeth*. Not angels. Not even doves. Teeth. Jack remembered his disappointment. He didn't want Tommy to experience it tonight.

His son continued to rattle the shell, his blue eyes bright. "Aunt Liza says a sand dollar is magic."

"Magic?"

"Yup. Aunt Liza says you have to open it in order to get the magic out, but once you open it, you can't close it."

Aunt Liza this, Aunt Liza that.

"That's true. Are you going to open it?" Jack asked.

Tommy gave the matter a great deal of thought, then shook his head slowly. "I wanna save my magic."

Jack wondered when he would stop being humbled by this amazing, precious child. With that, Tommy carefully placed the sand dollar on the nightstand, scooted under the sheet and burrowed into his pillow. Jack kissed his son's forehead, and like every other night these past three and a half months, the boy's eyes closed almost immediately, sleep a quick drop into oblivion.

Jack watched his son sleep. Tommy's thin arms were tan where they lay on the sheet, and there were freckles across his nose—both testaments to the fun he'd had that day, and the sheer normalcy of his life now. A week ago, there had been patches of bald spots on his pale scalp. Tonight, dark-auburn peach fuzz covered those places. Tommy's hair had been growing back for a while, but suddenly it was coming in all over, and the cold knot of fear was easing in Jack's gut.

He didn't know when his apprehension would disappear completely. A year? Five? Ten? Never? He could live with that, because Tommy was better. And Jack's days were beginning to feel more normal, too.

After turning out the lamp, he left Tommy's room. He paid a few bills, swept the kitchen floor, then stood for a long time beneath the warm spray of the shower. Donning a pair of his most comfortable old sweats, the fabric worn thin, the elastic long gone so that only the drawstring held them up, he settled himself in his leather recliner with Laurel's journal. After reading some of the entries again, he reread the last letter Laurel had sent to Liza.

My dearest Liza.

She'd crossed off the first two words, so it read simply, Liza. *No sense getting maudlin, right? Aw, hell, if I don't have a right to be maudlin, who does?*

She'd started again.

My dearest Liza,
    Well. This is it. The end of my beginning . . .

She'd known she was dying. Jack read each word carefully, putting them to memory, pausing where she'd written . . .

I came here to explore my life. And at the end of my quest, I find myself back where I started. Somehow, I think it must be the same for everybody. Everything I thought I knew is false, and it's as if I've reached this place inside me for the first time, only to discover that I've been here before.

These were deep, poetic, meaningful words that made Jack's throat close up one second and brought a feeling of peace the next. Laurel Cassidy had been exasperating and witty, and a joy to know.

I need you to do me one last favor. I need you to meet Jack. Go to the lighthouse on the Isles of Shoals next Wednesday at noon. You should be awake by then. He'll be waiting. You'll recognize him. Tall, dark and brooding. Give him a kiss for me . . .

You're going to love Alcott. And I love you. Take care of Nola. Tell Jack I tried.

She'd signed it with a flourish of loops and curves that spelled, simply, *Laurel*.

Like the fear that had evaporated on the onrushing ocean breeze that day when he'd discovered the secret legend of the sand dollar, Jack's anger had begun to dissolve this past week. Five years was a long time to be angry.

Five years was a long time, period.

He didn't know what had happened to Laurel's final letter to him. It no longer mattered. She'd loved him, but she'd died. She should have told him about the brain tumor, but she hadn't. He didn't have to like something in order to accept it. Finally, he accepted this, and that acceptance brought peace.

It was pitch dark outside by the time he closed the journal and folded the letter and put it back into its envelope. Tomorrow, he would return it to Liza. He couldn't remember when tomorrow had felt so full of possibilities.

He knew he would sleep tonight.

Not much had changed at Hal's Barber Shop since Jack was a kid. It still boasted an old-fashioned barber pole next to the door and a bench under the window where old-timers shot the breeze most summer mornings. Tommy sat on the same booster board that Jack and his brothers had sat on when they were small. His son enjoyed the haircut about as much as the rest of the McCalls, too.

The barbershop was a busy place on Saturdays, and everyone who came in was pleased to see the evidence of

Tommy's good health. Although his platelet counts were in the safe range, which meant his blood would coagulate if he suffered a scrape or cut; and his white blood counts were high enough to fight infection, Jack wasn't taking any chances. Hal used the electric clippers instead of scissors or a razor, giving the boy a cool, neat, safe buzz. They'd called it a butch thirty years ago when Jack had been Tommy's age. Tommy was immensely relieved when Hal was finished.

Jack paid for the haircut. Tommy chose his hard candy from the big glass jar, and his first haircut in a year was over. They were going to celebrate with ice cream.

Someone pulled the heavy wooden door open at the same time that Jack pushed. He found himself face-to-face with Roy Kemper. The two men squared off opposite one another. Everyone stopped talking, even Hal, while they watched the confrontation between their lawman and the meanest man in Rockingham County. Roy didn't back down. He never did. Keeping Tommy well out of the way, Jack stepped aside. Roy entered, his smile nasty and victorious.

It was common knowledge that Roy beat his wife and disliked his own son, the rising star of the high school baseball team. Nobody knew where Roy had acquired his mean streak. He was a braggart and a know-it-all who didn't do anything unless he was the center of attention. So of course he never went to Seth's baseball games. Roy made no secret of his disdain for the sport—and any sport—calling baseball players sissies, and calling his son worse things—mean, vicious, nasty, ego-sucking, hurtful things. The rest of the town did what they could to make it up to the boy. There wasn't much they could do to make up for the black eyes, the dislocated shoulders, and various other bruises Roy had bestowed upon his wife, Sara, over the years.

If she would only press charges, Jack would nail the bastard. But like so many other battered women, she wouldn't. As time passed, she stood up to her husband less and less. And yet the beatings hadn't lessened. The only place Sara had any backbone left was where Seth was concerned. As far as anybody knew, she'd never let Roy lay a hand on their son. She told everybody Seth was going to college someday. The people of Alcott agreed he had one hell of an arm, and would likely earn a sports scholarship. Seth delivered newspapers to earn enough money to pay for his shoes and baseball camp and special equipment. Like the sniveling coward he was, Roy pretended it was his idea, and made sure he pocketed any money that was left.

Jack would have enjoyed taking matters into his own hands, but he'd taken an oath to uphold the law, therefore his hands were tied. Roy knew it, just as he knew he was safe as long as Sara didn't press charges. And Sara never pressed charges.

Hitching his pants higher, he strolled inside and took the waiting chair as if it was his due. Jack clenched his jaw so hard it ached, and forced himself to leave quietly.

On the sidewalk outside, Tommy looked up at him. "You don't like that man, do you?"

Jack wished there was a way to shield his child from cruelty and wickedness and everything vile. The most he could give him today was the truth. "No, Tommy," he said. "I don't like him."

"Me neither!" The boy put his hand in Jack's, and father and son strolled to the corner to buy ice cream.

Abby Martin was there with her twins, Joel and Jenna who, Tommy informed his father, were already five. The children sat together, laughing and giggling. Abby invited Tommy to their house to play for the remainder of the morning. She assured Jack that nobody in her household had so much as a sniffle. Suddenly Jack had an hour or two to himself. He climbed behind the wheel of his SUV, started the engine, and pulled out of his parking space. His turn toward Captain's Row was as automatic this morning as breathing.

Liza would never be a morning person, and yet for the second day in a row, she'd awakened before nine. She took a long, hot shower, washing her hair with shampoo scented of honeysuckle, and her body with soap made from oatmeal and vanilla. When she ran out of hot water, she turned the tap off. Wrapping her hair in a towel, she dried with another, and donned a loose-fitting dressing gown.

Sliding her feet into slippers, Liza threw open the back door. She stood for a moment, breathing in the moist ocean air. The stillness and the fog drew her outside. She stood perfectly still, her feet moored to the damp flagstones.

She heard a car drive by, but this little section of land was secluded, surrounded by the ocean on one side and tall hedges on the other. Somewhere to the north, the shoreline came to a point. Slightly inland, and the tide ebbed and flowed through natural salt marshes that were visible on clear days, but not today. If there were ships on the horizon, she couldn't see them, for fog rolled across the ocean like steam falling over a bubbling caldron, the sea undulating, rhythmic.

It was almost as if she was standing inside a cloud, where she could smell the morning unfolding, the scent of wild-flowers and dew. She could see the morning unfolding, the sun a faint yellow haze in the milky white sky. She could hear the morning unfolding, birdsong and the gentle breeze, and footsteps muffled by the damp grass, and a deep, rich, masculine voice behind her.

"Somehow I knew I'd find you out here."

Heat spread through her at the sound of that voice. She turned her back on the morning, and there Jack was in jeans and a black T-shirt, his hair dark, eyes darkened by emotion. Once, she'd thought his eyes were unreadable, but today she understood what he'd been through, what he was going through, and what that look meant. And it warmed her, flushed her with heat at something so simple, so honest, so real.

"Where's Tommy?"

His next step brought him closer. "He's playing at a friend's house."

"So you're here alone?"

"Alone?" The man had sexy down to an art form. "Alone. With you."

"Quite a coincidence, your being here, alone with me, wouldn't you say?" She knew how that sounded—flirty and joyful.

Jack knew how it sounded, too. She was sexy and playful, and yet it was as if she was waiting for him to make the next move. Something was coming alive inside him, something that had been dead for a very long time. Desire poured through him, hot, heavy, pounding, roaring as if in direct relation to the waves that were breaking on the rocks far below.

"Know what I think?" he asked.

"Am I supposed to guess, Jack?"

Oh, that attitude. Her hair was wrapped in a yellow towel, her gown semitransparent, the wind toying with the fabric, her smile toying with him. "I don't believe in coincidence," he said.

"You believe everything happens for a reason?" Her voice was a sultry whisper, a sigh, a slow sweep across the part of him that was already straining for attention.

She'd obviously just come from her shower. She was standing three or four strides away, so he must have been imagining that he could smell her shampoo from here. That wasn't all he was imagining, for he wanted to lay down with her, stretch out beside her, glide his hand over her, and burn off his desire in her, while the sun burned off the swirling morning fog.

It was crazy. It was broad daylight. He couldn't, wouldn't, shouldn't.

"You didn't answer my question." She stayed where she was, joy in her eyes, temptation everywhere else.

"Yes," he said. "I'm beginning to think that everything happens for a reason."

The breeze fluttered through her gown, pressing it to the contours of her lush body. Her smile enticed, and yet she remained artful, patient and serene, waiting, it seemed. For him.

Jack did the only thing he could do. He walked over to her, hauled her into his arms, and kissed her.

CHAPTER 13

Jack's arms came around Liza and his lips covered hers. She felt herself being drawn up, folded into his embrace. Heat emanated from the entire length of his body. The breath rushed out of him, and her, his hands gliding over her from shoulders to hip, kneading, fitting her up against the hard ridge of him. There was something about kissing the right man, something that made sense out of nothing, that gave rhyme to reason, that changed everything without altering anything at all. There was something about kissing Jack that made Liza want to climb right inside him and experience him from the outside in, the inside out. There was something about kissing Jack that made her never want to stop.

Faint sunlight shimmered through her eyelids. Desire weakened her knees, turning any conscious thoughts into vapors that floated away with the fog. Somehow his shirt had come untucked, and her hands found their way inside, skimming over the corded muscles of his broad back and shoulders. The kiss stopped and started a dozen times, wet, wild, frenzied, somehow too much but never enough. Never that.

He kneaded her neck, her shoulder, one hand skimming to her breast. His other hand took a slow journey down her ribs, to her waist, her hip, her thigh. All the while, he kissed her, mouth open, breathing ragged. She held on to his shoulders, her body curling into his, her thighs bracing his, pelvis to pelvis, heartbeat to heartbeat. Reaching up, her hands went around his neck, gliding into his hair, then slowly down his back. He'd probably shaved that morning, but already there was a slight stubble that brought another level of awareness to her cheek and chin and neck, and along the vee of her robe where her skin was already sensitized by a touch, a kiss and a caress.

He led her, by fits and starts, toward the open door. They shuffled their way into the cottage with far more determination than grace. Men must have different instincts than women—that was the only theory she could come up with to explain the fact that he had enough presence of mind to want to move this inside.

She was barely through the door before he pressed her against the wall and kissed her again, and again, his feet straddling hers, his body seeking, hers accepting, both conforming to the other. He covered her breast with his hand again, his thumb moving in half circles, over and over, squeezing, skimming, until she arched her back and called his name.

If she could have, she would have reached a hand between their bodies, finding him, but he left her no room, or time, for he was kissing her again, and all she could do was respond, kissing him in return. Her towel tumbled from her head, her hair falling around her shoulders and into her face. He reached up, taking a damp, wavy tendril into his hand.

They were close, their breathing labored. She wondered if her eyes looked as dazed as his.

"Mmm," she said. "You definitely don't need to work on your hello."

Once again, she smiled, and once again, he almost did.

He smoothed her wet hair off her forehead and put a little breathing room between them. Now that he wasn't kissing her or touching her, she could almost think. His lips were parted, a muscle working in his jaw, and she knew it would take only one word from her, and he would resume this in the bedroom. Outside, in the weak morning light, fog all around them, she would have uttered that word.

Laurel had been the impulsive one—and Nola had, too, for that matter. Liza was the rational one, the one who always seemed to be cleaning up other people's messes. She didn't want to make a mess out of this. It was too important to allow it to blow up in her face. "There are a dozen reasons why I'd like to finish this," she whispered. "But only one reason that I won't."

He waited, already disappointed.

"It's too soon. I've only known you for a week. Now, I think I could be persuaded—"

He cocked an eyebrow.

"—to admit that mornings hold more appeal than I once thought."

This time he did smile. "But?"

Again, she said, "It's too soon."

He released an audible breath.

And she said, "I may be a modern-day woman, but I won't be a one-morning stand."

The shock of Liza's wit and wile ran through Jack, her statement so full of innuendo and double meanings that he didn't know where to begin. Her lips were still wet from his kisses, her breathing still heavy, her entire being full of attitude and spunk. He wanted to finish what he'd started, and draw out that spunk in other ways—either in bed or right here on the floor.

He looked at his watch and tried to regain a semblance of control. He flattened his hand on the wall above her right shoulder and straightened his arm. Less than three feet of air separated them, and yet he pinned her with his gaze. "You're sure?"

She nodded.

He gave her plenty of time to change her mind. She had

to know how badly he wanted her to change her mind. But she didn't change it, and maybe she was right; maybe it was too soon. But it didn't feel too soon to him.

"I could make coffee," she said.

"I didn't come here for coffee."

Her green eyes widened. "What did you come here for?"

"Not for what almost happened. I came to see you."

"That's nice, Jack."

Not many people called him nice. Most people saw him as one of those moody McCalls, the kind of man you could trust with your secrets and your sister, but not one who was often nice. Liza saw another side of him, and it made him feel seven feet tall.

"If I can get a sitter, would you have dinner with me tonight?"

"I'd like that."

He said, "And perhaps see a movie?"

She ducked under his arm and walked to the center of the room. "Why don't we see how dinner goes before we decide what to do after?"

There she went again with that attitude. And there went his breath, whooshing out of him, along with a sound that was part frustration and part admiration. "I'll pick you up at eight." He headed for the door.

"Jack?" The thin houserobe covered her, but didn't conceal. The towel that had covered her head now lay on the floor behind her. Her hair was long and wet and wavy from her recent shower. "If you can get a sitter earlier, why not make it seven?"

"Seven?" he asked.

"Unless you would rather wait."

He stood on one side of her threshold, she on the other. And they both knew it wasn't going to be easy to wait another hour, let alone until tonight.

One thing was sure. He would find a sitter or die trying. "I'll see you at seven." He strolled down the steps, past the overgrown rhododendron bushes hugging the front of the cottage, and along the crushed shell path where there were two nearly identical plastic pink flamingos now, instead of one.

"Strike one!"

A father of one of the players yelled at the umpire, and the rest of the fans held their breath, waiting for the next pitch. Eve held her breath for an entirely different reason.

Her push-up bra was uncomfortable. Her orange T-shirt was a V neck, enabling her to see the upper swells of her breasts when she looked down. Despite that, her mild flirtations hadn't garnered much success where Jack was concerned. It wasn't easy to flirt when the man with whom she was trying to flirt was sitting next to his brothers. Jack always attended the Saturday baseball games with Brian and Carter. And Eve always sat next to them. Just like one of the boys.

No wonder he thought of her that way.

That was about to change.

She had to make her move soon, because Jack was leaving at the end of this inning. It would have been nice if somebody had crowded in beside her, forcing her to scoot closer to him, her thigh touching his. It was going to be a little trickier to accomplish when they had most of the top row of bleachers to themselves. At least the breeze was on her side, carrying the scent of her new perfume in the right direction. Every time Jack took a deep breath, she held hers, anticipating his reaction, awaiting his realization that Eve Nelson most definitely was not one of the boys.

"Strike two!"

Eve crossed her legs, the right one over the left, her toes with their bright pink nail polish touching Jack's calf. Her ankle was better. To prove it, she moved her foot in half circles, her toe brushing Jack's leg with each pass.

"Boy," Brian said on the other side of Jack. "That kid sure can pitch."

Jack took a deep breath, and sniffed. He swore he smelled perfume. "Yeah," he said to Brian. "The college scouts have their eyes on him."

And Carter said, "If Seth keeps his nose clean, he'll make it out of this town."

Something nudged Jack's leg. He glanced down, wondering why Eve was fidgeting.

Seth Kemper started to wind up. Instead of pitching, he spun around and threw the ball to first. The first baseman caught it, forcing the runner to try to steal second. A game of cat and mouse ensued until the runner was tagged. The opposing team had their second out.

Nearly fifteen, Seth was a strong, accurate and talented pitcher. It brought to Jack's mind the streetlights that had been busted last week. Last night somebody had chucked a rock at the light on the clock tower in the village square. Anybody could throw a rock at a streetlight, but the clock tower was three times as high. Throwing a rock that distance and with that much accuracy required skill and precision.

Unease settled into the pit of Jack's stomach. He could think of only one person in Alcott who had that kind of strength and precise aim, and he was winding up on the pitcher's mound right now.

Jack hoped to God he was wrong. All along he'd said it looked like the work of kids with too much time on their hands and not enough sense. Seth Kemper had plenty of sense. He had to know that if he got into trouble with the law, he could kiss any hopes of a scholarship good-bye. And if Roy found out about it, battered, frail, worn-down Sara wouldn't be able to protect her boy from his father's wrath.

Jack scanned the crowd. He spotted Sara at the end of the first row at the same time Eve nudged him again. He glanced at her. She turned her head slowly, but she didn't smile.

"Did you want something?" he asked.

She leaned closer, and it occurred to him that she was the one wearing the perfume. "Actually, I was wondering what you were doing later."

"Later?" He had to talk to Sara, and to Seth. And he had to make a stop at the drugstore. He still hadn't found a sitter. And he *had* to find a sitter, one he could trust. He'd call Mrs. Pennington across the street. If she couldn't do it, maybe her granddaughter could.

"Yes, later this evening. As in tonight," Eve said conversationally.

"Saxon's playing canasta at Ben's, and both Carter and Brian have plans to do something."

"I didn't ask about Saxon or Brian or Carter. I asked about you."

Eve was acting strange. Now that he thought about it, she'd been acting strange for a few days. Everybody was acting strange: Brian, Carter, Eve, even the aunts. And what about Seth Kemper?

"Because I could come over tonight, if you'd like," Eve said.

"You could?"

She nodded and smiled.

Eve to the rescue. Jack didn't know how she did it, offering to help, somehow knowing it wasn't easy for him to ask. "You wouldn't mind?"

"Oh, quite the contrary."

Why was she leaning so close?

"What time?" she asked.

"Strike three!" the empire yelled.

The fans cheered. Down in the first row, Sara Kemper folded her hands as if in prayer. The breeze blew her hair off her neck. Jack could see a bruise on her jaw from here. Keeping an eye on Sara, he said, "Six-thirty?"

"Six-thirty sounds lovely."

"I appreciate this, Eve."

She sat back.

"And Tommy always loves it when you come over."

"You know how much I love Tommy."

Jack stood. "I'll make it up to you the next time your sink gets plugged."

"My sink?" Eve tipped her head back in order to see him.

"It's still working, isn't it?"

"Yes. Of course."

"Good," he said. "I'll tell Tommy you're babysitting."

Her mouth opened, but no sound came forth. He wanted her to babysit? That's what he thought her offer was for? But, of course—that was how he saw her, and no push-up bra, no fragrance, no amount of flirting had changed that.

Brian stood, too. And then Carter did the same, giving Jack room to get past them. It gave Eve a moment to collect herself. What was she going to do?

"Jack?"

He glanced back at her.

"Where are you going tonight?"

He looked at Brian and Carter before answering. "I have a date," he said quietly.

Carter called him a choice, brotherly name, like he always did.

Brian told Carter to watch his language, just as he always did, too. Nothing had changed.

With a sick feeling, Eve watched Jack navigate the bleachers.

"Look at that strut," Carter said.

"Yeah, so?" Brian said.

"He wouldn't be strutting like that if he wasn't confident he's going to find out if Liza is a natural redhead."

Eve's scalp started to tingle.

Far below, Jack took a seat next to Sara Kemper. Sara shook her head a few times. Jack must have said something encouraging, because Sara finally nodded. Jack ambled away. All right, maybe it did look a little like a strut.

Eve tried to take a deep breath, but her push-up bra pinched. She had a sudden image of whisking it off and flinging it at Jack's head. She had to get out of there before she did something she would regret.

"Excuse me," she said, standing.

Brian rose to let her pass. Carter was still chortling at his wit.

Eve gave him a scorching look. "Grow up, Carter."

Head held high, she made her way to the ground.

"What's with her?" Carter asked, his eyes trained on Eve's back.

"I don't know," Brian said. "Look. Our team is up to bat."

Liza hadn't planned to watch the baseball game. She'd been driving by, her windows down, her car nearly emptied of everything she'd brought with her from California and Nevada. The crack of the bat and the yell of the crowd had her parking down the street from the high school, and watching what appeared to be a high school baseball game from behind a chain-link fence.

The smell of fresh popcorn and the sound of the crowd brought back memories of the year Laurel had dated a first basemen in high school and had dragged Liza to all the games. Today, Liza looked around for a place to sit. There was plenty of room next to Brian and Carter on the top row. She didn't know any of the players, and knew only a handful of the fans, but she recognized the woman walking toward her, moving with an easy grace that tall women took for granted.

Liza smiled as Eve approached.

Eve didn't. Dislike glittered in the depth of her gray eyes. "Eve?"

She stopped. They were side by side, Eve facing one direction, Liza the other.

The crowd groaned, and a few fans yelled a complaint about a pop-up fly that was bobbled in the outfield. Liza's attention was trained on Eve's face. "Have I done something to offend you?"

"As if you don't know."

"What is it?"

"Pu-lease. No one is as innocent as you appear to be."

Liza didn't know what to say. This was good old Eve? Everyone's friend Eve? She certainly wasn't friendly to Liza. "I don't understand."

Eve's laugh held no humor. "You're not stupid, so cut the act, at least."

Liza felt her mouth drop open. "This is about Jack."

"See there? You do know."

"Are you and Jack seeing one another? Is that it?"

Innate sadness flickered far back in Eve's gray eyes. "Not exactly."

"What, *exactly,* are you to each other?"

Eve cast a surreptitious look around. "You've only known Jack for a week. I've known him all my life. And that's how long I've loved him."

She clamped her mouth shut. Liza wondered if this was the first time she'd said it out loud. "Does he know?"

Eve's voice shook as she said, "You've heard the expression, he can't see the forest for the trees? He must know, down deep, but he's never brought it to the surface and examined it. I was devastated when Jack introduced me to Laurel. I had to accept that she was the love of his life, and maybe you're one up on me because you look exactly like her. But Jack and I have a history together, and I'm not going to play dead this time."

Liza remembered thinking there was something between Jack and Eve that night when Liza had gone to ask about Tommy. He'd mistaken her for Laurel, and he'd kissed her senseless. Laurel had said it herself. No one could cuss or kiss like Jack McCall. And after that initial kiss, Liza hadn't given Eve much thought.

Eve had loved Jack for a long time. Liza had known him just over a week, and had only loved him for a short while. She was startled by the thought. But it was true. She'd fallen in love with Jack McCall. She wasn't certain of the exact moment it had happened. Maybe when he'd buried that mouse, or maybe it was earlier, when she'd read about him in Laurel's letters.

"Who does Jack love, Eve?"

Eve's eyes widened at the question. "That's what I intend to find out."

"And how will you do that?"

"I'm not sure, but I don't intend to hand him over without a fight."

Liza felt a burgeoning respect for the other woman. "That seems fair." She held out her hand. "May the best woman win."

Identical splotches of pink spread across Eve's cheeks, but she accepted the handshake and the challenge. The lines were drawn. The competition was on.

Dinner was delicious. Or perhaps it was the company. Liza took a sip of wine and studied her companion.

Jack wore black pants, a cobalt blue shirt and no tie. They'd driven to Portsmouth, a beautiful, charming old town that had once been a bustling seaport and was now a tourist town. Liza wanted to come back when she had more time to browse in the art studios and stores. Tonight, her attention was trained on Jack. She wasn't the only woman watching him. Jack McCall had a presence, an aura, a kind of aloofness that, when combined with his stature and physique, made women of all ages sit up and take notice.

Now that Liza knew about Eve's feelings, she was surprised more women didn't come forward, professing to be in love with him. Jack didn't seem interested in other women. In fact, sitting across from him in the old-fashioned restaurant that had once been the mansion of a wealthy merchant, the flicker of candlelight between them, he seemed to have eyes only for her.

They spoke of everyday things and important issues, and they didn't agree on all of them. Arguing with Jack was fun.

He seemed to be having a good time, too. She asked dozens of questions about Tommy's health and treatments. And he answered them all, an underlying sensuality in his eyes each time his gaze rested on her bare shoulders.

She'd spent a good deal of time deciding what to wear. She'd opted for dark purple pleated slacks in a thin fabric that looked elegant and never went out of style. Her top was cream-colored silk, the neckline cut wide, baring part of her shoulders. The garment flowed freely with her movements, making her feel svelte and sensuous. Or perhaps the way Jack looked at her was responsible for that.

Liza had been a little surprised to discover that Eve was babysitting Tommy tonight. She'd watched Jack's expression closely, searching for hints regarding his true feelings for Eve. He seemed to genuinely care about her. He wasn't cagey or evasive, leaving Liza to surmise that whatever love was between him and Eve wasn't the romantic variety—at least not on Jack's part.

Liza almost felt sorry for Eve.

Jack mentioned Laurel's name in passing. Contrary to what Eve had insinuated, Jack didn't seem to be pining after her any longer. Perhaps he *had* been drawn to Liza because she looked so much like Laurel. And while it was true that he'd kissed her differently those times when he might have mistaken her for Laurel, the man sitting across the small round table tonight knew the difference.

Liza felt that she was on the verge of discovery, and it was fun and exciting and new. She wanted to know everything about Jack. And for once, he spoke about his work and his family and his town. He was worried about a boy whose father had a mean streak nobody understood. Jack cared about the people he protected. His family exasperated him, the way all families did, but it was obvious the McCalls were a united front.

"How did you do it?" she asked. "How did you care for a newborn baby by yourself?"

He pushed his plate away, his hands steady where they

rested on the table, his gaze steady where it rested on her mouth. "How does anyone do it?"

He didn't want her admiration, at least not for his role as Tommy's father. That brought her to another question. "Who chose Tommy's name?"

"I guess I did."

"And Laurel gave you free reign?" That didn't sound like Laurel.

"She expressed her opinion that we should name him after me."

And yet they'd named their son Thomas John. Something in his expression made her curious, even suspicious. "What's your full name?"

He shook his head. He seemed uncomfortable, self-conscious almost, and it was terribly endearing.

"All right, now I have to know."

"No, you don't."

"I want to know everything about you."

His expression changed, his breathing deepened, his eyelids lowered partway. Liza waited until her quickened pulse had quieted, and then she leaned forward. "It can't be any worse than Liza Jayne."

He sat ahead, covering her hand with his. He didn't smile. She didn't expect him to. He stared into her eyes, his gaze bold, seductive, galvanizing. She felt a ripple of excitement as he signaled for the check.

Soon they were leaving the restaurant. He unlocked the passenger door, then kissed her before she could climb in. She was breathless by the time the kiss was over. He had a way of changing the subject. And he still hadn't told her his full name.

"Now, about that movie," he said close to her ear. "It's your call, Liza Jayne."

Not even her grandmother had called her Liza Jayne. She climbed onto the running board. From her elevated position, she looked down at him. "The idea of a dark theater is appealing. But I have another dark room in mind."

His voice deepened as he said, "Whatever you say."

They didn't talk during the drive back to the captain's cottage, at least not with words. They communicated in other ways. He found her hand and placed it on the shifting lever between them, covering it with his, his thumb stroking over her wrist, sending the most delicious sensations to places physically unconnected to where he was touching. He kept his eyes on the road, his other hand on the steering wheel. She knew, because she kept her eyes on him.

His window was down, the road smooth, the radio playing softly in the background. It was only twelve miles to Alcott. It was the most sensual, anticipation-filled twelve-mile drive Liza had ever experienced.

Until his cell phone rang, that is.

CHAPTER 14

"Jack? It's Eve."

"Eve. What's wrong?" Jack parked in front of the captain's cottage next to Liza's car. "Is Tommy all right?"

"He's fine," Eve said. "I'm sorry to bother you. It's not Tommy. It's me."

The only illumination came from the dials on the dashboard. Jack held the phone to his right ear. Whether she wanted to or not, Liza could hear both sides of the conversation.

"I was wondering if you could come home."

"Well, of course . . . that is, what—"

Liza looked at Jack, and heard Eve say, "I'm not feeling well."

"You're sick?"

"I'm sure it's nothing serious, per se, but I'm afraid I'm coming down with something, and I don't want to take any chances exposing Tommy."

Liza had underestimated Eve.

"I'll be home in five minutes." He turned his phone off, and looked at Liza in the semidarkness. "Damn. I have to go."

Her body felt heavy and warm, her senses heightened by

the darkness and anticipation. This was not the way she'd hoped the evening would end.

He opened his door, blinking in the flickering light. His features, always strong, looked chiseled; his mouth was set, his reluctance as tangible as his passion. He met her at the front of his SUV, walking her to the door like a true gentleman.

She turned to him with key in hand. "I enjoyed tonight, Jack. The food. The wine. You."

There was gentlemanly, and then there was the way his arms came around her and his mouth came down on hers. Every time he kissed her, she felt something brand new. One time his kiss was frenzied, the next instinctive, and then demanding, coaxing, masterful, each a purely sensual experience. His kiss at her door surely would have led to tangled sheets and pleasure.

There was no pleasure in his groan. "Do you know how sorry I am about this?" His hand went to her face, his thumb tracing her bottom lip. "M.," he said.

She studied his eyes. "Pardon me?"

"My middle initial is M. For Marshall."

She grinned—not because there was anything wrong with the name, but because of what he did. Sheriff Jack Marshall McCall was a lot of name. But then, he was a lot of man.

Liza didn't want him to leave. She could have suggested that Eve was up to something, but it was best to let Jack discover that on his own.

"Good night, Sheriff."

He practically tore himself away from her. "Good night, Liza Jayne."

She watched him drive away.

Eve hadn't been kidding when she'd said she wasn't going to play dead. And now Jack, aroused but not satisfied, was on his way home. Where Eve was waiting.

* * *

"I hope my phone call didn't interrupt anything."

The old floor creaked beneath Jack's feet, his voice quiet as he said, "We were just getting back."

He was checking on Tommy. Eve watched from the doorway. She'd been imagining all sorts of things. Jack. And Liza. And the dark.

"Did you have a nice time?" she whispered.

His nod didn't give much away. She'd calculated how long it would take to drive to Portsmouth, dine and drive back. She didn't think there had been enough time for . . . anything else. And Jack didn't look like a man who'd just crawled out of a woman's bed. At least, Eve didn't think he did. Oh, she wished she had more experience with this.

Tommy was sleeping peacefully, and the house was silent except for the wind chasing through the eaves and a branch rubbing against the siding like an out-of-tune violin. Eve backed up unobtrusively as Jack drew the door closed on his way from Tommy's small bedroom. He turned and ran headlong into her.

His hands shot out to steady her. His fingers were warm on her shoulders, his body a mere two feet away. Eve froze for a moment in indecision, feeling trapped between the past and the future. She'd dreamed of this moment for so long, had imagined it, choreographed it in her fantasies. Except in those, Jack had been the aggressor. Sometimes fantasies needed a little altering. She may not have been experienced, but she was a warm-blooded woman, and she was in love. She had instincts. For once, she was going to follow them.

She flung herself into his arms.

The impetus sent him stumbling backward. His elbow hit the wall first, his back second. The breath rushed out of him. Her entire body was pressed up against the entire length of his. Her height brought her face within inches of his. She could thank fate for her tall genes later. For now, she molded every long, womanly inch of her quivering body to his. And then she did what she'd been dreaming of doing for so long.

She placed a hand on either side of his face, reached up and kissed him.

The air rushed out of him all over again, and his hands went to her upper arms, his fingers tangling in her hair. Encouraged, she moved her hips in a manner that no man could misconstrue.

Jack's mouth was as firm as she'd imagined, his body as muscled and warm. As soon as he responded the way men responded, she would let him take over, leading her into a dance as old as time itself. He was the man of her heart, the man of her fantasies, the man of her past. Please, let him be the man of her future, her man, tonight.

His fingers tightened around her upper arms. He wrenched his mouth from hers.

She opened her eyes.

"What are you doing?" he asked.

"Isn't it obvious, Jack?"

He opened his mouth, but no sound came. He didn't need to say anything. She saw the truth in his eyes. The magazines were wrong. It took more than visual and physical stimulation to turn a man on.

He set her away from him. "You said you were ill."

She felt sick, but only shook her head sadly. She knew she was turning crimson. If only she could self-combust. "I thought, maybe. But I was wrong."

"Wrong about what?" He pushed himself away from the wall, then stood, baffled, feet apart, chest heaving, staring at her in the shadowy hallway.

"All this time," she whispered. "All these years, I thought, if only I could open your eyes, you would see me, the real me."

She'd opened his eyes. And he was looking at her as if seeing a complete stranger.

"Eve, I . . ."

"I was wrong. Wrong. And so, so stupid." She closed her eyes and wished she could disappear. When had her wishes ever come true?

She took a backward step, turned on her heel, and fled. It had all gone so wrong. The curl had slipped from her hair, her breasts bounced without her bra, and instead of feeling sexy, her new thong underwear chafed. She wanted to go home, climb into bed and hide under the covers for the next twenty or thirty years.

She had no idea Jack had followed until he caught up with her near his Scout. "Eve, wait, please."

She remembered the day he'd found the old four-wheel drive vehicle. It was ten years ago. She'd gone with him to look at it. The windows were busted out, one bumper missing, the muffler dragging, the passenger side dented. He'd been thrilled, insisting it was rare to find an International Scout in such *good condition*.

She had so many memories.

"Leave me alone, Jack."

"For God's sake, would you just talk to me?"

Oh, that was priceless, coming from him.

His hand went to her shoulder. He tried to turn her around bodily. "Eve, look at me."

"Don't tell me what to do, all right?" She shook his hand off with so much vehemence that she stumbled.

He reached to help her again.

"I said leave me alone." Any louder and it would have qualified as a scream.

Carter had just gotten home next door. Hearing the commotion, he jaunted over. "What's going on?"

"Stay out of this, Carter." Jack's voice was low and ominous, but he was gentle as he reached out to Eve.

"Don't touch me!"

"Jack, what are you doing?" he asked. "Leave Eve alone."

"Stay out of this, Carter," Eve yelled. She wrenched herself away from both of them.

"Eve, would you just wait, goddamn it!"

"No, Jack, you wait!" she cried.

Carter eyed Jack, who shook his head once. "It's all right, Carter."

"It is not all right," Eve wailed. "Liza gets the prize. May the best woman win, right? The contest was certainly short-lived, wasn't it?"

"What does this have to do with Liza?"

She ignored the question. "All these years, wasted. Who did you come to, Jack, in the eleventh grade, when Melissa Stevens took a date with Chad Mercer because he was the quarterback and you weren't good enough for her because you hurt your knee that year and couldn't play? Who listened to you, encouraged you, when you decided you wanted to go into law enforcement? Who comforted you when Laurel left? And who always lent a helping hand with Tommy? Who, Jack?"

"You did, Eve."

"You're darn right I did."

"I know that," he said. "You were always there. You still are." He looked at her, bewildered and baffled, as if seeing her for the first time. "My God, Eve, I'm sorry. You've been a wonderful friend. I appreciate everything you've done for me. You must know how much respect I have for you."

Respect. Right. Her throat convulsed and tears swam in her eyes. "Not just a friend. I saved my virginity for you." Her hand shot up, covering her mouth.

Jack and Carter took collective gasps.

Eve looked from one to the other. She'd forgotten Carter was even there. But of course, without a witness, her humiliation wouldn't have been complete.

"I don't know what to say," Jack said. "Except in all honesty, I never knew."

She released a shuddering breath. Her anger was dissolving. In its place she felt a deep, welling sadness. It was as if the old Eve was slowly returning. And Eve didn't want her. She didn't *want* her!

"But Eve, I never asked you to do any of those things."

All her years of standing on the sidelines, of watching from the outside, of wanting, dreaming, and denying herself rose up inside her. Her lower lip trembled, frustration and embarrassment turning into scalding fury. "I told Liza I wasn't offering you up on a silver platter this time. Guess what? She can have you! And one more thing. Go to hell, Jack."

She spun around and started toward home.

Jack went after her, only to stop at the end of his driveway. He couldn't leave Tommy alone.

"Carter," he said. "Would you stay with—"

But Carter was already running to the driveway next door. Tossing his helmet to the ground, he climbed onto his Harley, eased it off its kickstand, then putted in the direction Eve had taken. Looking at Jack as he passed, he said, "I'll make sure she gets home safe and sound."

Once Carter was abreast of Eve, he slowed down even more. She was walking as fast as her legs would take her, and those were long legs. "Get on," he said.

She increased her pace.

"Quit being so goddamned self-sufficient and get on."

He stopped when she did. She gave him a quelling glare. "I didn't ask for a ride."

"Tough. Maybe if you asked for help once in a while, everybody wouldn't dump on you. Did you ever think of that?"

Any second now her legs were going to give out. She must have realized it, because she slunk to the street and did what she was told. He didn't completely trust her. She was a woman scorned, after all, and women in her boat had been known to retaliate against men in general. On the alert, he moved up slightly, giving her room. She swung her leg over the seat, grasping a swath of his shirt on either side of his waist. He deliberately cranked the throttle and laughed like the brat everyone said he was when her arms went around him.

Every long, lithe, soft inch of her was pressed to his back. And the joke was on him.

Damn.

He putted toward the open road.

"You just passed my house!" she yelled close to his ear.

His hair blew straight off his forehead. A muscle worked in his jaw. "We're driving around for a while. If you have a problem with that, deal with it."

Eve didn't want to ride around Alcott on the back of Carter's motorcycle, but she didn't tell him that. She'd just lost every last ounce of her pride. What did she care what happened now?

It was dark; several of the streetlights had been busted by vandals. And it sounded as if Carter was counting backward. "Nine hundred ninety-nine. Nine hundred ninety-eight . . ."

She no longer pretended to understand any of the McCalls, but of the three brothers, she knew Carter the least. Bad-boy Carter, everyone called him.

Whatever.

She'd never ridden on the back of a motorcycle. She'd never made a complete fool of herself, either. She still couldn't believe her embarrassment, and she didn't know how she would ever face Jack again. First, she had to deal with Carter.

Her hair billowed behind her. She'd probably never get a comb through it again. Maybe she would shave her head. She could always join a convent. She wondered if monasteries accepted women these days.

Probably not. It was a man's stinking world.

She fit herself against Carter, the motion of the bike relaxing her by degrees. She was pretty sure he was taking it easy, driving more cautiously than usual, since neither of them wore helmets. Eventually he pulled his Harley into the driveway of her plain, adequate little house and cut the engine. Eve scooted backward and swung her leg over the seat. She just wanted to get inside her house without further incident. Silently, she begged Carter not to say a word.

She made it as far as the first step before he said, "Are you really a virgin?"

She kept her back to him. "So what if I am?"

Other than the blood whooshing through her head, and the crickets chirruping, and a june bug beating itself against her picture window, the neighborhood was quiet. Carter was the quietest of all. His silence drew her around.

She probably looked like a madwoman, her hair a riot of tangles, her bra obviously missing, her clothing askew. But Carter wasn't looking at her as if she were a madwoman.

Well, well, well.

He raked one hand through his hair. His eyes were narrowed, his lips parted slightly, his breathing deep for a man who'd just putted around the neighborhood on his stupid motorcycle.

He was definitely all man, stupid, sorry, pathetic though that might be. Worse, he was a McCall. And if there was one unfortunate thing to be right now, it was a man named McCall.

All the lonely years she'd been pining after one such man culminated, rearing up inside her. Something snapped, and she thought, to hell with it. To hell with everything.

She tilted her head slightly, wet her lips, and opened the top button on her shirt. "Why?" she asked. "Are you offering to take it off my hands?"

They both gasped.

She didn't know who was more shocked, her or him.

Him.

Definitely him, for he'd gasped louder. And then he raised up slightly in the seat, as if searching for a more comfortable position. "Your virginity?"

"Isn't that what we were talking about?"

"Is that what you want me to do?" he asked.

Of course, Bad-boy Carter McCall would never back down. "Know what I think, Carter? I think you're all talk and no action."

She gave her tangled hair a deliberate toss over one shoulder and strolled inside. Once her door was closed, she sank against it.

What was she doing? She'd made a complete mess of everything tonight. In the process, she'd made a fool of herself.

What difference did it make now? Jack didn't love her. She knew it for a fact. All these years, wasted. She had no pride left. Besides, Carter couldn't talk. He'd certainly gotten into his share of trouble over the years.

She could hardly believe she'd called his bluff.

Big deal. What did a thirty-five-year-old virgin with no dignity have to lose?

What if he accepted the challenge?

What if he didn't?

He wouldn't. Of course he wouldn't. She stood, her back against the door, listening for Carter's motorcycle to roar to life. Footsteps thudded up her porch steps and across the wooden floor.

He knocked so hard she jumped. "Don't make me break the damn door down, damn it."

She couldn't muster up a smile, but she found the courage to throw open the door. Carter stood on her porch, tall and angry, McCall jaw clenched, the rest of those McCall features arranged in fit-to-be-tied fury, one diamond stud earring visible through his tangled hair.

"Oh," she said. "You're still here?" She opened the next button on her blouse.

"Stop it. Just stop it, all right?"

She opened the next one.

"Look. Eve."

She noticed *he* was the one looking. She opened yet another button.

His Adam's apple bobbled. He stepped inside, kicking the door shut. "You want to rebel. Fine. I've been there. But your emotions are getting out of hand. Jack's the one who set you off. He's the one you love."

"Jack had his chance. Now he can go to hell." The last button came undone, her red knit shirt falling open.

"Eve." His voice was raspy, his breathing choppy, his expression darkened with a dangerous, intriguing emotion. Slowly, he reached a hand toward her.

Eve didn't move, not even to breathe, waiting for the heat

of his hand on her pale breasts. His fingers skimmed her breastbone. She nearly whimpered. A delicious shiver started in that sensitive spot at the base of her throat. It moved downward and outward, and downward again, all the way to her toes. Still, she waited for a more intimate first touch.

Nervous, she watched his eyes. What was taking him so long? She looked at his hands. A light dusting of dark hair grew on the back. A knuckle was scuffed, the fingers work-roughened.

"You don't want it." He drew her blouse together without touching her intimately at all. "Not like this."

She stared at him in disbelief. His hair was too long to be considered civilized, but even he was too civilized to take what she was offering. Damn him for that.

Surely, she held the record in Alcott for being the biggest fool. "I don't appreciate being told what I want, Carter."

"Come on, Eve."

"I want you to leave."

He visibly relaxed. If she'd been a violent person, she would have slapped him for that.

He slunk out the door like the coward he was.

"Get back on your pig, and go to hell!" She slammed the door so hard her windows rattled.

"Fine!" Footsteps thundered across the porch.

"Fine!" she screamed through the door.

And then he yelled, "And it's called a *hog!*"

It was only a matter of seconds before his motorcycle roared to life. When the sound disappeared, she dropped her face into both hands.

She felt cold, empty, awful. Her shirt hung open. Fingers shaking, she fastened the middle two buttons. At least it eliminated the draft. There wasn't anything she could do about the awful, empty ache in her chest, and the knot in the pit of her stomach. What had she done? And what on earth was she going to do now?

* * *

"Carter, for crying out loud!" Jack grumbled. "I've been worried sick. What the hell took you so long?"

Carter rocked his motorcycle onto the kickstand and growled right back. "Don't yell at me. These things take time."

"What things? Is Eve okay?"

"She'll live," Carter said.

"She was pretty riled."

He didn't know the half of it.

"I tried calling her," Jack said. "She hung up on me."

Carter raked his hair off his forehead with his hand, shuddering as he recalled what had almost happened. "I think maybe you should give her some time, Jack."

The brothers faced one another on their old turf. As far as Carter was concerned the cool night air was a welcome relief. A cold goddamned shower wouldn't hurt, either.

Jack didn't look any better than he did. Curious, Carter said, "What the hell brought that on?"

"I've been wondering that, too. Apparently Eve felt threatened by Liza."

That was the difference between men and women. When men were threatened, they took it outside, yelled unintelligible insults and then beat the crap out of each other. That, Carter understood.

"Women," he said.

"Yeah."

"How'd it go with Liza tonight, anyway? I figured you had big plans."

Jack ran a hand over his cheeks and jaw. "Dinner was good. Eve's phone call interrupted the rest."

Carter laughed.

Jack sent him a quelling glare. "I never guessed Eve had feelings for me. Did you?"

"What, are you kidding?"

Jack said, "Eve has always been Eve. But Liza must have figured it out."

"Women," Carter said again. And then, "Liza's probably pretty curious right about now."

Jack wanted to talk to her about that. "Can you stay with Tommy?"

Carter released a long-suffering sigh. "I guess. Just spare me the details later, all right?" He pulled at his jeans, then walked somewhat stiffly inside.

Liza opened her door halfway through Jack's second knock. "Oh, dear. You don't look so good."

He made a sound universal to men and buffaloes.

"Is Eve all right?" she asked.

"Yes. No. I guess. But then, maybe not."

She opened the door wider, and Jack went in. A lamp was on next to the couch, a bowl of popcorn on the coffee table, one of Laurel's old black-and-white movies playing on the VCR.

"You knew?" he asked.

"About Eve's feelings, you mean?" Liza nodded. She'd changed out of her silk shirt and dress slacks. Her face looked freshly scrubbed, and she wore what appeared to be cotton pajamas and slippers. Even if he would have had time, it was obvious the ambiance had changed.

"I suspected the first time I saw her with you," she said, motioning him farther inside. "Eve confirmed it this afternoon at the ball game. We even shook on it—may the best woman win and all that. I take it she wasn't really sick tonight?"

"You suspected that, too. I would have appreciated a heads-up. Instead, I walked into a bear's cave covered in honey."

He didn't think Liza's grin was at all necessary. "It was between you and Eve," she said.

Okay, Liza wasn't feeling too sorry for him, but she didn't gloat, and she didn't fight dirty. She had integrity, and a come-hither light in her eyes that made him reach a hand to her face, his fingers sliding through her hair, drawing her closer.

She resisted with just enough strength to get her point across. "Poor Eve. She must be crushed."

"I took her for granted, but we were never a couple. I came here to tell you that."

She eased away from him. "That's what I thought. And I appreciate that you've put my mind at ease. You're welcome to stay and watch the movie."

Jack hadn't had sex in a long time. A long, long time. If Eve hadn't called, Liza would have taken him to her bed tonight. Now she was making a stand of solidarity. He bit the inside of his cheek until he tasted blood.

"Carter's with Tommy, and babysitting on a Saturday night isn't his idea of a good time. I have to get back."

She walked him to the door. "We'll get the timing right, if it's meant to be."

"Oh, it's meant to be." He left her with a kiss and no good-bye.

Carter was sitting in Jack's kitchen, drinking Jack's beer when Jack returned. "That was fast."

Jack gave him a dirty look.

"What's the matter? Wasn't she in the mood?"

"I thought you didn't want details."

"Don't bite my head off." Carter tipped back his beer, then lowered it to the table with a loud clank. "Women!"

Jack made a sound of pure frustration.

"How do you think they do it?" Carter asked.

"Do what?"

"Annoy the hell out of us and still make us want them."

Jack helped himself to a bottle of beer. He popped the cap, then took a swig while standing in the open refrigerator.

"They're hot one minute," Carter said, "cold the next."

Jack took another drink.

"Unlike us." Carter was on a roll. "Same temperature all the damn time."

The back door opened. Jack and Carter looked over as Brian sauntered in, his arms, face and T-shirt paint-splattered. "What are you two doing?"

Carter held up his brown bottle. "Drinking."

"That much I can see."

"To a hundred reasons it's better to be a man," Carter explained. "You're welcome to join us. On one condition. No preaching."

Brian eyed each of his brothers. When Jack handed him a beer, he took it.

Carter said, "We can open our own damn jars."

Jack pulled out a chair and took a seat. Giving Brian a what-the-hell-we-don't-have-anything-better-to-do shrug, he said, "Our last name stays put."

"We don't give a rat's ass if anybody notices our bad haircut."

Brian and Jack looked at Carter, whose hair was wind-blown and long.

"Hypothetically," Carter said.

Brian got in on it. "Chocolate is just another snack."

Carter said, "Orgasms are real. Every time."

All three of them drank to that.

Jack said, "Mechanics tell us the truth."

It was Brian's turn. "We aren't expected to know what color chartreuse is."

Jack said, "One wallet. One pair of shoes. Every season."

"Porn movies were designed with us in mind."

Jack and Brian both looked at Carter, an eyebrow raised.

"Just stating the facts." Carter took another long swig of beer. Wiping his mouth on the back of his hand, he said, "We never feel compelled to stop a friend from getting laid."

Jack snorted at that. He tipped his beer up, draining the bottle. More bottles were brought out of the refrigerator. More tops were popped. Hot wax and wrinkles and tux rentals were mentioned, in different toasts. By the time they were all on their fourth beer, they'd grown quiet, having exhausted every way they could think of in which it was better to be a man than a woman.

They sat quietly, the clock on the stove ticking, the late-night breeze billowing through the faded kitchen curtains. All three had a woman in mind—Jack, a red-haired artist; Brian, a brown-eyed attorney; and Carter, a red-faced, hot-blooded *virgin*.

A virgin, for chrissakes.

"I have one more," Carter said, taking his bottle in hand.

Jack and Brian groaned.

"Trust me, I saved the best for last." He motioned for them to pick up their bottles.

Jack and Brian cooperated.

And Carter said, "The world is our urinal."

"Amen," Brian said.

They all drank to that.

CHAPTER 15

Natalie held the door for the movers. The younger man smiled at her in that come-and-get-it-because-I'm-shy way that let a woman know he found her attractive. She kept her smile friendly, and make-no-mistake-about-it professional. Mild flirtations aside, the extra care he'd taken with her Louis XIV desk, her Aubusson rug, Prateek lamp shade and cushion cover, as well as the rest of her office furniture was going to earn him and his partner a healthy tip.

"It looks as if the movers are almost finished, Natalie." Edward Harcourt, of Abbott, Harcourt and Smith, smoothed a well-manicured hand down his two-hundred-dollar tie.

Natalie eased away from Edward and looked out the window. She could see Tremont Street from here. At eight o'clock, downtown Boston was bustling, not that you'd know it from inside the thick walls of the glass-fronted building. It was hard to believe she'd spent six years in this meticulous though bland suite of offices. With the exception of her things, there wasn't a pure black or white article anywhere. Instead, the offices were done in shades of gray, a telling color scheme, if you asked Natalie.

Her office in Alcott was going to be different. She wondered how far Brian had gotten painting today.

"I take it you've discovered that all your precious antiques are present and accounted for. And you were worried." Oh. That's right, Edward was still here.

"I wasn't worried in the least," she said. "I photographed and catalogued everything before I left Boston."

"Such a shame you always feel the need to cover your ass, even around me."

Edward Harcourt was the last person she'd wanted to see from the firm tonight. At forty-eight, he had a fabulous physique—perfect teeth and enough gray in his hair to make him look distinguished. A powerful and cunning attorney, he'd won some of the most difficult cases on the East Coast, and for some of the guiltiest clients.

"You're making a mistake, Natalie."

"Are you referring to the fact that I turned down the partnership or the opportunity to sleep with you?"

He made a clicking sound with his tongue. "You can take the girl out of the trailer park . . ." He hadn't brought that up in a while. She remembered the first time he'd mentioned it, the insinuation alerting her to the fact that he'd investigated her past. He didn't know everything, though. Still, he always knew just how much to leave unsaid.

But then, so did Natalie. "Speaking of trailer parks, how *is* Helen, Edward?"

Helen Abbott Harcourt, wife of Edward Harcourt and daughter of Maxwell Abbott III, had been born, raised, and still lived on Beacon Hill. She'd attended Harvard, as had Edward. Unlike her husband, who went slumming from time to time, Helen had never set foot in tenements or the projects or a trailer park until last year when she'd convinced her daddy that the firm needed to take on one of the largest and most rundown areas in Boston, holding landlords accountable for housing violations and derelict buildings where evil seemed to fester and muggings and other violent acts were commonplace.

"You know Helen . . ." Edward said, "always on the lookout for her next cause."

And her husband was always on the lookout for his next lay.

The movers returned, immediately going to work covering her camel-back sofa, the sole remaining piece of furniture in the room. While they worked, Edward said, "It's always a chore to get out of the city on a Friday evening. Perhaps you should spend the night with a friend and leave in the morning. It's what Helen's doing in New York."

Edward's propositions were always brilliantly though thinly disguised. Natalie shook her head. "I'll take my chances with the traffic."

"You'll be back, you know." Edward just touched the tip of her shoe with his Cole Haan loafer. "You're too bright, too sharp, too energetic to spend the rest of your life being *satisfied* dealing with stiffs and gifts." These were what attorneys called wills and trusts. "You'll be bored out of your mind in three months."

She did bore easily. Not that she would admit that. But she didn't feel bored. She felt energized, and it wasn't entirely in a professional capacity. She held the door for the movers, smiling after the younger of the two.

"Surely it's not him," Edward said.

"What makes you think it's anyone?"

"Oh, someone's lighting you up, and whoever he is, he's very, very lucky, indeed."

It might have been a compliment if it had come from anyone else. Compliments didn't work with Natalie. Nothing Edward had tried had worked with Natalie. And Edward had certainly tried everything in his ongoing quest to drop his imported shoes under her bed for an hour or two. Or three.

She left Edward with a clipped good-bye, then followed the movers from the office, a pair of scuffed, American-made work boots, size eleven and a half in mind. Oh, but she was wicked.

Brian McCall didn't fill out the seat of his jeans, but when he turned around, now that was a different story. But it was more than physical. She liked his humor. She even went so far as to admit she was invigorated by the way he said one thing but suggested another. He didn't make her feel sleazy the way Edward did. Brian made her feel witty and just a little bit wild. She'd noticed the way his eyes had rested on her. A woman could always tell what a man was thinking when he looked at her that way. And if he agreed to a discreet affair . . .

She wondered if it was possible to have a discreet affair in a town as small as Alcott. If it was, Brian, with his smart-aleck comebacks and his devil-made-me-do-it retorts was her first, her only choice. She had three carved-in-stone criteria, and he seemed to meet the requirements on every point. If he was still interested the next time she saw him, she might just encourage him.

Time would tell.

All was quiet in Alcott the following morning. Even the dog lazing in a patch of sunshine failed to bark as Natalie walked by. Maybe there was an ordinance against barking on Sunday.

It had been well after midnight before she'd finally gotten back from Boston. She had too much to do to sleep in. Actually, she probably had too much to do to take a walk around town, too, but her walk had a dual purpose. She needed to pick up a few groceries. While she was out, she would stop at the diner as well. Now that she had her bearings and her offices would be spruced up and ready soon, she planned to frequent the local establishments, say hello to the people in town, so that they felt comfortable around her. She knew she was trustworthy, but they didn't—at least, not yet.

Her black sandals with their two-and-a-half-inch heels weren't made for walking great distances, which hadn't mattered, because the grocery store and diner were only a few blocks away. Except she hadn't stopped at either of those places. Instead, Natalie found herself blocks from the town square. Any girl who grew up in Texas hill country knew how to use the sun as a compass, so a mixed-up sense of direction wasn't to blame for the fact that she was standing across the street from a quaint old church.

She liked old things—liked their look, their feel, their smell. That wasn't the reason she gaped, either. The stained-glass windows were open. An old organ was belting out "Amazing Grace." She didn't believe in coincidence. Quite the contrary. She was of the opinion that everything that happened was a direct response to something that had gone before. She'd been humming the song for three days. And now people were singing it in that church across the street, although croaking would have been a more apt description.

Checking for traffic out of habit, she darted across the deserted street and ducked through a heavy side door. The smell of paste wax mingled with the musty scent inherent in buildings this old. She tiptoed to the doorway of the church proper and saw the usual stained-glass windows and uncomfortable-looking pews. She noticed there was room in most of them. She recognized Eve Nelson standing next to two little old ladies three rows from the front. A burly, white-haired man sat near the back next to Sheriff McCall.

Okay. Natalie had seen the church, heard the song. Both were almost over. Pews creaked, prayer books thudded and feet shuffled as the congregation prepared to leave. She'd turned to go when a movement at the front drew her gaze. The pastor started down the aisle toward her. Her steps froze in the vestibule. Like all preachers, this one was dressed in black and carried a Bible.

This pastor was a dead ringer for her handyman.

How many brothers did Brian have, anyway?

At that precise moment, his gaze found her. She felt the heat in his eyes, *Brian's eyes,* all the way from where she was standing. She couldn't breathe. She couldn't swallow. She couldn't move. It was the answering heat shimmering through her that finally thawed her frozen mind and body. While the organist was massacring the crescendo, Natalie got the hell out of there.

Natalie was on the stepladder when Brian showed up. He was on foot; she'd noticed him when he was a block away. Not that he looked the same in black dress pants and a white shirt.

He walked the same, though.

She'd gone to bed the previous night thinking about him. Every time she'd closed her eyes, she'd envisioned that jean-clad rear end. After a while, she'd imagined it without those jeans.

She'd been fantasizing about the pastor of the Pilgrim Church of God? If there was a hell, she would go there for that alone.

She wouldn't go alone, for he'd told her he was a handyman, not a holy man.

No wonder he'd shown such a keen interest in her religion. And he'd been whistling "Amazing Grace." And he didn't work on Sundays. There had been clues. Why hadn't she seen them?

Because he didn't act like a preacher, that's why.

He stopped at the stoop, one foot on the bottom step. "Why did you run away?" he asked.

"I never run in heels. I am busy, though." She didn't look at him, so she had to be imagining that his gaze climbed from one end of her to the other, pausing in a few places, both of which she was suddenly terribly aware. Teetering on the top rung of the stepladder, she finished installing the hook that would hold her shingle overhead.

He didn't say anything. Eventually she had to look at him. He was staring, all right.

"You're ogling, Reverend."

"You're angry."

"Don't be silly."

"Then cut the crap and tell me what's wrong."

She lowered the pliers and looked at him. "You failed to mention that you have another job."

"I supplied you with character references. Everyone of them knows I'm a preacher."

She hadn't checked his references. She'd trusted her instincts. "Did you come to pick up your tools?"

"Why would I pick up my tools?"

"Brian, I really wish you would just answer my questions."

Brian really wished she would come down off that stepladder before she fell off. She was upset, although she was doing an admirable job of pretending not to be. The question was, why?

She picked up the pliers first and another hook second. And promptly dropped them both. "Damn it. I swear tools know who's on the other end of them."

He bent down, retrieving both items. She held out her hand. He ignored it.

And she said, "I want this shingle hung today."

"I'll do it."

"You don't work on Sundays, remember?" She cringed, as if she was silently kicking herself for something.

He had to tip his head back in order to look at her face. And tipping his head back made the crick he'd gotten sleeping on Jack's couch hurt like a son of a bitch.

"How was Boston?" he asked, wondering if that might somehow be responsible for the change in her.

"It was fine, thanks."

Fine, huh? "What do you think of the rooms I painted yesterday?"

"They look good. You accomplished a lot in my absence. If you'd like to wait, I'll get my checkbook and pay you for the work you've completed."

"Why would you do that?"

"Because you're fired."

"I'm what?"

"Fired. There's no room for argument here. You're just going to have to deal with it." She swept down the stepladder and disappeared inside.

Brian followed.

Despite the doors and windows that were open, paint fumes hung on the air. He'd questioned Natalie's color choices when he'd picked up the paint. The color on the walls in the foyer, a huge room that would be the reception area, was called plum pudding. The first office on the right was burnt burgundy, and the powder room tucked under the stairs was chartreuse, which turned out to be green. The trim color in every room was called chardonnay. It turned out that every room looked rich and old and charming.

"You can't fire me, Natalie."

"I just did."

"We shook hands, the equivalent of a gentleman's agreement, and gentlemen's agreements still hold up in court."

"You would sue me?"

He angled her his best knowing smile.

"You're joking, right?"

"I won't sue you, Natalie."

"Thank God."

"And you said you're a vegetarian." Yesterday she would have come back with a sharp rejoinder. That was before she'd known about his calling. He was pretty sure he was getting close to understanding something important about her. "I won't sue you. But it wouldn't be good for business if the people of Alcott got wind of the fact that their new attorney isn't trustworthy."

She stopped riffling through a drawer and looked at him. "What would your congregation say if they discovered their pastor would resort to such underhanded tactics?"

"I doubt they'd be surprised. They don't like me."

"Imagine that." But at least she finally smiled.

"Why do you think I have to supplement my income?"

Brian didn't pretend to understand what went on in a woman's mind, and he especially didn't presume to have a clue what went on in Natalie's. But he knew exactly what she meant when she muttered, "Oh, hell," under her breath. She knew she couldn't fire him. She wasn't happy about it. She'd been flirtatious when she'd thought he was a handyman. Now that she knew he was a preacher, she was as cool and untouchable as an ice sculpture. It seemed to him that it would have been the other way around.

"This isn't helping my headache."

Natalie eyed him closely. He'd spoken out loud and, as he often did, seemingly without intending to. "Are you hung over, *Reverend*?"

"Carter tried to get me drunk last night."

"Carter?"

"My brother."

So there was another one. "Are there any more McCalls I should know about?"

"There's just Jack, Carter and me. And our father, and Tommy. Notice how we're sadly lacking in female companionship?"

"You won't get any sympathy from me."

"What can I get from you?"

"You can get a knee in the groin if you come one step closer."

He turned up his smile, but stayed where he was. "You must know I'm completely attracted to you, Natalie."

"You'll get over it, trust me."

He looked at her far longer than Natalie considered polite. And then he looked a little more. "I do trust you. You're just going to have to deal with it."

She was the attorney, and attorneys were noted for their eloquence and intuitiveness and quick, sharp tongues and wide command of the English language. All she could do was stammer and stare at his unholy swagger as he walked out the door.

"Here we go. Tea for three."

Eve carried the tray. Rose poured. Addie dropped two

lumps of sugar into hers, stirring delicately. "That color looks beautiful on you, dear. As fresh as the ocean breeze."

Eve had worn the lime green dress. She'd needed it to bolster her confidence. She always took the aunts to church. Not doing it this morning would have garnered attention, and right now, attention was the last thing she wanted. What she wanted the most was to disappear. That wasn't an option. What she wanted the least was to run into Jack or Carter. As it turned out, she hadn't come face-to-face with either of them. It was inevitable, she knew. Perhaps she would get lucky, and it could be put off for a while—say, ten or twenty years, give or take a day.

"Didn't you sleep well?" Addie asked.

Miss Rose eyed Eve sharply.

There was no getting around this. Eve finally said, "It's hopeless with Jack."

The aunts exchanged a look. And then Miss Addie said, "Now that you've brought it up, I feel you should know that people saw you riding on the back of Carter's motorcycle last night. Now, I can see where it might be a good idea to try to make Jack jealous, but pitting brother against brother is never a good idea."

Eve thought about the disastrous night. "I didn't ask for a ride on Carter's motorcycle. But don't worry, Jack would only be jealous if Liza was the one on the back of Carter's motorcycle."

"Liza?" Rose asked.

Eve nodded.

"Then he . . . ?" Addie's feeble voice trailed away.

Eve nodded just as feebly. "Jack doesn't love me. He never did and never will."

"Oh, Eve dear, are you sure?"

"I'm sure." Eve took a deep breath and released it through her mouth. Taking another, she said, "I finally told him how I feel."

"Why, that's so courageous."

"Yes, that's wonderful, dear."

"Not if he told her he doesn't love her, Sister."

"Oh, that's true, Rose, quite true."

Eve waited for the aunts to remember she was here. And then she told them how she'd offered to go over to Jack's last night, and how he'd mistaken the gesture as an offer to baby-sit so he could go out with Liza.

Both old women tut-tutted sympathetically. They really were dear, sweet, loving friends. They were also all ears. This was more interesting than their daily three o'clock soap opera. Except this was Eve's life. She explained how she'd called Jack home from his date, purposely leaving out the more sordid details, such as the way she'd thrown herself into his arms and then opened her blouse in front of Carter. Misery loved company, but humiliation was better suffered alone.

"All these years, I thought if only I had been more aggressive, sexier, prettier, *shorter*, Jack wouldn't have fallen in love with Laurel. I was wrong. It never had anything to do with the length of my legs or the size of my breasts or the color of my hair. He loved Laurel. She made him happy."

Eve didn't want to admit that Laurel had been good for Jack. But ignoring the facts hadn't changed them, and the reality was, Laurel had brought him to life in a way that Eve never could. It was happening with Liza, too, only in a different way. "It's almost as if Laurel guided Liza here."

"Why do you say that?" Rose said.

Addie must have noticed the bluntness in Rose's voice, too, for she cleared her throat, then softened the question. "What do you mean, guided, dear?"

Eve looked from one to the other. Something seemed slightly off, but she said, "Jack told me at the ball game yesterday that he and Liza found Laurel's journal at the captain's cottage. She wrote a last letter to Liza. Evidently, she sent one to Jack, too, explaining why she left, why she couldn't tell him about the brain tumor or about her mother and sister in Nevada. Only Jack never received the letter. All this time, he thought Laurel had left without a backward glance. So many years spent being angry would have been avoided if he'd known the truth."

"A letter, you say?" Addie asked.

"Sister!"

"It's time we fessed up to what we did," Addie said, voice shaking.

Fessed up? Eve thought. She recalled a conversation last week when she'd confided in the aunts about her feelings for Jack. They'd said something that hadn't made sense. She'd been so overwrought, she hadn't examined the conversation too closely. Now, she remembered that Rose had mentioned drastic measures they'd taken five years ago. What drastic measures?

"We feel terrible, Eve dear. Terrible."

"You have no idea how many times we've prayed for forgiveness."

"Guilt is a heavy burden, indeed."

"Ah yes, Sister, that it is."

"But we did it for you," Rose said. "We love you like a daughter. And any fool could see that you would be a wonderful wife for Jack and a loving mother to his son."

Eve stared at Rose, who said, "Remember how the whole town pitched in to help take care of Tommy?"

Eve remembered. The Pilgrim Women's Society took in meals. Saxon and Brian did what they could, but Saxon was still working then, and so was Brian. Eve helped after school. Everyone did what they could, including Miss Rose and Miss Addie.

Addie was wringing her lace handkerchief. Rose sat, stoic and pale.

"We were still driving then," Addie said. "Remember, Sister? We went over to Jack's house one day a week to care for Tommy. We took turns rocking the baby, and we did whatever else we could to help. We straightened cupboards, folded booties and blankets, washed bottles and answered the phone and brought in the paper and the mail."

"The mail?" Eve said.

Both women turned watery blue, sad blue, guilty blue eyes to Eve.

"You intercepted the letter from Laurel."

They closed their eyes and nodded stiffly.

Eve sat back, shaken. Tampering with the mail was a federal offense, not to mention a moral one.

"What if Laurel had needed Jack?" Eve asked.

"Then we would have put it back on his hall table, dear."

Eve and Rose both looked at Addie, and then at each other. "You read the letter."

Addie nodded forlornly.

Rose bristled. "Now that Sister has spilled the entire sordid tale, how well do you think we'll get on in prison?"

Addie nearly fainted. "Prison!"

"Now, Miss Addie."

"Will they put us in the slammer, Eve dear?"

They wouldn't last a day behind bars. No matter what they'd done, they loved her. Eve tried desperately to think of a way around this. "Do you still have the letter?"

Rose found her feet and walked carefully into the parlor. A drawer squeaked. She returned, a yellowed envelope clutched tightly in her arthritic hand.

Eve took the letter. She knew what she had to do.

It appeared as though she was going to have to come face-to-face with Jack a little sooner than she'd hoped—ten or twenty years, give or take a day sooner.

"Eve! Hello! Tommy, look who's here." Jack was still wearing his church clothes, and he was a lousy actor.

"May I come in?" Eve asked.

"You know you don't have to ask." But she noticed he watched her closely and gave her plenty of room.

Tommy bounded into the kitchen. "Hey, Eve."

Tears burned the back of her throat. "Hey, yourself."

"Guess what me'n Dad and Aunt Liza are doing today?"

"Tommy." Jack's voice was stern.

Eve caught his attention and gave her head a little shake before gliding down to Tommy's level. "What are you doing this afternoon?"

"Going whale watching!"

His blue eyes, so like his father's, were bright. He was happy. Eve smiled. "That sounds like fun. Maybe you could tell me all about it sometime."

He flitted into the next room. While Eve was rising, Jack said, "I haven't asked Liza yet."

Eve wasn't sure what Jack was trying to tell her. It didn't matter. What Jack did wasn't her concern.

"Jack, there's something I need to show you."

She supposed she deserved the assessing look he gave her. She rolled her eyes anyway. She was embarrassed beyond belief, but what was done was done. Slowly she reached into the pocket of her lime green dress—she'd worn it because she really did look good in it, and darn it all, she wanted him to know it.

She handed him the letter and watched him bring it closer, examining Laurel's loopy, distinctive handwriting. "How . . . what?" He looked at her. "Where did you get this?"

"Let's just say I found it." In Rose Lawson's hand. "And leave it at that."

"You haven't had this all these years, Eve. I'm not buying that."

She appreciated his faith in her character. "You're right. I haven't. I only *found* it recently. An hour ago, to be exact. It doesn't matter where it's been. That can't be changed. What matters is that Laurel loved you, and never intended to hurt you."

"You've read it?"

"No." But she knew it. In her heart, she'd known it all along.

There was no doubt in Eve's mind that Jack would figure out where she'd gotten the letter. But without proof, there was nothing he could do. Perhaps he wouldn't have tried to do anything. Just in case the vow he'd taken to uphold the law tied his hands, she kept quiet. She looked at him. He really was a fine-looking man. But at least this first encounter was nearly behind her. "I'll leave you to your reading."

"Eve? Thank you. For everything."

"Don't mention it." She pulled a face the way she'd been doing for twenty-five years.

And he gave her one of his rare smiles.

Jack heard the screen door open and bounce shut. Eve had gone. Tommy was watching his favorite whale movie in the living room. Jack stood in his kitchen, staring at Laurel's handwriting.

There was evidence that the yellowed envelope had been steamed open once. He tore into it, removed the letter and began to read.

My darling Jack . . .

CHAPTER 16

Liza was painting when she heard the crunch of tires on gravel. She completed one brushstroke—but only one—before the knock sounded on her door.

It had to be Jack. There was just something about his hard-fisted rap, impatient, aggressive, with a hint of restraint, that kept the window from shattering. Barely.

She opened the door. It was Jack, all right. He stood on the front stoop, hands on hips, head tilted slightly. There was nothing unusual about the angle of his chin or the cut of his dark hair. He was tall, but she'd met other tall men in Alcott, two of whom shared his last name. His shirt looked freshly ironed, but most of the men she'd seen on this side of the country were neatly dressed. So it wasn't his height or his clothing that made her feel this excitement. It wasn't really even his face. It was something far, far deeper.

"I'm supposed to ask you if you can come out and play."

Just then Tommy honked the horn, eliminating Jack's need to clarify. Tommy scrambled to the open window. "We're goin' to see the whales, Aunt Liza. Dad says it's a family day. Wanna come?"

Liza's throat closed up.

Jack said, "I cleared it with his doctor. He sees no reason

Tommy shouldn't ride out to sea in a covered boat to see his whales. There are two cruise lines that dock in Rye Harbor. The first boat leaves in an hour and stops at the Isles of Shoals."

"Where you and Laurel met."

He touched his pocket where the tip of an envelope was visible. "I finally received my letter."

"But how?"

"Eve delivered it after church."

"Eve?"

"She was only the messenger."

"But how—"

"I have a theory, but it's only that. I think I understand why I never saw the letter five years ago. I'll explain it later. I thought we could show Tommy his mother's favorite view of the ocean."

There was so much emotion in his eyes, that tears swam in hers. Tommy honked the horn again.

"Hold your horses!" Jack yelled. To Liza, he said, "The child has no patience."

She wondered where he got that.

She swiped at her tears and started in one direction, only to stop and head in another. "I have to put away my paints. And change my shoes. And I'll need a parka."

"We'll be waiting. Better grab a sweater, too. Even in June the Atlantic can be cold twenty miles out to sea."

They shared a long, searing look. They were family, the three of them. Not in the traditional sense, perhaps, but family just the same.

Liza dashed around the cottage, replacing the lids on paints; changing her shoes; and putting on a jacket, a scrunchy for her hair, dark glasses and sunscreen. All the while, excitement simmered deep inside her. That excitement was going to bubble over. The heat in Jack's eyes said he felt it, too.

And it was going to happen soon.

*   *   *

The Isles of Shoals were comprised of nine jagged out-croppings of rocks of various sizes six miles from shore. Cited as a maritime treasure, the islands were harsh and primitive and breathtakingly beautiful. Tommy was too young to appreciate the tale of Blackbeard's treasure, or the story of how the poet Celia Thaxter, the daughter of a lighthouse keeper, had grown up on White Island and later built a creative salon for nineteenth-century artists. A little boy wouldn't care about Celia's flowers that still bloomed in her former gardens. Not surprisingly, Tommy did get a kick out of the name of Smutty-nose Island. It would have taken days to explore the islands properly. They had an hour, which was just long enough for Tommy to fall asleep between Jack and Liza on a bench in a park overlooking the ocean.

This was the second time Liza had come here. The first time she'd been unbelievably sad and spitting mad at Jack for standing her up.

He hadn't known.

She wasn't angry anymore. And neither was Jack. He talked quietly about Laurel, his arm resting along the back of the bench, his hand on Liza's shoulder. There was a far greater connection between them. It had to do with the child sleeping, his head in Jack's lap, his feet in Liza's. And how much they'd both loved Laurel Cassidy.

When he was finished reminiscing, he took the envelope from his pocket and handed it to Liza. Huddled in her wind-breaker and sweater, she opened the letter and read her sis-ter's final words to the man she'd met on this very island nearly six years ago.

My darling Jack,

By now, you know I died. I've known about the tumor for almost a year, and yet it feels strange to be writing as if I'm already a part of the past. I'm here now, and for that I'm grateful.

The cottage door is open; warm spring air bathes my face and whispers through my hair. I smell the morning warming, the scent of daffodils and dew. I see the morning waking, one wispy cloud floating across the blue, blue sky. I hear the morning stretching, birdsong and wind and waves. I feel the glorious morning, and I'm sorry you're not here.

I'm sorry for many things. Sorry I was never able to find the words to explain why I need to do this this way, to die this way. I'm sorry I won't be here with you to raise our son. But I'm not sorry I met you. I'm not sorry I couldn't keep my hands off you, and vice versa. Meeting you, loving you, having Tommy with you, those are the best things that have ever happened to me. And that's saying a lot, darling, because so many good things have happened to me. Just ask Liza . . .

And that brings me to my last request. I need you to go to the lighthouse on the Isles of Shoals where we first met. My sister, Liza, will be waiting for you. You'll recognize her. She looks so much like me it's uncanny, except she's more beautiful and ethereal, except in the morning. Trust me, wait until after noon. . . .

She'll tell you about our mother, Nola, and this brooding, relentless dragon the doctors call a brain tumor, and my quest to uncover the words that are still inside me. And you can tell her about our precious son, and my most amazing final year. I read once that sorrow looks back, worry looks around, and faith looks ahead. I have complete faith in you, Jack McCall.

Know that I love you. And take peace in knowing that I'm not afraid. You're going to love Liza. And I think Liza will love you.

Come what may . . .

Laurel.

Liza folded the letter very carefully, touching it as she imagined Laurel had touched it, handing it, along with the envelope, back to Jack. "Why do you suppose she insinuated that I'm grouchy in the morning?"

It was the only thing she could have said that would have made them both laugh. Even Jack thought he was getting better at it.

And Liza said, "Do you get the feeling we're on a blind date?"

He nodded. And this time they both smiled, their thoughts turning to the exasperating woman they'd both loved.

It was time for the whale watching excursion to resume. Jack woke Tommy, and all three of them boarded the boat with the other passengers and several marine biology students earning college credit helping on these whale-watching tours. They had to travel fourteen more miles before they reached the area of the ocean where whales fed on plankton this time of year. Tommy would have stood at the rail, his face in the wind the entire way. When coaxing and bribing failed to convince him to save his energy for the actual sightings, Jack insisted. Tommy knew there was no arguing when his father was this stern, and they went inside the cabin, to rest away from the wind.

Finally, on the horizon they saw a spray of water and a dorsal fin—whales.

There was a flurry of excitement as everyone rushed outside. They watched, waiting for the next spray of water from the huge creature's blowhole. Ultimately, cameras and binoculars and video recorders were brought out.

Eyes shaded with one hand, an arm outstretched, finger pointing, a college student yelled, "There's another one. Starboard."

The captain set his course, zigzagging across the ocean, hoping to be closer the next time one surfaced. Sometimes it worked. Sometimes it didn't. But every sighting was a thrill. The creatures were huge. There were three kinds in all, all different, all magnificent, majestic in their strength, size and beauty.

It didn't take Tommy long to acquire his sea legs. He stood, feet apart, one hand on the rail, eyes on the ocean like so many sea captains of old. A pod of dolphins appeared, showing off for their spectators, jumping and flipping and grinning from ear to ear. Tommy stopped watching for whales, mesmerized instead by one of the dolphins. And strangely, it was mutual. Jack and Liza stood beside him, shielding him from the cool Atlantic wind. The dolphin swam alongside the boat, sleek and gray, effortlessly keeping up with the boat, an eye on Tommy. The dolphin didn't jump or flip or show off in any way—just went on swimming as close as he could get to Tommy.

One by one, several other passengers noticed the connection between the boy on the boat and the dolphin in the sea. It was as if they were communicating without saying a word. Everyone marveled at it. One woman said that dolphins have a unique sensory perception. Some doctors were using them to treat autism, and depressed and terminally ill patients.

The information knotted Jack's stomach, planting doubt and fear in him.

Tommy reached into his pocket and took out his sand dollar. Jack thought he was going to toss it overboard.

"What are you doing?" he asked.

Tommy looked up, the hood of his red parka covering his head, the bill of the baseball cap he wore underneath nearly touching his eyebrows. "I'm showing him the magic. Duh."

The knot in Jack's stomach eased. But he still couldn't bring himself to laugh.

Another whale-watching boat appeared on the horizon. The dolphins swam away to entertain a new audience. Jack was relieved to see them go.

The remainder of the afternoon passed quickly. Eventually the whales stopped surfacing. Most likely, they'd moved to different waters. The captain pointed the boat toward shore.

Tommy, Jack and Liza sat in the sun on a long bench out of the wind, their backs against the exterior wall of the cabin. Tommy turned into a veritable chatterbox. Tucked between Jack and Liza, his eyes were bright, his color good. The knot in Jack's stomach eased a little more. His gaze took to lighting on Liza, heating, delving, asking, promising.

Soon.

It was six o'clock by the time the boat chugged into Rye Harbor. Jack, Liza and Tommy peeled off their windbreakers and sweatshirts. Liza didn't know how it could be eighty degrees on land and fifty-five degrees out on the water.

It was at least a hundred and ten degrees in Jack's eyes.

There was something different about him today. Some people would insist he'd found closure. Liza knew from experience that it wasn't closure that saw a person through terrible losses. It wasn't even that old pearl of wisdom, time. Although those two things helped, it was love that made it possible to smile again, and mean it.

She loved Jack McCall. And she had a feeling that before the night was through, he was going to tell her he loved her, too. At the very least, he was going to show her.

Soon.

The evening passed quickly. For a man who was trying to appreciate every minute, it didn't pass quickly enough. Jack made no attempt to hide the fact that he was watching Liza. God, she was beautiful, her hair a riot of curls she claimed she couldn't do a thing with after their afternoon on the ocean.

"I have a suggestion for something you can do with your hair. Later."

Her eyes took on a glint that called to mind exactly what he was thinking. Thankfully, the sparks in the atmosphere went over Tommy's head. They ate at a little diner in Rye. When they got home to Alcott, Tommy had his bath. He accepted Liza's presence as if it was the most natural thing in the world. Perhaps that was because it *was* natural. Her being here felt right, more right than anything had felt in a long time.

They tucked Tommy into bed together. After fingering his sand dollar and finally placing it carefully on his nightstand, he snuggled beneath the sheet. As always, he was asleep before his head touched the pillow.

Jack would never so much as think there was anything good about childhood cancer. Even in remission, it was a sniveling, cowardly monster that lurked beneath beds and in closets and in the back of a father's mind. It was a dragon that had to be slayed each time it breathed fire. A long time ago Jack had made a vow that he would fight that dragon every minute of every day for the next year, the next ten, the rest of his life. Just so long as Tommy got well and stayed that way.

He felt Liza's hand on his arm, warmth settling into his skin, layer by layer. That one touch doused the flame of worry that had been plaguing Jack ever since that dolphin had taken such a shining to Tommy. His son was happy. He was safe. And he was sound asleep.

"I know men hate it when women ask this," Liza whispered. "But what are you thinking?" There was sass in that whisper. There was sass in her gaze, too.

"I'm thinking that Tommy usually sleeps a good ten hours. That ought to give me enough time to start."

"Enough time to start what, pray tell?"

He drew her closer. "Enough time to start loving you good, loving you slow, loving you deep."

"Ten hours?" She took a step away from him. "What are you waiting for?"

She darted from the room one step ahead of him. He caught her from behind just inside his bedroom. Wrapping his arms around her, he drew her to him. She leaned her head back, fitting it to the right of his chin. One hand squeezed his forearm, her other hand smoothed along her hip, and down the length of his thigh. They stood that way, hearts beating, their bodies absorbing the heat in each other, enjoying this moment, anticipating the next.

Liza had never been inside Jack's bedroom. Like the rest

of his house, it was sparsely furnished with comfortable old things. There was a dresser, a nightstand where a driftwood lamp was turned low, a filing cabinet, a few pairs of shoes, one of Tommy's toys. The only extravagance was the king-sized bed. Liza rather liked where he placed his priorities.

He turned her slowly, and it was as if, no matter how much he enjoyed the fit and feel of her, he needed to touch her face-to-face.

He skimmed his fingers across her cheek. Lifting her chin slightly, he covered her mouth tenderly with his. She felt the tenderness in her bones, in her heart. And when the kiss was over, they'd both had their fill of gentleness.

She went up on tiptoe, diving into a frenzied kiss, her arms gliding around his waist, her body straining against his. She felt his hands go around her back, too. He peeled her shirt from her jeans, and then drew it over her head. She kissed his mouth, his cheek, his neck, her fingers, making short work of freeing the buttons down the front of his cotton shirt. And then that was peeled off, too. Belt buckles were unfastened, front closures undone.

Locking the door was probably just a precautionary measure. She liked a man who was thorough. Oh, she liked this one a great deal. In fact, this one she loved.

They kicked off their shoes, shimmied out of their jeans. He was naked first. She went perfectly still as she watched him move toward her, the epitome of confidence and pure animal grace. Two more steps brought him directly in front of her. Her eyes fluttered closed, her hands brashly gliding over flesh that was amazingly warm.

It landed her in bed—one second she was standing, the next her back was being pressed into a soft quilt, her legs tangling with his. She unhooked her bra, he helped with her panties, and finally they were thigh to thigh, breast to chest, woman to man. He kissed her mouth, her breasts, her stomach, the curve of her hip and the length of her thigh, in that order, and in every order, until she lost track of where his mouth ended and her flesh began. She writhed and moved, returning his kisses, caress for caress, pleasure for pleasure.

He brought her to the brink of completion before sliding to his side and reaching into the nearby drawer. Realizing what he was doing, she moved close to him and wrapped her arms around his waist, pressing herself into his back. "I'm on the Pill," she whispered.

He lay down. What she did after that brought a moan from a place so deep in his throat, she felt its vibration in each place she kissed on her way back to his mouth. His jaw was clenched, his face so taut she smiled.

Leave it to Jack to take that smile as a challenge. He turned the tables and had her underneath him before she could gasp. He settled himself between her legs, raised up over her, his expression hard and beautiful and intense in the dim light. She couldn't see what he was doing after that, for her eyes closed, her hips finding that age-old rhythm.

"Kiss me, Jack."

His mouth covered hers for a moment. A moment was all it took for her, and then he followed. Or had he led? Regardless, they danced the most primitive of dances, on and on, and when they were spent, they grew still.

He eased his weight off her, but only partially. When she could think again, she said, "That was a profound performance, Sheriff."

Jack lay back, an arm over his eyes. "That was no act, woman. That was the real thing."

Eventually, they had to move. He kissed her, then climbed out of bed and raided the refrigerator buck naked. Liza freshened up in the bathroom, then joined him in the kitchen. He was about to take a bite of his sandwich. He looked at her instead, her hair glowing red, her green eyes warm, her legs sexy as hell beneath the hem of his shirt. His sandwich didn't get eaten, and his shirt didn't stay on her for long.

Some time later, the clock in the town square chimed

midnight. The doors were locked, Tommy had been checked on, the lights were off and Liza's body was tucked close to Jack's in the middle of his big bed. She felt his lips brush her hair as he planted a kiss on the top of her head. She didn't have the strength to move that much.

"I'm glad you came to Alcott, Liza Jayne." His voice was a deep rasp that echoed all the way through her.

"I know." Her eyes were closed. "I'm glad, too." And just in case he couldn't tell, "I love you, Jack."

"I know."

She smiled sleepily.

And he whispered, "I love you, too."

Liza drifted to sleep first. She didn't even consider going back to the captain's cottage. There was no question this was where she wanted to be, where she belonged.

Jack fell asleep, too, his heart full, his mind at rest, his dragons slayed—at least for tonight.

CHAPTER 17

On Monday afternoon Brian was seated at his desk in the pastor's study. The blinds were partially closed, awarding privacy while directing sunlight onto the ceiling next to the water stain from the last rainstorm.

He'd finished painting Natalie's offices an hour ago. He would still be working there if the aunts hadn't called him, requesting an emergency meeting. Several members of the congregation had stopped by these past several months to complain about his sermons, his car, his younger brother, the way he held his mouth, and anything else they could think of, but nobody had expressed an interest in meeting with him in a ministering capacity.

He'd hurried home, scrubbing as much of the paint splatters off his arms and face as he could. If Rose and Addie Lawson noticed any that he'd missed on the fingers steepled beneath his chin, they didn't mention it. Something was on their minds. They both wore little net-covered hats, and they were missing their favorite soap opera. This must be serious.

"We appreciate you seeing us on such short notice," Rose began.

He nodded encouragingly.

Addie said, "We've thought about what you said last Sunday, how our places in heaven can't be earned."

"Although I have to say," Rose interrupted, "I'm disappointed that Peter won't be standing outside the pearly gates with a tally sheet."

Brian lowered his hands to the arms of his chair. What he'd said in his last sermon was that a seat in heaven couldn't be bought by a number of good deeds. Instead it would be awarded, rewarded to those who have faith. It was heartening to discover that somebody had been listening, even if they hadn't understood his exact meaning.

Miss Rose sat straight as a board, her countenance severe, while Miss Addie's face was as crumpled as the lace handkerchief she clutched in both hands.

"Perhaps if you tell me what has you concerned about your final judgment, I can help in some way."

Addie looked at her sister, who nodded briskly. "We've done a terrible thing, Reverend."

Brian couldn't imagine either of these frail old ladies doing anything bad, let alone terrible. They were generous, civic minded and for the most part nonjudgmental. "What did you do?"

Rose said, "We hurt someone."

"And we've been praying for forgiveness for nearly five years."

"But then you said there are two parts to forgiveness."

Brian nodded. "Divine and human."

Good one, Rev. They've been asking for forgiveness for five long years. Now you've got them worried they won't get their extra credit points.

"Is everything all right, Reverend?"

"Yes. Go on."

"As we said, we've asked for divine forgiveness, but we can't ask for human forgiveness," Rose said.

"I'm sure you—"

"Trust us. We can't."

"Why?"

"Because we could go to prison!" Addie exclaimed.

And they're thinking about opening a whorehouse next door.

Brian shook his head slightly. At least he was getting better at keeping such thoughts to himself.

"Why don't you tell me what you've done, and perhaps we'll find a way to avoid a future that includes prison."

Don't forget that whorehouse, Rev.

"You won't tell anyone?" Rose asked.

"Of course he won't tell anyone, Sister," Addie admonished.

"But Jack is his brother."

Jack? Brian thought.

"I know that, but Brian's a minister, and ministers have taken an oath of confidentiality." Addie looked at him. "You have taken an oath of confidentiality, haven't you, Brian? I mean Reverend."

Brian's mind raced. What on earth could these prim and proper little old ladies have done that involved Jack and a potential prison sentence?

"Why don't you start at the beginning. I promise, whatever you say will remain between us."

"You won't tell Jack?"

"I promise I won't tell Jack."

"This involves Eve, too," Miss Rose said.

"And the mail."

They took turns doing the talking, sometimes arguing over certain aspects, such as who did what and when. At one point they veered off on a tangent about someone Brian had never heard of but they once knew who married their third cousin who used to live next door to a house that was said to be haunted, which, as far as Brian could tell, had no bearing whatsoever on their confession. When they were finished, they both sat, pale as the ghost they'd mentioned, blue eyes faded and watery and full of remorse.

They stared at him in waiting silence. Brian had never felt such pressure to produce the magic words that would absolve them and help them make everything right. Where was that voice when he needed it?

Steepling his fingers beneath his chin again, he considered his reply. "You're sure Eve delivered the letter to Jack yesterday?"

Both women nodded gravely.

And Brian said, "Then he's read it. I saw Jack early this morning. He looked pretty happy to me."

Of course he looked happy. He had his tongue down Liza's throat and one hand on her ass.

"Welcome back."

"I beg your pardon?" Addie asked.

Brian refocused. "I was thinking out loud. Perhaps there's something you could do to make it up to Jack."

"But you said we can't *earn* our way into heaven."

"I believe that's true," he said. The point he'd been trying to make on Sunday was that people shouldn't remain stagnant. Instead, he wanted his congregation to strive toward personal and spiritual growth. To that end, he said, "I believe there's a third part to forgiveness. I didn't have a chance to mention it during Sunday's service because I ran out of time."

"You do tend to get long-winded, Reverend."

"Addie!"

"Well, he does."

"You were saying, Reverend," Rose said with obvious disgust at her sister, "about the third part to forgiveness?"

Brian sat ahead, elbows on his desk, straining to be closer to these two white-haired felons who truly needed his guidance. This was the reason he'd gone to the seminary: to help, to nurture and to console. "The third part is forgiving yourself. Perhaps you would be able to do that if you felt you'd compensated Jack in some way."

Addie and Rose looked at each other, and then at Jack.

"Compensate?" Addie said.

"With some act of kindness or gesture." Damn, but Brian felt good.

"We could give him money," Addie said.

"Sister!"

"That isn't what I—"

"We're filthy rich, you know."

"Adeline, really!" Rose exclaimed.

"Well, we are." Addie looked at Brian. "Papa left us very comfortable. I took half and bought Intel at six. Sister was so angry! Until I sold it and rolled it into our bank account, that is. Now, we'll never have to worry about money, but does Rosalie thank me?"

Brian knew his eyebrows were probably hovering above his head, but he felt it was his duty to say, "In all honesty, I don't think Jack would accept charity."

"That's true," Rose said. "But I believe Addie might be on to something."

"Why thank you, Sister."

"You're welcome. I do give credit where credit is due."

Addie looked pained.

Rose rushed on to say, "What if we put money in a trust fund for Tommy's education?"

"Why, that's a marvelous idea."

Rose smiled. "That's what we'll do."

"We'll be helping Tommy, and Jack in a roundabout way, and forgiving ourselves at the same time."

"We'd need to make sure it's legal," Rose said.

"And we'll have to make certain Jack doesn't realize it's coming from us. I don't think I'd enjoy prison."

Both turned to Brian once again. Before the session had concluded, they'd used his phone to call the only attorney in Alcott. Somehow, they'd convinced Miss Harper that this couldn't wait until she was technically open for business.

Natalie agreed to see them at two forty-five. Five minutes later, they'd both squeezed into the passenger seat of his Corvette, and Brian was driving them to the former merchant's house where a new shingle hung over the front door:

NATALIE HARPER, ATTORNEY AT LAW.

* * *

"This is working out wonderfully. I can't tell you how pleased this makes Sister and me!"

"And relieved! You're certain that's all there is to it? We just had to designate the amount and sign on the dotted line?"

"Yes, that's all."

"And Jack won't know where the gift came from?"

"It's an anonymous gift, yes, and will remain in the trust as well as draw interest until Tommy graduates from high school." Natalie glanced around her outer office. Brian was oiling hinges, and wasn't even looking at her. It should have been easy to drag her gaze back to her clients.

"How much do we owe you, Miss Harper?"

"I'll send you a statement."

Rosalie and Adeline Lawson shook their heads sternly. "We prefer to pay in cash."

"Cuts down on the evidence," Addie whispered.

Natalie hid a smile. The Lawson sisters were in their eighties, had waning eyesight, arthritic hands and creaky knees. They were still cagey old birds.

She named an amount, and Adeline snapped open her purse and counted the money carefully. Rose recounted it, then handed it over.

Natalie was aware that Brian watched from across the room. "Are you ladies ready?" he asked.

The sisters glanced at each other, then raised their fleshy chins. Addie said, "We thought we'd do a little shopping."

"I'll drive you."

"It's a lovely day. We'll walk."

"But how will you get home?"

"We'll call Eve," Rose said.

Addie said, "Do you want us to get ticketed for failing to wear seat belts?"

"Really, Reverend," Rose added, "It's high time you considered driving another kind of car."

They clattered and shuffled out the door.

Natalie thought he was taking his sweet time oiling the

top hinge. With the tip of one finger, he snapped the little tin closed. Since she couldn't very well sit around gawking, she busied herself in front of a carton of file folders. As far as hints went, it should have been quite obvious.

He didn't take it and leave. But of course not!

He didn't get back to work, either. Not that she expected him to. He wasn't dressed for physical labor anymore. He wore black pants and a black shirt, complete with a Roman collar. Even in that getup, he didn't look like a minister. It was the way he was looking at her. He was staring openly at her in a very unholy way.

His face was made of interesting planes and hard angles. He had long eyelashes, a firm chin and cheekbones to die for.

"You can thank me later."

"Thank you?" she said.

"For bringing you your first paying clients."

"I appreciate it, Reverend."

Brian popped the top on the oilcan again, and oiled another squeaky hinge. It awarded him a little time to try and figure something out. This wasn't the first time Natalie had called him Reverend. It had felt like an honor when Rose and Addie Lawson said it, but there was a cool edge of reserve in Natalie's voice. It wasn't disrespectful. In fact, she'd been minding her p's and q's since she'd discovered that he was a pastor.

He preferred the old fire.

"What are you doing tonight?" he asked.

"Working."

"You know what they say about all work and no play."

"That's right, I do know."

"I miss you."

She stared at him, mute.

"What's the matter? No smart retort?"

"You haven't known me long enough to miss me, Brian."

"Wanna bet? I miss the smart-alecky, sassy, witty comebacks. Why the change?"

"I don't know what you're talking about."

"Liar."

She gave him a dirty look. He figured that was progress.

"You know I'm completely attracted to you, Natalie."

"You'll get over it."

"What if I don't? What if I only want a woman who wears high heels and tight skirts and jangley bracelets, a woman who has black hair and brown eyes and a sharp wit and soft, full, lush lips."

"Women like that are a dime a dozen, Reverend."

He noticed she wet her lips, though. "You're kidding, right?"

"Do I look like I'm kidding?" she asked.

She didn't. She looked dead serious. He would think about that later. Now, he said, "I want *you.*"

"As I said, you'll get over it."

"I don't want to get over it. I want to get on it, under it, inside it."

Her breath caught in her throat. "Tough."

Brian grabbed her wrist before he had time to think about it and she had time to prevent it. He brought her hand to his mouth, and nipped one finger.

"I can be tough." He kissed her palm next. The kiss wasn't tough at all. It was gentle, warm, enticing, luring her to want more. He hoped. "Tough, rough. Gentle, slow. I can be anything you want."

"Brian, you don't want an affair."

"Meaning you do?"

"That isn't the point."

What was the point?

But she was right. He didn't want an affair. He wanted a hell of a lot more than that, but he kept it to himself for now.

"We're both adults," he said. "Both single. You are single, aren't you? I mean, you don't have a husband and half a dozen kids somewhere, do you?"

She waited a heartbeat longer than he'd expected before she rolled her eyes. "I was born Natalie Harper and I'll die Natalie Harper."

"You want to keep your maiden name, it's no skin off my nose." But he'd heard that hesitation. He'd felt that hesitation. He didn't understand it, but he was getting close. And close is where he stood as he brought two fingers to her cheek, her jaw, her chin. He didn't touch her mouth. He left, wanting to.

And he was positive she wanted him to, also.

The aunts were waiting for Eve when she pulled into the parking place in front of Sharla's Dress Shanty. Unfortunately, they weren't alone.

Eve used the time it took her to get out of her car to prepare herself to be polite to the overaged adolescent charming the support stockings off both of them. Carter McCall was all she needed.

"Hello, Eve dear," Rose said.

Addie giggled like a schoolgirl. "Carter McCall, you always were the most outrageous young man."

"Boy," Eve said to Addie. But she looked at Carter as she said, "In many ways, Carter is still a boy."

Carter gave her one of those all-male up-down-up-again looks he was famous for. "Jealous?" he asked.

"Not at all," Eve said so sweetly she almost gagged. "I don't know what you three were talking about, that's all. I missed the main act."

"You should be thanking me, not insulting me."

Eve practically had to drag Carter's gaze above her shoulders. "Excuse me," she said, "but my eyes are right here."

"I know where everything is, Eve dear," he said.

"Knowing is only half the battle, isn't it? Talk is cheap and all that."

"I don't think I like that insinuation." Carter's hair was in a stubby ponytail, his sunglasses hooked in the neck of his white T-shirt.

"I don't think I care what you do and don't like."

"Know what I think?"

"Of course I know. I teach first grade, remember?"

"I think you're jealous of Miss Addie and Miss Rose, here. You don't want anybody else honing in on your territory."

"You are so full of it."

Downtown Alcott wasn't bustling with activity on this late Monday afternoon, but people were beginning to notice them arguing. Lyle and Otto O'Leary stopped complaining about the weather in front of the barbershop, and their wives stopped complaining about Lyle and Otto on the steps of the post office across the street.

Addie and Rose exchanged a high-eyebrow look, too. "We'll just walk on over to Samantha's flower shop."

"Yes, that's what we'll do, Sister. It always smells so lovely there. Perhaps we could be of some help. We've missed our stories, anyway."

"We've bothered you enough, Eve. Carry on, you two." Unmindful of the fact that they were jaywalking, they tottered on across the street.

Eve and Carter stared after them in stunned silence.

"Did Rose Lawson just tell us to carry on?" Carter asked.

Yes, that was exactly what she'd told them. Eve didn't know what was happening to her. She'd spent thirty-five years trying to blend in. It wasn't like her to raise her voice. It wasn't like her to argue about nothing in public. It wasn't like her to bare her breasts to just anyone, either.

He said, "You okay?"

"Why wouldn't I be?"

"I just wondered."

She got a glimpse of Jack's cruiser rounding the corner at the end of the square. Carter noticed it, too.

"It's all over town," Eve said.

"I haven't told a soul."

She gave him a cross look, because she hadn't been referring to *that*. She'd been talking about Jack and Liza.

"Grow up, Carter."

"I'm damn sick of hearing that. You think you're the only person in Alcott who's stuck?"

Eve knew about Carter's superstition that Tommy's remission somehow hinged on his Uncle Carter's return and subsequent stay in Alcott. She wasn't superstitious herself, but she couldn't really blame him for sticking around. It was even kind of admirable, or would have been if somebody else, anybody else would have done it.

"Stuck in Alcott, you mean?" she asked.

"Stuck is stuck. In a town. In a reputation."

The breeze lifted Eve's hair away from her neck and fluttered through her plain cotton shirt. She was wearing a bra again, and she'd thrown the thong underwear in the trash. It was hopeless anyway.

"You're saying that no matter what I do, I'll always be good old Eve?"

He scoffed that bad-boy scoff.

And honestly, Eve never saw the kiss coming.

But that was what Carter did, kissed her, right there on Main Street in front of God and everyone. It was a hard kiss, an in-your-face kiss. It was over as quickly as it began.

"Carter, for God's sake." She smacked her lips in an effort to get the feeling back in them. "You think that's going to change people's perception? Being kissed by Bad-boy Carter McCall? That's exactly what the town expects from you."

Something glittered far back in his eyes, so far back she couldn't tell if it was anger or disappointment . . . or sadness.

"Yeah, well," he said, hands going to his back pockets, "maybe everything isn't about you. Maybe you're not the only person in Alcott who's invisible."

He ambled away with his long legs and narrow hips, a rebel in cowboy boots, holey jeans and T-shirt. And she watched him, cheeks pink, heart erratic. But her mind was crystal clear.

* * *

It took Eve an hour to find Carter, partly because it had taken her ten minutes to decide to go after him in the first place, and by then he'd ridden out of town on his motorcycle. Or at least that was what Lyle and Otto O'Leary said he'd done.

It was a fluke, really, that she'd noticed his Harley parked behind Dusty's Pub. Eve hadn't been inside Dusty's since her twenty-fifth birthday, when Samantha and some of "the girls" had taken her out for a drink. Not much had changed inside the hole-in-the-wall establishment since then. She recognized the man holding up one end of the bar. Eve was more interested in the loner playing pool at the back of the room.

She didn't doubt for a moment that he knew she was there. He continued racking the pool balls, though.

She stopped at the far side of the billiards table. "People don't see you, either," she said quietly.

He spread one arm slightly, elbow bent, palm out. "This is what they see. This is what they get."

She stared at him, the long hair, the earring, and was reminded of that article in *Cosmo. "Give me a man with an attitude and an earring,"* she whispered. "But there's more, isn't there Carter, more than that attitude and an earring?"

"So what if there is?"

"Show me."

He lined the cue ball up for an easy shot. "Three in the corner pocket. Is this the old I'll show you mine if you show me yours?"

"You've already seen mine."

He scratched on the easy shot. Very carefully, he lowered the pool stick to the table. A muscle worked in his cheek.

Eve smiled. Bad-boy Carter was blushing.

"Come on, Carter," she whispered. "How dangerous can a thirty-five-year-old virgin be?"

Carter glanced around the bar. He and Eve were too far away from anyone else to be heard. He still didn't answer, at least not out loud. The fact was, she was a hell of a lot more dangerous than she realized. She was trouble with a capital T. The problem was, she was exactly the kind of trouble he wanted to get into.

"Double-dog dare you." She winked.

She knew what she was doing. She knew nobody double-dog dared Carter McCall. "Don't say I didn't warn you."

"Warn me? I was just praying you wouldn't make me beg."

He had her out the door and on the back of his bike before either of them could change their minds.

CHAPTER 18

"Okay, just listen up." Man, woman and machine crested a hill and started down the other side. Man and machine both growled. "I'm laying down a few ground rules. I'm not taking your virginity. That's not even an option."

Eve kept her arms around his waist and more or less hummed.

"So you can just get that notion right out of your head. I mean it, Eve. This isn't about your virginity." He eased the motorcycle around a curve. They'd driven past the salt marshes and were a few miles north of Alcott. "And it sure as hell isn't about sex. You and I aren't having sex. Got it?"

Eve decided that the wisest course of action was to be agreeable. "Whatever you say, Carter."

He was angry. If he was anything like Jack, his anger was a cover for what he was really feeling. He had a good reason to be agitated. For all his ground rules, he wasn't immune to the feel of a woman snuggled up against his back. Oh, he'd tried to keep his back ramrod straight and his shoulders as solid as a brick wall, but halfway into the ride, his shoulders relaxed and his breathing deepened. And no matter how hard he tried not to, he was enjoying it.

He didn't speak again until he pulled onto a weedy path and cut the engine. "We're here."

Here was about three miles north and half a mile west of Alcott. *Here* consisted of overgrown bushes and weeds that surrounded a house with crumbling chimneys and rotting porch steps and old wood siding that hadn't seen a coat of paint in God only knew how long.

Eve climbed off the back of the Harley and glanced at Carter. He wasn't looking at the house. Following his stare, she noticed another path, this one much more trampled. It led to what appeared to be an old barn or shed in about the same condition as the house.

He secured the motorcycle, then got off, too. He placed his hands over his head in a stretch that was casual. Maybe too casual. Eve wasn't fooled. He was nervous about something. Perhaps *vulnerable* was a better term.

Boy, could she relate.

"Who owns this land?" she asked quietly.

"I guess I do."

She couldn't help her double-take. Carter McCall being sheepish didn't happen every day. "You bought property?"

"I won it in a poker game up in Portsmouth."

She could picture that. "Do you come here often?"

"Every day. I needed something to do while I was stuck here and I figured this was as good a place as any to do it."

They took the path toward the barn. When they rounded the other side, she noticed new overhead power lines and an old flatbed truck. Carter slid a huge door open, then flipped on the lights. She entered what appeared to be a workshop. It had open rafters, a dirt floor and a loft that had probably held hay or straw in another time.

Tools were lined up neatly on an old bench. Steel and iron and large sheets of tin and other metals were everywhere. There was a cot in one corner, and a minirefrigerator and hot plate nearby. She didn't recognize the other machines.

"What do you do with these?" she asked.

"I use them. That one's an arc welder. This is a mig welder." He showed her different grinders and tin snips and hammers, an anvil and other tools she'd never seen or heard of.

"But what do you do with welders and anvils and grinders?" she asked.

He stared at her. Scowling, he led the way through a large hole in the wall that opened into another room. Dust floated on slanted beams of sunlight that streamed through every broken window, every crack, every knothole. It was nature's track lighting, and it touched upon an intricate iron gate depicting an ocean scene. The gate leaned against the wall, and an iron table with curved legs sat next to it. There were wall sconces and cupolas and freestanding iron sculptures.

"You did all this?"

He didn't answer. But of course he had done all this. It was what he wanted to show her, what he was nervous to show her.

"My God, Carter. It's beautiful."

"Shucks."

He was making light of it.

"I mean it," she said. "You're an artist."

"I just putter around."

"You've puttered masterpieces. You're talented. You're beyond talented. Why keep it a secret?" she whispered.

"Why ruin a perfectly bad reputation?" He seemed pleased, though.

She'd looked at Carter hundreds of times in her life. Today, she was seeing him anew. He wasn't just Saxon's youngest son, Jack's youngest brother, Bad-boy Carter, the McCall least likely to be important. There was more to him than the earring, the hair, the attitude. He was thirty-one years old. Physically, he didn't look it, and yet the eyes looking back at her looked older.

Why, he was an old soul.

Her heart seemed to rise up into her throat. Of its own volition, her hand went there, one finger touching her erratic pulse.

His blue eyes darkened, heating about twenty degrees. "Stop right there. I'm not warning you again."

He'd assumed she was going to unbutton her shirt. The thought hadn't even crossed her mind. "It bothers you that I'm a virgin."

"Sweetheart, I passed bothered days ago. I'm well on my way to full-scale frustration."

"But wouldn't having sex relieve that?"

"If all I wanted to do was relieve my frustration I could do it on my own."

She stared at him, her eyes widening as his meaning sank in. "Show me."

"What?" They were only three feet apart. There really was no need to yell.

"I want to see you in action."

"You want to *what?*"

This time her ears rang. "Not that. Geez Carter, I want to watch you create one of your masterpieces." Just in case he was considering making a joke, she pointed her finger at him as if he were one of her first graders.

"You want to watch me weld?"

"I want to watch you create."

For the longest time she didn't think he was going to move. Finally he went to the workbench, fumbled in a drawer, then returned with helmets and earplugs. "You have to shield your eyes or you'll go blind."

"So it *is* a lot like sex, then." She noticed he grimaced, and then, as if he couldn't help himself, he grinned.

Two hours passed.

He welded, hammered, cut and explained. And Eve took it all in, mesmerized. He was creating a fireplace screen out of wrought iron, sheet metal and copper. It would be a true work of art when he finished. He was a work of art unto himself, his muscles corded, the sheen of perspiration on his neck and arms glowing amber beneath the lights and the sun.

He talked as he worked—about his life, about the people he'd known, the places he'd been. She talked, too. Amazingly, she had a lot to say. Before another hour had passed, she realized her life wasn't so stagnant. There was something missing, but it was a good life. From now on, it was up to her to make it better, richer, more meaningful.

Eventually he took a break from his work and got them both an ice-cold bottle of beer from the little refrigerator in the corner. Eve tipped it up, savoring the taste of discovery.

He stopped drinking when he caught her staring at him. "Now what?" he asked.

"If you could be anything, anything at all, what would you be?"

"You ask the damnedest questions."

She continued watching him.

"I guess I'd be an artist who sculpts with metals."

"That's what you are. Do you know how lucky you are to be exactly what you want to be?" She swallowed, wishing he would ask her the same question. When he didn't, she said, "Know what I would be?"

He sighed as if he knew better than to go there but was going to ask anyway. "What would you be, Eve?"

"A wanton, shameless hussy."

"Eve."

"Just once, I'd like to be wild and free and uninhibited and demanding and voracious—really." She shrugged. "Pretty stupid, huh?" She gestured with a flourish of one hand. "I mean, look at me. My legs are too skinny and my breasts are too small." She spun around, pretending an interest in her surroundings. "Forget I mentioned it. I don't want pity. It's not so bad being invisible. Little kids love me. I have wonderful friends. Your brother's one of them. But he's not the only one. Plenty of people like me. I can't think of one who's ever really seen me, though. Other than my sister, no one even knows what color my eyes are."

"They're gray. Not hazel. Gray, like liquid pewter."

She kept her back to him as emotion caught her in the hollow between her breasts. So this was desire, this gentle warming, this soft mewling. So this was need, and it was so very real.

Carter heard a sniffle. He reached a hand to Eve's shoulder, and slowly drew her around. He'd sworn to God he wouldn't do this, wouldn't touch her, wouldn't get close enough to want to.

He'd wanted to all day.

He removed his welding glove with his teeth, dropped it to the dirt floor, and cupped her face. Tears glistened on her lashes.

"My brother is a blind fool."

She wavered him a smile and blinked away her tears. "Would you believe me if I told you it was all in my mind? There was never any romance between Jack and me. I realize that now. I wasted a lot of years being stupid. Are you going to kiss me, Carter?"

Carter never saw the question coming. She did that— lured him into a false sense of security, then *wham*. "Oh, hell."

But he kissed her. And it just got deeper, and richer, and darker. He'd kissed a lot of women—he didn't want to brag, just think of it as a fact. Okay, maybe he was bragging in the back of his mind, and maybe they hadn't technically been women. They'd been of age, but they'd all been young. Those were the women he attracted—sexy, nubile, twenty-somethings in tiny bikinis or short skirts and tight shirts, females on the prowl who knew how to work the bar crowd with their lush round breasts and tattoos of daisies and toe rings and pierced belly buttons. Every one of them had been experienced in sex but not in life.

Eve was the opposite.

Her hair was long and the texture of silk. He wrapped it around his fingers. Her arms were long, too, and God help him, so were her legs. They went on for miles. There wasn't anything about her that wasn't long. There wasn't anything about her he didn't want.

He kissed her, with his lips, his mouth, his tongue. That brought a little gasp. But then she got gutsy, and kissed him back the same way.

She was the one who stopped long enough to take his bottle from him and place it on the workbench with hers. Then she strolled right back into his arms and started all over again.

"Honey, you're a fast learner."

"I've been studying up on it. And practicing."

"How do you go about practicing this?"

She swatted him for his naughty look. "Remind me to tell you later."

Somehow, her shirt wound up on his workbench. This time, he'd been responsible for unbuttoning every last button. He got them both naked from the waist up. And although he'd sworn to God he wouldn't do this, and he knew a woman like Eve deserved to lay down on a blanket of rose petals in a room flickering with candlelight, they ended up on top of the sleeping bag on his cot in the corner.

Carter usually went for women whose heads fit beneath his chin. Eve was only about three inches shorter than he was. She fit him perfectly, long legs to long legs, chest to breasts. And oh, those breasts. He tasted one, but once wasn't enough.

"They're not very big," she whispered.

Why did women think breasts had to be big? "Beautiful." He covered one with his hand, squeezed gently. "Perfect," he said. "Soft, so white. How does this feel?"

She hummed an answer. Moved slightly. "Yes, there."

He coaxed her to do a little exploring of her own. His zipper rasped as she lowered it. Her touch was tentative, but not for long. There was no way she could have been practicing that.

His breathing hitched. "You're well on your way to becoming a wanton hussy."

She smiled. And it wasn't shy.

She moved. And it wasn't bashful.

She kissed. And it wasn't enough.

He intended to be careful. He *tried* to be careful. Her eagerness made mincemeat out of his best intentions.

She shimmied out of her jeans and panties, moving against him in a sinuous way she might have learned while "studying up on it." More likely it was instinctive. One thing he was discovering about Eve was that she may have been lacking in experience, but she wasn't lacking in instinct, or anything else. She was eager, warm, willing, hungry.

A wanton hussy. God, he loved it. Almost too much.

"Eve, wait."

"Don't make me wait, Carter." She slid on top of him, then down on him. "Now," she whispered. "Please?"

He had protection in his jeans. Where in the hell were his jeans? He eased her off him, fumbled around for his jeans and got it.

"Now, Carter."

He'd run out of patience, out of coherent thought. She wanted to be bossy. Fine. He parted her legs and did what she asked and what he couldn't have kept from doing if trumpets were blaring and the end of the world were imminent.

He tried to be gentle, watching her eyes, watching her accept him an inch at a time. She shuddered once. He stopped. But then her tense expression eased and she started to move.

And so did he.

It wasn't a profound performance. Such things required forethought and planning. And Carter couldn't think, let alone plan. He could only react, and move, and tangle his arms and legs with Eve's, moving, moving, drawing toward her sighs and moans, her heart beating against his. He'd been creating metal sculptures in this very room for months. Today, together, they created a masterpiece, the most original work of art known to man.

They stirred, eventually. "Mmmmm," he said.

He felt her smile against his shoulder.

"You okay?"

"Mmmmm." And then, "I wish I had a warm washcloth."

"A what?"

"There's blood."

He fumbled to get up. But couldn't. His hands were tangled in her hair and his legs with hers. "Christ, Eve. I'm sorry."

"Sorry? Are you crazy? I'm not—crazy or sorry. I'm happy. It was wonderful. I feel wonderful. Don't you feel wonderful?"

Carter felt as if he'd just been kicked in the head. And not the one he usually thought with. Eve wanted a warm washcloth. The house had running water, but only cold.

She must have read his mind. "A cool cloth would do."

He got up, bent back down, and kissed her. He threw on his jeans and boots. She shot the rubber band that had come out of his hair at him, then leaned back like a queen and watched him snag it out of the air and stuff it into his pocket.

Carter felt jittery as he headed for the house. He felt winded, hungry, thirsty, and weak in the knees. He was spent.

Damn, he felt good.

He returned with what she needed, then awarded her some privacy. When she was dressed, they finished their beers. She wanted a tour of the house, so he showed it to her in all its decay and disrepair. And somehow they ended up naked, on a bare mattress, legs tangling, hearts beating, bodies straining all over again.

Staring down at her, he smoothed her hair out of her face and looked into her gray, gray eyes. "Before this day is through, I'm going to show you how this is done on a proper bed."

She only smiled.

Well, that wasn't all she did. But it was what Carter would always remember.

Much later, when darkness was just starting to creep across the sky, they climbed onto Carter's motorcycle, Eve more stiffly than Carter. Sated and languid and in need of nourishment, they returned to Alcott.

It had been an idyllic day.

Jack stood at the counter waiting for the coffee to stop dripping, his ankles crossed, his breathing steady. He'd had a shower, and yet he swore he could smell Liza's perfume and shampoo. Perhaps those scents were permanently imbued in his nostrils, the way the rest of her was imbued on his mind. He'd awakened around three, fully aroused again, and had proceeded to awaken her. And now, at six-fifteen, while the sun was starting to streak the sky with the palest shades of pink, Jack was dressed for work and waiting for his first cup of coffee. And he would have liked to awaken her again.

Tommy would be up soon enough. Saxon had gone to Atlantic City with two of his cronies for their yearly gambling stint. Liza was going to spend the day with Tommy. Everything felt right with Jack's world.

A low rumble sounded down the street. Carter was just getting home. Jack had heard about the scene Carter had made in the town square yesterday. Didn't he know that Eve was fragile? Jack had hurt her deeply. If there was a way to make it up to her, he would. Eve Nelson deserved respect, care, gentleness and consideration.

Jack glanced at the clock on the stove. Perhaps he and junior should have a little talk. He took a sip of coffee, then headed across the dewy grass next door, letting himself in the way they all did.

Carter glanced over his shoulder and eased into a sleepy smile. "Hey, Jack. What's up?"

"I need to talk to you."

Carter's face showed the first signs of trepidation. "About what?"

"About Eve."

"This isn't necessary, Jack."

"I appreciate everything you've done for me, Carter. You've helped with Tommy, you've put up with Saxon. And me. And Brian. You've made an impossible situation almost bearable."

"No problem."

"I heard about the scene between you and Eve yesterday. I'm worried about Eve. Have you seen her?"

A door opened. Footsteps sounded softly. "Carter? Is that you? Did you get the mocha?" Eve froze in the doorway.

For the first time Jack noticed the Styrofoam cups in Carter's hands. Eve's hair looked tangled. Now that Jack looked, Carter's did, too.

Recovering, she moseyed on in wearing Carter's white T-shirt, and from the looks of things, not much else. "Hi," she said.

"Hi." Jack looked at Carter again.

Eve said, "Don't worry about me, Jack. I'm fine. In fact, I feel quite wonderful."

Three adults cleared their throats.

"Yeah, I can see that." Jack backed up. "I guess I should be going." He looked at Carter. "I'd hate to see anybody get hurt."

Carter drew Eve to his side. "I'm not going to hurt her, Jack. I'm going to marry her."

"Marry me!" This was obviously the first Eve had heard of it.

"Hell, yes. You don't think I'm going to let you get away."

"But we've only . . . for a . . . it hasn't even been twenty-four hours!"

"I've known you all my life. I've loved you for twenty-four hours, and will for the rest of my life. Do you have a problem with that?"

"You love me?"

He nodded.

"Really?"

He nodded again.

"Oh, Carter, I love you, too."

Jack took his cue to leave. He didn't bother slipping out the door quietly. He figured Eve and Carter were so wrapped up in each other, they wouldn't notice anyway.

Eve and Carter getting married. Would wonders never cease?

Tommy was standing at the railing, staring into the ocean. He was shivering. Where was his coat? Why was he alone?

He was with the dolphin.

The sea was choppy and the boat was rocking dangerously. The wind was blowing and huge waves washed on board. Liza tried to move, tried to get to him, but she slipped on the deck.

Tommy.

She called his name, but the wind carried her voice away. The waves were going to drag him overboard. Where was Jack?

She writhed, the sheet tangling around her body. She tried to reach out to the fragile child. He stared at the dolphin.

Before her eyes it changed form, turning into a shark, its eyes cold and ugly, its teeth sharp.

"Tommy!"

Her scream awoke her. She bolted upright in bed, her heart racing.

She'd been dreaming. She could still see it so clearly. The boat, the shark—and Tommy.

It was only a dream. She wasn't on a boat. She was in bed. Jack's bed. In Jack's house.

She looked around. The room was gray in the early light of dawn. It had been a dream. Just a dream.

A dream.

Oh, God, no. She hadn't dreamed of Tommy in months.

Dread filled her. Taking a deep breath, she tried to make sense of the dream. Tommy had been in danger, of that she was certain.

How could that be? She'd helped tuck him into bed just last night. He'd giggled.

And after he fell asleep, she and Jack had made love. She could smell his piney aftershave and woodsy soap, and the scent of lovemaking and sex. Underneath those she tasted fear.

She threw back the covers. Where was Jack?

She pushed her hair out of her eyes and her arms into the sleeves of a long robe. Barefoot, she rushed into Tommy's room. She took one look at him, touched him, and darted out again, a sob lodging sideways in her throat.

Oh God, Jack where are you?

She checked the living room, the kitchen. She ran out to the driveway. His car was here. Finally, she saw him coming across the yard from next door. She raced to meet him.

Jack took one look at her face. "What's wrong?"

"Tommy's still asleep."

He continued to watch her closely.

She said, "He doesn't usually sleep this late."

Jack looked at his watch.

"I dreamed."

"A nightmare?"

She shook her head. "Like before I came to Alcott. Before I knew Tommy existed. Before he went into remission." When he was close to death. "I just checked on him. Tommy's sick, Jack."

They ran all the way to Tommy's room.

Jack threw the door open with so much force it banged against the wall. They rushed to Tommy's bed, Jack on one side, Liza on the other. He was still asleep. He'd thrown the sheet off. His hair was damp with sweat.

Jack touched his forehead. "He has a fever."

Just then, Tommy opened his eyes, and they looked glazed.

"Hey, buddy."

"My tummy hurts."

Liza whimpered. Jack grabbed Tommy up, and noticed the bruises. Oh, no.

"We'll get you to the hospital where they can make you better."

"I don't wanna go to the hospital."

"I know, buddy. I know."

Just then Carter and Eve entered the room. They must have seen Liza meet Jack in the side yard, and their mad dash back here.

Jack said, "Carter, call Dr. Andrews. Tell him to meet us at the hospital in Manchester."

Carter ran to do what Jack said.

Jack was getting Tommy dressed. Liza needed to move, too. But first, Eve grasped her hand. "We'll all help. We have to believe."

Liza nodded, thankful for that brief connection. She glanced at Tommy's fever-induced, sweat-dampened sheets. Just before leaving the room, she grabbed Tommy's sand dollar from his nightstand. She'd told him about the legend of the sand dollar, about the angels and the doves and the magic.

She squeezed it in her hand. Squeezing her eyes shut, she repeated what Eve had said. "I believe."

She broke the fragile shell open and released the magic.

CHAPTER 19

Tommy cried—big, fat, wet, silent tears.

He huddled in the stainless steel bed, small and scared, imploring Jack and Liza with his blue, teary eyes. *Why are you letting them hurt me? Make them stop.*

Liza felt helpless. She wished it was her, wished she could take his pain, could make them stop. She ached for him. In an effort to distract him, she talked about whales and dolphins and the magic in the sea. He'd listened for a few seconds, then sobbed when the next needle arrived. Magic was magic. But needles hurt.

He cried.

Jack and Liza cried, too.

When the nurses were done inflicting their pain, their eyes weren't dry, either. At least that part was over. Tommy's blood had been drawn. His IV was in. A sample of his spinal fluid had been extracted. Although Liza would have gladly held him, ached to hold him, he wanted Jack.

Jack held his son and rocked him and reassured him. He would never tire of the warmth and weight of his child in his arms. But none of those things brought him a semblance of peace.

The leukemia was back.

Dr. Andrews had been waiting at the hospital in Manchester when they'd arrived this morning. He'd checked Tommy in and checked him over, listening to his heartbeat, scrutinizing his symptoms, studying the thermometer, examining the bruises that hadn't been there the day before. They wouldn't have the final analysis back from the lab until tomorrow, but Kevin Andrews had seen enough of this to know. He'd looked at the slide under the microscope himself. Little Thomas John McCall's cancer was no longer in remission.

"But how?" Liza implored. "He was fine yesterday."

Jack knew how. This dragon was cunning and sniveling and vile. And it was patient. It had been waiting beneath the surface of normalcy, of happiness, and of hope. And then it had surged up from a seemingly tranquil sleep and breathed fire, not at night when most monsters struck. Instead, it had waited until the gray light of early morning.

There was an endless stream of nurses coming and going. Forms were filled out. Carts and gurneys creaked by out in the hall. Liza stayed with Tommy and Jack. Saxon and Brian and Carter and Eve all arrived to help in whatever way they could.

Hours passed. Dr. Andrews returned after lunch. Finding Tommy sleeping, he asked Jack and Liza to follow him. The others went, too. When they were all in the glassed conference room, Liza repeated the question.

"How, doctor? Why now?"

"Sometimes it happens this way," Dr. Andrews said. "Some ALL patients go into remission and stay there. With others, the second round of chemotherapy does it. The leukemia is knocking on Tommy's door. We're going to knock it right back out again."

"On its ass," Carter said.

The doctor glanced at the others, then nodded. "This is a setback. It's not an indication of the outcome. Tommy's chances are still very, very good."

Jack and Liza clung to those words and to each other.

Tomorrow, next week, or next year, this would all seem

like a blur to Liza. But today, she listened to every word Dr. Andrews said. She'd read about acute lymphoblastic leukemia, and understood that the disease caused the body to produce too many immature white blood cells, which in turn crowded out the healthy white blood cells, red blood cells and platelets, which were necessary elements for healthy blood and life. Dr. Andrews talked of intrathecal medication, induction, consolidation, and new combinations of chemotherapy.

"We're going to hit the ALL hard. And then we'll draw another vial of Tommy's blood and see how the disease has responded."

They all dreaded more needles. But at least they had a game plan.

Some game.

"What about a stem cell or bone marrow transplant?" Liza said.

Dr. Andrews looked compassionate as he said, "Those procedures have shown a modicum of success, although improvements are being made every day. Autologous blood stem cell transplantation uses cells harvested from a patient's own bone morrow or peripheral blood. Allogeneic blood stem cell transplantation uses a donor. Tommy's strong. He's had a good rest. I've seen a lot of success with the drugs he's taking. It's far too soon to consider transplantation."

"I want to be tested as a donor just in case," Liza said.

Everyone else in the room echoed the same wish. Dr. Andrews removed his glasses, cleaned them on his lab coat, and replaced them. Liza was reminded of something Nola always said to the girls' grandmother. *If I can't see in, you can't possibly see out.* And suddenly, it was as if her mother and grandmother were right here.

Dr. Andrews said, "Your insurance may not cover it."

"I'll pay for it." Saxon had finally spoken. "I won in Atlantic City, more than enough to pay for it. The McCalls are lucky, in love and in cards. Tommy will be lucky, too, but we might as well get tested, right?"

Liza was proud to be part of this united front.

"Probably, he won't need it," Saxon insisted. "But we're not going to lose that precious boy later because we've waited for the results of a test that can be done now."

"Very well. I'll set up the screening. Again, I've seen great success when daunomycin is added to the chemotherapy cocktail. I know you're worried. We're all working together, doing everything we can. Now we have to give the medicine time to do its job."

"Don't forget the power of prayer," Brian said.

The doctor's handshake concluded the meeting. Jack and Liza wanted to go back to Tommy. Eve hugged them both good-bye. And honestly, she was glad they had each other, especially at a time like this.

Saxon, Brian, Carter and Eve left then.

Carter took Eve's hand. Saxon had his card-playing buddies. Brian seemed so alone.

Natalie heard the weak knock. She hadn't seen Brian all day, and was surprised to find him at her back door at ten o'clock at night.

"When I didn't see you today, I thought you'd finally wised up and deserted the proj—" The lighting was poor in the back, and she stopped when she got her first good look at his face. "What's wrong?"

"I didn't plan to come here."

"What is it?"

"It's Tommy."

She remembered that name. His nephew.

"His leukemia is back."

"Oh, Brian, no."

He didn't even try to enter, just stood there beneath the bare bulb of the outside light where moths and other night insects fluttered. "We found out this morning. It's all over Alcott. The outpouring of love and compassion has been wonderful. The youth group is going to sponsor a car wash, and the Pilgrim Women's Society is organizing food. I just came from their emergency meeting."

The pastor of the Pilgrim Church of God looked done in. He needed a friend. Natalie glanced at her offices behind her. Her furniture would arrive tomorrow. The hardwood floors had been buffed, the carpets professionally cleaned. "We'll be more comfortable upstairs."

She closed her office door and locked it, then led the way up to her apartment. Brian began to talk as soon as she opened her door. He spoke of many things, his worry over his nephew, his father's recent trip. "Oh, and Carter and Eve are engaged." He settled on the sofa.

"Eve and *Carter?*" She turned on a lamp and opened a window, then took the overstuffed chair.

"Who knew?" Brian said.

"Evidently, not even Eve."

He shrugged. "That's one of the nice things about Alcott. Every woman gets her man, not necessarily the one she thought she wanted. I want you, Natalie."

That had certainly come out of the blue.

"If you don't want more than friendship, I'll abide by your wishes, for now."

"My, you are tired." Tired or not, he looked good on her sofa. Where on earth had that come from? But it was true. His shoulders took up half the area, his long legs a good deal of the rest. He also looked exhausted, worried, done in. She tried to prod a grin out of hiding. "So you decided to come see Aunt Natalie."

"You're too young to be my aunt."

"That isn't the point."

"How old are you?" he asked.

Prodding never worked with Brian. "In case you haven't heard, women don't like to answer that question."

"You don't like to answer any questions. Come on, how old?"

"I'll be thirty-seven."

"When?"

"In October."

"You're two years older than I am. That's nothing."

"We're getting off track."

"Know what I think, Natalie?"

"I shudder to ask."

"I think you like me."

"I like a lot of people."

"No, you don't. But you like me."

"Don't let it go to your head, Reverend."

Sure. Now he smiled. And she knew that wasn't where it was going.

"Do you have a problem with the social perceptions and differences in our chosen professions?" he asked.

"You know, you really don't sound like a preacher or a handyman."

"What do I sound like?"

"More like every man. And no, in answer to your question. I'm not a snob. That's my mother's specialty."

This was the first Brian had heard mention of Natalie's mother. The apartment was small, the furniture comfortable and expensive. There was dust on most surfaces; lamps on the end tables; a glass sculpture in bold, vivid colors; and the usual magazines and junk mail on the coffee table. There wasn't a single family photograph in sight. Perhaps she hadn't unpacked them yet. Or perhaps she didn't like her family.

He'd asked where she'd grown up before. Her reply had been vague. He tried again, wanting to know everything about her. But Natalie was easing him away from conversations about her and bringing him a pillow and a stiff drink.

The stiff drink turned out to be warm milk. "Are you trying to get me relaxed so you can have your way with me?" he asked.

"Is that any way to talk to a doddering old aunt?"

He leaned his head back against the pillow. "You're good with people. I bet you'd be good with kids."

She'd started to slip out of her shoes and draw her feet underneath her, only to stop. He thought back to the other time she'd hesitated like that. He'd mentioned children then, too. So whatever her supposed sin, it had to do with children.

He took a sip of warm milk. "You call yourself a doddering old aunt. Do you cook, too, Aunt Bea?"

"Sometimes."

"And bake?"

"I open a mean box of Jell-O."

"I hear that's great in a bathtub for two." His eyes closed.

Natalie leaned forward, taking his empty glass as it started to slide from his lax fingers. His face was made up of interesting lines and hollows. His nose was straight, his chin strong, his cheeks and jaw darkened by whisker stubble. He wore blue jeans and a blue chambray shirt. He didn't look like a preacher. He didn't always act like one, either.

"Brian?" She shook his arm.

He opened his eyes and looked directly into hers.

"You can't fall asleep here."

"Why not?" he asked.

"What would you tell your congregation?"

"I'd tell them what I always tell them. That they don't have to drink and swear to have a good time. Did you know I was thinking about quitting? Thinking seriously about it. Came that close to doing it."

She sat back again. This time, she drew her feet underneath her. "But you're not going to?" she whispered.

He shook his head. "I don't think so."

"Why don't you tell Auntie Natalie all about it."

He scoffed. But he started to talk. "I thought I'd go to Paris and find some gorgeous, sensual woman who had a minimum mastering of the English language and a major mastering of erotic arts. That's what the voice of my alter ego was telling me to do. I finally told the voice to take a hike. And it worked. Do you know what else? I don't want to go to France. I like it right here."

Natalie let him ramble. Erotic arts and Jell-O, indeed.

*   *   *

Brian showed up to help with the unloading and place-
ment of her office furniture the next day, and arrived at her
door about the same time the next evening, and the next day,
and the next evening.

"Brian," Natalie said when she opened the door the third
night in a row, "don't you have anything better to do—like
people to save, sins to forgive?"

"I have good news. Tommy's spinal fluid came back
clean. Evidently Liza's still having some sort of dreams of
Tommy, so she and Jack aren't resting easy, but I think the
test results are a promising step in the right direction. I'm
not staying. I just wanted to give you an update on his illness. Oh. The way you dress? The straight, tight skirts and
high heels and fishnet stockings? That wild and sexy hair?
The red lipstick? I know why you do it. It's to scare off the
good guys. It attracted me. So I guess it backfired, didn't it?"

"I don't know what you're talking about."

"Sure you do. I don't scare easy, Natalie. I came to tell
you that, too. Oh, and one more thing. I've fallen in love
with you."

He kissed her lax mouth.

"I'll see you tomorrow."

He closed the door before Natalie closed her mouth. She
sank to the Aubusson rug. She'd seen clients today—just
wills and trusts, but it was a start.

Brian claimed he loved her.

He didn't listen! He refused to see reason. Before this
went on much longer, she had to set him straight, once and
for all.

Brian led the final prayer. His congregation prayed along,
voices raised. He'd kept his sermon short and sweet. He
spoke of Tommy's illness and the miracle of love. He
thanked everyone for their prayers, their generosity, the food
they'd prepared and the help they'd given.

He'd had to clear his throat in order to say, "I'm proud of

all of you. And I'm proud to be your pastor. This past week, I've come to understand what that means. I've renewed my commitment to the church and to you. God help us all."

Everyone smiled. And the service came to a close. Edith Hungerford raised both hands and brought them down hard on the organ's keys. Unfortunately, they were the wrong keys. People winced. A few even ducked. Edith finally found the proper notes, mostly, and Brian started down the aisle, his gaze steady on the woman watching from the back row.

Only Natalie would wear fishnet stockings and four-inch heels to church. He'd hit the nail on the head a few nights ago when he'd told her why she dressed this way. The question was, Why would she think she was unworthy of a good man?

He greeted the members of his congregation as they left, shook hands and thanked them for their kind words. All the while he wanted to hurry, for he'd seen Natalie slip around back and into the pastor's study. It seemed the moment of truth was close at hand. As soon as the last parishioner left, he followed the path Natalie had taken.

Natalie heard Brian enter the room. He turned on a lamp, then tossed something onto his desk.

"Did you know that by law," he said, "Joseph could have had Mary stoned to death because she was pregnant before they were married?"

No, she hadn't known that.

"Laws are man-made. Laws of any given church. Laws of the state. They all change as society changes."

She finally looked at him. He was arguing law with an attorney?

"It's my nature and my line of work to constantly analyze these things. And I truly believe that what's right comes from here"—he touched his chest—"And there"—he pointed to the sky.

She rolled her eyes. "Thanks for the tip."

"Anytime."

"I have a past, Brian."

"Who doesn't?"

His glib comment failed to move her.

"Come on, Natalie . . . what's your big secret? Were you a hooker? A man? Tell me your sin and I'll absolve you."

"I didn't come here to be absolved of my sins."

"I figured that. You came here to scare me off. I told you before, I don't scare easily, but go ahead, give it a whirl."

She stared at him, angry, and not quite certain why.

"What did you do, rob a bank?"

She looked him in the eye from twelve feet away. "I had an affair."

"A lot of people have affairs. People make mistakes. Not all mistakes are sexual in nature, but many of them are."

"I would appreciate it if you would wait to hear what I have to say before you wave your magic wand and make it disappear. I had an affair with an older man."

He nodded, and she could see that he still wasn't put off by her past.

"A politician," she said.

The slight lift of his eyebrows prompted her to tell him the rest.

"He was married."

"Most older politicians are."

"To my mother."

He closed the study door very quietly. Next, he reached for her hand and led her to two chairs that faced one another. He lowered into one as she lowered into the other. When they were both seated, he said, "I'm listening, Natalie."

CHAPTER 20

The pastor's study was old. It looked it and it smelled it. Like the church next door, the rectory had probably been around for 150 years. The wooden blinds at the windows were closed part way, causing the cloudy day to seem darker. To Natalie, the gloom and doom seemed fitting somehow.

"I don't talk about my family, Brian. Other than tying one on once a year, I try not to think about the past. I'm not one of those women who blames everything wrong in her life on her childhood. Not that I couldn't. But what good does it ever do? It was just my mother and me, and whatever boyfriend she happened to have at any given time. And Brian? The way your fingers are steepled looks very pastor-like."

"A downfall of the trade. Go on."

"Oh, hell. I don't know why I'm doing this." She rose, paced, then finally dropped back into the chair.

"I take it there wasn't a father in the picture?"

"I had a father. I saw him once. I was born in Arizona. When I was three, my mother met some guy in a bar in Abilene. I don't know how, but we ended up with his trailer in one of the most rundown and decrepit trailer parks in Texas. Still, my mother always ended up with more than she brought into a relationship. She aspired to be a lot of things, and not one of them was trailer trash. What she never seemed to understand was that trash can live anywhere, and many of the people in that park were decent human beings. I liked it there. I had friends there. Who was it who said that what we need is not a clear plan but a clear intent? My mother had both. She was a barmaid, and I was a bratty, smart-mouthed kid. She got it in her head that we deserved better. Or at least that *she* did, and since she was stuck with me, I was along for the ride."

"I take it she knew a way to improve her current lifestyle?" Brian asked.

"She always said the ticket out of poverty was class. She figured that the way out of our situation—that was what she called it—was to improve herself and marry well. As if it was all in the presentation. She studied her customers, the way they talked, the way they acted. We were to dress a certain way, behave a certain way. As I grew older, we moved up, as she called it. Her next boyfriend had his own house. It wasn't in a great neighborhood, but it was a step in the right direction. With every *step*, it became more difficult for me to make friends. She enrolled us both in charm school. Can you picture me in charm school?"

What Brian pictured was a lonely girl.

"When I was fifteen, my mother hit pay dirt. His name was William and he was in state politics. Charm school must have cost her a fortune, but by God, we'd learned to speak correctly and smile demurely and drink tea with our little fingers in the air."

"And you didn't like that?"

"What's not to like? Becoming a total fake?"

"You rebelled."

"Big time. I refused to dress tastefully and behave demurely. And I dated anyone I pleased. I was a wild one. The wilder I got, the more terrified she became that I would spoil her chances with William, who was her ticket out of the trailer park of life and into the high life she felt she deserved. She finally kicked me out of the house, which was a nice little story and a half in the suburbs by then. She told me not to come back until I saw reason. It wasn't the first time in my life I knew real fear, and it wouldn't be the last, but it was one of the most memorable."

"How old were you by then?"

"Almost seventeen."

"You were a baby." A look crossed her face, causing Brian to dread the rest of her story. "And did you go back?"

"For a while. She was engaged, and the thing was, William was a nice man, older, and kind. Kindness wasn't something I was accustomed to. My mother told me I could stay as long as I followed her rules. I was never real good at following rules."

"You don't say."

"One day when I was a senior in high school she caught me with an unsatisfactory boy. She gave me an ultimatum. I moved out again, got a job, dropped out of school. I was hungry. I was scared. And I guess I was lonely. One night William knocked on my door. He stayed for a while. And he left some money for food and rent. And I noticed I wasn't as lonely after he was gone. He started coming around a few times a week. One time, he kissed me good-bye."

Brian's eyes narrowed—not in judgment of Natalie, but of an older man who'd known exactly what he was doing.

"During that time he married my mother."

"But he continued to visit you."

She nodded. "Not at first, but after a time, he started coming by again. I wish I could say that was the end of my sordid tale."

"You thought you loved him," Brian said.

He heard Natalie's sigh. "I didn't know what love was."

"The asshole used you. God, no wonder you're a vegetarian."

"Reverend, your language. It's true that a man who was married to my mother but continued to stop by for a young piece of—well, suffice it to say he was a user. He was also kind to me. He talked to me about politics and law. He convinced me to go back to school and when I couldn't make the rent, he was gracious about giving me the money. He called it a loan, but I knew I never had to pay it back."

"How long did it go on?"

"A while."

"What finally ended it? Did your mother find out and throw him out?"

Her laugh was bitter. "You're kidding, right?" After a long silence, she said, "I got pregnant."

"And kind old William offered you money for an abortion and then washed his hands of you."

"Not even close. My mother found out. Evidently she'd been having me watched for a long time. It was nearing election time. She told William she would go to the press if he didn't end the affair."

Brian sat back. "What a mom."

Natalie looked at him, and strangely he saw little bitterness in her brown eyes. Instead, there was a look of acceptance. "She was very focused on what she wanted and needed out of life. They came to see me together to tell me."

"And he," Brian couldn't bring himself to call the bastard by his first name, "he agreed to this, to ending it?"

She shrugged. "He liked his life. His real passion was politics. There would be other young women, right?"

Brian called the man a choice name under his breath. "Did they stay married?"

"As a matter of fact, they did. He won the election, and stayed married to a woman who might as well have had scales."

"So he got what he deserved."

"I guess."

"And your mother?"

Natalie brought her hand to her collar, smoothing her thumb over the skin above it. "William died a few years ago, leaving her independently wealthy."

"And the baby?" Brian's voice was soft.

"That night, she wrote me a check for twenty thousand dollars and handed it to me under William's nose. She said to take care of it. She was washing her hands of me, and I was never to show my face in Texas again. I'd like to say I did something noble, like tore the check into little pieces. But I didn't. I left town with three suitcases and a full tank of gas. I drove until my car quit. That happened to be in Indiana."

"You had the baby."

She nodded. "I interviewed several middle-class couples, and chose one of them. The adoption was very tidy and legal."

He was quiet. Natalie was glad he didn't say anything trite. She was glad he didn't mention the moisture in her eyes. When he finally spoke, her first thought was that his voice sounded strangled.

"What was it?"

She looked at him. "Pardon me?"

"Your child. Was it a boy or a girl?"

No one had ever asked her that, as if it mattered, as if what she'd done had mattered, as if her child mattered.

"A boy." It escaped on a short breath. "I was like a rock. More like a stone. I didn't hold him. I thought I wouldn't miss him if I didn't get attached to him. I was wrong."

"God, Natalie."

It was all he said. She stared at her fingers clasped tightly in her lap. He sat ahead, knees apart. Slowly, he reached for her hands. She didn't look at him at first. He waited. And when she finally raised her eyes, he said, "You're not a rock or a stone. What you are is an incredible woman."

Natalie hadn't felt exactly like this since she'd gone into labor during a thunderstorm seventeen years ago. She didn't dare lean forward, not even slightly. Her heart felt strangely still as she waited.

"I love you, Natalie."

She made an unbecoming sound.

"As a pastor, I preach waiting until after the wedding. A week ago I wouldn't have been able to practice what I preach."

She stared at him, stunned. "What are you talking about?"

"This past week I came to a realization about my calling. I was going about it all wrong. If I want them to treat me like a pastor, I have to start acting like one."

"That's nice, Brian."

"It's awful."

"What?"

"I can't expect seventeen-year-olds to wait if I won't, and that means I can't sleep with you until after we're married."

"You're not marrying me."

"You think I'm put off by circumstances and decisions you made when you were a teenager? Which you handled damned admirably, if you ask me. I loved you before you told me. I love you even more now." He reached for her.

"Brian, wait."

"We can wait. And we will wait. I'm not like William. I'm not looking for a roll in the hay. You've brought something into my life that had been sadly missing. Now that I've found it, found you, I don't plan to let it go. I want to marry you, spend the rest of my life with you."

He was kissing her, touching her. And she was melting, responding, yearning. "Brian, wait. There's more."

He stopped what he'd been doing to her with his hands, but he didn't release her. "Go on."

She looked into his eyes, those Atlantic-blue eyes. "Two weeks after I left the hospital in Indiana, there was an infection."

He continued to look at her. She wasn't certain either of them were breathing.

"It almost killed me. And there's a good chance it killed my chances to have another child."

His lips parted. He drew a breath through them. And then another. "Then I guess we won't need protection on our wedding night."

Her throat had closed up, making it next to impossible to speak. "You don't care?"

"I care a great deal. You'd be a wonderful mother. I love you. Marry me."

"Brian."

He got that look in his eyes, the insolent glint that she loved. He put his hands back where they'd been. And he took up where he'd left off. "I love you. You made me sure of who I am, what I am, what I want, and what I need to do. I can give up fatherhood, although there are other ways to have children. I won't give you up. Come on, Natalie. Do you want me to beg?"

"You mean you would?"

He swatted her behind.

"Ow."

"Want me to kiss it and make it better?"

"For a man of God, you're very sick."

"I don't feel sick. I feel healthy and energetic and strong enough to conquer anything, just so long as you're with me. Are you with me?"

She nodded slowly.

"Care to put your money where your mouth is?" Great. The voice was back.

She smiled the way she'd been taught back in charm school. "I have a better place in mind to put my mouth. Now aren't you sorry you renewed that commitment to the church?"

He groaned deep in his throat. "That isn't the only reason I'm going to wait. There's a greater reason, and it has to do with you."

"With me?"

He nodded. "You're worth waiting for, Natalie. You're the kind of woman who deserves honor and respect. I'm not judging anybody else, but it seems to me that maybe a lot of marriages fail because people don't respect each other enough to wait, maybe don't respect themselves enough to wait. You hear a lot about commitment. Part of that is willpower. Maybe if we abstain now, we'll be able to abstain when one or both of us are tempted later."

"That's the most pastoral thing I've ever heard you say."

"How long before you can marry me?"

"I haven't actually said I'd marry you. A pastor's wife,

me?" They'd ended up on the leather sofa. She cocked one eyebrow. "What are you doing?"

"Practicing. And persuading."

"Won't that just make it more difficult?"

She could tell his attention was already elsewhere. Where she had her hand, actually. "I can play the organ, Brian."

"Don't I know it." When she didn't swat him, he looked at her. "You mean at church?"

She nodded. "I learned that in charm school."

He started to laugh. And she joined in. The laughter faded and their passion grew and grew. Before he got completely carried away, he said, "Will you make an honest man out of me, Natalie?"

"I think I could be persuaded."

"I'm taking that as a yes. I love you, Natalie."

"You're crazy."

"Do you love me, too?"

"You're obviously not the only one who's crazy here."

"Meaning you do?"

"Yes, I love you, Reverend."

"Hallelujah!"

CHAPTER 21

Jack was near the hospital's entrance when he noticed a young man helping Sara Kemper into her rusty old van beneath the portico. "Afternoon, Sara," he said.

"Sheriff." Only half of Sara's mouth moved when she spoke. Her lower lip was cracked and swollen. The dark glasses didn't hide the bruises around her eye, either.

The young man turned around.

"Seth!" It took Jack two seconds to sum up the situation. The hospital emergency room. The scarred face. The battered woman. And her son.

At nearly fifteen, Seth Kemper was an inch shy of six feet tall. He had a lot of filling out to do. Jack didn't know what to make of the belligerent stance or the cool reserve.

"Your mom okay, Seth?"

Seth's answer was one small nod.

"You sure?"

The boy sighed. "This time. How's Tommy, Sheriff?"

A few days ago Jack wouldn't have known how to answer. Yesterday they'd gotten some good news. But even if they hadn't, Liza hadn't dreamed of Tommy last night. "He's better. The new chemo seems to be working. He's five today."

"Five, huh? I'll be fifteen next week."

Jack thought about the broken streetlights and the shattered light in the clock tower. Just last night, somebody had thrown a baseball through the stained-glass window of Brian's church.

He looked at Sara. "Can I borrow your boy for a minute?"

She nodded, looking small and frail in the driver's seat.

Jack waited to speak until he and Seth were several paces away from the van and the curb. Seth had sandy blond hair and the beginnings of a strong chin. His Adam's apple bobbled. Right now, he was halfway between being a boy and becoming a man. He met Jack's gaze, though, and it was as if he knew what Jack was going to say.

"I heard your team won the game yesterday."

Seth's brown eyes showed his surprise. He nodded guardedly.

"I missed it, myself," Jack said, "But I heard you pitched a no-hitter."

The boy nodded again, and this time there was pride in it.

"You have a future, Seth. And chances are it won't be in Alcott. They'll probably bring you up to the varsity team next year. And after that is college, and who knows, maybe the pros. Maybe, if you get out of this town, get yourself a house somewhere, your mother will go with you."

"Maybe she'll be dead by then."

They both turned their heads, glancing at Sara. She was huddled down in the seat, her head back.

Seth said, "She thinks that as long as he doesn't hit me, it's okay."

"It's not okay," Jack said, his voice barely controlled. "My son is lying in a hospital bed, and Roy Kemper has a son like you, and a wife like your mother, and this is what he does to show his appreciation."

Seth took a shuddering breath.

"I'd hate to see you do anything that might jeopardize your future, Seth."

The boy had to know what Jack was saying, that Jack was

pretty sure he was responsible for the broken glass, all of it. He wasn't cowering. He wasn't backing down.

"Getting into trouble with the law wouldn't help somebody in your situation. No college is going to offer a baseball scholarship to someone who has a criminal record."

Seth's chin quivered slightly, but he recovered. "You do what you have to do, Sheriff. And I'll do what I have to do."

It was then that Jack realized that Seth wanted to get caught. Getting caught would force the situation to change, one way or another. His father would most likely come after him with his fists. If he hit Seth, Sara would leave him. Even if Roy didn't, Sara would have no one to protect if her son was in the county detention home for juveniles. Seth was trying to save his mother from any more beatings.

My God, Jack thought. Seth wasn't even fifteen. He was far too young to carry this weight on his thin shoulders.

"Take your mom home, okay? And don't do anything else until I've had a chance to talk to some people."

"What people?"

"My brothers. Liza. Some others."

"What good will that do?"

"Maybe we can find a way to keep Roy from ever laying a hand on your mom again *and* keep you playing ball."

"You think you can do that?"

"I'm going to try. Do I have your word you'll lay low for a few days?"

Jack held out his hand. After a long moment, Seth took it. His fingers were cool, though, giving his nerves away.

Jack watched the kid amble to the old van and get in. Life, Jack thought. Sometimes it just wasn't stinking fair.

"Do you think I'm gonna die, Aunt Liza?"

Liza lowered the letters from Laurel she'd been reading to Tommy. He sat cross-legged on the bed. The corners of his eyes drooped. His hair would inevitably fall out again. Until yesterday, he'd upchucked everything he'd eaten. The antinausea drugs were helping. Today's breakfast and lunch had both stayed put. Happy birthday.

Some birthday. She hated to think about the poison inching through his veins this very minute. But the poison was also killing the cancer. Did she think he was going to die? he'd asked. Until yesterday, her answer would have terrified her. But today, she eased onto the bed next to him, upsetting the discarded wrapping paper, the party balloons and disinfected toy boat and the snap-together model of a ship and coloring book and crayons. There was hardly room for her.

"I don't think you're going to die, Tommy. Not until you're very, very old."

He stared into her eyes. And although he was tired, weak and very sick, she knew he believed her.

His head grew heavy. Resting it against her shoulder, he said, "That's good, cuz I've been thinking. About what I want to be when I grow up. And I think I'm gonna buy a boat. A big one." He spread his arms wide. "And I'm gonna live on it out by the whales, and take it around the world."

"Can I come?" She grinned at his big plans. Thomas John McCall reminded her more of his mother every day.

"Uh-huh. And when I get done sailing around the world, I'm gonna be a doctor. I'll help kids who are sick. And I'm gonna get the dolphins to help me. It'll most likely take a long time to do all that sailing and all that learning. I figure it'll go pretty fast once I get to kindergarten."

Liza knew he was disappointed because he wasn't going to be able to start school in the fall. Eve, bless her heart, was going to tutor him, instead.

He grew quiet. The next time she looked, he was asleep. She hoped he was dreaming about his whales.

A movement drew her gaze to the doorway. Jack stood in it, eyes hooded, chin set, shoulders squared. "You're smiling," he said.

"I just listened to Tommy's plans for what he's going to be when he grows up."

"He's a dreamer, is he?"

"He'll make his dreams come true."

He stopped at the foot of the bed, his gaze on the sleeping child. "And your dreams?"

She shook her head. "Two nights in a row, dream-free. I'm on a roll."

He released a breath of air so loudly, she half expected Tommy to stir. The preliminary test results looked good; the new chemotherapy seemed to be effective. She hated those words: *appeared, seemed, apparently, thus far.* The results were in for the bone-marrow matches, too. Jack, Saxon, Brian and Carter's weren't even close. Liza's was a perfect match.

Of course hers matched. It all had to do with the miracle that had taken place during that millisecond nearly thirty-four years ago, when two children had been created at once.

Perhaps a bone-marrow transplant wouldn't be necessary. Most likely it wouldn't be. She prayed it wouldn't be. But if it was, they were ready. The fact that she hadn't had children was a plus, for it meant that her body hadn't produced anti-something-or-others that would have impeded the new bone marrow from doing its job if it ever had to make its way into Tommy's bones.

Jack sat on the edge of Tommy's bed opposite Liza, one leg dangling. "I've been thinking . . ." he said.

Him, too? Tommy hadn't gotten everything from his mother.

"What have you been thinking about, Jack?"

"About what you said last night."

She'd said a lot last night. She'd told him she loved him, and she'd told him her dreams had stopped. She'd told him that Laurel had endured the pain of childbirth to give Tommy life, and Liza would endure the pain of a bone-marrow extraction to save it.

"I was thinking about Laurel," he said.

Their eyes met, their gazes held.

"I'm glad she came to Alcott," he said. "For so many reasons." He looked at his son, and then he looked at Liza. "She brought you here. To me and to us."

She smiled and sniffled.

"I know the future is uncertain," he said. "But I'm certain of one thing. I love you. More than I thought I could ever love anybody. No matter what happens, I want you in my life. Will you marry me, Liza?"

She clasped his hand, and since she couldn't speak for the tears, she nodded. Although she hadn't told Jack yet, Liza had dreamed a short while ago while she and Tommy were dozing. This time, she'd dreamed of Laurel, and she'd been smiling. It had been a peaceful dream, a joyous dream. She would tell him later. For now, she savored this moment, their fingers entwined, Tommy asleep between them. She'd come to Alcott, a woman completely alone. And she'd found a family. Her family.

It was all mind-boggling, really. If Laurel hadn't had that brain tumor, she wouldn't have come to Alcott, she wouldn't have met Jack, and Tommy wouldn't have been born. She wouldn't have written those letters, and Liza wouldn't have come here, too. And if Tommy hadn't been born, Carter wouldn't have ridden his motorcycle into town and stayed, and Eve wouldn't have gotten desperate enough to try to open Jack's eyes, opening Carter's instead. And Brian wouldn't have won over his congregation, and the congregation wouldn't have a new organist, and Brian a future wife.

None of it would have happened.

But Laurel had come here, the curator of her own destiny. She'd fallen in love and had a son. She hadn't written the book that was inside her. Liza was going to do that. She'd already started it.

At the top of the first page, in her own smooth, legible handwriting, she'd written, *Come what may . . .*

Dear Reader,

Many of you have asked me where I get the ideas for my books. I wish I knew. They come to me as notions from a place outside of myself, and arrive at the most inopportune times—in the middle of the night, in the middle of supper, during conversations, and at traffic lights, to name a few. The first glimmer for COME SUMMER filtered into my mind while I was waiting for the doctor to remove the cast from my son's hand a few years ago. The idea had me scrambling for a pen so I could put on paper a sister's last letter to her identical twin. From that letter, the story of Laurel and Liza, Jack, Tommy and the rest of the McCalls unfolded.

COME SUMMER became my fourth full-length novel. Coincidentally, four is a significant number for me. I was the fourth child in my family; my husband was the fourth in his, and we have four children. The four-leaf clover is synonymous with St. Patrick's Day, which just happens to be my birthday. Is it any wonder COME SUMMER is so special to me?

Although the ideas for my books come to me from out of the blue, I must search for the settings for each story. (Yes, it's as much fun as it sounds!) My quest for the perfect setting for COME SUMMER took me to the Atlantic seacoast. There, I discovered salt marshes and ocean spray, interesting people and quaint towns with charming old buildings and hilly streets with views of the ocean. From these elements, Alcott, New Hampshire, was born in my imagination. I was so taken with this town and these characters that I couldn't leave them after only one book. As if by magic, another notion came to me . . .

They called themselves the Three Potters back in Alcott High: Brooke, the achiever, Sara, the nurturer, and Claudia, the free spirit. All three had plans, big plans. Big plans have a way of toppling. As the dust is settling, these long ago best friends reunite in the small seacoast town where they grew up. Brooke is leaving an unfaithful husband. Sara is leaving an abusive one. And Claudia is fleeing from the scariest thing of all—the most wonderful, perfect, delightful man on the planet . . .

The story became JUST BETWEEN FRIENDS and will arrive in bookstores in January 2005. I cordially invite you to join me and everyone else in Alcott for Eve and Carter's wedding. Look in on little Tommy McCall, and root for Brooke, Sara and Claudia as they discover strength, humor, and themselves. And oh, did I mention passion?

For a complete list of my titles, family photos, and for more about my future events and contests, visit me online at www.sandrasteffen.com. I leave you for now with my sincerest and warmest regards. Until next time, and always . . .

Sandra

Please turn the page for a sneak peek at
Sandra Steffen's next novel
JUST BETWEEN FRIENDS
coming in January 2005!

CHAPTER 1

Brooke Valentine's eyes opened before her alarm went off, just as they had every morning this past year. She moved to get up. Instead of finding the edge of the bed, she encountered a warm, solid obstacle, namely her husband, Colin, who was lean and athletic and had the physique of Adonis, but was a barricade just the same.

"Out of bed is that way," he mumbled, ninety-nine percent asleep.

She lay back down groggily, trying to get her bearings. This new bed was going to be the death of her. She never could seem to find her way out of it. The problem wasn't really the lovely antique four-poster with a thick mattress and luxurious Egyptian cotton sheets. She couldn't even blame it on exhaustion, although she had been incredibly tired lately. The problem was that she was sleeping on the wrong side of the bed. An entire year and she still wasn't accustomed to the change.

An entire year.

Their move to one of Philadelphia's most picturesque and historic neighborhoods a year ago had been a symbol of their new beginning. Society Hill was a magnificent area. Sophie loved her school. Colin loved the prestige of living in a Main Line town. And Brooke loved her husband and daughter to be happy.

Colin sighed in his sleep, and yearning welled up inside her. If only she could stay right there and forget about the rest of the world and all the outside forces that pulled at them. Sophie could sleep in while she and Colin *didn't* sleep, like they'd done so many years ago. Later, they could make up excuses not to go into the office, and she would fix an enormous breakfast for the three of them and never once worry about the calories. They would all lounge in their bathrobes, and she wouldn't even think about donning her smart, pencil-slim gray skirt and jacket and the gray-blue silk blouse, the one that matched her eyes, the one she'd bought specifically for today's meeting.

Today's meeting.

Her eyes were wide open now. Still, it was a shame she couldn't stay in bed, for her husband was an incredibly fit and exciting man. She'd known it the first time she'd laid eyes on him fifteen years ago at college. Brooke's roommates had warned that she would never be able to keep him. She'd kept him. But there had been a price.

That was behind her, and behind them.

The clock-radio came on. Listening to the quiet music, she wondered what time Colin had finally gotten in. Poor man worked as hard as she did. Leaving him to get another half hour of much-needed sleep, she swung her legs—left this time—over her *new* side of the bed. Rising with as little jostling as possible, she pressed the radio's off button, her hand going to the book on her nightstand. *One Hundred and Ten Ways to Sex Up Your Marriage.* Tonight, she would suggest they try number seventeen again.

She had it all planned. The bottle of Chateau Latour was already chilling. And since Sophie was spending the night at a friend's, Brooke and Colin would have the house and the evening to themselves. They had much to celebrate, for they'd spent their first year in their new home, their marriage was solid once again, Sophie was flourishing, and Brooke's career in advertising was on the rise. Malcolm Klein was making an important announcement at today's board meeting. Brooke's colleagues agreed that all her hard work was sure to be rewarded. She smiled tiredly in anticipation, for she had worked hard, giving one hundred percent to every aspect of her life.

A glance at her watch told her she'd started her day a few seconds behind schedule. She made up for it by bypassing the window where she usually took a minute to greet the dawn. By rote, she drew her nightgown over her head upon entering the large master bathroom. Naked, she stepped on the scale. Next stop, the shower. Thirty minutes later she was clothed, made-up, scented, and ready for the daily juggling act of marriage, motherhood and career.

The lights were on in the kitchen when she got there. Twelve-year-old Sophie glanced up from the window seat where she was petting the family cat.

"Morning, Shortstuff. You, too, Fluffy."

"I'm the second tallest girl in my class. You have to stop calling me Shortstuff." Her daughter rose on gazelle legs—God, she was beautiful, and Fluffy skulked off, skirting Brooke entirely, gray tail straight in the air.

They'd had the cat a year, and she still hadn't warmed up to Brooke. No matter what Brooke tried, she couldn't seem to win the feline over.

"What would you like for breakfast, Sophe?"

"Blueberry pancakes with real maple syrup and hash browns and do we have any more glazed donuts?"

Brooke opened the airtight container and handed the donuts over. "Are you sure you don't have a hollow leg?"

"I have a high metabolism."

Sophia Nicole Valentine had her father's metabolism and her mother's eyes. She'd most likely gotten her self-confidence from Colin, too, but her quirky personality was all her own, and had been apparent when she was still in the high chair.

Wearing an old-fashioned apron, a cherished artifact from her teen years when she'd dreamed of becoming a world-renowned chef, Brooke took down the skillet, turned on the stove, reached into the cabinet for a bowl, and cracked an egg with one hand. There was a rhythm to cooking, a timing of movements and a blend of scents and sounds.

Sophie was an early riser, too. She sat in the pale yellow sunshine slanting through the windows, prattling on about any number of things. Today she complained about her best friend's annoying little brother.

"I used to wish for a baby brother or sister, but now Makayla wishes she was an only child."

"Toby's seven, Sophe. He'll outgrow pretending he's Spiderman." Brooke flipped the pancakes then stirred the hash browns, now perfectly golden on one side. "What are you and Makayla going to do today?"

"Get our tongues pierced, pick out a tattoo, hitch a ride out to the race track, talk to our bookie. You know, the usual."

Yes, Sophie had her mother's bone structure and her father's brains, and as they used to say, *the pool boy's sense of humor.* She and Colin didn't refer to the joke anymore. Not because it wasn't funny, per se, but because Brooke had discovered firsthand that there was nothing funny about infidelity.

Sophie sputtered. "You know today's Thursday, and—"

"Every Thursday Mrs. Prescott takes you and Makayla riding."

"—takes Makayla and me riding."

Mother and daughter spoke at the same time. They smiled the same way.

Sophie continued to talk while her breakfast was being prepared. And laugh. And gesture and giggle. And Brooke thought, was it any wonder this was her favorite time of the day?

Arranging everything on the plate, she stood on the opposite side of the counter, watching her daughter take her first bite. Sophie's eyes rolled back in her head. Born dramatic, everything the girl felt showed on her face. Brooke took a bite of her dry whole wheat toast and wondered what she'd done to deserve this child.

Colin entered the kitchen just as she was cutting a banana in half. "Good morning, ladies."

"Hey, Daddy."

He kissed Sophie's cheek and handed her a napkin, then waited to see that she used it before continuing on his way to the coffeemaker. The cat appeared, wending around his ankles, purring. Brooke stared at the creature, and then turned her attention to Colin. He wore a dark Italian suit and crisp white shirt. His eyes were deep-set, his hair the color of rich coffee. If Adonis had turned gray, Brooke had no doubt he would have done so as Colin was, with a slight brush of white at the temples. His cheekbones were as prominent as his lineage, his jaw angular and symmetrical. Few men on the planet were as handsome.

He laced his coffee with cream, took a satisfying sip, then placed the cup on the counter near her dry toast. "Are you dieting?"

Nothing got past Colin Valentine.

Two stinking pounds, she thought as she sliced her allotted half banana. "I probably had too much salt yesterday."

Colin moved directly behind her, his hands gliding to her hips covered by the new pencil-slim skirt. "The scales don't lie. But you sure feel good to me."

It was a compliment. She knew it was a compliment, and yet it burned like a slap. Something she couldn't name seared the backs of her eyes.

"You smell good, too."

He nuzzled her neck, and she relaxed. "You know I'm ticklish in that spot."

"I know another spot where you're ticklish." His voice was deep and quiet, loud enough for her ears alone, and sent those first, delicious flutters of desire swirling low in her belly.

From across the island, Sophie polished off the last of her pancakes and went to work on the hash browns. "I'm trying to eat over here."

Colin winked, Sophie grinned, and in that moment, everything felt right with Brooke's world. She poured batter onto the skillet while Colin settled himself at the table and shook out the *Wall Street Journal*. He called himself a glorified number-cruncher, but the truth was, at thirty-nine years of age, he was a brilliant problem solver with a long list of credentials including an MBA from Columbia. He had a reputation for getting results, and was sought after by major corporations both in the city and across the country.

He'd been extremely affectionate these past few weeks. Probably because he knew that although she'd forgiven him, the indiscretion still weighed on her mind sometimes, and on her heart, especially at this time of year, for it had been early summer when she'd discovered his affair. He'd tried so hard to make it up to her these past two years. It had taken months before she'd been able to make love with him without crying afterward, and a full year before she'd stopped wondering if he was comparing her to his former lover. Counseling had helped her deal with the hurt. She'd forgiven him. Not that she would ever forget. She'd discovered that forgiveness didn't miraculously wash down from the sky. It was a conscious decision, requiring strength and tenacity on her part, and patience on his.

When it came right down to it, he'd won her over all over again. No other man had ever made her feel the way Colin made her feel. She loved him. Deep inside she'd always known her life would have been simpler if it wasn't true.

Sophie ran upstairs to get her riding clothes. Alone in the kitchen with Colin, Brooke removed her apron and carried the plate to him. He thanked her, squeezing her hand.

"You know those ticklish spots you mentioned?" she said. "I was thinking I'd dab them with the new Chateau Latour before our celebration tonight."

A look crossed his face so quickly she wondered if she'd imagined it.

"Is something wrong?" she asked.

He turned his attention to his coffee, his hand steady as he stirred cream into his second cup. "McCowan invited me to accompany him and the new vice president to dinner. I'll let him know I can't make it."

Brooke smiled as she stacked the dishes in the sink for Portia, the housekeeper who came over two hours each morning. Leaving Colin to his breakfast and his paper, Brooke brushed her teeth in the half-bathroom. She was checking her appearance one last time when Sophie raced into the kitchen carting a bulky nylon duffel bag that held everything she would need for her overnight stay at her friend's.

"Are you moving out?" Colin asked.

"No silly. I'm going to Makayla's. Bye, Daddy." She kissed his cheek.

Brooke reached for her own leather bag. "I'll see you tonight, Colin. Wish me luck."

He rose to his feet, smoothing a hand along his tie, his blue eyes giving her a thorough once over. "We make our own luck, Brooke."

Why on earth did the statement leave her feeling empty? She started for the door Sophie had left open.

"Brooke?"

She glanced over her shoulder. He'd picked up the cat and was stroking its sleek fur. She understood the cat's rapture.

"You look beautiful, and if it wouldn't smear your lipstick and make you late, I'd prove it to you. I'll be tied up in meetings all day, but I should be home by seven. We can begin the celebration then. Don't uncork the wine until I get here. I'm going to enjoy watching you apply it to those ticklish spots almost as much as I'll enjoy sampling it."

Brooke's knees went weak. She wouldn't have cared if her lipstick smeared and she wouldn't have minded being a few minutes late. Pride and experience kept her from saying it.

He put down the cat, folded his newspaper and carried his plate to the sink. She walked out the door, her makeup impeccable, her schedule intact.

Brooke's cell phone began to ring just as she was entering the lobby of the building that housed Wilson Advertising Agency. The drive downtown had been harrowing. The founders who'd dubbed Philadelphia the city of brotherly love obviously never endured a typical morning commute.

This life in Philadelphia was a far cry from her life in Alcott, New Hampshire, where she'd grown up. She and her sister, Eve, had been born late in life to straightlaced parents. They'd had a quiet childhood, but not an unhappy one. Back then, it had seemed as if the long, lazy summer days would go on forever. She'd had caring parents, a loving younger sister, and two best friends who'd understood her better than anyone else in the world. Until Colin, that is. She couldn't remember the last time she'd talked to Sara or Claudia. The Three Potters, they'd called themselves. Sometimes she got so busy she forgot how much she missed them. It occurred to her that she missed Colin, too, which was strange considering she lived with him, slept with him, shared her life with him. She was in a weird mood today, no doubt about it.

She reached into her bag for the ringing phone as she was rounding the landing at the top of the first flight of stairs. Placing the small device to her ear, she said, "What did you forget, Sophe?"

"Close but no cigar."

"Eve! I was just thinking about you." Brooke paused for a moment at the top of the second flight of stairs, damning those blasted two pounds!

"Really?" Eve asked. "Listen, I know you're busy." Her sister knew her well. "I have good news. I'm getting married."

"You mean Jack McCall finally—"

Eve laughed, and Brooke could picture her in her mind, five-feet-eleven, and most of that legs, hair down to her waist, eyes the color of pewter.

"Not Jack," Eve said. "His brother, Carter."

Brooke entered the suite of offices on the third floor where she worked. "You mean you? And bad-boy Carter McCall? Are you kidding? Are you crazy?"

"Crazy in love. You know how that is."

In her reflection in the window, Brooke's smile lost its brilliance. Placing her heavy bag on her desk, she lowered into her chair. "When? How? My, you've been busy."

"You don't know the half of it. He asked me two weeks ago, and I hardly know where to begin, Brooke. Tommy's cancer is back, but he's doing better again."

"Oh, Eve, that precious child. Leukemia, isn't it? And you've really been engaged for two weeks?"

"It came about suddenly. I'm so happy I wanted to wrap it around me, around us, just us for a few weeks, savor it, relish it."

Brooke had misgivings about Eve's news. She voiced a few as gently as she knew how. Eve sounded very sure of herself, secure in her decision, and very sincere in her feelings for Carter McCall.

They talked until Mr. Klein opened his office door, his signal that he was ready to begin the meeting. "Eve, I have to go. Congratulations, sweetie. As long as Carter really loves you, and you really love him, I'm happy for you."

"We do, Brooke. Neither of us had any idea love could feel this way."

"All right, then. I'll call you later."

She replaced the phone. Rising, she smoothed her skirt into place, rehearsed her acceptance speech in the back of her mind, and followed her coworkers into the conference room.

*   *   *

"Brooke. No one can believe this."

"Yeah. It's so unfair."

"We all know the economy has been horrible. It's inspired us to work even harder. None of us dreamed it would come to this."

"It's a shock, all right." Brooke didn't look up from the box she was filling with personal items from her desk. If she did, she knew she would lose the battle of restraint and cry. She felt it coming, the welling up, the hot throat, the tight, aching chest. Pain was trying to get in. But she didn't let it. She couldn't. Not yet.

She hadn't gotten a promotion. She'd gotten . . .

She couldn't even form the word in her mind. It hadn't been easy for Malcolm Klein to do. She was certain his remorse had been sincere, for the president of Wilson Advertising possessed an honor she'd always respected.

"Money is tight," Malcolm had said.

Evidently the agency was hurting. Consumers weren't buying, and only a handful of companies could afford to pay top dollar for advertising these days, and those wanted talking ducks or mud wrestling. This morning Malcolm had announced that he'd hoped the agency could ride this out until the days of tasteful advertisements returned. Evidently, that wasn't the case. The bottom line was money. It was nothing personal. It had been a corporate decision.

It felt personal to Brooke. Intellectually, she knew it had to do with seniority. She'd left the Pratt Agency a year ago, shortly before she and Colin had moved, because this commute was much shorter, and she and Colin had agreed that it would be better if she were home more with her family.

She wasn't the only one to get the ax. Doogan, the still-wet-behind-the-ears college graduate in design, and Polly from accounting, were both filling boxes, too. Others wondered if they would be next.

With nothing more to say, the two colleagues hovering around Brooke's desk shuffled away to their own cubicles. Brooke picked up the last item on her desk. Colin didn't like clutter, so she'd brought the framed photograph of The Three Potters taken the summer after high school graduation here. She stared at the smiling faces in the photograph, then tucked the momento into her bag along with her pink slip and severance check. Biting her lip, she cast a look at all her coworkers—make that her *former* coworkers. She nodded a quick goodbye, hefted the cardboard box into her arms, then followed Doogan out the door.

"This sucks," he said at the elevator.

Brooke nodded.

"I've got bills, man."

In the lobby, Brooke said, "Well, good luck."

"You, too."

What was it that Colin had said that morning? *We make our own luck.*

Tears stung her eyes. The thought of Colin kept them from falling. She dreaded telling him about this.

In the parking lot, she fumbled for her keys, only to drop them, nearly dropping everything. By the time she deposited the carton on the backseat and managed to unlock her door and get behind the wheel, her hands were shaking.

She wanted . . .

What? A friend to talk to? A shoulder to cry on?

She wanted Colin to hold her. She wanted that so much she ached.

Gripping the steering wheel with both hands, she watched for traffic and kept her mind blank. She wasn't surprised when she found herself near the office building where Colin worked.

Parking was always a problem downtown. Today she didn't mind, for looking for a parking space gave her a focus. She found a spot three blocks from Colin's building. Calmer now, she began to walk, noticing for the first time what a beautiful day it was. The weather, at least, was lovely. It was a sunny, breezy eighty-two degrees. Perfect July weather. She would find another job. Of course she would! Meanwhile, she had her health, her family, and sunshine.

She was going to have to rethink the private celebration she'd planned for tonight. She felt vulnerable and disappointed. She needed Colin to hold her, and make her feel cherished and safe. The counselor she'd seen had told her she had to learn to ask for what she needed. She was working on that.

She waited with the hoards of other pedestrians for the WALK sign to light up at the intersection. Keeping pace with everyone else, she breathed in the scents of ginger and orange and teriyaki wafting on the breeze from the outdoor café at the end of the next block. It was eleven-thirty and she was starving. Perhaps Colin would have time for an early lunch. Perhaps, now that she was between jobs, she could meet him for lunch often. That sounded lovely, actually. She was thirty-six years old, and she couldn't remember the last time she'd had an extended vacation.

She would get through this. Hadn't she worked through worse things?

Her steps quickened and spirits lifted somewhat. It didn't take long to catch up with a group of tourists from the Midwest. Since she now had all the time in the world, Brooke slowed to a stroll and breathed deeply again.

She was close enough to see the patrons enjoying lunch at the small umbrella tables in the little courtyard up ahead. A mix of tourists and businesspeople, most appeared to be enjoying the food and fresh air. A blond woman in a stunning red suit caught Brooke's eye. She could have been Marilyn Monroe reincarnated, complete with full lips and plenty of cleavage. She was with a dark-haired man in a dark suit. The man looked good from behind, but it was the way the woman moved, sinuous and seductive, that captured Brooke's attention.

The Midwesterners stopped in front of Brooke to admire something in a window. Brooke stopped, too, intrigued for reasons she couldn't name. Perhaps it was the way the blond woman's fingernails flashed bright red as she slid one inside the man's cuff. Perhaps it was the way the man reached toward her, indulging her, exciting her, luring her to lean across that small table and kiss him in front of God and everyone.

The kiss went on and on. When it finally ended, the woman smiled breathlessly. Giving him an extended view of her breasts, which were straining the buttons of her bright red jacket, she reached over and wiped her lipstick from his lips with her thumb. He said something that made her smile broaden, then handed her his napkin. There was something familiar about the way he did that.

Just then the waiter appeared. The lovers turned their heads and looked up, smiling. And Brooke got her first glimpse of the man's profile.

The tourists moved on. Brooke was frozen in place.

Colin. The man was Colin.

She darted to the cover of a nearby store, then stood, hiding, as if she had done something wrong. What she'd done was witnessed her husband kissing another woman. Her husband, who hadn't kissed her goodbye for fear of smearing her lipstick, had just kissed another woman senseless in broad daylight. He certainly hadn't been concerned about *her* lipstick.

The realization burned Brooke's eyes, her throat, her chest. She turned, stumbling. Righting herself, she fled back the way she'd come.

He'd promised, *promised* it would never happen again.

Today was the anniversary of the day they'd started over. A year ago they'd recommitted to each other, turning over a new leaf, embracing the future instead of the past.

There would be no celebration tonight.

Damn you, Colin Valentine.